LAEL

J.S. McGOWAN

Copyright © 2016 J.S. McGOWAN

All rights reserved.

ISBN-10:1535236698
ISBN-13:978-1535236690

DEDICATION

This book is dedicated to our parents.
Jessie and John; David and Anna.

ABOUT THE BOOK

I started to write an action novel called 'The Marmalade Swan'. The story was about an ex-commando who became a government assassin. There were some really violent episodes in it so as a light relief I started another story alongside. Within the alternate story the main character was the exact opposite of the commando in the Marmalade Swan.

I was walking through the real world forest of Lael when I first thought about it so I called the main character Lael. As my writing progressed I found I spent more time writing Lael than I did the Marmalade Swan.

I was always interested in the elements and the night skies and I had worked for most of my life on the sea. I was regaled with stories of faeries and mythical creatures from my grandparents and religion and superstition were never far away.

The book of Lael is a blend of fantasy and spirituality it is an imaginative tale which deals with the age old struggle of good and evil, of male and female status and the love of the natural world. Or in this case… three worlds……

ACKNOWLEDGMENTS

I wrote this book because I enjoyed doing it. I never did any research for the writing just put it together using a lifetime of memories.

However I will give thanks for the wonderful environments I grew up in and the fantastic tales told to me by my parents and grandparents; the stories nearly always had spiritual connotations.

My love of nature and the elements further enhanced the writing of Lael – my boyhood in the north of Scotland with the winter nights in total darkness. From an early age I was fixated with the romance and the mystery of space.

I give respective thanks to all the creative authors of books and magazines I have read in a lifetime.

To Doridh MacLennan Angus without whose support and encouragement the book would never have been published.

I thank Leanne Maxwell for the artwork which she matched perfectly with the descriptions of the characters and the setting for the book cover.

CONTENTS

Chapter headings are the tree names taken from the old Celtic alphabet. I have made a change to the letter D, which is usually Dara in the modern alphabet – the older version was Darach (oak). My substitute is Draighean which in the old language refers to the Sea Buckthorn, it is a plant that was prolific on the shoreline of my place of birth.

Prologue: Magimatrix of Space………Pg 1

Ailim (Elm)……………………………..3
    Liath and Lael………………………30
    Daralonadh……………………..........44
    Worlds Apart………………………46

Beith (Birch)………………..………...53

Coll (Hazel)…………………………......82
    Suilval……………………………... ..88
    Too Much Puflic………………..........90
    The Bana Ger……………………....101
    In Elids Bower……………………..106
    A Walk with Elid…………………..118
    Faol Warriors and Shade Elves…......126
    Coonie and Enderli………………...128
    Lael and the Bana………………….131
    Gruflics……………………………....134
    The Death of Senna………………..155

Draighean (Sea Buckthorn)...........190
   The Sword of Elid..................198

Eadha (Aspen).........................208
   Scaravban...........................234
   The Crossing of
     the Tanaron Sea...................254

Fearn (Alder)...........................263

Gort (Ivy)...............................283
   Derca's Story   283
   Part One of the Search for
     the Tears of Apuss...............286
   The Exodus...............................294
   Part Two of the Search for
     the Tears of Apuss...............301
   The Landing........................ 309
   Mirma's Story......................317

Uath (Hawthorn)
   The Battle of the Fochd Pass..... 337
   Esir-amit and Riora................340
   Spearhead...........................342
   The Firedraig.......................347
   The Trio of Light..................347
   The Words of Tiathmor,
     Queen of the Bana...............351
   The Battle is Over..................353
   The Song of Draigs in
     the Voice of Nal..................354

Iogh (Yew)...........................365
   Semora's Kiss......................378
   Casualties of War..................386

Luis (Rowan)..........................391

Muin (Vine)...........................399
   The Orb of Ascendency...........423

Nuin (Ash)............................425
   Epilogue...........................425

PROLOGUE:

MAGIMATRIX OF SPACE

The blackness sucked the cosmic energy out of the spinning orb of light and fire.
That was in the beginning when the mighty burning orb was always there.
Surrounding it was a weave of dark energy, both it and the orb locked together in timeless duality.
Then light and dark made contact. The weave formed itself in conical shape its apex fixed at the orb.
Expanded gasses and fire from the orb raged in a storm of cosmic violence, finally it blew and burst asunder. The weave inhaled the fragmented orb within its conical blackness and formed a vortex of pushing - pulling - crushing energy; then at last for a second time - another mighty explosion.
This time the eruption fanned out - ever outwards its

expansion took the light, heat and energy of the broken orb until at last the elasticity of the weave began to slow it down and within that magimaterial space another beginning took place.

Out of the expansion of the mass and energy two entities took form, retreating away from each other, one favoured the light and clung to the brightness, she was Ica of the light.

The other entity was drawn to the dark side of the magical weave and he became Ulas of the dark.

Once again through the fusion of two opposing energies the forward and backward motion of time is determined by light and dark, always one accompanied by the other.

It is the combination of the opposites that eventually leads to ascendency of the highest - then light and dark separate - the purity of light surrounded by the totality of darkness, then--------

AILIM

Every Saturday morning I got up early and after a wash and shave followed by a light breakfast, set off with my pet German shepherd on one of my favourite walks.

The town where I lived was situated on a headland and was in fact a peninsula, at one time in the far past it had been an island. The sea was virtually all around and I had seen and heard it all my life, never tiring of the sense of freedom it gave me.

I grew up in the town of my birth and had a great childhood roaming the beaches and exploring the seashore. When the tide was all the way out we scoured the rock pools for the small fish darting in and out of the fronds of seaweed.

Very occasionally a heavy sea mist would descend on the shore and I would go to the last point of rock at the tide line. My dog would sit beside me during those special moments; we both would listen to the silence and feel the stillness of the air.

The outside world was closed off to me and I was

untouchable - free - breathing in that space in time that had been reserved for me.

There was a great tract of forest to the landward side of the town which my friends and I would stray into on occasions.

There was always an eerie, magical feel to the forest. The beaches, rocks and cliffs of the seashore were open and airy. In the forest we felt closed in, most of the trees were ancient pines and we saw them as long dead druid warriors, rooted to the earth forever by warlocks.

Within the wood there were areas where trees had fallen in ages past and we could make out bits of the trees on the forest floor. One in particular looked as if it had tried to rise out of its blanket of moss. On either side of its buried trunk a pair of rotting branches reached out like arms.

The wood was okay when the sun shone through it but it was scary on dull days and even more frightening if we got caught as the dark came down.

The gnarled twisted limbs of the trees creaked and moved as area winds teased them about and moving shadows gave life to the wooden warriors – we were off before our imaginings came to life.

Then childhood days all too soon came to an end and so departed thoughts of magic and make believe as I ghosted into teenage years. Change of body and change of mind-set produced confusion and scattered emotions.

I got to my thirties, and by that time I was well into what I called my domestic period in which I enjoyed the pleasantries of a wife, daughters, cats and a dog.

I also had a successful career but it entailed a car journey to the nearest city, a journey I did there and back every weekday for many years.

My release was the Saturday morning walk on my own with the dog. I would walk for hours - usually up one of the beaches which extended for miles on each side of the town.

No matter what the weather was like, the energy of the coastal elements dissipated all the stress and strains of the working week. I very seldom used the forest walk, much preferring the openness of the sea which stretched to the opposite shore where I could see the hills of the northwest highlands.

However, after one particularly harrowing week at work I found I had to squeeze my Saturday morning walk into a forty minute sprint due to unforeseen circumstances.

I went out that morning for a short walk with my dog and we went through a part of the pine wood - I had taken a liking to the forest walk of late. The day was crisp and clear, the sun was shining and a scent of pine pervaded the air. The dog was ahead of me snuffling and dodging among the trees and bushes, a twitter of birdsong was in the background.

The few recent times I had used the forest walk I had felt what I would describe as a deep longing for my youth.

As I got deeper into the wood I noticed a slight change in the air, although it was warm and still I felt it had been rejuvenated by an injection of oxygen. The song of the birds had changed, they were still calling but it sounded as if they were in unison singing one song.

The trees were bigger in every respect; taller, thicker and their foliage was startlingly green. I had walked this wood at various times in my life but I could not remember being in this part of it. Then I missed the dog - that was unusual as she was never more than twenty feet from me; the last time I saw her she had regarded me with a puzzled look on her face.

I called her a few times but got no response but I did not feel worried, the song of the forest kept on going. In spite of my calls, nature paid no heed to the sudden noise of my voice.

I walked on through the wood which got bigger and bigger, by that I mean the trees were taking on gigantic proportions, as were the shrubs and bushes of the forest floor, but strange as it was I felt I knew the direction I was taking as if I was being called! My step was lighter my breathing clean and easy, the air was crystal clear and vibrant.

I felt as if the whole inside of my body had been spring cleaned, now and then I caught glimpses of creatures and birds but I could not identify them - it was as if I had stepped through a door leading to another dimension.

I should be anxious about the dog or indeed myself as I know now that I am completely lost, and yet I feel I am going on a predetermined path; the forest that I am in is light and airy. Why can't the whole world be like it? Never before have I experienced such a belonging to the natural world and beyond. I could hold my hands skywards and float to the tops of the highest trees, such was the lightness of mind and body.

The further I walked the more I accepted the forest as my home, by that I mean it was to be my new walk, I was going to explore the forest during all my spare time, I liked it so much, in fact it felt better than my favourite place by the sea, and that was a statement!

The dog had probably made her way home by now so she will be there to welcome the girls home from school - I just need to go little bit further now. I can always run back to make up lost time, I really want to enjoy this sensation for a little bit longer.

I am intrigued by the daylight, it is clear and blue; the tops of the trees seemed to pierce the very fabric of the azure sky. I could not see the sun but by the amount of light which was present it had to be there somewhere above.

Then the air around was charged with a new sound - voices speaking in a strange tongue, there was something hypnotic about the speech, so much so I felt myself drawn to the source. Had I been in a normal state of mind the sight that I beheld would have made me run a mile, however their voice tones were like musical notes to my ears and I was pulled towards the sound.

Standing by a large rock was a very tall woman, she was at least twice my height, her face was beautiful and noble, her dark coppery hair was pulled back from her forehead at the front, thick strands of hair bound together with some kind of braiding hung down the sides of her face over her shoulders and on to her chest.

The rest of the hair looked as if it was bound at the back of her neck as I could see a metal pin of some kind protruding behind her head. Her tight fitting outfit consisted of a jacket with a material that looked like a cross between leather and metal.

It had a high collar like a polo neck and was fastened with a metal clasp of a design I could not describe. Her tight fitting trews reached down to her calves and her feet and ankles were bare.

The body and clothes of the woman had a colouring of copper all over - she looked like a living statue.

Her companion in speech was every bit as awesome, a male, and one right out of my childhood imagination. Almost as tall as the woman stood an elf, and what an elf he was. Brown skinned, in a tunic of forest green, dark hair pulled back from the forehead. He looked back at me with laughing eyes and a reassuring smile and what identified him the most was his long pointed ears.

Apart from the elf's smile, the pair showed no surprise at my sudden appearance! I could not understand what they were saying; they seemed to be communicating with each other in musical speech. It was enthralling and although I could not make head or tail of it I felt it was in harmony with everything around - the air, the trees, birds, and animals - even me.

Then the tall woman spoke in words that I could understand, 'Hello young spirit, you join us, I trust your transition was enjoyable?' At the word transition I shimmered a bit and that was the appropriate word because I felt I glowed when really I should have had a feeling of discord.

I was awed by the sight of a giant woman and although it was she who spoke to me I could not take my eyes off her elfin companion. He stood by the woman and although not as tall as her, his bearing was regal, but not aloof, and he kept smiling at me as the woman spoke.

A thought passed through my mind at that point - I am definitely in the dream world? No I am not, the strangeness of the forest, the light, worry free feeling and the missing dog.......

'What do you mean by transition?' I was hardly able to mouth the question. The reply was immediate and to the point.

'Young spirit, your earthly body died while walking through the forest. You suffered a fatal heart attack. You were called to the spirit world through the door of the forest of Lael, every spirit is met by a known spirit and the journey softened by using an environment that was known or loved on Earth. In your case your path was through the forest of Lael into the spirit wood of Celdis.'

'You mean I am dead? I can't be - I am still myself - I can see, feel and hear; nothing has changed.'

'You are no more an earthen human, you have come into the spirit world of Ulana and your earthly shell has expired. But you, dear spirit, are very much alive and have come home.'

The woman's words took me aback and I struggled momentarily to take them in, however I was lightened by the smile and expression on the face of the elf who then spoke to me.

Holding his open hand in the direction of the woman he said. 'This is Roscranna, she is a dimensional guardian and a keeper of the channels of time and I am Teric, an elf of the forests of Ulana. We were asked by Elios the faerie to meet you at the gate of reality and Roscranna herself is obliged to take you to her.'

Although the words of the elf reassured me a bit, my immediate thoughts forced me to voice fears not for myself but for those I had left behind. 'I have to go back. I have a wife and children and I cannot leave them.'

Roscranna came towards me and laid her hands gently on my shoulders. 'They will have their own journeys to make when it is their time to be called. You are the spirit of life and you have come home, for this is Ulana the spirit world of Earth. You cannot go back, only after the seventh generation of your line on Earth has passed might a spirit guardian ask you to go back and bring life to another.'

Teric then approached and stood behind me holding my head in his hands, I felt such an energy pulsing through me at the touch of the two spirits and in that brief flicker of time an aura of perfect peace settled over me. A golden light misted over the three of us and I worried no more.

Teric then said to me that I would now be known as Lael, as that was where my earthly body expired and my spirit walked into woods of Celdis and so this place would always be sacred to me.

'We will meet again Lael in Ulana somewhere but for

now'---He held up his hand and was gone.

'Come Lael let me take you on your first journey in the world of the spirits, we have much to see and I have much to tell you.' Roscranna motioned me with a slight movement of her eyebrows 'let us explore a little more of Ulana.'

Dutifully I followed her. I had no choice as the powerful presence of Roscranna was all encompassing. My mind and body were filled with a spiritual euphoria and I was floating along in a cloud of pure joy, never ever had I experienced anything like it on Earth.

My excitement knew no bounds when I beheld two elves at the edge of the wood, it brought a quiet laugh from Roscranna, all my reading and storytelling about elves and faeries and now I see two elves out of my imagination right in front of my eyes.

Under the leaves of a huge spreading tree the two elves, one obviously female crouched on one knee, the other a male standing behind her with his hand on her shoulder and both dressed in hues of green and russet brown.

'Lael meet Aris and Ner, they are elves of the wood of Celdis.' Aris and Ner drifted across to make contact with me and contact they did, they caressed my face and body and Ner brushed my lips with hers - then to my amazement she floated upside down still holding my lips, it was a wonderful introduction. On Earth contact as such would have attracted attention of different sorts, but here it was the touch of spiritual bodies giving and receiving energy and it felt so natural.

I said my goodbyes to the elves and watched them stepping lightly through the trees laughing and talking.

I turned to Roscranna and said. 'Will I see them again?'

'Yes at some point in eternity you will see them again but until then enjoy the space in Ulana that you occupy now.'

I asked her about the hours of the day and how the year was divided----but she cut me short.

'Lael, Ulana is a vast world and as such reality is here in the form of spirituality. You are in everlasting time now, you no longer need to look ahead to the future and dread old age and infirmity.

You don't need to think about life after death because you have left death behind. The hope of mankind has been achieved and in this place all of the creatures that were born of Earth live in eternal joy'.

At this she laughed and said. 'Well maybe not so much man but more woman, in the older ages of Earth in some of the races the female was dominant. In Ulana man has reached out and has now found his feminine side. We walked on in silence for a while then a thought struck me, 'Roscranna can you tell me in Earth years how long will my walk with you take?'

The answer she gave made sense. 'There are no segments of time here as you live the life in spirit in the space you occupy now. The curvature of time flows in perfect motion with spirit and forever keeps the balance in Ulana.'

I replied. 'So there is no measurement that I can use to work out when my wife and children will arrive here?'

'Lael, this is your real time. The world of Earth is still with you because you have just entered Ulana. Believe you me as we leave the woods of Celdis you will have left all earthen thoughts behind you and begin the reality of Ulana. When the real awareness of where you are and what you are comes upon you, tiredness almost like a stupor will weaken you. It is a transition from the dual individuality you had on earth – of self and ego – to the wholeness of spirit. It is nothing to fear, in fact there is nothing to fear in Ulana ever.'

I still persisted with my questions. 'Will I ever meet my children and my wife or even my mother and father?'

'Your wife and children will be met in comfortable surroundings just as you were and so also your parents before you. You may meet them in Ulana; it all depends on what movements they have adopted.

Some spirits wander the vast forests and mountains, others sail seas that are alive with the wonders of marine life. Others prefer to stay in one place surrounded by trees, animals and birds and are happy in their spiritual solitude.

You, I think will be a wandering spirit and the faraway terrains and seas of Ulana will pull you into their magnificence, not for you to be a forest hermit or an island castaway.'

'Yes Roscranna I like the sound of that, I would

have liked that life on earth but I was too insular to make it happen, it sounds exciting and carefree but who will I be responsible to?'

'Lael I must explain something to you –listen awhile and ponder on my words.' Roscranna motioned me to sit. I sat down on the root of a tree and fairly jumped when it moved upwards under me!

Roscranna said. 'Settle down Lael, the tree is only making you more comfortable - his name is Huil. Say hello to him.'

I said hello to Huil and Huil shook his leaves in response, I was truly amazed at that and by the fact Roscranna knew his name, so my next question was if she knew every tree by name in the forests and woodlands of Ulana.

She answered me in the affirmative. 'Lael in your short life on Earth how many creatures and plants did you know by name? I have been here before the dawn of man's time on Earth; I know Ulana - I am a guardian of the spirit world and a wanderer of the universes.

I know all the life forces within my domain, all their names and all their thought. If one blade of grass ever cried out in pain I would know of it, you will understand this after a while in Ulana.

When on Earth you recognized a rowan tree or a birch you called them by their collective names, here all of the life have spirit names be they tree, bush, bird, animal, elf, faery or woman / man spirit.' She then picked up the conversation we were having before I had sat down.

'You are responsible to yourself and every single

spirit form in Ulana and they in return are responsible for themselves and others of the spirit.

When you lived on Earth you were an Earthman, you were yourself, you belonged to a Celtic race, and you had family and friends. Spirit is the essence of life - it was in you as it was in every other human on Earth. In the majority of the human race, ego-self was dominant, Spirit tried hard to speak but ego-self seldom listened.

Hate, jealousy, vanity and materialistic values were all part of the ego-self, that same self ruled supreme. Now in Ulana that egotistical self that was such a big part of you in human form is gone.'

She paused and watched my reaction for a moment or so. I did not reply immediately, just looked around me at my surroundings and breathed in the soothing air of my new home. I looked into Roscranna's eyes and said. 'I am glad that ego has not accompanied me to this world and I am also happy that there are no vices in me, I feel as if a great weight has been lifted off me.

My mind will no longer be cluttered with meaningless thoughts of how I look or what people think of me. It is now open to the natural order of things, it is a truly wonderful feeling that I hope lasts forever.'

Once more Roscranna smiled and said, 'Yes Lael, it could quite well do that. Now let us be on our way as there is much to see and plenty to tell.' I responded to her words right away as I wanted to see so much and I had so many questions to ask her. I was elated and I knew that I would be in that state forever - everlasting bliss.

I had another question for Roscranna, 'Does every new spirit that enters Ulana carry the name of the place where they died on Earth?'

Roscranna replied. 'You came to Ulana through the earthen forest of Lael; happenings there long before your time will become significant as events will show. You are Lael, others may call you by another name and that is acceptable here.

For example the mountain people may use another name for you depending on how they see you as a working spirit. On the other hand the sea denizens of the great oceans may know you by another name and so on.

That is so for every spirit that enters Ulana, irrespective of how they conducted themselves during their Earthly existence; no entity is barred from the perfection of the spirit world.

That would be against all universal law if rules were in place to bar entry, because self and spirit were in contention within a human body. Light and dark, love and hate, good and evil, life and death, all exist in duality, take away dark, hate, evil and death and you have reality, the reality of Ulana.

Spirits take many forms and so names are given by their mentors on arrival, they can be given place of death names or condition of death names or even names their guides feel is right for them.'

Roscranna gave me one of her penetrating looks and asked me what the Earth I left behind most needed. I gave her the first thing that came in to my mind and the strange thing was that had I been on Earth and been asked the same question, I would not have given the answer I gave Roscranna.

'Healing' is the answer I gave her and I gave it with conviction, Earth definitely needs healing.' She told me that I gave the right answer and that the spirit of Ulana was working in me.

We continued our walk, for how long I could not tell. Roscranna talked and pointed things out to me, it could have been forever and a day and I was beginning to understand what she had said about time - it was meaningless. I saw creatures that I was familiar with and many more that I thought belonged to the realm of myth and legend.

Roscranna told me that every living thing that had been born on Earth in every age ended up in the spiritual world of Ulana.

I laughed and said. 'Even T-rex and half the dinosaurs he killed?'

'You are right about that Lael, but it's a very watered down T-Rex - no aggression and no need to hunt for his living.'

The next question I asked her was one I needed to know. 'Roscranna are there such beings as angels?'

Her answer nearly overwhelmed me with emotion. I could see by her eyes that she was in a far distant place and was reliving an event of great magnitude. Her whole demeanour changed as she tilted her head skywards and in a voice that carried such an abundance of joy began to describe her meeting with an angel.

'The moving darkness took shape in front of my eyes; in the isolation of that space - the heavy darkness manifested in the form of an angel.

Beautiful and awesome she was, her dark form and features glinted with silver light, behind her the darkness of wings began to flutter in hues of black and platinum.

When she spoke it was in a voice the like of which I had never heard or sensed in thought. In beguiling tones her words and the loveliness of her face were almost too much to bear. The dark contours of her body shape began to mimic the backdrop of the starry universe, a movement of wandering stars all over her.

I who had travelled in the beauty of Ulana and wandered in the mystery of space was held spellbound – and at the same time humbled so much that I wept at the angel before me.

She came down to my size and took my face in her hands, I felt I had been touched by the highest power in infinity and for all my great powers I was as a child again.

I had met many creatures during my inter-dimensional wandering, all shapes and sizes, but until then I had never met an angel. There in that part of time and space called Satus I encountered finality in the form of an impenetrable barrier and a formidable guardian.

She turned my head slightly so that I could see over her shoulder and between her wings, I could feel an energy coursing through my senses. Her words were in my mind telling me to look beyond the far reaches of space through mists of galaxies and the magimatrix of dark energy and to tell her what I saw.

With the power of the angel in my mind my eyes beheld a wondrous sight – a red glow of light as if a mighty sun was rising on the edge of infinity. The voice in my head told me I was looking at the beginning of everything in existence.

The angel was Seronis, keeper of the outer darkness; time and dark matter merged in that place, I had happened on a space curve and I could not get through it. I followed a great arc and it was like I was moving inside a round room; getting nowhere!

What I am telling you Lael, is that no matter how high you think you are in spirituality there is always going to be a level above which you will gain more love of the universe, indeed all of creation, than you would have thought possible. Time, space, matter and magic are all words but when words translate into great depths of meaning then the wonder of it all flows through your very being.

Since you left the heaviness of Earth did you not feel a lightness of mind and body even before you met with me, and did not that lightness continue as our journey got nearer to the bower of Elios?'

There was something nagging at me in the back of my mind so I voiced it to Roscranna. 'What do the spirits eat in Ulana? They must have sustenance of some kind.'

Her reply was in the form of a question. 'Did you ever see a tree eating on Earth Lael?'

'Not physically' I replied 'because the tree drew life from its roots.'

'Well you are getting warmer Lael; now ask yourself, the tree had its roots in the earth so where was its trunk and branches?'

Slow dawning came as I contemplated her words. 'The roots were fed by the energy of the Earth and the leaves of the tree absorbed the sunlight.'

'Exactly Lael and that is the way the spirit world functions. We take our energy from the earth, nobody wears any kind of footwear on Ulana's soil nor do we wear any kind of head cover, the light of the day is enough to sustain our spiritual bodies.

The magical night air and the starry sky energize our feelings during our medi-slumber when the day's light has gone. We are then connected to every source of energy in the universes and that same energy fills us with an abundance of wellbeing.

We all have lush heads of hair; some wear their hair down their back or draped over their shoulders some prefer it piled up on top, others - usually the males, wear their hair tied up behind their necks. It does not matter, either way it attracts the spiritual light which feeds the body just as the leaves sustain the trees. There are no bald heads in Ulana by the way.'

'What body shape will I develop?' I asked

'Whatever spirit entity you feel at one with, it is usually the spirit mentor that guides you in your early life in Ulana. Many men and woman of the human race keep their own human image, though they are far healthier looking than they ever were on Earth, we are all ageless in spirit.'

'Are you to be my mentor Roscranna, surely I could not assume your shape as we are opposite sexes?'

Roscranna laughed at that then answered. 'No Lael, I

am a dimensional guardian and so have other tasks to perform. Erim Elios asked me to meet you at the gate and accompany you to her bower in the MoAraian forest; it is she who will appoint a mentor not I'. Then she went on tell me who Erim Elios was.

'Erim Elios is the faerie guardian and keeper of the MoAraian forest; it is she who is the interface between the spirit world of Ulana and the higher reaches out-with. She is strong in spirit and her magical power can penetrate through the dimensional veil.

'When you meet her you will feel the aura of one who was a queen long before the feet of men walked the Earth. Erim and her faerie band were the last to leave Earth after the coming of the elves.'

'So why was there never any evidence of faeries and elves to be found?' I asked.

With good humour Roscranna answered me. 'Lael you ask so many questions and that is good, but Erim Elios will answer them for you and maybe ask you a few, but suffice to say that the eyes of humans have always been clouded as far as the spirit goes. The first of the human race were very aware of the faerie folk and the elves and they all lived together in the garden of the evolving Earth. As the ages of men and women moved through time and occupied more of the planet so the faerie bands and most of the elves left the Earth.

In time the human race forgot all about their ancestors, faeries and elves were the stuff of legend kept alive by a few beings that held on to their spiritual selves – and they were mostly women.

Man may sow the seed but women bear the essence of life within, they retained the strength of mind and spirit which gave them intuition and powers of healing. They alone held on to the ancient ways of spirit and some paid dearly for it.'

We walked on in silence for a while then we approached a dell which emanated yellow light through the greenery of the forest and at a point where the yellow light melted into white stood a hind. She also was white and so gentle looking, I was hypnotised by her. Roscranna's voice took me out of my trance.

'Lael this is Minver, the hind of Erim Elios, she waits at the pathway for all those who are called to the bower of Elios and she will take us to the guardian.' Roscranna looked at Minver but did not speak. Minver made a sound like the whisper of leaves being ruffled by the breeze, then moved ahead of us.

We followed her along a pathway of what felt like moss, but it was white and the energy I felt through my feet was far greater than the feeling I had experienced on the journey to here, then abruptly Minver stopped and I saw the reason why.

In all my dreams I ever had on Earth nothing in them ever came close to what I saw there. Only this was no dream, it was another world experience in more ways than one. I could only stare at the figure before me, Roscranna's voice sounded far off as she introduced me to Elios the faery. I was transfixed with wonder by the magical being standing tall and elegant in front of me.

I had no voice to answer her with as she welcomed me, her tone was soft and hypnotic as she thanked Roscranna for escorting me to her, then her attention was on me, 'Welcome to my bower Lael, I hope your journey pleased you?'

I could have listened to the melody of her voice forever, it seemed to touch chords in the very air itself; in that bower I could feel an overwhelming sense of spiritual energy not only in Elios herself but from the trees, plants, crystalline rocks and the very earth I stood on. All I could muster in the presence of such majesty was - 'am I still dreaming? I have to be!'

At my comment and dumbstruck look Elios laughed and came forward to me. The laugh shimmered in the air round about and I am pretty sure the trees joined in, she stood in front of me and put her hands on my shoulders.

I know I had already died but for that glorious moment I would have died again, Roscranna was tall but Elios was easily a head taller. Standing in front of me was a faerie of my imaginings, of storytelling and of make believe and all I could do was stand and stare.

Elios literally broke into my thoughts because that is where she was, I could hear her inside my head but her lips were not moving, just a smile as she beheld my wonder. Then she laughed again and broke into speech.

She motioned me to a mossy bank saying. 'This is your reality now Lael, each part of your new exiting life will be filled with spiritual learning, your friends will all be spirits like yourself also the animals and birds, the sea and the earth. Now do you think you can make that tongue of yours work?'

I answered her right away and was amazed at how melodious I sounded, 'What do I call you?'

She laughed again, that oh so thrilling sound that touched everything round about.

'I am known by many names but Elios will do, now tell me how you feel in your new life?'

The question was easily answered in my new voice tone I said. 'I feel as if I have been cleaned out, all the way in my journey with Roscranna I felt light and airy and at home. I suppose I am totally bewildered as to why I am allowed into this beautiful world.'

Elios cut across my words.

'Lael, on Earth you loved the animal kingdom, you respected the trees and the birds of the air, you were at home by the sea and on the mountain tops, you felt at one with the natural world. No one person on Earth will ever be barred from Ulana.

But every once in a while on their journey in the world of Earth certain women and men feel the elements in them, a feeling of a higher power at work that they cannot put a name to, but they know it is there.

Although they are not aware of it they are standing on the cusp of the physical and spiritual divide, within them is love of all natural things so they tread easily and lightly with little guidance when they arrive into the world of spirit.'

My numb look seemed to amuse her as she laughed aloud and when she laughed it sent musical ripples all around the bower and beyond, then she spoke again.

'Lael settle down, we are all spirits together so take your time, breathe the air; the tree next to you is called Herel a tree of destiny, feel his bark and he will know your energy mark.'

I did as I was bid, Roscranna had introduced me to many trees on my journey to the place of Elios so I knew how to address them, finding my voice I called him by his name.

'Herel I touch your skin and ask you to transmit some of your wisdom and energy to me'. I embraced the tree and was straightaway locked into a spiritual embrace the like of which I had never experienced with any tree so far.

My mind felt as though eons of time, worlds and lives were being fed into my memory, as if entering Ulana were nothing compared to the hyper energy that filled my whole being in my connection with the tree of destiny.

I felt the rush of living through other lives which Elios informed was the spirit of me occupying physical bodies in past lives. I was an old spirit and had passed through many humans before being called back to Ulana.

As we broke contact I knew that in the space of a heartbeat I had changed, I felt bigger in stature, confident in mind and a sense of belonging from a long time ago.

Erim Elios came forward and took me by the

shoulders and looked me straight in the eyes, she held me for a time before saying…

'Lael, your destiny is not forever in Ulana - your journey does not end here, you are bound to be an ascendant spirit, come walk with me and I will explain my words'.

We walked along the path of light which wound its way up to a knoll, from the top we looked over the trees to a distant sea, the blue green of that distant ocean seemed to be a continuation of the forest roof. The soft undulating movement of leaves and branches seemed to blend with blue-green water that stretched as far as the eye could see.

Water that looked placid and still and yet there was motion, movement that was so slight it was as if it was waiting for some event. Then Elios was in my thought telling me, 'Look further Lael, across the MoAraian Sea. Use your mind to extend your vision and tell me what lays there?'

I focused with my mind and my eyes told me what was at the end of the sea, I was excited by the picture I saw. 'It's a range of mountains of different shapes but there is one prominent one right in the centre, it is conical and higher than all the rest.'

Elios entered my thoughts again 'Your eyes have seen what is there, now tell me what your spiritual mind tells you about that distant shore.'

Again I looked at that far shore and this time I sensed something mystical about the land, as if it was apart from Ulana but not separate, there seemed to be a presence about the conical mountain but I could not ascertain what it was, I voiced my thoughts to Elios.

She answered me once again in thought. 'The mountain is known as MoAra and it is the abode of a faerie guardian called Sonal, she was here before I came to the MoAraian forest and you sensed her presence from afar, Herel was right, your eternity is not in Ulana.

Sonal was the progenitor of the elves on Earth and her name then was Dris-mir; she was the first faerie to leave Earth. With her band of faerie females and males she formed the circle of light high up on the peaks of MoAra.

They are called the Ailim faeries as they were first of our race to occupy Ulana, Ica herself gave Dris-mir her new name of Sonal to mark her identity in the evolving spirit world of Ulana.'

'Who or what is Ica?' I asked.

'You will learn of Ica when you are ready, now you must learn to project your thoughts.' So saying she turned to face me and I looked up at her green sparkling eyes, the russet brown skin, the thin high-arched eyebrows and a pointed ear just showing through the thick auburn hair. The face was beautiful and the feminine body shape was perfect in every detail.

The green mantle that she wore clung to her all the way to her feet. On her bare arms she had a tattoo that resembled a snake, one on each arm that wound their way up to her shoulders, disappearing into the green.

In her hand she carried a long slim wand which had a green crystal stone set on the top. I looked into her eyes again and saw with my spiritual vision a beautiful mind, wise beyond belief and very powerful. I was about to tell her it was no good when she held up her hand and said.

'I thank you Lael for the complimentary scan of mind and body but I will remind you that we are all beautiful in spirit, your spirituality will increase at a great rate. I have already appointed a mentor for you.'

'You are going to be together in spirit with Liath, a blue elf of the mountains and he will be here soon to take you on a journey of fulfilment, you will grow to be like him in stature and in spirit. He will suit your mind set as you were infatuated with the idea of elves and their pointed ears when you were of Earth.'

She went on to say, 'Liath will be here to take part in the meditation of the night with myself and with you. Every single spirit in Ulana lifts their faces up to their guiding star - we are in the first quadrant so our star is Iaphalon.

Opasania is the guiding light for the second quadrant; Irius for the third and Ebinis for the fourth quadrant. Every area in the World of Ulana is watched over by a guiding star.

It is the nearest thing we have to sleep but it is deeper than sleep. In meditary slumber we send out our messages to the universe and all the spirits in Ulana are united in this trance-like state.

We give out all our goodness and energy to the myriad of stars in all the universes; know this Lael, there are worlds of physical beings and worlds of spirits out there in the great cosmos. Life entities of all shapes and sizes and intellects and all of them share what you had when you were on Earth, a physical frame that housed both self and a spiritual essence.

Always remember when in thought communication with another that as the universe receives so also it gives. Along with Ulana all other spirit worlds send out their spiritual vibrations to all the universes bound together by the unseen matter that is alive in the great vastness of space, it is older than time and it is the creator of all things.'

Even though I had heard most of what she said from Roscranna I was staggered by her statement and I told her so. 'Elios I cannot take in something that can be older than time.'

Elios replied. 'Time is the illusionary guide for the machinations of the human race, there are many things in the spirit world that defy the Earthly logic of physics, but heed this.

Spirit was at work long before the Earth was formed, like the spiral in its steady rotation it knows no end or beginning as its motion is both upward and downward, so it is with the spirit, ever present and everlasting. Liath will teach you so much and you will enjoy your journeys with him.'

My mentor-to-be arrived just before evening. He took council with Elios first then they both came to me. I had been spending some pleasant time with Minver practicing my thought speech.

Minver returned to her position at the foot of the white path and I accompanied Elios and Liath to a place where we were to meditate. I liked Liath immensely the moment I was introduced to him. All spirit creatures that I had met on the journey were pleasant of countenance but Liath had a face that looked as if he was laughing all the way from the soles of his feet.

He was taller than me but smaller than Elios, he had the blue pallor to his skin which was the mark of his race. His hair was black as the raven's wing, tied back behind his neck with what looked like the feathers of the same bird. He wore a skirted tunic of some kind pulled in at the waist with the same feathery cord that adorned his hair.

His tread was light but his upper body bent forward as if it was trying to get ahead of his legs. Elios said it was an eternity of climbing hills that made him walk that way and he only comes down into the plains when he is asked.

My first meditary state was an event that bound me to the spiritual continuum - I was part of a whole world of spirits, trees, animals, plants and all the denizens of the seas.

Every single lifeform facing their guiding lights sending so much love to the mighty universe - if only the human race could emulate such a feat!

Liath and Lael

After the meditation Liath took me by the arm and practically hauled me away from the bower of Elios.
He said. 'C'mon Lael, let us run through the forest all the way to the foothills of Eilisel and there we will ascend to the highest peaks. My legs are telling

me they need stretching.'

I said. 'I should surely say goodbye to Elios before I take leave of her, maybe she needs to tell me more about Ulana.'

Liath laughed to his very ears - because his pointed ears actually lifted up slightly - it was really funny.

'Do not think too much about the doings of faerie Lael, if Elios has something to say she will contact you in thought. Now is our time, come away with me to the high hills and the majestic glens of Ulana.'

Then we were off on my first great journey in Ulana out-with my entry, and it begun just as Liath said - we took off at the run. We went through the MoAraian forest at great speed and some of the times we were joined by elves and at other times deer and antelope.

We were even joined by a pack of afghan hounds and they looked so well and happy in their environment; legs stretched to the limit and long flowing hair, their long pointed faces surging forward reflecting the joy of a whole world to run in with no constraints whatsoever.

We burst out of the forest into a wide open glen and I had to stop to take in the wonder I saw before me. Liath must have anticipated that I was going to stop running as he had already stopped slightly ahead of me.

My eyes took in the biggest, greenest and most fantastic glen I had ever seen. It was gigantic - a great deep valley stretching as far away as my eye could see, shouldered by high- high hills of variegated hues of purple, green and yellow.

In the distance I could make out silver wisps of water threading their way down from the hills to the valley floor. A faint shimmering reflection told me a lake of water had formed and from that spilled the gently flowing river that wound its way to where Liath and I had stopped.

Everywhere in that glen were life entities - earth spirits, elves, dogs, horses, in fact so much life I could not list them all. But for all the activity that was going on it was not crowded. The glen absorbed them all, they were part of it and it was part of them, a wonderful amalgamation of life forms.

I felt tremendous joy when I beheld two earthen spirits and an elf with a cocker spaniel and a German shepherd - how real was that? On the walk with Roscranna she instilled in me to think of the reality of Ulana and the unreality of Earth.

Now my mind never dwells on the unreality of violence, destruction, hatred and alienation of the land and the disempowerment of the animal kingdom. I know and love the reality of Ulana.

Liath said. 'Lael this is the great glen of Eilisel, I call this glen the gateway to the peak of enlightenment, see with your far away vision, away beyond what looks like the end of Eilisel.

Through the shimmering light of Ulana's sky you may discern a very pointed hill - I call it the peak of further enlightenment. Its proper name is the Sky Pinnacle - because it seems to reach up to the universe.

At night, as you will see when we get there, you would think you were in amongst the starry clusters.'

Then we were off at great speed, I was exhilarated by the sheer spiritual motion of our movement and yet I was taking in everything as we swept passed.

Such was our speed that it felt as if the two of us were static and the scenery was a series of visionary pictures flashing past.

In what seemed like the twinkling of an eye we reached the head of the glen of Eilisel and there we paused for a while by the side of a great loch which Liath called Sonal.

He told me that the climb to the top of the pinnacle would take in many meditary slumbers. This was due to the fact that the pinnacle had many levels of learning and he named a few.

Liath said. 'We begin the climb where all climbs begin – at the base, we will linger at the start and you and I both will take in what is going on there. Then, when you feel you are ready, we will head for the next level.'

I asked him what it was like at the very top and his answer fairly took me aback.

He said. 'Lael I have never been to the top, I go as far as the level that is known as the Window of the Crystal Cave. When I reach that level I am contented with the beauty and the vision I get from where I stand, I have never felt any readiness to go any further.'

I said. 'So I might not even get as far as the Window of the Crystal Cave, I thought it was a straightforward climb to the top.'

Liath stood up and held his arms outstretched and said. 'Lael look around you, see the life entities that wander about here by the side of Sonal water, what do you feel about them?'

I said. 'They all look so happy and contented the vibration of absolute joy is all around.'

'Exactly!' said Liath. 'They came into the spirit world with the perfection of their own souls and companionship of the natural world. The animal kingdom which most of them knew nothing about, the elements of nature that was taken so much for granted on Earth. For many, this is the Elysian fields of the Romans, the Heaven of the Christians and the Tir Nan Og of the Celts; all of them are here now under the name of Ulana -   who would ever want to leave it?'

I said. 'How many pinnacles are there to climb, I thought when I came to the spirit world and accepted that it was the land of eternal youth, that would be journeys end?'

'We are the kindlings of a fire, as we rise in spirituality so we get closer to the light. Until finally the light consumes us, we become part of the light and the light shines on forever, its speed reaches far into dark space to who knows where.

You Lael are an old soul, your spirit form has passed through many human bodies when on Earth. You have learned much during these transitions and that is why you have been called back to Ulana. Your stay will not be long, of that I am sure you, will become part of the light in this side of the Fire Glow - in its race to the final destination.'

Liath laughed that laugh that made his ears lift and I laughed with him, then he went on to explain about the pinnacle.

'Lael we are not the only spirit world within the universes, I am sure Roscranna made you aware of that during the walk to the MoAraian forest. When your life on Earth ended your death was not the end - it became a new beginning right here in Ulana. We are proof that there is life after death, so if that belief is projected on a higher scale; visualize a world that has shed all its physical beings into its relevant spirit world.

Now that all the life entities are gone the world dies, usually by explosion, but where does all the mass and energy go? Most of it will be dissipated in space, some minute grains will be recognised by other ones far away and they will gravitate to that source.

Even though a world has died - its shattered parts will evolve and live again in one form or another.

So it will be with the spirit worlds, all the life entities will congregate as one, eventually all will be consumed within the light then it will be as it began – light and darkness, then who knows?

Lael the pinnacle of Ulana is a stepping stone to the greater glory, later when the age of stars comes near to their end, all will have ascended in love and light.'

I knew what Liath said would come to pass, and as I stared past him at the great pinnacle I got a brief flicker in my mind of a place and name akin to where I stood then.

It was a very green land across a vast ocean, but it was not in Ulana! I also knew I was ready for the top of the pinnacle and I told Liath so.

He did not show any emotion at my statement but

he did say a few words of reason and a warning.

'Lael, I believe you will ascend and it will be rapid. However I saw in your aura - black shapes that were all over you. Wherever you go out-with Ulana tread warily, always be on the alert.

Come, let us be off and make for the base of the pinnacle - we meditate at the first level.'

It did not take us long to reach the base of the peak, we arrived just before the meditary sleep and it was great to see all life that had gathered there.

Just before I fixed my gaze on Iaphalon I glanced around and noticed a few wolves sitting amongst a gathering of elves. It enhanced my pleasure seeing them sitting there, and just like me they were looking upwards to Iaphalon, the guide to Ulana.

At certain times during the meditation the spirits take up chanting, it is a mixture of the voice tones of the various life entities. The elves usually lead the chant as their sounds are sweet and melodious. Within the mellifluous assembly, the rising and falling howl of the wolves blended well in that sacred huddle at the base of the sky pinnacle. The meditary night gave way to the light of day and the spirits dispersed, Liath asked me what I wanted to do - as if he didn't know!

I said. 'I have to climb the pinnacle now that I know what it is about; I know I am ready to go. The tree of destiny said I would continue to ascend the levels of spirituality and in the magic of space find my zenith.'

Liath said. 'We start now Lael, at the foot of the pinnacle is the level of earth and it is where we all are. The next level is water, the level after that is air and that is where the Crystal Cave is. That is my level so we must wait and see what my feelings are when we get there.

The top of the pinnacle is the level of fire.'

At the mention of the word fire I almost shouted at Liath.

'Liath - how can there be fire in Ulana, it is the abhorrence of trees ------

I was cut off in mid-stream by Liath, who held up both his hands in mock surrender and said.

'Lael I do not know too much about the level of fire because I have never been ready for it, and because I have not been ready I do not ask of any creature what it is about.

But I do know that in the beginning of all things fire was an entity that was present in the making of the worlds.

In our mother planet of Earth, stone and rock was the foundation of all the life forces. The destiny of the planet was written in fire, from a solid spinning core a burning event drove an ever moving melt of stone to a mosaic of churning - flowing - molten evolution. That event moulded the crust of the world and on that outer skin all life began.

The stones and rocks of the Earth were living entities that were formed in a cauldron of energy before any creature walked the Earth. More knowledgeable spirit entities than I have said that great Ica herself formed powerful life forces that breathed fire into the worlds.

Again I heard the mention of Ica, Elios did not

elaborate so I tried Liath to see how far I got with him.

'Who or what is Ica Liath?'

He replied in his usual enthusiastic manner. 'Great Ica took the light of the beginning of all things and made the worlds, it is she who gave us all this.' As he spoke he held his arms outstretched palms up, and wheeled himself round in circles shouting thanks to great Ica.

I got caught up in his exuberance and started shouting along with him, and no sooner had I joined him in praise than other life entities round about took up the joyful chanting. It seemed as if all of Ulana had taken up the shout.

After the euphoria I asked again about Ica but Liath would not elaborate, he started where he left off before the mention of Ica.

'I say to you now that this journey will take many nights of meditary slumber but it is a wonderfully stimulating climb of self-discovery, so let us begin.'

The lower part of the pinnacle began with a graceful, afforested slope that beguiled me as to the height gain. It was after five nights of meditary slumber that we came out of the forest and I was able to see the blue loch of Sonal so very far below.

We climbed ever upwards for another five meditary nights, but this stage of the journey was open country. Grass and moss carpeted the slope and many colourful flowers and bushes added to the ambience of the hill.

We did not see many beings or animals during the forest hike but out on the open hill it was different.

We saw and had meditation with a few members of the animal kingdom. Then we met with a party of spirit people and some elves and they joined us for a fair bit of the journey.

I got in conversation with a female called Ess and she took me by surprise by saying that I faintly resembled an elf! I told her that I was human Earth spirit like her and that I was not that long in Ulana.

Ess then asked if I had been close to Liath in mind and body for long and had I shared in many meditations.

Roscranna had said that the spirit shape grew to resemble another entity that it respected and felt comfortable with, however I did not feel myself changing nor did Liath make any comment on my appearance at any time.

Ess told me she was not a nice person on Earth, and as she grew older she abused her body with strong drink and general debauchery. She eventually died on a bench by a sea shore.

When she passed through the veil she was met by an elvess at a shore on the fringe of one of Ulana's great seas. This was her first time on the pinnacle and she was enjoying it immensely.

Liath came back from where he had been standing away from the company, acknowledged Ess and told me it was time to ascend.

With a wave to Ess I was off after the lord of the hills, who had set off at yet another cracking pace. He took the time to say to me that one more night of meditation and we would reach the level of Water.

In the light of day after meditation we were off again, we gained height for a while and then we arrived at what I would describe as a huge shelf that pushed itself into the body of the pinnacle.

The first thing I noticed was a very long drop of sparkling blue water that ended its headlong plunge into a loch. The loch curved itself around a bastion of silver rock which was the backdrop of the falling water.

Many small plants and trees grew at the edge of the shelf, as we got nearer to the loch I saw small, tender looking trees with silver trunks and branches - they were no more beautiful than the other trees but they contrasted well among the gold, brown and green trunks of the rest of the trees.

The combination of all the coloured trees and bushes and the magnificent backdrop of tumbling water; the blue mirror like surface of the loch that absorbed the weight of water without as much of a ripple - it was perfect tranquility .

All around were elves and spirits, the tones of their laughter and talking added to the perfect ambience of the place. As we walked forward I saw that there were smaller pools of water out-with the loch.

White cranes and pink flamingos stood in and around the waters, their bright plumage adding to the ambience of the level. I felt a touch and realised it was a pied wagtail perched on my shoulder, his wagging tail fanning my ear.

He hopped off my shoulder and perched himself on Liath's head and then flew to the grassy flat to the front of us. He skittered among the cranes with the eccentric gait which marks his kind.

Liath watched the bird and shook his head; he turned to me and said. 'Come Lael; let us to the water's edge.'

We looked into the water from the top of a rock which was grey in colour but was speckled with flecks of a coppery colour. We stood side by side, mirrored in the blue water and immediately I saw the difference between us.

Liath was tall and athletic his blue pallor merged in the water, his pulled back hair exposed the pointed ears. I was smaller and paler in comparison and although my ears had lost their roundedness they were not quite pointed.

Liath got behind me and pulled my ears back we both laughed and carried on with our antics watching the images in the water.

We stayed at the level of water for many nights of meditation and had the kinship of many elves, spirits, birds and animals. I loved the place - it was so real and although we were still in Ulana I felt as if I was on a separate plain and I told Liath what I felt.

'That is what you will feel when you are in the state of readiness and I know you want to go further upwards to the level of Air.'

I agreed and in typical Liath fashion he pushed me in the direction we were to take amidst a chorus of laughter from some elves and spirits.

We made our way through a clump of silver trees which led to a winding path somewhere behind the waterfall rock. There are no defined paths in Ulana so I was surprised to see the path leading upwards looked a bit contrived.

Liath saw my look, and accompanied by the effervescent laugh said. 'Lael what better way to reach the level of Air than by an open-air staircase, and I think you will enjoy this one.'

The way to the level of Air proved to be an experience even by Ulana's standards, we followed a zig-zag path which was totally exposed on one side all the way.

Ivy and other creeping plants hugged the side of the rock but the greatest feeling came from the changing energy of the air. All the way up we were caressed by differing waves of motion from the air, it felt as if we were being breathed in, not the other way about.

We could not see the earth below because a haze of some kind obscured the view and likewise the summit was blinded to us. We had a window of light which kept on a level with us all the twisted way to the Crystal Cave. …….It seemed as if every bird in Ulana flew into that band of clear view at one time or other. Carried in and out by the wafts of the energetic air I could feel their emotions as a spirit form sharing their freedom of the sky.

The level of Air was well named as for most of the time I felt I was floating in a window in the sky of Ulana.

I was taken out of my reverie by Liath saying. 'Here we are Lael, the Crystal Cave at your disposal.'

I looked inside the cave and was dazzled by the splendour of the light reflecting off the crystals. On the opposite side to the opening I stood at was another opening and through the glinting, gleaming show of light I saw two more openings, one on either side of the dazzling cavern. In the middle a spring of water flowed softly from a source in the crystal wall.

But the level of Air had filled me with a need for more and I knew then I was ready for the level of Fire, I told Liath what my feelings were.

He did not seem surprised at my statement and straight away said if my feelings told me I was ready then follow them to Fire. He tailed off by saying he would still be at the Crystal Cave when I came down.

I resumed the path that we had followed all the way to the cave but this time the air around me had changed and I had no longer had a window of light.

A haze enveloped me I could not even see my feet - I was drifting up the pinnacle, not walking. Then with a suddenness that stopped me dead, the mist cleared and I was at the top. It was exactly the top; enough room for my two feet to stand comfortably and when the mist had cleared I saw that the evening sky of Ulana was passing into the night of meditation.

I can safely say I stood among the stars that night, I was so high up I felt I could have reached out and touched some of them. Never in my spirit or Earth form have I felt so much a part of the mighty universe as I did that night.

One movement in particular drew my attention, within a cluster of brilliant white stars I could make out a shape blending in and out of the starlight. A body with a flicker of wings, so brief in my vision I was only able to make a comparison with the description of the angel that Roscranna told to me.

Most wonderful of all was a red glow far away past all the universes that ever were and like Roscranna's description - the afterglow where time began.

I watched the fabric of starlight fade away into the light of day then my senses were heightened by the redness of the sky - it was fire and such a fiery sky I had never seen, it was like a mirror of what I had seen during the night - the brief glimpse of infinity.

I felt as if I was breathing in the whole of creation and with that feeling hard on the departed starlight spectacular I was so humbled that I wept in the wonder of it all.

Although I knew my feet were planted on the tip of the pinnacle, all of the time I was there I felt I was suspended. Floating in my own space completely detached from below but totally absorbed in the upper limits.

Daralonadh

In another world somewhere in space two figures stood on a lonely hilltop. One was a female of the elfin race and she stood slightly taller than her companion – the other a furred being that resembled a giant cat standing upright.

The elvess was standing with a staff in her hand, around her waist hung a very potent looking sword. Her poise showed she was totally focused on the land in the far distance, she was searching not only with her eyes but also her mind.

'Have you found where the malice is coming from

Elid?' The question was growled out from the cat being.

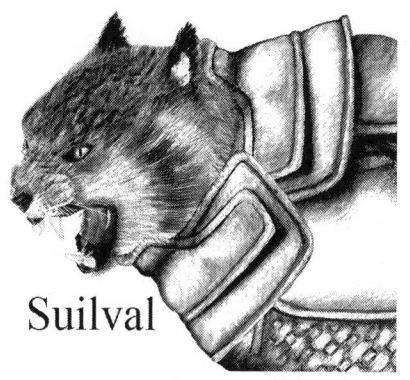

Suilval

The answer came slow as if the elfin woman was coming back from a long way away in her mind. 'Yes Suilval it's out there somewhere but whatever it is – is very powerful because I cannot track the energy.'
Suilval said. 'What can we do about the bad energy if we do not know where it comes from, surely you Elid, who has the magical power of the faerie can trace this badness?'
'Ah!' said Elid. 'Remember after the last great battle when the faerie folk and a great number of our elves left to go their own ways?'
'Yes Elid I remember well, even after the battle there was great upheaval in the lands of the Laic and beyond. I will never forget the sight and sound of the warrior elf Cimer as he led his elves from the battle field. With the weird sound of their war pipes and the steady beat of the drums of the Lael elves following on, it was an unforgettable event.
Many other creatures of the land followed Cimer to the wild wastes of Dargal, most of the faeries, or

maybe all, returned to the spirit world of Ulana - wherever that may be!'

The elvess answered Suilval with a hint of a reprimand. 'Do not scoff at the mention of the spirit world of Ulana Suilval, it is a wonderful place filled with blissful energy. However I must take blame for allowing the bad energy to get a grip on the lands out-with.

After the last great battle I made my bounds in the lands of the Laic and surrounded it with allies, I took no interest in what was going on in the wastes of Dargal or the Black island.'

Suilval said. 'Well I know a place of blissful strong drink and I think that is where we should go now and forget about the black magic for a while.'

With no more said, the elvess and the giant cat turned about and headed down the steep hill to wherever Suilval's bliss was.

Worlds Apart

I came down from the Pinnacle of Fire and true to his word Liath was waiting for me at the level of air. He looked at me and gave a laugh saying 'Lael, you went to the level of fire like an Earth spirit and you have come down looking like me, you have been transformed into a blue elf.'

I wondered at myself on the way down - I put it down to the euphoria of what I had experienced at the fire pinnacle, I had not realised that my spirit body had transfigured.

We retraced our steps laughing and talking as we did on the way up, not once did Liath ask me what I saw at the level of fire. I felt within myself that my time with Liath was nearly over, and yet it had hardly begun.

We had many, many nights of meditation with each other before I got the call. It reached me one evening before the night gathering. I was with Liath and a brown bear called Ura when Elios's voice came softly into my mind.

'Lael, your journeys in Ulana are now almost ending, you are now ready to begin a new one, one which will take you on a great adventure and ultimately to greater heights of ascendancy. After this nights meditation Liath will accompany you to the MoAraian forest.'

And then she was gone and I breathed long and slow, taking in all that was around me. I methodically thanked every tree, plant, animal, elf and earth spirit that was round about me at that event. I sent out love to each and every one and it came back to me in abundance from all.

I asked Liath why Elios was able to project thoughts from so far and was most surprised by his answer.

'Lael, not only in Ulana can Elios project thought but almost anywhere in the universe, all that is needed is an entity that recognises her thought essence and will answer her.'

Liath took me to the edge of the MoAraian forest after the spiritual slumber and said that was as far as he was coming. He wished me love and said that we would meet in the great fusion of light.

I entered the forest and chose my direction to the bower of Elios, my journey was a lot slower than the one I took with Liath. I had one meditation in a belt of Scots pine along with a gathering of elves.

Not long after the meditary slumber Elios came for me and told me it was time for me to go out-with the bounds of Ulana.

As we made our way through the forest Elios told me not to look back, she said the way is forward to another part of my journey and the meeting of new life entities.

I walked alongside the faerie of the MoAraian forest and part of me remembered the first time I met her, but now the greater part of me was filled with a new sense of purpose. She had already told me about the boulder field and what its purpose was in the great workings of the universes.

She said the mighty sea that swept over the boulder field marked the way of portals leading to other worlds. As she spoke we appeared at the edge of a great expanse of rocks. Elios turned to me and motioned outwards with her staff saying.

'Here Lael is the great seashore - forward is your direction now and I will give my thoughts to you when you cross the great divide. Go in light and love.'

I did as she said, without a backward look I walked to the start of a new journey and another world. I stopped after a while and took it all in.

A giant pebble beach that stretched out to the eternal sea, it was linked to the tunnel which carried the ascending spirits into the eccentric world of Darwan. Elios had told me I had to spend the darkening in amongst the rocks of the boulder field.

I do not know why I had to spend a night in the

boulder field, I felt no difference round about me and Iaphalon shone with its usual brightness high above.

After the night in the boulder field I came out of my meditating slumber, the air was sharp and bright and the tang of sea air filled my senses.

I was refreshed and exhilarated by the thought of the new experience about to happen. I thanked the rocks and sands beneath my feet, the still and running waters of land and sea and the innumerable universes for who I am and where I go. May I be worthy of the part I play.

I vacated my rocky refuge where I had spent the night calmed by the luminance of Iaphalon. Skipping lightly from boulder to boulder I came to a halt atop a rock which was higher than the surrounding stones. I had spied its pointed summit from the moment I stood up after my medi-sleep.

Red and rugged looking it seemed massive against its lower companions and yet even it was but a pebble on that vast shore. Like its brother boulders it waited patiently for the refreshing taste of salt water from the incoming tide of the mighty sea that would spend itself on that gigantic foreshore.

Elios told me that I would be catching the tide, it would be still and waiting for a while, building up its impetus for its white foaming charge to the boulder field. Watch for the violet elvettes - they will be heading for the tide line and they will be your escorts.

Those had been the parting words from Elios the faery as we had stood on a rocky plateau before the boulder field. It was not a sad parting because I was elated with the knowing that I had been chosen for ascension in spirit. I had been chosen to take an upward path that many had trod before me.

Elios would be in thought communication with me from time to time and told me I would meet friendly entities on land, sea and air wherever I went. There are creatures of physical body who love the plant, animal and bird kingdom, they may be in the minority but they are there.

They endeavour to keep a semblance of order in the chaotic life system of Darwan. She also told me Elid Silverhair would be expecting a visit from me, however I could not draw her to give out any more information on whom or what Elid Silverhair was.

As I made my way across the boulder field a thought took me, I go ultimately to a greater place, if I fail I will be whisked back to Ulana - only the greater spirits of the universes will know of my success, the rest may only guess. Well as Elios said, there is no success or failure only a state of readiness.

I was aware of beings skipping and jumping over the boulders - and sure enough it was the violet elvettes. Like bundles of pure energy bent on having fun they swarmed past me, some shouting. 'Come spirit - come with us to meet the wave.'

I joined the melee and got caught up in the euphoria of their excitement, jumping over boulders, sliding down dried blades of seaweed, skipping over shells and all the time shouting and laughing with the elvettes in pure delight - and then abruptly we all stopped and gazed ahead.

There in front of us in all its blue glory - the sea - a great expanse of passive water waiting to begin its mad rush to the shore. The elvettes waited as well, they ride the wild waves to the shore with the same childish energy they used on the boulder field.

Then they got excited at something else, a huge turtle had surfaced in front of us and some of the elvettes had climbed on its back, they are so light they can skip on the surface of the water. 'Spirit, spirit, the turtle comes to carry you over the great water —come – come!'

Their twittering never stopped, even when I got on the turtles back they crowded on with me, singing and dancing; others splashing and happy in the water, some swimming and diving. It was so funny seeing their pointed feet sticking out of the water. Then the turtle headed out to sea and my happy violet friends jumped off waving and shouting their farewells.

Then the sea moved and I saw the small creatures poised ready to catch the first wild wave, still screaming and shouting to each other. I opened my thoughts to the turtle. Turtle's thoughts matched the speed of his movements however; he was a gentle spirit and told me he had carried many spirits on their upward journey.

I made a mental calculation based on the vastness of the sea around us and the turtles speed, then ventured the question.

'When are we likely to reach Darwan turtle?' I could almost hear turtle's thoughts gathering before he even thought them out to me - I said to myself. We will be there before he answers.

However Turtle did answer eventually, he started by giving me a mini reprimand in the nicest - slowest way. 'Spirit Lael, I don't need to remind you that time is meaningless here - did not Elios of the faery folk tell you that we exist in readiness - forever readiness.

Time is for Earth mortals to live by, it is important to them and they wear time on their wrists; they have time on their walls; they build towers of stone with faces of time on them.

They are ruled by segments of time and it never occurs to them that they are bound by the hands of time. But time scoffs at all their instruments and streams past oblivious to the human attempt to stretch it out or harness it.

Now in answer to your question I will ask you a question. Look to your front spirit and tell me what you see?'

I did as turtle said and was surprised to see a bright, shining, elliptical shape hovering over the sea.

'The power of the rushing sea provides the energy to open the portal of light and so the veil is parted for a short time. Step off my back spirit of Ulana - go in love.'

BEITH

I stepped into the light and in an instant all changed, I was in a tunnel - at least it felt like a tunnel, only it was a downward spiral of purple and indigo haze. Lights twinkled like mini-stars through the mist of colour, then I was on solid ground.

I looked up and beheld a watery blue sky, a yellow sun was hovering over distant hills and all was quiet. My feet felt the bare rock; eyes took in the sparse vegetation and tall willowy trees, no fragrance in the air or moist taste on my lips. I felt despair all around, I didn't know then if some of the despair was in me or the land I stood on.

I took my first heavy steps in the stark landscape, from the delight of the elvettes, the serenity of turtle and the wonder of the starlight tunnel to drab air and bare earth. I was amazed at how heavy I felt, the lightness I was used to in Ulana had left me the instant I had set foot in Darwan.

A voice in my mind told me that this is not the way it is meant to be, however the voice was my own, so

I quietened it and focused on my surroundings.

To one side were a group of sad trees, and under my feet grass with no life, whatever events occur in this Darwan world this is where I make my entrance. Lael of Ulana has arrived here and has the power of healing. I spoke out loud so that my vibration would be carried through the air all around, all life within voice range would hear what I had to say.

'Mineral earth, shrubs, bushes and trees take my healing - feel my aura of spirit which is the essence of all life.' I stooped low over the grass and gave it my touch until I felt a flickering of life. I projected my light through the green blades down into the root systems - from the roots the light spread to the earth beyond, cleaning it for all time.

Next I turned to the bushes, encompassing them in my aura, filling them with the magic of the spirit, they responded instantly to my healing. The trees were already feeling the tremors of energy through their roots as I turned my attention to them - walking among them - soothing - feeding - energising - talking.

'Trees we are linked to you, we need you as you need us, you are a universal life force just like us and you will grow in splendour; you are the start of a magnificent forest in which you will always stand tallest.

Physical creatures and spirits will live and care for your kingdom of plants; growing under your guardianship the birds of the air will return and nestle in the shelter of your ample spread and you will be known far and wide as the Forest of Lael.'

When I finished healing I sat down under the trees, I could feel their mood, pulling life force from the newly energised earth, filling their trunks with growth and wellbeing. Their leaves gratefully accepting the energy of the yellow sun which was now high above; I felt it was smiling down on my little world.

I meditated well in that little copse and although I knew I would not pass this way again it did not matter because part of me which is spirit and light will always be there. Then I got a surprise, a peculiar twisted tree which had its branches wrapped around its trunk started to unravel its boughs.

I looked on with wonder as I saw the tree's twisted branches reach upward to the sky, but even more wonderful was the stone that was revealed which had been hidden within the bosom of the tree.

The stone was ancient looking and had markings of some kind on it; I couldn't make out what they were. The top end had bits sticking out of it as if there had been arms of a cross and I wondered what race of life entity had put it there and for what reason.

I stayed in that small huddle of spirituality for the remainder of the day's light and when darkness came I stayed there under the trees with my back against the stone. I was still aglow with energy from the day's work and that was further enhanced when I saw the night sky of Darwan.

I was so impressed with the starry night - a myriad of twinkling lights, stars, planets and a moon that was full and low in the sky. The moon was not completely round; it was more oblate than spherical and it was ringed, red ochre was the nearest colour I could think of, it had a slight corona which made it look as if it was floating and it gave an eerie reflection to the land.

With no Iaphalon to fix on I turned my focus on a star shining brightly above all the rest. It had a very blue light but it was restless, at times it held its colour then it would twinkle with green light tinged with white; then back to blue again, a truly wonderful sight. My mind and body went into suspension that night under the watchful eye of that star which I named Artel.

In the early light of the Darwan day I left my little flourishing kingdom and went where my intuition took me, with the forest of Lael behind me I took an upward path by a rocky ravine of falling water.

The higher I climbed so also the ravine at my side steepened and the fall of water accompanied me with its noisy bubbling motion as it careered in splashing whiteness in its hurry to get off the hill.

Finally I arrived at a plateau, although it looked more like a huge bowl had been carved out of the hill itself, I made out huge shapes of random boulders scattered about the grey basin. High ramparts of stone reared up on one side, to the front I could make out a peak through the drifting grey mists.

On the other side a long low ridge of undulating stone wound its way like a never ending rampart to disappear into the obscurity of greyness 'Where did that yellow sun go?' Everything was grey, even the one or two lochans that glinted at me reflected the same grey gloom that haunted the place.

My eyes lingered on the stone shapes that lay all around and at first glance I surmised they had rolled off the high slopes at one time in the past, but as I focused on them I began to realise each and every one had been carved to form shapes and symbols of some kind.

Then as that realisation came I began to make out shapes of living creatures moving and working amongst the boulders. The reason I didn't see them to start with was because they blended in with the surrounding drabness, short two legged beings very reminiscent of the men of earth.

I made my way towards them and as I closed the distance they became aware of me. They chattered in a language I felt I knew from a distant time, more of them appeared out of the mists alerted by the words of their companions.

Then awareness that they could see me hit my mind with mild curiosity - I was supposed to pass through Darwan unseen by the physical life entities that inhabit it.

The power of the spirit enables me to communicate in thought and voice and even if I haven't heard a language before I can understand it immediately and communicate -such is the way of the spirit.

It came to me that they were dazzled by my appearance as in their drab world any semblance of colour would stand out. Questions were coming thick and fast and short thick hands were touching me, it wasn't really me they were touching, only my aura which emanated and followed my body shape. I told them who I was and they were greatly excited when I told them I had come up from the land at the bottom of the mountain.

One, who told me his name was Ser, informed me that they used to live in the lands below but their masters moved them up to the hills to labour on the stones. They lived in caves and stone houses all around the grey plateau and survived on the scant vegetation, small animals and birds.

Ser said the masters used to come to check on them for a while but they stopped coming long - long ago. I told them that there was no one at the bottom of the mountain now and that I had created a new forest which would need caring for, I addressed them all saying.

'Go, take yourselves and your possessions to the land at the bottom of the mountain and claim what is rightfully yours, live in harmony with the new born land; take care of it and it will take care of you. Go now and allow yourselves to grow alongside the forest of Lael.'

It gave me so much pleasure to see the grey people collecting their meagre possessions and start heading down the hill to a life of colour and meaning. Ser lingered with me a while and gave me another piece of information, he told me when the masters sent the people to the hills there were other people who were put on a ship and sailed away to who knows where.

He then said goodbye and followed on after his companions. I watched them until they disappeared from sight then walked on in the direction of my own journey. I passed over the peak that I had spied when I arrived on the stone plateau and wound my way down to a flat, bleak stretch of grass and stone.

It seemed endless; stretching as far as my eye could see was an undulating landscape of grey stone devoid of any life - silent - sinister. The air matched the mood of the land, in shared grief they seemed to be waiting for some event to break their sombre bond to release one from the other.

The change from the beauty of my first night in Darwan to this dismal atmosphere was hard to comprehend. I had been warned by Elios about the drabness of the land and that it would hang heavy on me, my feet would feel heavy and the air that I breathed would be cold and damp at every intake; well that was upon me now.

Probably the euphoria of the healing session then the magic of the night sky followed by the release of the stone people had blinded me to the reality of the harsh land I was in. It felt as though I walked forever on that stony plain, a grey mist clinging to me, no horizon, no birds, no animals - silence.

I was a grey spirit in a grey world; my mind was a mud of near despair until suddenly!!! I hadn't felt their presence - they were on me it was as if they had appeared out of the air and when they came at me it was like the air itself was charged with evil intent. I had the reflex to charge my aura outside my body - this managed to stop the initial onslaught.

Fierce demented black shapes that threw themselves at my spiritual aura like things possessed, which I'm sure they were, like demons from childhood nightmares. Features contorted, green barbed teeth set within wide slavering jaws, chomping and chewing out what I imagined were hideous screams - at least I was spared the noise because of my protective aura.

There were dozens of them and when they smashed against my aural shield their body shapes grew bigger and more sinewy, their arms were long and ended in huge taloned claws with which they hammered and scraped at my defence. All around me were harsh horrible faces pressed against my invisible bubble of safety.

The faces were doglike, their angular muzzles like black ebony and yet when they crashed into my spiritual aura their faces squashed and became almost flat which made them wide and more terrible looking, exposing the deadly looking green fangs.

The gums that held them were blue and slimy with a constant flow of saliva which seemed to spray everywhere. The skins of the creatures were black and jelly like, their black eyes bore at me with malignant intent.

I tried to project my thoughts to any friendlies that might be about, but the combination of trying to maintain my protection and keep my mind off the horror of the creatures, whatever they were, was too much; I could not keep my mind-set and I knew I was weakening.

The shield was starting to bend because I was beginning to doubt the strength of my aura; the black shapes seemed to sense my weakness and redoubled their efforts. Now I could hear their piercing screams - like so many daggers the demonic shrieks stabbed at my protective bubble.

Not long now - when sound breaks the aura it's not long before physical force will penetrate the defence, and the aggressive energy of the creatures would certainly do that.

Escape was the answer - I thought if I was quick enough I could drop the shield and take them by surprise, and maybe move quickly through them - but I knew that it wouldn't work as I was getting weaker and they had doubled their numbers since the first onslaught.

Just when I thought all was lost I heard a different sound coming from behind the black hounds. Not the demented cries of the frontal assault but more like sounds of alarm - and it was coming from the demons at the back of the pack.

The panic of the cries was infectious because my attackers were breaking off - something was scaring them. As the black shapes disappeared from my aura I couldn't at first make out what was going on, but whatever was causing the turmoil with the demons they had started to flee in all directions.

The air was filled with panic stricken shrieks as they knocked and jostled each other in their haste to get away. My vision had cleared and I saw what was causing the creatures distress - and what a sight it was.

Two figures in the midst of the black confusion, wielding swords the like of which I had never seen before. Their movements were orchestrated as in fast and fluid motion they cut down the black devils, blades cutting and slashing, bodies dodging and swirling -pure energy and beautiful to watch - if it were not for the slaughter.

All around me I could see the results of the weird duos fighting prowess. Decapitated bodies; arms and legs lay about, some demons had actually split in two - cleft from head to groin. Others had been sliced across the waist - the torso separated from legs.

Entrails and black treacle-like blood spewed everywhere and a horrible rotten smell pervaded the air. I was so fascinated by the rhythmic pair of warriors that I had not noticed that my aura had slipped, I was outside my protective shield but I felt safe now that I could see who my saviours were.

All the surviving black creatures had run off, leaving their dead or dying companions on the wasted plain where they had fallen, the dying had not long to wait as one of the fighters, a catlike creature, was moving about the scattered bodies finishing off any that still clung to life .

Being of spiritual mind and body I can see the essence of life leaving the body after death and I had seen many of the creatures departing to wherever they go after death; I had to marvel at the glorious colour their spirits took, especially since the bodies were so gruesome looking in their physical form.

A powerful looking elf came towards me, he was very tall and reminded me of Liath my blue elf friend and mentor, the elf's body looked as if it was made of flexible steel. His face bore the fine lines of the elfin race but they looked as if a hard lifestyle had chiselled them from stone.

There was no expression or softness of voice when

he faced me to ask who I was, although it was more of a statement of fact rather than a question.

'You are Lael, spirit of Ulana?' 'I am Ruis of the blue elfin and this is Suilval, a warrior female from the tribe of Selma and we have come to escort you to the lands of Elid Silverhair.'

His companion who he had introduced as Suilval had been padding round about me after she had finished her handiwork with the devil creatures and the acknowledgement I got was an offhand snarl.

They were a most intimidating pair and if it was not for the fact that I recognised the name of Elid Silverhair I would have been very much on my guard. However I was not allowed to dwell on my thoughts as Ruis told me to follow his lead and stay close; Suilval said she would follow behind me.

I did as I was bid and dutifully fell in behind Ruis, who had already set off at a cracking pace before the words had hardly left his mouth. The big cat was close behind me, and yet for such a large creature she so was so very light in her tread that I had to look behind me to see if she was still there - I got a stiff rebuke for my troubles.

'Never mind what I am doing spirit, just watch out for yourself, I thought Ruis was light on his feet but you - you seem to float along, I think I will call you air-boy.'

'And I might call you snarl face!' I said that to myself, because I did not want any kind of dialogue with Suilval, I then tackled Ruis to see if I would fare better with him.

'How far is the place of Elid Silverhair, Ruis?' I used

my best voice tone to ask the question. I got a better response from him.

He pointed upwards to the yellow sun which was melting its way through the grey air.

'That, Lael, is Apuss - he is our daytime guide and when he appears for the third time we will be in sight of the Laic land.'

And that was it, the elf called Ruis clammed up and sped off with me trailing behind and conscious all the time of the furred, snarling entity at my back. I must say - thinking back to that seemingly endless journey I felt useless, redundant and any sense of purpose I had was dissipating fast into the grey stillness around us.

We trailed on throughout the day never pausing or communicating. I kept looking upwards to the sun - Apuss, as Ruis called it, shimmered behind the thickness of the atmosphere all during our journey. I tracked its path from overhead to where its curve had taken it as our journey progressed.

Ruis was obviously using Apuss as a guide and as the said guide dipped low to our immediate front the elf broke the silence.

'Apuss will be leaving us soon, we are coming to the pass of Fochd and we will stop there for a while and rest up.'

Suilval stuck her oar in with. 'Tell me air boy, do you sleep floating above the ground?'

'No, standing up or sitting down' was my curt reply, it got no response from the cat.

Ruis found a sheltered nook within the approaches of the Fochd pass, he and Suilval wasted no time in digging out bits of food which had been concealed on their persons. They sat side by side and started eating their fare, Ruis did ask me if I wanted anything to eat, I declined and he accepted that.

After they had eaten they stretched out and got into a sleeping position it was not long before both were sound asleep and silence reigned.

I moved out of the sleep area a bit and found a place where I could see as much of the now darkened sky as possible. In the quiet of that bower in the dark of evening I looked up at the sky. Across my field of vision the starry backdrop was alive with twinkling light and the hidden movement that only the spiritual eye can see.

Then I realised something was missing, the red ringed moon I had seen during my first night in Darwan, oh well, it might rise later on.

My mind went back to the advice Elios gave me before I entered the boulder field, it had been touching my thought waves from time to time during the passage to here.

Spirits passing through Darwan watch and during their passing can touch life entities by their unseen presence. When that happens healing can take place if it is needed.

However it is not appropriate for an ascendant spirit to meddle in the affairs of a world in turmoil such as Darwan, which is why the invisible corridors are created impenetrable. The faster speed of the life energy in the spirit body does not allow a spirit to break through to the heavy world of Darwan.

In contradiction an entity that has slow-moving life

energy, such as any Darwan creature, can pass through the unseen barrier with only a mild feeling of change which vanishes as quickly as it is felt.

It is the magic essence of light as it makes its way from where it was born to wherever it goes. It is an infinite energy that lives and breathes and carries the past, present and future of all it encompasses.

Elios was informative about the paths of spirits passing through Darwan and likened it to ley lines on Earth, whereby spirits walked well beaten tracks observing all events. Spirits pass unseen but some creatures feel their presence as they pass.

Then another thought struck me, Elios, when she spoke about the passage through Darwan, always spoke in the plural as regards spirits. At no time did she refer to the journey as - my journey or your journey; and nor of course to the strange pair that were out looking for me - confusing indeed!

I thought back to the meeting with the grey people of the mountains and their reactions - they could see me; the wild black creatures that attacked me - they saw me as well. Why have I been exposed to all of the creatures of the land?

Even more confusing was what Suilval had said during one of her rare utterances during the march. She told me that she had sensed the lines of spirit occasionally but as far as she knew neither she nor anyone else had ever seen a spirit passing through.

She and Ruis had been told by Elid Silverhair to be on the lookout for me appearing from the grey plains of Slar-fel and they were told to escort me to her lands in the Sloch. She went on to say that it was the noise of the black slarcs (as I had learned they were called) that drew them to me.

They were most surprised to see the black creatures so far from their lands and attacking a spirit. I breathed in the night air and once again turned my thoughts and eyes to the sky.

The dark energy that weaves in and out of the mighty cosmos has many purposes. It keeps the stars and galaxies apart at the same time it keeps the worlds, moons and planets in their ordained places.

Elios told me that it has corridors that dimensional guardians pass through to access the windows that allow them to journey through the spiral of time and so enter other dimensions. She also said the energy can reveal messages by shifting its shape in the form of dark pictures, and in that place by the pillars of Fochd the dark movement began to manifest to me as I thought on her words.

The main shape was dark and ominous looking even in that dark quadrant. The entity was being chased by creatures, some were familiar and some were not, but they all seemed to have a purpose and that was getting rid of that menacing shape. Then the vision was gone and all I could mutter was 'Brudair', I must have said it louder than intended because I woke up my companions.

'What did you say Lael?' Ruis asked. Both he and Suilval sat up, mildly interested.

I repeated what I had seen in the sky to my two companions. Ruis looked as if he understood but said nothing. Suilval, who told me in no uncertain terms she did not care much for spiritual feelings or sightings, snarled out a bit of bravado by saying she would catch and kill the shape.

As she spoke I looked hard at her and got a feeling that Suilval would kill anything that got in her way - she stared back at me and I said. 'Yes Suilval I believe you would.'

Then I asked them what the cloud in the sky was; it had the shape of a head with a hat on it and although I could not make out any visible stars in its mass - something was going on.

It was Suilval who answered again. 'That is known as the 'Witches Head' and marks the way of Ulas, you do not want to be looking that way too often air-boy or, spirit or not, it will suck you up and spit you out like puflic froth. Now turn yourself upside down or sit on your ass, whatever you are comfortable with and just shut up and leave us to sleep.'

They both went back to sleep to dream about whatever they dream about. I was left gazing at the sky, willing the shapes to come back. I have retained memories of Earth because my physical body lived and died there. All throughout my earthen journey whether in happiness, anger, work or play the cold dark winter nights were a solace to me.

I lived on the edge of a great sea and the village I lived in was built into the hollow of a shoreline of high cliffs. Light pollution was non-existent, the rocks of the foreshore were the world to me and my favourite outlook was to the north.

To me the stars were shining lights in the heavens; I used to gaze up at them in awe, these twinkling auras that lit up the darkness. I knew that many of them had died a very long time ago but their light lived on through time to brighten my nights and fire my imaginings.

I now know that physical death does not signal the end, as with the stars we make the transition to a new beginning in light and spirit.

Looking back I think I must have had some kind of spirituality because when I sat on my favourite perch on top of a mound of large boulders I felt as if I was part of the mighty universe.

The stone beneath me, the sea to the front and the starry northern sky above me, my thoughts had a habit of turning to the past and I would wonder if any of my ancestors had sat where I sat.

They certainly would have sailed the seas and they would have used the stars and moon as guides. All my ancestral line through both of my parents was fisher folk, and both my father and mother could recite by name their main line to three hundred years in the past.

And now as I drift back to my present situation my sense of awe has not changed in any way, in fact it is stronger than it ever was. I could never imagine a world without a night sky, how sad that would be. It is in seeing the night sky with its innumerable stars that we are reminded we are part of a wonderful creation.

I then fixed my attention on one particular star; it was the one I named Artel that I had seen on my first night. I lapsed into my meditary slumber focusing on that bright object and I left the darkness around me to the spirits of the night; that is if

Darwan has any.

Suilval was first to waken, Ruis was not far behind her and they both faced the sun god Apuss and bathed their faces in his light. Suilval pulled some food out of a leather pouch and offered me some. It looked like meat of some kind so I declined.

Suilval fired a comment at me as she divided the food between herself and Ruis. 'Air- boy you don't sleep and you don't eat - you would be at home in a gruflics hut'

I had to ask what a gruflic was and it was Ruis who answered.

'They are creatures who live in the Laic lands, they busy about all day and well into the night achieving nothing, they do eat and sleep but not very often. They scavenge the land and collect things that appeal to them, and that means just about everything, they decorate their huts with the things they pick up - in fact some of their huts are bursting with their finds, so much so that there is hardly any room for them to sleep.

Suilval had eaten her fill and was now going through the motions of fighting imaginary foes. Cutting and slicing the air with sword and knife she was fascinating to watch. For such a large creature she was amazingly agile, but I knew that already having seen her in action at Slar-fel.

She deftly sheathed both weapons and with the obligatory snarl indicated that it was time to get going. We set off, Ruis and Suilval abreast and me at the rear.

As I followed in the footsteps of my strange

companions I could not help my thoughts returning to the conversations of the previous day. My escorts had been describing the place where we were heading, also mentioning some of the life entities and their doings.

The Sloch! It conjures up images of drudgery and debauchery, gruflics that never sleep and river gaists - slimy black creatures that spend most of their time in muddy waters and bogs. 'What am I heading into?'

I turned my attention to the surrounding land. It was not as bleak and barren as Slar-fel or the Fochd pass. The track we were on was bare and tedious but it was bordered on both sides with small, creeping plants and some upright shrubs.

How I wish I could stop and spend time healing the bare land, I had felt its pain when I first appeared in Darwan. I took action then and healed all the growing things - but now I am being rushed along to meet someone I don't know and with a pair of very aggressive guardians.

As my thoughts dwelled on the confused state of the land and myself, my eyes took in the changing scenery, it had become more fertile the further we progressed. As well as striking greenery there was blooms appearing and hedges were flanking the path.

I asked the twosome where we were and if it had a territorial name, it certainly looked and felt more nature friendly. I could smell the aroma of healthy plants and the air tasted better on my lips.

It was Ruis who enlightened me; he called the land

Daralonadh and added it was the most fertile and beautiful land in the known world of Darwan.

We walked on and the path continued to take on a life of its own, it had ceased to be tedious a while back and the more we followed it the greener and softer it became. It eventually turned and twisted us through to a wooded copse where trees of wide spreading branches resided.

At the edge of the copse just inside the tree line, my companions stopped at a huge stone slab. The edges were silver grey in colour and the table top of the slab had an even covering of moss. In the centre of the table was a tree growing out of the slab of living rock, it was a truly amazing sight.

On closer inspection I saw handprints in the moss, clearly defined as if they had been imprinted the very time we entered the copse. I felt very aware of the presence of spirit in that tabernacle, something very significant had taken place here.

I was aware of Ruis and Suilval being muted so I asked what was the meaning of the handprints. I put the question to both of them but it was Ruis who answered and he spoke in the most reverent tone I had heard in the short time I had known him.

'This is the stone of departing spirits; long before the fighting and violence culminated in the great battle at the Fochd pass, many of the elves and faeries had enough of the slaughter of life entities and the devastation of the land.

They recognised it was the end of an era for some and the start of a new journey for others.' Ruis moved closer to the stone and pointed to each hand print in turn. 'These hand identities were made in a time long past.

Here is the elfin hand of Eperna, high elf, and here the long fingered hand of Meadus, queen of all faerie folk. As you can see their path was in the direction that we are taking now.'

Ruis moved to the other side of the table and once again indicated the direction these handprints were pointing, which was where we had come from. He pointed to the two elfin hands, recognisable by their slightly curved hand prints.

'This was Loir, king of the mountain elves and this was Vuris, queen of sea elves and here are the two faerie chiefs. One of whom was Tress, leader of the faeries of the daylight and the other Ilo, watcher of the night faeries and protector of sprites and lost spirits.'

Ruis had a faraway look in his eyes as if he was reliving the events. In a quieter voice he continued. 'They led their elfin and faerie bands out of Darwan forever. Elid Silverhair and her retainers stayed behind in the land. It was she who planted the tree in the rock as a symbol.'

I thought to myself if it can survive and grow with nothing but the rock to nurture it then it surely sends out a powerful message. If we nurture and respect the rock and the soil of the land then it will sustain us. It further convinced me that the stones of ages live and evolve.

'All the faerie folk and some of the elves left. Most of them went to the spiritual world of Ulana but Eperna and Meadus chose the upward path and so passed out of all knowing.

Elid and two other elves remained. Meren of the sea elves chose to live well beyond the waters of Cunig and made her bounds all along the coast of the sea of Meren. She, after many ages, took the upper path. Isilis now rules the Meren elves.

Cimer was a soldier elf and he stayed on after the last battle, after which he led his warriors and others to who knows where. Not a whisper has been heard from him or any of his elfin people ere they parted in that age.

Ilo had to leave the lost spirits in Darwan as they were not elfin or faerie, however they have refuge within the boundaries of Elid and Meren. They are shy and retiring shapes and seldom reveal themselves unless summoned. However there seems to be some doubt as to the leaving of Darwan by Ilo and Tress as some have felt strong faerie magic at times.'

I interrupted Ruis at that point. 'But surely you and Suilval would have seen or heard of Cimer during your journeys.' No reply from Ruis but Suilval broke silence.

'Faerie tales and tall elf stories', said with a snarl of disdain 'Ask Ruis what he thinks happened to Cimer.'

I turned to Ruis and said. 'Well?'

Ruis turned away and lifted his face skywards, a habit he had, I had noticed, when it involved avoiding a question.

'It's only a thought, but when thoughts get intercepted by curious cats they get turned into words and words can be dangerous if picked up by other ears.'

'What he is trying to say Lael; is that Cimer is the source of the dark energy that is making itself known out-with the land of Daralonadh by the way of Ulas. He can't get his head round the idea that an elf can be turned to the side of Ulas.' Suilval growled off by adding. 'If you ask me, no race is spared when it comes to magic and enchantment.'

I changed the subject by asking yet again how far it was to the Sloch.

Suilval said. 'We have to take a route which Elid gave us that diverts us over mountainous terrain and brings us in sight of the Meren Sea. It is slower but it is not a passageway that many creatures use so you are safe from prying eyes.'

Ruis broke the moment. 'Come, let us be on our way to Silverhair's inn, I can taste the puflic already.' And with that he was off. Suilval needed no second telling, at the mention of puflic she was alongside him and matching his pace.

They chattered away in a strange sounding language and whatever they spoke about they never shut up all the time they marched together, I found if I focused on it I could follow it if I wanted to!

At least it's a break from having Suilval behind me snarling sweet nothings. They must have regarded the land as safe after the pause at Fochd because since then they seemed alright with me bringing up the rear.

After we left the tree on the rock I began to notice a difference in the landscape. There were more trees, bushes and an abundance of flowers. The air was clearer and the land was more alive, I could feel it reaching out to me. *I wonder how the Sloch fits in with this?*

We carried on for another day of Apuss and one of Ara - the moon which displaced the red one I first saw, the following day of Apuss saw yet another change in the scenery. I was informed by Suilval that we were headed in the direction of the sea of Meren, sometimes known as the Shores of Cunig.

On the way to the shores of Cunig we passed through some rugged landscapes, for all the goings on in the land which had scarred it badly, the higher parts had a rare beauty about them.

We were ascending a steep slope which led onto a ridge, this Ruis assured us would take us to the shores of Cunig. It was at this point we encountered the lavender snow. What a sight, I couldn't believe my eyes. Huge wonderful flakes of twinkling snow, sometimes indigo, sometimes lavender and in the shadow of the hill, mostly purple.

I asked Ruis why it was that colour. He answered me in a very offhand manner.

'Why is the sea blue Lael?'

'Well!' I said. 'It could be that the light might have something to do with it or maybe that the land is not ready for the purity of white.' I added the latter part for a reaction - which I didn't get. I was dimly aware of Suilval saying. 'What's that sluin bird doing so far from the sea?'

Having got no response from either I shifted my gaze and through the feathery snow I saw the sky coming down to meet the land, its colour was only a fraction lighter than the snow.

Outlined against the sky was a rounded hill topped with skeletal trees, black and stark in contrast to the colours behind and in front. My body is not capable of shivering but the sight of those trees stopped me for a moment.

It looked as if they had gathered at the top of the hill and in a despairing last gesture raised their black boned arms upward, imploring the light to fill their darkened trunks with life. As I looked on I could hear the despair in the creaking boughs, the sound carrying through the air, and knew they had been abandoned by all.

'What's wrong air-boy?' Once again I was scoured by Suilvals recycled question.

'Just pondering on things Suilval, that's all.'

'Well ponder up past me so I can keep an eye on you.'

'Keep your eye on this Suilval.' And as quick as the eye could see I made a lavender snowball and threw it straight at her.

The cat exhaled and blew it apart before it could get within three feet of her and I got a fine spray of violet snow all over me for my troubles.

We got to the other side of the ridge and started to descend. It was an easy path down to a wide plain which stretched on either side as far as one could see. We had lost the lavender snow long since and the colouration of the plain in its patchwork of brown and faded green was drab to the senses.

Beyond the plain I could make out a sea. It was not a

regular line, so I assumed it punched its way into a foreshore making inlets and bays.

Suilval told me it was the home of the Meren elves. They were elves of the great seas of Darwan. She went on to say that they shared the coastline with a tribe of the Bana Ger and there - she pointed a furred hand to a white mountain - a tribe of the same bana warriors. 'That is the great halls of Arcil; it is where the queen of the Bana lives.'

I detected a bit of respect in the voice of Suilval as she passed the information on to me. So I surmised the Bana must be a force to be reckoned with.

'Are we going into the settlements of the elves or the Bana, Suilval? 'I asked hopefully.

'No, growled Suilval, Ruis and I would like to but Elid told us to shepherd you by the paths that are least frequented by creatures, that is why we have taken the long way to get to the Sloch.

She went on to say. 'You might be lucky and meet some of the Bana at the Cat Bough and sometimes a few of the Meren elves show up. Both of the tribes are masters in the art of warfare.'

Ruis butted in with. 'They are also masters at throwing strong drink down their throats.'

Suilval replied heartily by saying. 'So are we.'

We carried on through some dreary landscapes, my two companions had stopped talking for quite some which suited me fine, and I was left to my thoughts and observations.

Eventually we came to a river and Suilval broke silence saying that we would be holding the side of the river we were on all the way to the Sloch.

Yet again the scenery had changed, since we joined the river it had become more fertile looking. Trees and bushes whispered their energy to me in passing and I in return acknowledged them.

Now and then we came across crystalline rocks of various colours and I marvelled at how the light of Apuss danced off their glossy facets. I could feel a strong spiritual energy all around.

I was further surprised when we came upon walled enclosures, whoever constructed them had no notion of symmetry; they certainly were not straight nor did they conform to any regular shape.

I was informed by Suilval that the plants inside the enclosures were the stuff that was used to brew the puflic and rotgut the walls were to stop the Bos from eating the plants. I was about to ask who the builders were when Suilval shouted.

'Look Lael, the smokes of the Sloch - and I can smell the brew of puflic from here.'

I saw many wisps of white, airy looking smoke curling up into the atmosphere and for the second time and in two worlds I shouted out loud-------------

'Fire - the destructive element of mankind and the abhorrence of trees!'

'Shut it and lighten up air-boy, there are worse things than fire in this world, nothing like a goblet of puflic and a bone of shard and your claws in front of a good fire.' Suilval almost purred out the last part of her statement.

The question I asked was directed at either of the two. 'What exactly is the Cat Bough? I imagine it to be a rest house and meditation centre for weary travellers.' Ruis took up the question and laughed as he did so.

'Lael this is not Ulana, this is a country of tribal societies with more than its fair share of bad entities. There are places of ill repute that trade in all kinds and the drink they barter for is very basic. It is vile to consume and tortures the mind, but creatures who are vile in the first place do not mind drinking it.

It doesn't take much to twist their minds and it results in them being thrown out. They had been hunting or fishing for many risings of Apuss for something to barter with, then, in hardly a good sized gulp, they are tossed out the door.

That is why Elid runs the Cat Bough the way she does, it has a fair barter system with laid down rules on how much drink you can get - take for instance a croonyal. A croonyal is a fish and it's a rare delicacy and so is worth many goblets of puflic.'

'So what other drinks or food does the Cat Bough deal in?'

Suilval answered the question with enthusiasm. 'Rot gut is served in smaller measures and can be very strong, puflic is the better of the strong drinks because it is pleasant to the taste and gives the mind pleasant thoughts. It serves the flesh of the Bos - I have that on the bone, the shard is the best part of the bos and I have that sometimes-----

'Sometimes more like all times.' Ruis's comment brought a snarl of agreement and the pace quickened even more.

I had noticed at times during my journey, huddles of timid looking creatures similar to earthen deer, Ruis had told me they were the Bos and were the main source of food to the eaters of meat in Darwan. He added on that Suilval can eat a herd of them at one sitting.

Ruis told me Elid formed the settlement after the last battle of the Fochd pass, he went on to tell me that there was always an inn at the place but it had been sadly neglected and the previous owners had gone with Cimer and his elves.

Many of her retainers live within the habitation of Rotten Sloch while others live in the forests and plains. Her lands are bounded by ranges of hills and mountains and are known as the Laic Lands, they in turn are part of the greater land of Daralonadh.

COLL

The Cat Bough was fascinating to behold. It looked like it was put together with no notion of regularity; a shambles would be an apt description. Most of the building was made of wood of some sort, a russet brown colour all over; that is except for the roof which had a life of its own.

On closer inspection I was totally razzled when I realised; yes - it was wood alright, however the wood was alive - in fact the whole building was made up of trees. Its roots were foundations, trunks for walls, branches for a roof. The whole building was a living, breathing weave of branches and leaves, no wonder it looked higgelty-piggelty.

The nearest shape could be described as triangular and it had the height of a two story inn. The roof had an apex of a kind as all the trees had woven their top branches together and produced a ridge which resembled a hedge.

There were no fine angular lines on the Cat Bough, trunks had parted here and there to allow a door and

The Catbough

windows. It looked like four mighty trees, one at each corner, provided the mainstays of the tree house, their boughs extending well above the roof and branched outward. Huge copper coloured ovate leaves adorned the branches of these giants.

It was then I made out shapes, I had been aware of movement within the treework of the building 'The Growing' would be a better word - then I saw the shapes.

Lots of tiny cats were stalking along the random branches, the cats all shared the same background colour but were characteristically spotted or striped. Their ears were placed more to the sides of their heads and were long and pointed in the elfin way.

I asked Suilval what kind of cats they were and as well as information I got a reaction.

'They are the pixal cats, pets of the Malvin pixies - pests just like their masters and I don't like them!' So saying Suilval hissed in the direction of the small creatures, the mini-cats scuttled off into the foliage.

I noticed that the windows consisted of a stone of some kind within the frames. 'Does the stone in the window let the light in Ruis?' I was struck by the ingenuity of the Cat Bough inn.

Ruis's reply was quite sharp. 'Lael, can you stop asking so many questions, you will make good company for Traig of the bana - and yes, the stone lets the light in and yes, you can see outside when you are inside, now can we go inside? Suilval and I haven't tasted brew for an awfully long time.' With that he gestured towards the door.

In anticipation I entered the Cat Bough inn. The moment I set foot inside the dwelling I felt a strong spiritual presence. It was the same energy that I had felt when we first joined the river, but one thing I was sure of, that the hub of the energy was here in this place or close by. Not since leaving the tree in the rock had I felt the like.

Ruis and Suilval strode past me straight to the bar, I stood where they left me to take in my surroundings. It had a magical ambience about it - like being in a wooden cavern. Stone tables and chairs were scattered about that had creatures of various sizes and shapes partaking of the food and drink which seemed to be in abundance.

I could feel the heat of a fire somewhere to my right. My vision was blocked by the throng of living creatures that populated the bar. A mingling of bodies and a burbling of chatter pervaded the space that I was in and I was caught up in the happy melee.

I joined my two companions at the bar where they were being served the famous puflic by a very attractive elfin woman of the forest people. She had russet brown skin, and at the fringe of her hair there was a lighter colour.

'Ah!' I said. 'You must be Elid Silverhair?'

'Yes I am.'

The voice came from behind me. I turned and beheld an elfin woman as beautiful and as charismatic as Elios of the MoAraian forest. She regarded me with an amused smile on her lips.

'And you must be Lael of the spirit world of Ulana.'

The voice was feminine but the tone authoritative. I didn't hear her approach nor did I see her in the large stone mirror behind the bar - she was just there.

It was noticeable that the ongoing chatter stopped when Elid spoke and all eyes were on her and no wonder. I was transfixed by the fantastic elfess who stood in front of me.

I looked directly at her enchanting face, taking in the almond porcelain skin, the high cheekbones, the strong line of the mouth with only a slight darkening of the skin colour to define it.

The eyes were moss green with eyebrows that arched upwards in a fine line to her temples. Her metal white hair was short on top and sides, showing her long pointed ears to perfection.

Standing as tall as Ruis and Suilval she was dressed in the garb of the forest elf, tight fitting green leggings and a short tunic to match. Across her body from shoulder to hip was a band of woven dark green material and from that hung a sword. What awed me a bit was within the greenness of her eyes a slight misting of violet appeared and disappeared as she regarded me - maybe a trick of the light.

My attention was diverted by the voice of Suilval.

'Remember me Elid?'

Elid laughed and, typical of elves and faeries, she laughed with her eyes and mouth but never a crease appeared on her perfect skin. The laugh was thrilling to hear.

'Of course I remember you Suilval.' So saying Elid took the big cat by the shoulders and gave them a squeeze, the cat dipped her head slightly, exhibiting the first display of respect since I had met her.

Taking in Ruis as well, Elid expressed her gratitude to both for getting me safely to the Cat Bough.

With that she was gone, melting into the crowd and bang on cue the chatter started again in full flow.

Ruis took me by the shoulder and said. 'Lael meet Casa the elf, maid of the Cat Bough and companion of Elid, with her help we are going to get melted - starting now.' After his announcement he looked around and asked more to himself than to any other person. 'Now where are the gaists hiding?'

I introduced myself to Casa. Who immediately asked me if she could touch me to feel how substantial I was! She added. 'You have the look of the blue elf people, but much paler.' Then she took my hand in hers and said. 'Yes, you are solid enough to take a few goblets of puflic' and with that she laughed and told me to go and sit with Ruis.

I could see Suilvals head and ears above the throng so assuming Ruis was with her I headed in her direction. I didn't get far when I got a hail from Ruis who was sitting in an arbour by the wall.

'Lael sit here, Suilval will join us soon.' He pointed

to a goblet foaming over with puflic 'She has left her drink.' He then picked up his own drink and started to gulp it down as if the Cat Bough was going to dry up before he finished it, although he did leave a meagre drop in the bottom of the goblet.

I took the opportunity to study the table, it was stone and the colour of red ochre, swirls of silver ran through it and I needed to touch it. When I ran my hands over it the stone responded by sharing its energy briefly.

'Never mind shaking hands with the table air-boy, get your mouth round this.' Came the plaintive tones of Suilval, armed with a foaming pint of puflic which she deposited in front of me. 'Casa gave me puflic with clear instructions to deliver it personally to yourself well what else would I do?'

Ruis laughed at Suilval's speech and made haste to enlighten me as to why Casa emphasised that the brew got to me. 'You are very fortunate that the drink has got this far completely full, when Suilval gets her furry paws on a goblet of brew it very seldom gets further than her own throat.'

Suilval didn't comment, she sat down and got stuck in to her own drink. I just looked at mine for a long time before I attempted a tentative lick at the stuff, it tasted okay - and that was as far as I got.

Suilval yanked the goblet from me and drained it in one easy movement, banged the goblet down on the table and said. 'That's how you drink puflic Lael, you don't lick it -you swallow the stuff.'

Then she turned to Ruis and said. 'Shift your ass elf man and get some more of the brew before I die of thirst.'

Ruis just laughed at Suilval's orders and replied in like style. 'You have a way with words cat woman, what choice have I got but to obey.' Then he drained what was left of his first drink and said. 'That's the best drink of puflic I have had all day.'

Suilval noticed the look on my face, I was confused because I knew it was the only puflic he'd had.

'Never mind him Lael he often comes out with nonsense information.' Suilval finished her statement by flicking her head in the direction of the bar.

Ruis took the hint and headed for the bar.

He returned in a remarkably short space of time with a clutch of goblets in his hands, much to Suilval's satisfaction. They savoured some of the puflic in silence for while then they locked heads in deep conversation and I may as well have been invisible.

Suilval

Suilval has a lot of anger in her. She has a perfect right to nurse that anger. Her whole tribe had virtually been wiped out and the remnants sent scattered to the wild wastes.

She lost all her kin and her lover 'Lunas.' Lunas had fought well in defence of her Queen, Selma, they both had fought well and killed many of the enemy before they were overwhelmed.

The observer was Senna the hunter, himself being a master of merging into the land around him. He saw all from his hiding place, none of the enemy saw him.

Along with Selma and Lunas was another of Suilval's tribe, Senna named him as Scarus and somehow he got away from the killing ground clutching the sword that was given to Selma from Elid Silverhair. He ran the opposite way to the others, thinking perhaps the enemy would chase the greater numbers and maybe he was right.

According to Senna the survivors ran in the direction of the dense forest of Moress, once in the forest they would be safe.

Senna said the enemy consisted of black elves and others the like he had never seen before. Big ugly warriors long in the legs and the arms, not as skilful as the black elves but brutal and savage fighters. Screaming out war shouts in a language he had never heard before they battered and hewed at the Selma with heavy clubs that had blades embedded in them.

Senna said that he had been paralysed with fear at the onslaught, not because of the wild warriors but something else that pervaded the air. Suilvals tribe were fierce and fearless fighters but they looked as if they had been weakened by an invisible force of some kind.

He spied a strange looking figure at the back of the horde, he was not sure if it was male or female, cloaked in black it seemed to be guiding the screaming throng with hand movements. He had not dared to look too closely at the weird spectre as he felt exposed even though he was well hidden.

When the information was relayed to Elid she immediately identified the club wielding creatures as grelenim warriors. They were a tribe from the direction of Ulas, well beyond the lands of Dargal. A primitive people that were part of tribal society residing in a land of rugged hills and moorland, the place was named Grela.

As to the fear in the air that Senna spoke of, she made no comment and when questioned about it she held her hand up and silenced all.

It did not take much to work out that the help of some kind had to be some power other than physical prowess. The tribe of Selma were fast and furious fighters and they could easily have dispatched the numbers of black elves and grelenim warriors that Senna had estimated.

The tribe of Selma had lived in the region known as Argall, it was well out-with the land of Daralonadh and was close to the wild forest of Moress which marked the border of the wasted lands.

As Told To Lael By Ruis

Too Much Puflic

I watched the two of them and noticed the more they drank the more sublime they became. Ruis became more laid back and had a silly smile on his face and he used his hands a lot when describing some of his exploits.

Suilval had a contented expression on her furred face and conversed easily without the usual snarled expletives. They were well away with whatever the topic was, so I took the opportunity to look around me. At the table opposite sat three black, shiny beings and I deduced they must be river gaists.

They were bigger and bulkier than I had imagined, their heads were large and fishlike, bulging eyes on the side of their heads and teeth that were large and formidable looking; not sharp and pointed but solid and even, more useful for grinding bone. I noticed they had goblets of foaming puflic.

'Hey rot-gut you finished your foam yet?'

The high pitched voice took me by surprise and so did the shape that it emanated from.

'Who are you?' I asked in an amused tone.

Before the strange little bundle could answer it was lifted up by the scruff of its collar by Suilval. 'This is a malin pixie, raised to cause mischief of one kind or other; they also brew the puflic and distil the rot-gut. This little twitterer is called Bila. Bila meet Lael he is a spirit ---'

'So is rot-gut!' Exclaimed Bila, and not in the least fazed by Suilval's speech or her rough handling.

Neither was Suilval; she dropped Bila from a great height. He quickly regained his feet, gathered the empty goblets and with a high pitched 'byeee' he was gone.

No sooner was he gone than another pixie appeared with three foaming jugs of puflic. I knew this one was different by the colour of his cap.

Ruis intercepted my thoughts. 'Yes Lael, this little one is Rosa and is the leader of the little band that run the Cat Bough. Rosa was the rascal who laced the gaist's puflic with rot-gut.'

At that Ruis hailed one of the gaists 'Hey Gular!' at the same time he flicked Rosa up with his toe and caught the pixie in mid-air 'Would you like something to dip in your brew?'

Gular's voice sounded like gravel. 'No Ruis, you keep him - pixie not taste good.' At that the gaists, elf and cat all laughed uproariously. Ruis let the fidgeting pixie go. Then he invited the gaists to join us, they pulled their chairs up and I was introduced to them.

The biggest of the three was called Gular the other two were Yuris and Tagga. They seemed affable enough although they had difficulty pronouncing my name - they settled for Laee, I was okay with that – *obviously two Ls were too much for them.*

Darwan could have been anywhere in space to them - *of course it is*. Suilval told me they have never been outside Elid's bounds.

The gaists are very slow, deep voiced individuals. They spend most of their time in the river and lochans around the Sloch and the surrounding Laic lands. Ruis told me that they live quite comfortably in turf houses by the banks of the river.

I asked Ruis once why it was called the Sloch but he had no answer other than adding on - ask Elid. Then he changed the subject by saying. 'Remember the stone walls we passed, well the grass that grows inside is what the pixies use to make the drink.'

'Do the pixies build the walls as well; their build is a bit erratic?' I ventured a smile when I said it. But I got a surprise when Tagga droned out.

'We do walls is erratic good?'

Oh yes Tagga, erratic is good, in fact it matches completely with my present surroundings. At my words the gaists nodded with approval at the perceived praise and clanked their goblets together.

Ruis got into conversation with the gaists and I lost interest in their talk, it just seemed to go round in circles - fish-drink-smoke-more smoke-more drink-more fish. 'Help get me out of here!'

By this time Suilval had taken herself off to another table, probably having anticipated the conversation. She had seated herself with a group of fantastic looking beings. Tall mercurial-skinned warriors with some kind of symbols painted on their bodies in different colours. I learned soon enough that they were of the Bana-ger, a tribe of warrior women.

They must have been speaking about me because some of the warriors were turning round and looking me up and down. One in particular, sitting tall in her chair in the middle of the group, had an air of authority about her - definitely a leader. Another thing that drew my attention was the presence of weapons in the group.

Ruis told me Elid did not tolerate weapons in the Cat Bough and the only two apart from herself that she allows to have weapons are Ruis and Suilval. Customers who have weapons go to the back of the inn where the pixies take the hardware and rack it.

Suilval noticed me looking and motioned me over to join her at the table. The puflic was obviously pleasing to her because when she spoke the snarling was not so aggressive or cynical as usual, the voice was lighter and laced with a bit of humour.

'Here Lael!' As she said it she reached behind her and yanked at a stool ejecting the unfortunate creature who had been sitting on it. Seeing my sympathetic look at the poor creature spread-eagled on the floor. She reassured me saying that it was only Coonie who had too much to drink anyway and he would sleep it off on the floor.

Coonie summerly dismissed she went on to say. 'Sit down and meet the warriors of the Bana-ger.' then to the group she said 'Meet my friend the air-boy, a bit light headed at times - at this she gave a laugh of sorts. Most times he does what he is told and sometimes he answers to Lael.'

The tall warrior was first to speak. 'Why is a spirit of Ulana in the company of a giant cat and a mercenary elf?' I felt like saying that I had no idea why I was here but before I could gather my wits to answer Suilval cut in. 'Lael saw a picture in the sky when we slept at the pillars of Fochd - he called it 'Brudair.'

At Suilval's words one of the warriors said 'Bheir sees pictures in the sky sometimes.' She looked at one of her companions as she spoke the words.

The warrior she looked at nodded in agreement so I assumed that her name was Bheir.

Suilval, sensing that I was a bit intimidated by the blue warriors introduced each of them by name. The tall one was called Eils and the deep looking one that sees pictures in the sky was Bheir, so I got that right. The other two were Suila and Nal, I thought Nal was very aggressive looking.

Each one as they were introduced took me by the

shoulder and repeated my name.

When Suilval mentioned the word brudair I noticed the group had given me some odd looks.

The one called Eils asked me where I had learned of brudair.

I gave the answer straightaway. 'It is a word from an ancient language of Earth where I lived in physical form; it means 'vision."

And that was the end of the conversation as regards the 'brudair.' Elid told me later that the Bana show respect for the bright objects in the sky but they do not believe in an afterlife. They do not comprehend other worlds that are populated by life forms, nor do they show any interest if the subject is brought up.

When Suilval introduced me - she referred to them as the 'Bana five' - I asked where the missing warrior was; it was the warrior called Nal who answered.

'Traig is absent from our table but she will not be far away, probably quizzing the ass off somebody. Come with me and we will find her and see what she is up to.'

Nal was a fraction taller than me, but close enough with a slight stretch from me to be at eye level. Her eyes were clear and cool and the colour of indigo, her smooth, silver-tinted skin caught the light of the tallow candles, softening her features.

She had a strange, attractive face; hair colour a striking blue-black; slim, arched eyebrows; nose slightly squint against the regularity of the rest of her features and a fine line of mouth was set in a firm angular jaw. The physical energy emanating from her was so exhilarating I found myself drawn to this dynamic warrior.

'Are you examining me Lael?' She said in a low methodical voice.

'I am enjoying the moment Nal.' As we talked we had started to move about, the inside of the Cat Bough was as erratic as the outside. Twists and turns abounded in the bar space, creating little arbours here and there. I got the impression it was bigger within than out.

Nal said. 'Ah ha, I see the missing warrior' She motioned me to a table where sat Traig the fifth warrior and an elf, the elf looked relieved when we arrived. Nal introduced me to Traig of the bana and Enderli the shade elf. I noticed Enderli had a few empty glasses in front of him but only one of Traigs had been touched.

'Have you been stretching Enderli's ears with your tongue Traig?' Nal asked.

'Only looked for a few answers to questions asked.' Replied Traig.

'The point is Traig, did you give Enderli time to answer one before you asked another?' Said Nal.

Enderli shook his head and said. 'The only question I have answered so far is when she asked me if I wanted a drink.'

Nal carried on with the subject, saying that Traig

says she can tell by the face and eyes of the person she is questioning what the answer is, and the curious thing is, Suila and I have tested her and she does get a lot right.

We sat down and the first thing Traig told me was to watch Enderli. 'He is a mischief maker of the highest order.'

The elf smiled at that but said nothing.

'Enough of this let us drink and dance.' Having declared this Nal hailed a pixie. 'Bila, be quick and get drinks for this table.'

The pixie scuttled off at the double and in what seemed an impossibly quick time reappeared with a tray laden with the foaming stuff.

'Now.' said Nal. 'Let's see what this stuff does for you.' Placing a goblet of puflic in front of me she added. 'Get it down your throat.'

Oh well, I thought, it can't affect me, and so I took a good gulp of the stuff, they all watched in silence as I downed it, I licked my lips and declared it was good. They all cheered and cheered again when I took a second gulp.

I could safely say that puflic was good stuff, whatever Elid puts in it certainly works, as the events of the evening were to prove.

By this time we had the centre stage. Suilval had appeared, joined by the creature by the name of Coonie, who had sobered up a bit after being ejected from his chair. 'Drink the next one down in one gulp.' Suilval shouted, and when I did she said. 'Oh well done air-boy I am impressed.'

Then Enderli spoke up. 'Lael, if you take off your

tunic would we see the puflic going down your inside?'

Taking off my tunic I proceeded to slowly drink another goblet of puflic, to the noise of whoops and shouts from the audience watching the puflic zig-zagging its way down to my stomach. But Enderli hadn't finished with me.

'Lael, the river beings and Ruis are still performing in the alcove, they haven't been watching here.'

I heard Traig saying. 'Enderli what are you thinking now?' Once again the elf just smiled.

At this point most of the drinkers had gathered round our table, and were eager to see what was going to happen next - they hadn't long to wait.

Enderli said. 'Lael, why don't you float up to the roof along to where Ruis and the gaists are drinking, then turn upside down, and with your upside down head ask the gaists if they want a drink? 'This I did, and as I floated under the roof towards Ruis's company the audience followed me on foot to the alcove.

When I descended upside down the effect was better than anticipated, Ruis laughed, when I asked the gaists if they wanted a drink and Gular nearly answered. 'Yes mo—' then jumped up in a panic and along with his mates made a bolt for the door amid howls of laughter from the spectators.

Enderli said. 'They will go straight to their burrows and not emerge until the next day!' But I was not ready to come down yet, I was still hyped up with the attention and I didn't need any prompting from Enderli.

I floated back the way I came and when I saw Nal I remembered the two elves of Celdis, so I floated upside down again and rubbed noses with her, she laughed and taking me by surprise caught my lips. I rotated back to the floor still touching lips and I found myself liking it. I was aware of Suila saying. 'That's a new one.'

Then through my puflic induced joy I heard another voice in my thoughts. Instantly I became aware as the soft faerie tones of Elios vibrating in my head, telling me to go outside to the rear of the Cat Bough. I excused myself to Nal and made my exit through the rear door of the Cat Bough and straightaway looked to the night sky. Elios came again and asked what I saw in the starry night.

In the thoughts of my mind I answered Elios. *'I see a starry sky.'* I replied.

'Look upward beyond the near stars and tell me what you see.' Elios voice was soft and compelling.

I looked again and answered. *'I see the light of many universes, I feel a motion and a rippling of life in the dark places between the brightness; there is no evil intent there – it is life waiting to evolve.'*

Elios answered. *'That is the spirit speaking, in the bar of the Cat Bough your human ego came back for you, you drank the liquid of joy and briefly you felt a longing for Nal of the Bana. It cannot be, it must not be, you need to draw your power from the air, water, earth and the fire of Apuss.*

The light is your sustenance; it is your very being and you need it as much as fish in the river need the water. You have only begun your journey and you will be tested many times, so you need to be aware and ready for whatever comes.

There are enchantments going on in Darwan. Elid has told me that creatures are gathering in great numbers and others are migrating in from the dark wastes of Dargal. She fears there is a singular power at work and she will be talking to you. Remember who you are and where you are going.'

Then she was gone and I was left wondering *how does she know these things?* Liath told me that not a branch falls in the MoAraian forest but Elios knows of it. I think I would agree with that.

I was still looking at the night sky and breathing it in when Nal came to me; I felt her presence, quiet as she was.

'What are you seeing Lael?'

'I am looking at the beginning of everything we know about and everything that is to come which we don't know about.'

'Do you want to know about events that have still to come, are you not happy with the event of where we are now?'

Nal's logical question made me smile. 'Yes Nal, I am happy at where I am now but I am a restless spirit, I need to know what higher power made all this possible' as I raised my arms upward.

Nal replied saying. 'We were made powerful long ago and we still are - this we accept. We live our lives in Darwan and when we expire we are fed to the sea. The stars will still shine when we are all gone.'

'I expect they will Nal, and who knows you might be part of them. On Earth, people who lived long before me used to believe that great warriors were put into the night sky as a reward for their brave deeds.'

Nal's retort was swift and to the point. 'Had the Bana lived on Earth world we would have filled the sky with our warriors.' Then she said 'Come Lael, we will sleep together tonight' and that settled we returned to the Cat Bough.

I spent the night not only with Nal but also with her four companions, Suilval and a shade elvess called Derli. The elvess and Traig kept a steady ripple of chatter for a very long time. It didn't seem to disturb the slumbering bana or Suilval. I heard it like a gently flowing stream in the background during my medi-sleep and it didn't bother me either.

The Bana Ger

The Bana are a warrior tribe with a difference, the fighters are female, and very fierce fighters at that. They are probably the greatest fighting force in the known Darwan world, the only force that are on equal ground with them are the Guita, Geala and Lael tribes of the race of black elves - they also claim the right of being the greatest fighters in the known world.

The Bana were an island race at one time but due to eruptions and disturbances on the island over a period of time they decided to leave the island and settle elsewhere.

The queen of the Bana is called Tiathmor, she and Elid Silverhair, ruler of the lands of Laic, had great respect for one another. She approached Elid and asked her if the three tribes of Bana warriors could populate the extremities of her lands from the coastline of the sea of Meren, through the forest of Cubin and on to the high lands of Arcil.

Elid was pleased to grant the outer lands, but there were

two clauses that had to be agreed on. One was that Isilis, queen of the meren sea elves had to be consulted as they had hereditary right to the coastline of Meren.

The other was that if any force invaded either the Laic lands or the havens of the sea elves then the Bana would be required to help. Likewise if the Bana were attacked then the forces of the Laic and Meren would march to their aid.

A deputation from the three tribes of the Bana accompanied by Elid met Isilis and her retainers at a headland which lay at the extreme end of the Meren coastline.

Isilis explained that the coastline from the headland in the direction of Ica was originally settled by a faction of sea elves called the Vour. They were always a restless tribe and it came as no surprise when they announced that they were going to sail away in the direction of the Salacian Sea to find a new land to sustain them. They also said that the Meren should occupy their coasts as they would not be returning; such was their longing for new seas to sail…

After a silence she then said that a tribe that looked as if they were to be dispossessed of their island should take advantage of the empty coastline. She further asked as a memory to the elves that left, that the tribe of warriors who occupied the shores of Meren would henceforth be known as the Bana Vour.

This was readily accepted by the Bana who saw it as a great honour to carry an elfin name alongside their own. Rhu, a very extroverted warrior, leaped up to the high point on the headland and with arms outstretched, shouted to the sea and the sky. 'I am Rhu of the Bana Vour and here will be my home!'

Tiathmor said to the others. 'Well that's settled which tribe is going to be living here.'

Isilis added. 'From now on the headland between us will be known as The Rhu.'

'Hear that Rhu, now you have a rock called after you – matches your head.'

At Tiathmor's quip the company laughed and clapped each other's shoulders and retired to the settlement of Isilis and her elves.

Rinnis was in the night sky and her red light shone brightly on the sea of Meren as the group drank and feasted with their new neighbours. Standing with Isilis by the water's edge Tiathmor pointed to a blue star shining brightly above Rinnis.

'That is our guiding star Turis, we do not see it for many changes of Rinnis and Ara, I must get the stone masters to track its rise and fall; it is indeed an omen at this time.'

By consensus of all present Isilis and her aides were invited along to view the other 'pits of land' as they were called.

The Cubin plain and forest were parted to the Bana tribe who inhabited the interior of the island, it was felt by all that they would be more at home in the forests and plains of Cubin.

Two of the Bana men called Gedi and Onir, who were two of the foremost workers of the land, were well pleased with the fertility of the plain and the lushness of the forest. They wandered away on their own to feel the energy of the land and discuss what would be pasture and what would be arable.

Tiathmor said to Elid. 'We will be lucky if we see them again before we leave your lands.'

Elid corrected her saying. 'Your lands now Tiathmor and I

take it you have settled for the mountains of Arcil?'

'Yes Elid, my clan lived in the rocky part of Moula, not exactly mountainous but the hills of Arcil certainly appeals to us. What is the significance of the high one in the middle that looks as if there are caves dug into it?'

'Ah' said Elid, 'the halls of Arcil, they were dug out by the garg people many eons ago. They laboured long and hard at the work. Not only did they carve out the rooms and halls of the mountain. They used the stone that was taken from the mountain to decorate the plain in front of Arcil. When you see it you will be amazed at the intricate carvings on the boulders, they easily match the skill of your own stone masters.'

Tiathmor was intrigued. 'What happened to the garg people that they left such a place?'

'Well!' Said Elid 'that was a strange tale, Apuss rose on a morning and received the thanks from the gargs but ere Ara had set the following morning the gargs had gone - just up and left.

I knew of the race of garg but did not have much to do with them. Aior anor the Green woman enlightened me to their ways. She said that the garg people are workers of stone, they carve out caverns and halls out of the solid rock and use the excavated stone for outside decoration.

Their carvings follow a set pattern but when Aior anor asked them what they meant the gargs told her they had no idea, they were just doing what their ancestors did before them.

The gargs believe they have an affinity with the stone; as they do the carving they say that the stones guide them during their labours.

They told her that when their time was up at a place they

just leave it to whoever wants it and wander off to the next mountain range. So there you are Tiathmor, you have inherited a readymade palace for yourself and your tribe. Since the gargs left, nobody has claimed Arcil.'

Tiathmor was very happy about all the events that had transpired since they had met Elid and Isilis. Rhu had more or less claimed the coast on behalf of her tribe and they in turn would be satisfied with her choice.

Gedi and Onir, along with the warrior Cer, were delighted with their pit of land. Tiathmor herself was very taken by the heights of Arcil, even though so far they had been viewed at a distance.

However she could see the value of the place as far as strategy was concerned. Arcil itself was a natural watch tower, it had an all-round visionary aspect and the territories of the two Bana clans lay below the halls of Arcil. We can see them and they can see us - couldn't be better.

Isilis asked if the Bana had need of ships for the move.

Both Tiathmor and Rhu thanked her for the consideration but informed her that they themselves had enough ships for all of the Bana and they also have Big Jon Beet, master mariner of the Oliv losai, to act as a boat of passage.

After three risings of Apuss the Bana deputation had worked out a safe haven where all the ships could offload the three tribes. Where the Meren coast ran by the way of Ica, as it hit the foothills of Arcil it turned in the way of Apuss. Within the turn, the waters of the river Losa poured into the Meren Sea.

Tiathmor said to Isilis. 'The mouth of the Losa is an ideal place for all of the three tribes, Rhu and her clan coming out the best of course. It is the tri-point of the three territories and makes it easier for the baggage to be distributed.'

At that point Elid made a suggestion. 'I can get the river gaists to come down river with their skiffs. Their boats are made for the river waters and it will save time and labour hauling everything over land. Filling them up to their ears with puflic will be payment enough.

That was many eons ago when the Bana arrived on the shores of the Meren sea and it was not long after when they had to fulfil their bargain and take part in the fighting to preserve the land – but that is another story .

In Elids Bower

After the riotous night in the Cat Bough I took myself out to the clearness of the day. Apuss was bright in the sky, so in keeping with the creatures of the land I turned my face and let the light wash over me.

I was relishing my time with the sun god, I call Apuss a god at times but I remember Suilval picking up Ruis when Ruis mentioned Apuss as God. She had said that as far as she was concerned Apuss was a Goddess as she was warm and friendly like the females of Darwan. Her statement was a bit incongruous as it was tailed off with an aggressive snarl. My train of thought was broken as I was hailed by a familiar voice, Ruis coming from the direction of the river looking as fresh as the morning I was enjoying.

I returned his greeting and asked him where he ended up after the antics in the bar. He told me he spent the night in a turf lodge by the river.

I asked Ruis about his night with the gaists. He was very taken by his night in the burrow by the river, although I suspect it was not his first visit there. Before he started his story he took a puff out of the strange looking pipe that appeared by magic every time he was being questioned by me. The melancholy look on his face after the inhalation was something to behold; then he went on with his tale.

'Coonie, Enderli and I were invited into the burrow of Gular and there, amidst a swirl of reek and damp air, we joined the gaists in pipe smoking and drinking.'

I asked Ruis If they had recovered from their fright. He answered with a short laugh 'They forgot why they left the Cat Bough once they were in the burrow.' My next question was to ask what they did all day.

Ruis's answer came readily and by his tone he was with them in heart as he described their way of life.

'To sit with a pipe and a goblet of puflic is the height of contentment to river gaists. Puflic can be carried out in certain measures, but rotgut has to be consumed in the Cat Bough.

The gaists drink copious amounts of puflic in their time off, which is not often. When two moons are in the sky they are never out of river and lochs catching fish, in particular the strange looking croonyal, which is a delicacy here.

In their damp underground burrows when one moon has left the sky the gaists will drink puflic and smoke pipes. Their ponderous conversations will go on for days during the breaks.'

I nodded in agreement with Ruis's statement 'A simple but happy life by the sound of it.' I said.

'Yes!' Ruis answered 'Were it so with all creatures.'

Once again I saw that far off look in his eyes. He walked away from me, probably wanted solitude for a while. I looked in the direction of 'Under Sloch' which is where the gaists live, and reflected on Ruis's words.

I wandered round the back of the Cat Bough and watched the bana warriors and Suilval going through their imaginary fights with their weapons. At that moment poor Enderli chose the wrong door to exit from the Cat Bough.

Quick as lightening Traig grabbed him and, in an astonishing display of strength, lifted him above her head and shouted to Nal.

'Hey Nal, catch this elfin twister. He was sipping our drinks last night when we were not paying attention.'

With that she threw the elf in the direction of Nal who caught him with ease and hung the luckless Enderli by the scruff of his jacket from a spar on the wall of the Cat Bough.

With a glance at Enderli I shook my head and departed, but not before a retort from Suila brought me up sharp.

'What's up Lael, has Nal scared you off?'

Traig backed up Suila's comment by saying 'Nal scares every male in Darwan Lael so you are not alone.'

That was enough for me so I took off with a backward wave of my hand amidst a chorus of good natured cheering.

I was told not to wander too far by Suilval, who seemed to have assumed the task of guardian to me, well she was instrumental in saving me from the slarc warriors. But so did Ruis and yet the two of them more or less split up when we reached the Cat Bough.

The selective company of each one of them was so diverse - Suilval with a dynamic bunch and Ruis with the ponderous gaists - oh well, each to their own.

The gaists are simple beings, but that makes no difference to their status in the great spiritual plan which allows the spirit of every living identity a place to reside after death.

I spent the rest of the day at Under Sloch, where I was a celebrity to the gaist children. They were shy at first but after a few glows from my aura they approached me and sat in a half circle. It was really funny, because after I had glowed a few times the little creatures held the palms of their hands up to me as if they were warming their hands at a fire.

On the way from the Cat Bough I had picked up a stone it seemed slightly out of place where it lay. It was elliptical in shape and very flat, the background colour was a sky blue and it was dappled with miniature clouds of white. I showed it to the gaist children and did not expect the reaction this drew.

They all got up as one and rushed off at a rate of knots that would have left the violet elvettes standing. I had hardly time to take a second breath when they appeared laden with flat stones similar to the one I had.

The stones were spilled out at my feet amidst much

jabbering and facial expressions it was so funny and yet so innocent. I saw a chance to jump start the evolution of the gaist dyke building fraternity.

I got them in a semi-circle around me and began to separate the stones in size as it was my intention to build a hollow cairn. My first layer of stones I laid end to end in the shape of a circle. I knew I had their attention as the burbling voices went silent and all eyes were on what I was doing.

Then for the second layer of building I made a great show of taking two stones - one in each hand and laying them on top of the foundation stones. I laid the second layer with a space between each one and took great care to emphasise the space between had to be smaller than the stones themselves.

Silence reigned all the time as I built the second tier of stones then ever so slowly the tangled murmur of sounds started to get louder as I got into the third layer. Once they saw the space between the stones being bridged they got the message and began to build their own creations.

I did a few more tiers on my own structure and sat back to watch the young gaists in action. It was like a beehive, little bodies running back and fore to where the stone reservoir was. Little hands sorting out stones, others building shapes and all the time a non-stop chatter.

I was delighted to see what I had started, albeit a very small step but the creativity shown by the young gaists was most amazing. I was witnessing first-hand the distribution of labour, leadership and imagination. Lines, squares and circles were appearing in front of me.

Suilval appeared on the scene and the new generation of wall building gaist children scattered. 'It is okay Lael, I have that effect on them, and they know I wouldn't hurt them - I just give them a snarl now and then to keep them on their toes. Looks like they have a better idea of stone building than their parents have.'

Suilval said we were asked to gather in Elid's quarters, which were high up in the roof of the Cat Bough. I had seen what looked like a tree limbed tower above the rest house when I first arrived. It seemed to merge into the rock behind it.

I followed her lead and had to smile at the avoidance of any creature coming the other way. Most crossed to the other side and some ran away.

I said. 'You have a powerful personality Suilval, what does it feel like to be so popular?'

She answered me without the customary snarl. 'They can't avoid me in the bar but they fall over each other to buy me drinks so I just say - keep it coming.'

By the time we reached the Cat Bough the Bana had joined us, lastly Ruis tagged on behind.

We filed up a twisted stairway made up of a tree trunk which had grown in a spiral and sent out a branch for every step needed. The background was made up of hanging and creeping plants of all colours, the most prominent of which were russet brown, emerald green and red ochre.

The last turn of the stairway led us into Elid's bower and I noticed the walls were no longer tree. Her dwelling was a spacious cavern which was part of the hill behind the Cat Bough and cleverly hidden by the tree tower.

We were welcomed in by Elid and Bila the pixie was waiting to take orders for food and drinks. The Cat Bough felt good to me when I first saw it and inside was equally as good, but here in the bower of Elid there was such a sensation of pure spirit emanating within. All things relating to light and spiritual energy were at work in that space, it gave out such an aura of well-being.

Out of the rock flowed a delicate stream, it whispered its way over a bed of blue and white crystal and formed a small mirror of water at the centre of the cavern, then meandered out of the cave at the opposite end to our entry point.

The pool was adorned with flower heads of white and gold which glowed briefly with the slight movement of the water. The walls hung with the wild flowers of the forest of Laic. Behind the plants the stone of the cavern was alive with tiny flickers of light which must have come from minute crystals in the rock. The air was fresh and clear, giving its breath of life to all.

Elid is almost pure spirit I felt it for the first time during that gathering in the bower. I felt the emotive power of the faerie at work, of that I was sure. We were all lined in front of her as she welcomed us to her bower and asked us to be still while she delivered the prayer of light.

The Prayer of Light

Great Ica who restored the light to the universes

WE THANK YOU!

And in this gathering we will endeavour to walk in your energy path.

May your light shine on everyone and deliver us from the wells of darkness

The prayer said, Elid engulfed us all in an aura of orange light which felt so good, even the bana warriors expressed wonder at the effect produced. She then consolidated the prayer of light by telling us how Ica, goddess of all the energies in all the universes, drove Ulas into the well of darkness. Ica is a benevolent goddess - that is why we have to look to the sky if we need to ask for anything or to give thanks.

It was a time like that in the bower of Elid that I could have talked all night about the glory of Ulana, it is such a part of me and I miss it so much. I know I am in the company of beings who are doers and know what each other are capable of but to them I am still an unknown entity.

My thoughts were interrupted by Bila asking what I wanted.

I said give me the sweet nectar of Ulana or the blue light of Iaphalon.

'Can't do it Lael' was the sharp answer, then having got the orders from the others of the company he was off.

Elid bade us sit down and relax, I was relaxed already. I enjoyed the magical atmosphere of the bower and the prayer of light was well accepted by all. I felt we were all united during that interlude and it did me good to hear the word of spirit and to feel it.

Bila appeared accompanied by another pixie, one that I had not seen before, both of them bore trays laden with food and drink. They began to distribute the food to suit the differing tastes of the assembled company. Bila's companion asked me if I wanted puflic or rotgut. I declined both saying my days of strong drink are over.

Suilval, ever on the alert shouted, 'I'll have Lael's drink Aja!' I took it Aja was the pixie who served me as he went right to Suilval and presented her with a goblet of puflic and one of rotgut. That prompted the rest of the company to stamp their feet and shout - 'we want more - we want more.'

Elid's voice rose above the clamour and said to Bila and Aja. 'Give everybody except Suilval another drink.' That brought cheers from the company and a good natured snarl from Suilval.

I felt good sitting there watching and listening to the mixed company having a good time. I was most interested to hear two distinct accents from the bana.

When Traig and Eils spoke together, although some of the words used were the same as the speech of the other bana, I detected a marked difference in the dialect and words of these two warriors.

I asked Ruis why the two warriors spoke as they did

when they were together.

He told me Eils and Traig were blood sisters and they belonged to the tribe known as the bana vour. They were the people who lived by the sea and they are a race apart he said with a grin.

Ruis seemed to be in a better frame of mind so I pushed him for more information. 'So where are the other bana warriors from, I take it they are from different clans?'

After a good swallow of puflic he wiped the foam from his mouth with the back of his hand and stated. 'That was easily the best goblet of puflic I have had all day.'

I had heard that statement before so made no comment, I just gave Suilval a knowing look.

Suilval returned my look and with a sympathetic glance at Ruis said. 'I know Lael, he will keep making that silly statement to you and any other company that he gets a reaction from, just ignore him and he might give it up.'

Having got the required reaction, Ruis returned to my question and began to enlighten me about the bana-ger.

He pointed to a stern looking warrior sitting by Elid. 'That is Bheir, she is from the halls of Arcil, notice that she is very different in looks from the rest. All of the tribe of Arcil have blonde hair - so blonde it is almost white and their eyes are deep indigo. They tend to be more serious minded than the warriors of the other tribes.'

'The two by the water in deep conversation are Nal and Suila, Nal is the bowmaster and the other is the tracker of the section, they are from the forests and plains. Do you remember speaking to them last night?'

Ruis question caught me off guard. 'I remember being at the table with Traig and a shade elf called Enderli, but not too much after that, although I remember the sleeping quarters - was I that bad?'

Ruis laughed then allayed my fears by saying. 'As I said earlier, we were all worse than you - I ended up in Guler's burrow. Nal certainly took a liking to you and that is a bit odd as she doesn't have much time for men in any shape, tribe or other world.'

He went on to say that Nal and Traig were the youngest of the bana, Suila, Bheir and Eils are about the same age. But no matter which tribe they are from they are all bana warriors and there is no envy or dislike among them, they are very much all for each other.

'So tell me Ruis, why does the section of Bana have a mixture from the three tribes, I would have thought if they are three distinct tribes then they would all be same within a fighting section?'

My question brought a short laugh from Ruis. 'Yes Lael, well spotted but it is the Bana we are talking about and apart from the fact that they are an all-female fighting force, if they have to perform any task or quest out-with the culture of the race-----'

He paused to light up his smoking pipe and I had to wait until he took a good pull at it, then after he had inhaled the goodness he tilted his head back and blew the smoke back out. With a contented expression on his face he carried on to answer my question.

'Elid has obviously asked Tiathmor if she could borrow a bana section, by coincidence there was one already on the move. Apparently the hunter called Senna has stolen a possession from the outside of the halls of Arcil. Not the best of things to do because the bana will hunt him to the ends of Darwan and when they catch up with him his death will be swift.'

I realised then what he was talking about and finished off what I thought he would be telling me. 'So Ruis, the bana have a representative mixture of the three tribes when something happens that has an effect on the race as a whole such as the happenings of now?'

'You have it Lael the sections we speak of are called 'Arrowheads' I do not know how many of them the bana have. They live all their lives in each-others company and when they are not occupied they take it in turns to spend time in each of their tribal lands. The section you met had just come from the coastal lands of the bana vour where they were resting up with the tribe of Eils and Traig.'

'So why don't they have equal pairs, if they had, Bheir would have another Arcil companion?'

Once again I had to wait for the exhalation of pipe smoke before Ruis answered. 'Suilval knows more about the ways of the bana than I do, she and her tribe had close relationships with them.

However I can tell you this, I have met a few arrowhead sections out and about and they all have the same number, the thing is the single warrior can be from any of the tribes. Before we encountered you at Slar-fel we spoke briefly with another arrowhead and the single warrior in it was called Rhu and she was of the bana vour - two from Arcil and two from the forests.

A Walk with Elid

After we left the bower Elid took me aside from the company and told me we were going for a walk. I excused myself from the others, amid some raucous comments and whistles from Suilval and the bana warriors.

As we passed outward some of the pixal cats appeared and started circling around Elid's legs, purring and meowing softly, they even gave me a cursory rub and it was amusing to see their 'what's that?' reaction when they touched me.

'They are giving me a better reception now than I got when I arrived with Ruis and Suilval.'

Elid smiled and said. 'Suilval can be brusque at times but wouldn't hurt any creature she considered less able than herself, but pity the foe that comes up against her.'

I added on. 'I know, I have seen her handiwork.'

Elid gestured me in the opposite direction from where we arrived. The pixals left us at the corner of the Cat Bough. I watched them scamper up the twining branches that were the walls of the inn. They stopped and watched us from their living perches, their strange triangular faces held slightly bewildered looks and then the moment passed and they were gone.

Funny little creatures, I said to Elid.

'They play their part' said Elid. 'They are the eyes and ears of the Cat Bough and the surrounding land along with the pixies they get around within my bounds. I think the cats have more sense than the pixies at times.'

I have noticed in the short time I have known them that the pixies are very sarcastic to the gaists.

Elid agreed. 'It's not for the first time I have had to stop Gular from eating one of them. The pixies don't understand that the gaist's memory spans are short. They catch fish more by instinct but as to learning new skills, they have to be reinforced regularly.'

'They are very good at swallowing puflic and smoking pipes, when Ruis told me that I couldn't believe it.'

'There are many things that beggar belief in this world Lael. As you have seen, the Cat Bough is bigger than it looks. It is widely used by travellers, not only the inhabitants of the Laic but much further afield, some come by skiffs down the water of Losa and others come from territories beyond the Fada hills.

Not all are bad, but tribal warfare and loss of family and friend produces hardness in all creatures. In some it comes to the surface in acts of violence to their own kind; crimes within a society usually ends up with the perpetrators being banished from the tribe.

Unfortunately the rejects gravitate to others of the same kind and form bands of brigands that cause death and devastation to others.

None of them dare enter the bounds of Daralonadh, I have too strong a grip in my own lands. I also have the power of the Bana ger and the Meren elves guarding the coastal lands. Faolwarriors and shade elves are spread out along the forests and plains and I also have a handful of guardians who keep a very low profile.

Of late these bands have got bigger and more organised, I suspect there is a dark force behind it and it would have to be a very powerful to control the energy of such beings.

'Was the force of creatures that attacked me part of the dark anger?'

'I know it was! Slarcs are very dangerous entities, they forage in the wastes of faraway Dargal. They hunt in packs but are seldom seen anywhere near the lands of Laic. They know I can wield a terrible power if needed and as I have said I have Ruis and Suilval, faolwarriors, shade elves and others who can be called upon.

The three tribes of the bana warriors and the sea elves of Meren are ever watchful. An incident occurred when a tribe of crills ventured too close to the lands of the forest bana and did some damage. Retribution was swift and deadly – maybe too deadly!'

Elid then paused and went silent; I remained quiet and stood in her silence knowing she was far away in thought. Then as abruptly as she entered the trance like state so also she quickly reverted to the former conversation.

'Slarcs are cowardly creatures by nature, they need strength of the pack and they certainly wouldn't venture anywhere near such a strong force of tribes such as ours. It further backs up feelings that a power is at work guiding these creatures.

But what bothers me the most is that somehow the slarcs knew you were coming and how they had come so close to my border without me knowing.'

As we walked through the settlement Elid went silent again so I respected her silence. I started to notice the diverse life forms that inhabited the Sloch. Obviously they were all wondering who I was, I could see huddles of them pointing at me and talking, at the same time I observed the reverent way they looked at Elid.

A group of young creatures had been following behind us, some of them mimicking Elids poise, others touching her clothes.

'The children of the Sloch follow me when I choose to be seen, it gives them a sense of security I suppose. They call me the cat-elf as they think the cats are mine.

And this is another reason they follow me' - so saying she turned about and with a flourish of her hand threw a sparkling dust at them.

The children laughed and screamed as they gathered under the twinkling silver cloud that settled around them. Whatever it was, it encompassed all of them and it was having some effect as they seemed to be revelling in it.

'What kind of dust was that Elid?'

'What is amiss with Elios when you haven't been told about 'elvin dust'?'

I was ready to defend Elios until I caught Elid's look.

'Cool down air-boy.' She said in a very good imitation of Suilval, even tailing off with a snarl. 'The dust is something I made up for the children as it excites them and makes them feel good about themselves.'

With that she switched back to the previous subject again. 'Yes Lael I think your arrival had something to do with the slarc attack. Something I am missing!'

'What can you possibly be missing Elid, you know what is going on in your own territory and you have others out watching?' Even as my words came out I knew that Elid was not listening, she was far away in mind thought. I followed slightly behind and wondered who she was in thought with, I had not long to wait.

By this time we had wandered out-with the limits of the Sloch habitations into a depression by the banks of the river Losa, when a huge shape landed in front of us, and what a shape it was too! It reminded me of an earthen raven but it was huge - it could easily carry Ruis and Suilval on its back.

The beak was long and pointed, a formidable weapon in its own right, and the claws were more like the cruel talons of a falcon. Elid approached the bird and in respect the huge bird dipped its head.

They stood looking at other in thought communication. It was a 'need-to-know' thought pattern in which I was not included. So obviously I didn't need to know.

I gazed around the land from the gravelly dip we were in by the river bank. The bank on the opposite side sloped up to plains of pink and red flowers, tall willowy plants with flower heads spiralling up the stalks for at least half their length. Behind them in the middle distance was a forest, which lent a mossy green background to the field of vivid red flowers.

Beyond the forest, low purple topped hills snuggled against higher sentinels of jagged lavender peaks, which etched the blue skyline and formed a curve on my visual horizon. The only break in that natural fortress was the gap at the Fochd pass.

It was, in spite of the bad goings on, a beautiful land. Rugged in some places but tame and domestic in others. A loving sun by day and a mother and daughter moon by night, truly wonderful!

But I miss Ulana; the never ending goodness of the spirits and the land itself, all my friends to wander with in endless time, an infinity of gratitude. At times I wonder why I made the decision to leave that wonderful world but in the recesses of my mind I knew that I had to.

If all the spirits in all the spirit worlds stayed where they were there would be no ultimate spiritual development. My mind harked back to the words of Elios and Liath; both had told me many times that ascendency is paramount.

The spirit needs to burn brightly and the higher the ascendency it attains the more it will shine, until it reaches the ultimate level and there it will burn with incandescent fire in commune with others.

Elid is a powerful entity - why does she need to stay here - she can leave any time she wants and return to Ulana.

Elid stays where she is because she believes she can make the land better for all. Elios is in my mind and I am instantly calmer.

Where there is hope there will be strength and Elid has both, she also has strong allies to help her, some she knows of and some she does not, but they will show themselves when needed. Elid will show you the way Lael - you must keep to the path of the spirit at all times.

The land and the air outside of Elids land will lie heavily on you. There will be others who are strong and will support your strength and will help you along the way. I will speak with Elid now.

And with that she was gone and I was left in meditary silence for a while. Then the voice of Elid took me back to the event of now.

'Lael, come and meet Croin, he has come a long way to speak with myself and Elios.' Croin spoke in my mind and it was a surprisingly soft tone for one so big and I told him so.

His head reared back and he reverted to vocal, with a cruel laugh he went on to say.

'You tell that to a thousand Gurks that I gutted in mid-air. Yes they would be happy to hear they were destroyed by a black storm hawk with a soft voice.'

I took a step back as Croin was an entity I was not sure of.

'Lael! Go back the way we came, stay in the Cat Bough until I get back and do not mention Croin's name to anyone.' Elids tone was commanding. 'Go now!'

With a last look at Croin, who gave me an amused look and dipped his beak at me, I departed.

As I made my way back the way I had come I could not help but wonder at the strange meeting - a huge black bird in conversation with Elid - what next?

As I walked back the way we had come my thoughts took charge----*When I first entered the land I was so sorry for it, I felt its hopelessness but I set about to heal it and I did. I produced a lush growing forest which blossomed in front of my eyes.*

I was in a high state of motivation later in semi-med with the starry night above me and I beheld its wonder and felt its magnificent presence.

However, during the slarc attack, although my actions were quick, I did feel vulnerable and at one stage before Suilval and Ruis appeared it crossed my mind that I should try and kill them. That awful thought stayed with me for a long time and began to eat into my mind.

The walk with Suilval and Ruis was enlightening, but I was confused as to why I was being escorted to a place which was well off my spiritual path.

I met many colourful characters in the Cat Bough, but my mind was affected by strong drink and thoughts drifted back to earthen days.

The world of Darwan has many parallels with Earth, the struggle to stay spiritual for one. Another was my encounter with Nal of the bana and the desire I felt for her. In Ulana I had no dark thoughts, but here I feel I have a shadow side and I have to call on the sun and the universe all the time to dispel my doubts.

Elid has created a safe haven here in the Sloch and the life forces here all seemed to be happy. They have a powerful protector and two warrior tribes on the borders of the land that could ward off any enemy that might try to invade.

For a fleeting moment I am thinking that this would be a safe place to stay, free from responsibility of spiritual ascendancy --- No – no - no, I am responsible, responsible and answerable to the universal spirit, I cannot allow myself the luxury of self-indulgence.

I am here for a reason and whatever that reason is then I will be here for it, no doubt Elid will enlighten me in her own good time.

Then my thoughts evaporated as I spied Enderli and Coonie coming out of the Cat Bough, laughing and talking away in their colourful language and obviously on a mission of some kind as their pace quickened. Faolwarrior and elfin trickster, an unlikely pair but they share a bond of some kind and nothing seems to faze them.

Faolwarriors and Shade Elves

The shade elves were essentially wanderers of Darwan, preferring the vast forests of the land. They were smaller and slighter built than others of the elfin race. Their skin had a russet hue about it and they did not like to be out in the light of Apuss too much - hence the name *shade elfs*.

They had to fight at the battle of the Fochd pass because they had no alternative, it was fight or die. These were the words of Elid to the shade elves and the faolwarriors. Both tribes had blotted their copybooks with the black elves of dar-guita and as

Elid told them, they couldn't have picked a worse lot to fall out with.

If the battle was lost, the dar-guita elves would chase the shade elves and faols to extinction. Those few chosen words had the desired effect and so Elid placed them on the left flank as far away from the elves as possible. To their credit they fought well and held their ground.

The shade elves have as their emblem the depiction of a black and white bird called a fantail. The fantails choose their locations they are to be found in great numbers close to shade elves and faolwarriors.

Like the shades they are mischievous and like the faolwarriors they are fearless. The birds have a distinctive hopping manner when they are on the ground. The head bobs and the tail fans out and wags up and down.

Enderli is a well-known character among the shade elves he is a trickster and loves drinking puflic.

Their neighbours the faolwarriors, or wolf people, are fierce fighters when antagonised but like the shade elves most of the time they are laid back in their social habits. They are taller than shade elves and more muscular, wolf-like in appearance and like Suilval they are furred all over and have ears that stick up on the sides of their head.

Whereas Suilvals fur is smooth and well-marked that is not so with the wolf people. Their fur is coarse with sporadic marks through it and it comes in many random colours throughout the clan.

Two warriors called Coonie and Fennis are friendly with Enderli and Suilval and all four were drinking companions in the Cat Bough in peacetime

Coonie and Enderli

I asked Suilval about Coonie and Enderli because they interested me both in appearance and mannerisms.

She started off by saying that they were good drinking companions and they had some harrowing experiences together. Then she said, Enderli can sharpen the sword but Coonie is the one who can wield it!

She related a story about how the elf and the faolwarrior met. It was told to Suilval by Rusa a female warrior of the red shelc tribe that lived in the lands of Emul dun. The meeting of the two took place in a rest house; although it sold strong drink and had entertainment it bore no resemblance to the Cat Bough.

The master of the house was a large ugly male of the red shelcs called Gurt, he was an uncouth bully who revelled in his physical strength, he liked nothing better than to get stuck in to any trouble makers, although more often or not it was he who started the fight in the first place and mostly his opponents were so drunk they were useless.

I interrupted Suilval to ask if she had been troubled during her visits to the bar. She gave an answer in no uncertain terms. She said during the few times she does venture into the place, Gurt has been known to jump over the bar counter and stay there until she departs.

She also said that she never needs to barter for drink she gets a full glass when she comes in and a new drink appears whenever the last glass is emptied. She muttered - maybe something I said about ripping his head off.

Anyway Enderli was caught out obtaining strong drink by deception. He had appeared in the bar with a selk cub, now an adult selc is much prized and worth a lot in barter trade. A cub is smaller but is still a worthy swap, especially if you have a taste for strong drink.

Enderli struck up a deal with Gurt, which was the amount of goblets of drink from the nose to the point of the tail of the selc. If he could not finish the drinks by the time Apuss had set then Gurt could take the left over drinks back - he certainly did not realise the drinking capacity of the shade elf.

The story goes that Enderli had just about finished the drinks and Apuss had hardly moved. He approached Gurt again saying that he had another cub which he was going to barter with the bana but because he had a big thirst he would consider another deal with Gurt.

Greed and getting one over the Bana moved Gurt to make the same deal, because he felt sure the elf would leave most of the drink, considering what he had already consumed.

Suilval told me Rusa could hardly speak for laughing at the next part of the story, it was so funny.

When the hunters catch a selc they cut their throats

right away and hang them up to drain away their life essence, so when they are bartered they are completely dried out. Enderli knew where Gurt stored the selc cub so he went round the back of the bar housing. He took the cub and cut part of its tail off - the tails of selcs are very bushy so the cut would not be easily seen.

Gurt was taken in and probably congratulated himself that he had a goblet less to bargain with. He even left the selc stretched out on the bar counter with the goblets lined along it.

That's when Coonie came on the scene he wandered into the bar with a meagre bargaining object which only realised one goblet out of Gurt. Enderli invited Coonie to join him and that was the start of a very chequered lifelong friendship.

As the drink took effect Enderli got louder and bolder and he produced the tail end of the selc saying to all in the bar. This piece of tail lost me a drink but gained me many more at the same time. There was a chorus of laughter from all in the bar.

Gurt's face was a picture to behold, first bewilderment then slow dawning which broke into a full rage. He leapt over the bar and charged at Enderli. Now Enderli could not match Gurt in head-on physical strength but he is quick - very quick, unfortunately he was also very drunk.

He was good at leaping up in front of an attacker and planting both feet on the head of an assailant - well, this time he got up in the air all right but his feet were well short of Gurt's head, so he turned upside down and landed on his head and that was

him out of the fight.
But not to Gurt, who picked him up like the dead selc and was ready to throw him through the door. A voice growled from somewhere at the side of him. 'I wouldn't do that if you are a wise man.' It was Coonie. Gurt dropped the elf like a wet rag and aimed a balled fist at Coonie's head, Coonie caught the fist in his hand and twisted it violently to the side and the crack that echoed through the bar let everybody know that Gurt's wrist was broken.
Coonie slung Enderli over his shoulder and carried him out of the bar, Rusa so enjoyed the affray in the bar she invited Coonie to her dwelling to get Enderli in a fit state.
Suilval finished by saying, 'When you see Coonie and Enderli at a table with a jug of rot-gut and their heads lowered in deep conversation then you know some creature in the land is going to be the poorer for meeting them.

Lael and the Bana

I entered the Cat Bough and was surprised by the subdued atmosphere; there were creatures seated at tables but all seemed to be engrossed in eating. I spent a happy interlude with Casa who was very patient in answering my questions. My conversation was halted by the appearance of Suilval who said once again she had been summoned by Elid to take me to her bower.
I did ask her what it was about but all she said was that she got the idea that I was going to wander.
Suilval would say no more on the subject, she took me to the bower of Elid and we were told to enter.

Suilval gave a polite nod to Elid and said. 'Here is Lael, he has survived a night and a day in the Sloch and he is raring to go again.' She then turned to leave but Elid stopped her. 'Suilval I would like you to stay.' Elids tone belied her looks, it was a command said in the politest way.

Suilval came back and stood beside me. In spite of her brusque behaviour I had grown to like her and somehow I felt easy with her, saw her as a very dependable entity. Especially now because clearly Elid had something on her mind and it must involve Suilval.

'Lael I want you to accompany the bana, they are on a search for a hunter who they think has stolen an artefact from them. It will do you well to see how the bana operate and you will get a feeling of the land and how changeable it can be.'

I have already spoken to Eils and she and her warriors are waiting for you at the end of the Sloch, so go now and do what the bana tell you. I have words to speak with Suilval.'

I nodded in respect to Elid and to Suilval. Suilval said. 'Go get em air-boy, see you when you get back.'

That was me dismissed, I caught up with the bana at the road end and straightaway Eils said. 'Lael, you will march beside Nal seeing you get on so well with her, but do exactly as she tells you in the event of attack. I have been tasked to take you back to Elid in one piece.'

That prompted a comment from Traig. 'He won't be in one piece if he is left alone with Nal.' There was a consensus of agreement from the warriors on that one. The response from Nal was. 'You got that right Traig.'

Then we were off at a steady run. Suila was ahead of the pack, acting as a lead scout I thought.

They fascinated me by the way they moved, heavily armed

as they were, their weapons hung easily on them. They were scantily clad, what clothes they wore were made from the skin of a selc. It was a material I had never seen before; it was also body armour as apparently it was extremely tough.

They all wore selc on their upper bodies and round their pelvis, some of them had it on their forearms and lower legs too. Around their necks and wrists they wore necklaces and wristlets of a thin metal woven in distinct patterns.

Swords were worn at the sides of all the warriors some had short knives around their waists or diagonally across their bodies. Also belts of various sizes were worn to enable the weapons of choice to hang the way they wanted.

The warrior Traig carried an array of spears ranging from a very short one to one about the length of herself. I counted five and they were carried at her back like a quiver of very large arrows.

Nal was the bow-woman of the section and what a bow it was that she carried, deeply curved with short, wicked looking spikes along the length of it. The arrows in the quiver were long and dangerous looking - I shuddered at the thought of these weapons in action.

Bheir and Suila were armed with two swords each, at least the long weapons at their backs were swords, but the ones carried at their sides were short and the blades were curved at the top. I noticed Suila carried a short handled axe as well.

Eils wore a sword on her waist belt, and diagonally across her body an armament of grim looking daggers of various sizes.

They were all fine looking, I would not describe them as

beautiful women but they certainly were striking. The hair was mostly worn shoulder length and could be braided or pleated, some like Nal had it pulled back from the forehead and fashioned into a hairtail, the tail could be decorated or be left plain dependent on the likes of the wearer. The hair colour of the Arcil bana was blond - so blond it was almost white and worn very short. With their mercurial coloured skin they were a very distinctive looking clan.

The two other tribes of bana were similar to each other in looks, both of them had very black hair, totally the opposite to the clan of Arcil. The eyes of the bana vour were slightly paler than the eyes of the other two tribes.

The wearing of selc skin and types of weapons carried were common to all three tribes, as were all other customs that prevailed.

We had not been on the move very long when they made an abrupt turn. I asked Nal what was going on. She said that we were headed for the habitations of the gruflics, as Traig had made a suggestion that Senna might have offloaded the icon with the gruflics for something in exchange.

I was quite excited by the idea of a visit to the home of the gruflics. I had heard various stories about them and their eccentric behaviour. I made my feelings known to Nal who assured me that nothing I had encountered in my two previous worlds would match what I was about to witness.

Gruflics

We held the open ground for a while then we entered a forest of very strange looking trees. Nal told me to kneel down very low as the trees were the outer guardians of the forest, their branches and the tips of their leaves were armed with deadly sharp thorns.

Suila was already about to crawl under the branches - I asked Eils to call her back, she gave me a penetrating look but she hailed Suila and waved her back. I got the warriors to stand behind and then turned my attention to the trees.

The trees had already sensed my presence and were already open to my mind and I thanked them for their attention. The inner spirits of the trees were called 'Eam' and despite the threatening outer exterior they were very soft and receptive to what I requested.

Once I had thanked the trees for their help I turned to Eils and told her that the trees would allow us to walk through them. Suila assumed the lead again and with hesitant steps walked into the tree line.

The lower branches of the trees swept upwards and formed an archway to the inner forest, giving us ample room to pass through. I turned to thank the trees and was answered in a shimmer of leaves as the archway was closed.

'Nice trick Lael, now brace yourself for the greatest culture shock you are ever likely to have - the gruflic village to your front.' Eils backed her words up by pointing one of her swords dead ahead.

I could not believe what I saw; a village of sorts, its random huts scattered between the trees and in front of them creatures moving towards us.

The Gruflic

The gruflics were the strangest looking creatures. They were grey and spindly; body, arms and legs were all long and thin. Their heads were large in proportion to their bodies. From their eyes their foreheads swept backwards to the crown, no hair, very long pointed ears sweeping up and almost past their heads. Broad faces adorned with large eyes, long pointed noses and laughing mouths. These tree-like beings were designed for pure nonsense.

The huts they lived in were the most erratic looking buildings I think I had ever seen, they had a vaguely rounded shape but there symmetry ended with a vengeance. Some huts had trees growing sideways out of them others had the same but in company of bushes, flowers and birds' nests.

All manner of collectable stuff adorned every single dwelling, benches and seats were stuck higgelty-piggelty into the roofing. Some of the gruflics were actually sitting on them. Suila told me it's not unusual for them to fall through the roof, seat and all.

'When that happens it is a great upheaval and the whole village turns to, they all muck in to assist the owners of the broken roof. It occurred once when the five of us were passing through so we stopped to watch the goings on.

They managed to free the benches from inside the hut and got to work thatching the roof, we were very impressed by the speed with which they had acquired the fresh thatch until Traig pointed out that they had robbed the house next door of its roof, with the stupid owner's permission.

Finally they managed to fix the roof and drag the benches back onto the roof and every gruflic in the village was present. Nal said that we were not going until we witnessed the coming disaster - we had not long to wait.

They were singing and dancing and much blowing of the hooto things that they play constantly. We could not say how many were on the roof or sitting on the benches - when the whole singing, shouting, hooto blaring ensemble fell through the roof, but this time the hole was a lot bigger.

All in all, the gruflic village was very much like the gruflics themselves, full of random parts. Male and females shared in all things with no particular dominance from either gender.

I was told by Ruis that the gruflics were punished by Elid for chopping down trees when they first came within the bounds of the Laic. As they were under her protection they had no option but to comply with her rules. They were told - no more cutting down trees or branches.

They could build their huts with the twigs and branches cast off by the trees. The use of turf was permitted as it was used to bind the framework of the huts and to aid the growing of plants which decorated all of the huts.

The insides were amazing, very cosy in spite of the exterior chaos. The gruflics are scavengers of the land; they clean and look after the forest floors around Elids borders. They also help themselves to anything that lies around. If anyone is missing something there is a good chance it will be in a gruflics hut.

They don't mind showing their collections to creatures that have lost anything and they usually get left a substitute in place of a claimed article.

They are a happy lot, always laughing and shouting to each other and moving about their business in an energetic manner. They are friends with the skarling birds and the skarling birds share two things in common with the gruflics.

One is that they both communicate at high speed - vocal chirping is a good imitation. The other shared trait is they are both collectors. Skarlings decorate their nests with all sorts of things, but mainly bright articles. The gruflics on the other hand collect anything and everything.

The bana searched through the huts but found no trace of the missing artefact. The presence of the bana and I caused a great stir with both gruflics and skarlings. The birds were flying and chirping above us, the gruflics dancing and weaving about us on the ground, eager to show us round their particular hut.

Suila took out a gurks feather from her belt and aimed it at the sky, it didn't get far - a skarling zoomed in on it, grabbed it with its claws and took off heading for its bower. A gurks feather is a prize indeed!

This caused a great buzz of chatter from the gruflics and a pathetic display of fawning and pleading to the warriors for feathers. Eils told the warriors to give the gruflics the feathers as their belts would be filled again before their journeys end.

So saying, she threw her three feathers at the nearest bunch of gruflics, the rest of the warriors followed suit, throwing their feathers all around. Bheir, in a rare display of humour, holding on to the last two feathers shouted. 'First two to reach the Salacian Sea get the feathers!' As one – all the gruflics took off in what I imagined was the direction of the Salacian Sea—or not.

'Come back you fools, you'll take a lifetime to get there; anyway you are going the wrong way.' Bheir's shout was answered by an about turn by the horde - and two got the feathers.

Nal turned to me and said. 'Watch what they do with the feathers.'

I watched their antics with great amusement. They were sticking the long feathers between their toes and were tickling the ears and noses of gruflics who didn't get any feathers. Laughing and dancing the happy throng followed us out of the settlement, blowing on the peculiar looking instruments called hootos.

Suila told me the gruflics annoy the backsides off the gaists when they are fishing in the river, they throw things at them and even use the gaists heads as stepping stones to cross the river. They have to be quick though, because although the gaists are clumsy on land they are very agile in the water.

'Do they ever catch a gruflic?' I asked.

Suila said. 'Oh! All the time, the gaists hold them under the water until they almost drown, then they throw them out onto the river bank, but the grufs keep going back for more.'

'Where did they come from?' I asked.

Suila grinned when she answered. 'They say they came from a hole in the ground in Dargal.'

'But that's nonsense.' I said, although I was laughing at the stupidity of the statement, in fact I hadn't stopped laughing from the moment we entered the village. Whatever spiritual entity created the gruflics must have had one zany sense of humour, they were pure enjoyment.

Once outside the bounds of the gruflic village the bana stopped and had a discussion as to what direction they were to take for the trail to find Senna.

We carried on in silence for a while. After the euphoria of the gruflic village we all took the opportunity to retire to our inner selves. I had noticed earlier on that the bana went into a mode which I can only describe as - 'inner alert.'

They go quiet but they are not lost in thought, they are intense, all the senses are active, eyes watching; ears hearing; noses smelling. Suilval told me even their skin bristles if there is danger about. They are well and truly a deadly fighting force and I was soon to be informed just how unforgiving they were in their methods.

I as always was in a contemplative mood. Here I

was, a spirit entity and a healer of nature's land and bound by the law of the universe not to take lives; that was the job of a higher deity than me.

Nal had questioned me on the point of killing. She had said if I knew when a creature died that it went to a better place after it died; then why not kill everything I met to send them to that better place.

She then went on to say that she could not think of a better life than the one she had now. Part of a fighting section within the most powerful tribe in the land and if Ara was kind to her and she had to die in battle then that would be a triumphant end to her life.

I had never seen a bana warrior dying - yet! So therefore I could not say what shape or colour their spirit is when it leaves the body. No matter what they say about death the spiritual law of the great cosmos states that death is the beginning of a new life, the life force is taken from the body into the universe where it placed in the dark energy of space to begin a new journey - I am proof of that!

We had been marching in file for some time. Bheir at the point slightly ahead of the rest of us then Eil, me, Suila, Nal, and Traig at the rear, even she was quiet.

I came out of my thoughts and caught up with Eil and asked her what the next plan was.

Eil's reply was straight to the point. 'We must hunt down Senna and kill him.'

'But if you kill him and he doesn't have what belongs to you how are you to know what he did with it.'

'It matters not, he stole from us and broke our trust, so he will pay for that with his life. After that we will find our property even if we have to waste the whole of Dargal.'

'Do you ever give up Eil?'

'No, not ever. It was not so long ago we had to pursue a whole tribe who had done us wrong.'

'What did they do?' I asked fearing the worst.

Eil explained in no uncertain terms. 'A tribe of creatures by the name of crills came across a family of our name. The warrior woman was called Sar; the man was called Col and they had a child with them. They had been out on the fringe of our land when a very large band of crills came upon them.

Crills are similar in looks to Coonies people but bigger and they have a very aggressive nature, although they are not the fighters the faolwarriors are. Sar ordered Col to take the child and run to call the bana to arms - she had already shielded Col and the child and in doing so had taken a barbed arrow in the leg.

When Col got to the trees he looked back and saw Sar attacking the crills - she did not wait for them to come at her. Col got to Arcil and raised the alarm but by the time we got to the place of the ambush it was too late, the crills had killed Sar and despoiled her body. The crills had left many of their dead at that place, Sar had taken many of the carrion out before she was felled.

Tiathmor had led us there herself and an angry queen she was. But before we decided on a course of action we first gave thanks to the sea, air and the earth for what Sar did in life.

Tiathmor dispatched her guard warriors to carry Sar back to Arcil. When they departed she addressed us. Warriors; she cried, drawing her sword. We must teach this savage tribe a lesson; it will also be for others to think long and hard before they attack any of us - ever! Because when we finish what was started here today there will be no crills left in this Darwan world.'

I got a very bad feeling about what I was going to hear next.

'Come bana let us hunt them down at the run. Those were the words of Tiathmor as she led us on in the direction of the crill horde.

A warrior called Rhu ran ahead with me as we acted as scouts and also to pick up the trail, it was easy to read as they were a band of great size. I knew by the direction they were taking they were heading for the Fochd pass and once through that they would cut across the Heddon plains and then to their homeland on the Erdon heights on the fringe of Dargal.

Rhu and I doubled back and I reported my thoughts to Tiathmor. She had soldiered in Dargal in far off times so she was knowledgeable of the terrain. She agreed with me and Rhu that the crills were headed for home with their spoils and she proposed we would beat them home by running over the mountains of Ranmos.

She also swore by the sword of Elid which she carried, that the crills would feel such fear before they died.'

As Eil continued I could feel the energy off Suila, who was behind me, and I interrupted her story to ask a question.

'Were all five of you there Eil?'

'Yes, Bheir and Suila were behind Rhu and me, Nal and Traig were young warriors at the time so they were at the back as rear-guard watchers.

We were at the run all through the night and we held the trail by the eerie red light of Rinnis. In the light of morning when Apuss was at his highest we came upon the settlement of the crills - we had beaten the crill band home.

Then the anger of the bana vented its fury on the crill population. We fell upon all in the crill settlement. We killed males, females, children, animals and birds.'

Hearing Eil's words, devoid of all sorrow for such slaughter, I felt the pain of all that death in that far off age - can this story get any worse?

Eils carried on with her account of what happened next.

'When we were done we retired behind that place of death to await the crill force.

We had not long to wait. The crills came to the camp of the dead and when they saw the devastation they set up a wailing, but it was short lived.

Lead by Tiathmor we walked slowly into the camp. The crills went silent they had the dread of death upon them. Some dropped their weapons, others tried to run but we had them encircled, they had seen what one bana warrior could do now there were many of us so they were beaten before we closed in.

Rhu had asked Tiathmor to have the first go at the crills on her own. None of the bana will ever forget the way Rhu strode out in front of us. A striking warrior even among our ranks, her weapon of choice was a long handled two bladed axe the cutting blades were each end of the handle and faced in opposite directions.

'Hear this, crills.' Her voice was strong and steady as she gave her short message - 'Sar was my blood sister and I saw how many of your carrion tribe she killed. So in her name I will take as many of you or more before my tribe takes part.'

And then she was on them, she had speed, power, aggression and accuracy and even though the crills fought with the desperation of those who know they are going to die they were no match for Rhu - Tiathmor had to shout to us 'quick, get in there before she kills them all herself.'

When all were killed we left the bodies to the dead eaters of the land and air. We put the signs of the bana all around the land to warn others not to linger in or inhabit that place.

Before we left we found an old crill who had hidden himself well, but not well enough to hide himself from Rhu. She hauled him out from the hole he had crawled into, but before she could deliver the death blow Tiathmor stopped her.

'Hold Rhu, do not kill him, he chose to hide as his tribe were being killed off so let him live alone and he will eventually die alone. There are no females left for him to sire - he looks too old anyway.'

We left him on that bare hill and as we left a wind blew up and carried his wailing grief to us.

> Stay - stay a while wild wind
> Blow my shame and grief across the plains of regret
> And onward yet - to remorse and pain
> On sorrows moorland bare - my soul and spirit to forever share
> with carrion - and desperate cold

When we returned to our own lands we extended the bounds far beyond the settlement areas. Any armed force entering the bounds without permission would suffer the consequences.'
'A whole tribe paid the price for the death of one bana - Eil?'
'Yes Lael, a whole tribe for one bana warrior.'
There was no emotion in her voice and her face was as impassive as usual
The words were said - and that was it!

Suila proposed that they should head for the woodlands of Creroc as it was heavily wooded, hilly terrain, perfect for someone who does not want to be found.
They were all in agreement with Suila's words, so with her in the lead we were off again to wherever the woodlands of Creroc lay. I liked the description of the place - trees and hills, the lungs and heart of any land.
Once again we moved across a sparse undulating landscape, no bird life or animals to be seen. Suila

called a halt and we all gathered round to hear what she had to say.

She said. 'As Apuss will be going down soon I think we should sleep the night at the whispering trees. Before the darkening I will zig-zag round the land at the other side of the trees with Nal, to see if we can pick up any sign.'

I liked the sound of the whispering trees and asked Suila why they were called that. Suila replied with grin and said. 'Ask Traig, she has been silent too long, she must be about ready to burst.'

The said person did exactly what Suila said; she burst into a torrent of vocals which nearly carried me away in a wave of emotion at the meaning of her words.

She said. 'The whispering trees are a like a mini forest in the midst of a landscape bereft of any other kind of greenery. They are exposed on all sides to winds from all directions and it is said that they pick up messages from the breezes and pass them on to unseen entities.

There are no permanent residents in the wood but many creatures, both birds and animals, rest for the night there or take shade during the heat of Apuss. Even when there is no wind you can always hear the leaves whispering.

Inside the ring of trees there is a spring of water which bubbles up from beneath the ground and returns the same way, it is the best water you can ever taste. So Lael, you will be spending the night under the soothing chatter of the trees and drinking water that is as pleasing as puflic.'

By this time Suila and Nal had sped off, leaving the

rest of us to trot up to the whispering trees that were just ahead of us. I could see a goodly cluster of trees sitting on a slight knoll and just as Traig had described, it looked like a mini forest that had been stuck on a small hill.

We entered what turned out to be a triple ring of trees and in the middle was a carpet of soft green moss. Scattered about were some good sized stones, alive with twinkling crystals. They were well named the whispering trees because not a breath of wind was about and yet a gentle murmur was trembling through the mini forest.

I stood in the middle of that ring of tree energy and breathed the life-giving air, then knelt by the spring and tasted the water and in an instant I felt I was back in Ulana; with such overwhelming feelings of space and the elements of air and water in proportion within my spiritual form.

I was aware that Eils, Bheir and Traig had already picked their spot and were languishing on the mossy bed with their backs against the trees. Eils and Traig were in light hearted conversation; Bheir in silent contemplation.

I broke the mood by asking Bheir what she thought was the purpose of an island of lush trees in the middle of nowhere.

Bheir took her time before answering me and I noticed the other two stopped their chatter and turned their focus on her.

She said. 'It is a refuge for all creatures, as this place is neutral to all life forms - birds, animals, elves and us. There seems to be an aura round about that repels really bad entities, but that I do not understand. Maybe you, Lael, can feel what the whispering is all about?'

The appearance of Suila and Nal interrupted our conversation they had not taken long in scouring the flat terrain.

Suila said that they had come across two traces of dog fouling which could have been discarded by one of Senna's dogs, but no footprints. She added that Senna could have killed the dogs after keeping the fouling for later to distract us.

Eils agreed with Suila's reasoning because Senna would have known that the bana do not give up and would be on his trail. According to Nal and Suila, the two fouling's were many leg spans apart. The line of the two did not make sense as it was bare land with a great distance on either side.

Nal said that she thought Suila's first idea about Senna heading for the woods of Creroc was the right one, and that is the direction to go.

Eils spoke. 'We sleep the night here under the whispering trees and head for Creroc when Apuss rises. The red maiden will be in the sky for many nights, after we take care of Senna we will make for the bowl of Rinnis. We need to be careful not to be caught out in the open by the red winds.'

I did not understand what Eils was speaking about and I didn't question her as they all, as one, got stretched out. Only Nal fired a quip at me saying 'Don't turn into a tree during our sleep Lael, each one of us will be awake at different intervals but we will leave you to your standing sleep.'

The bana had named my meditary slumber 'the standing sleep'. I suppose it was as good a description as any, although I do sit down sometimes. I waited until they all settled down before I got comfortable and ready; the bana sleep with their eyes open so I couldn't tell which one was awake.

I was well into my medi-slumber; my eyes gazing upwards through the canopy, focused on the stars that were visible through the veil of murmuring leaves. Then an event took place which altered my focus, wisps of mist flowed through the upper branches of the trees.

Trees, mist and leaves were merged in a swirl of natural energy - the whispering turned into a soothing pulse that gradually faded away altogether.

An aura of peace and stillness settled in that little dell, my eyes were drawn downwards to the trunks of the trees. Shapes began to manifest within them - misty images that had body shape in the trunks, then filled the branches and end twigs like arms and fingers.

The spirits of the trees had revealed themselves to me, and for a short space in my great journey I was at one with them. I gratefully accepted their energy and thanked them for sharing their knowledge with me.

I came out of my communion of spirits just as Apuss was rising his welcoming light filled the little island of trees. A very confused bana five were debating why none of them had been awake during the night.

I told them not to worry as they had been well protected through the night. I also said that whatever events happened in Darwan, all of them would come through together and would be held in high regard by their tribe.

My words were accepted with no comments from any of them, but I could tell by the looks I got that their minds were working.

Eils said. 'Come, let us cross the sandy plain to Creroc without delay.' And that was the signal for all of us to move. We moved quickly and Apuss was quite high in the sky before we were halted by Suila, who had been leading a short distance ahead of us.

She shouted back. 'Eils, the sands are moving.'

Eils cried back. 'What direction Suila?'

Back came the reply. 'Half the way of Ica.'

Eils again. 'Suila, head for the torn rocks - Lael run like you have never run before - Nal and Traig alongside him - Bheir the tail.'

I knew by the tone of Eils commands that something serious was going to happen and it was something to do with the shifting sands. All the time I was thinking, we were hammering down the plain. I was conscious of Nal and Traig by my side and I could feel the tension coming off them.

Then I started to feel a resistance in my feet and ankles, as if they had encountered a force of some kind. Nal shouted to me that the winds of Rinnis were on us and that it was a wild wind that runs along the sands and that the higher it reaches the stronger it gets.

No sooner were the words out of her mouth than I

felt the wind thumping into my body and the force was very powerful. Nal and Traig had joined their hands behind my back and were helping me along.

The wind had reached our faces and with grains of sand from the plain smashing into our eyes it had slowed down our running. I could not see Eils or Suila I could only feel Traig and Nal beside me.

The wind was a shrieking frenzy as it tore at our bodies, it had slowed us down considerably and was threatening to lift us off the ground. We had closed up in a huddle of bodies, Eils and Suila were in front of Traig and Nal, pulling them by their belts; Bheir pushing from behind.

Then the commanding voice of Eils shouted out - 'The rocks, we have reached the rocks - everyone lie down at the same time.'

The bana all dropped as one, dragging me down with them, I got a sense of relief as the pressure of the wind eased off; and then I was hauled under an overhanging rock by Bheir.

We remained under cover until Apuss was ready to set; the sound of the wind was deafening as it pounded the rocks then ricocheted off, howling - proclaiming its irresistible force to all that was caught by it.

We emerged from our safe haven in time to hear the distant wailing of Rinnis's wild wind and I gave a silent prayer to the higher spirits that none were caught in the pathway of that tempestuous energy.

Suila was first to comment on our appearance, she said we were like a band of dust hoflics, I wondered what in Darwan a dust hoflic was!

I looked around at the immediate area which had been our refuge, and saw layers of serried rocks that looked like they had been savaged by winds and weather from a long distant past. They were well named the torn rocks.

The bana were shaking the dust off their bodies and checking their weapons; all seemed to be well as we took off straightaway and I supposed in the direction of the woods of Creroc.

We deviated from the rocks to take the direction we lost during the wind storm and made good headway with the red maiden dead ahead of us. I took the opportunity to ask Bheir about the wind that had hit us and why it was referred to as 'The winds of Rinnis.'

Bheir told me that when the moons changeover they are the harbinger of erratic goings on in Darwan. When it is Rinnis's turn to rule the night, chaotic winds and rising tides occur.

It only happens for the first two nights of the red maiden then everything goes back to normal. So it has to do with the changeover and yet for some reason it does not happen the other way round.

Bheir also said that she thought it had something to do with Rinnis being nearer to Darwan than Ara. At certain times when they pass in the sky she noticed that Ara always passed behind Rinnis, therefor Rinnis must be closer than Ara.

Before we could debate any further, once again the voice of Eils got our attention.

She said. 'We are now at the fringe of the woods of Creroc so from now on we go quietly, Suila and

Traig have gone on ahead to feel out the land; we will follow their lead.

Lael, stick close to Bheir. There have been reports of an eathie demon residing in Creroc and he has a particular interest in Ulana spirits.'

I turned to Bheir and asked her what in Darwan was an eathie demon? I didn't like the sound of it.

Bheir said. 'She is after a reaction from you and by the look on your face she got it, do not worry Lael, as far as I know eathie demons vanished from Darwan in an age long past.'

As we entered Creroc I could not get 'eathie demons' out of my mind, Bheir said they were long gone and Eils was only baiting me. However, having experienced the slarc attack and having never got a satisfactory answer from Elid at the time, I guarded my thoughts well.

Plenty talk of dark energy, even Elios hinted at it. And me - why have I been seen by all in Darwan? All very confusing, and now we're creeping through a wood by the light of the weird moon Rinnis.

Once again Eils broke my thoughts. 'Lael, you will be pleased to hear that Suila and Traig have found a suitable place for us to spend the night.'

We moved through a belt of trees into a space of mossy banks and large boulders and there we spent the darkening. There was no escaping the red glare, it was everywhere; it sketched thin red lines on the branches and trunks of the trees and its reflected light glared at me off the rocks.

I decided I needed to make friends with Rinnis and concentrated my meditation on the ring of the red maiden which was all that was visible from where I stood.

In the brightness of Apuss we were up and moving; we trailed up a tree lined gorge with Suila in the lead again. She stopped when we were half way up and had words with Eils. My ever present shadow Bheir said. 'Suila has found a sign, Senna is an able tracker and hunter, but Suila is easily his equal - it won't be long now.'

We closed up a bit and continued up the gorge and at the top we stopped for a while. Suila, accompanied by Nal, had forged ahead once more. After what seemed a very short time the two warriors appeared, they all gathered round and a short debate took place.

When the debate was over Bheir came to me and said we had to move fast for a spell, so I got up and tagged behind Traig and with Bheir behind me we took off at speed.

The Death of Senna

In a wooded hilly region we came to a break in the trees. We were higher up than I had realised. Scattered rocks and small plants were on the elevated feature we stood upon and a great view was before us. An azure sky was the backdrop to a range of rugged mountains and before them were smaller rounded hills with trees in a mixture of green and copper----

'Senna!' The muted warning came from Traig. To our immediate front the ground fell away from us forming a rocky steep, it was if the trees had parted to form an avenue.

As we looked down the corridor, far down at the bottom of the cut we could make out the figure of Senna and his two hounds.

'Your kill Traig.' The curt command came from Eils. I wondered how Traig was going to going to carry out the kill. I would have thought that Nal, who was the bow master, would have been the choice.

What happened next was a show of supreme strength and accuracy, Traig took about six steps back with her long spear in her hand, held it well back then rushed forward at an astonishing speed for so short a distance. Stomping her lead foot hard she came to an abrupt halt at the same time body and arm came forward to launch the javelin into the sky.

I caught a flash of the razor sharp black tip as it left the knoll we were standing on, in no time it found its height, then like the falcon when it sees its prey, it swooped, and we watched as Senna the hunter fell before the spear of Traig of the bana.

No movement from Senna but I sensed his spirit had left Darwan, I knew death had released him - I wished him peace and love on his way home.

When we reached the body of Senna we saw the spear had done its work well, it had pinned his body to the ground. Suila commented on the absence of Senna's dogs - we had expected to have to kill them as well - they must have run off, she mused. I said to myself I hope they run all the way to Slar-fel.

Senna had been a huntsman first and foremost; he wandered in far off places with only his two great hounds for company. He was a very able fighter - he had to be because his wanderings took him into dangerous places; he was a hunter of tree selcs - what made him steal from the Bana?

One of the most prized animals in Darwan was a tree selc. The selc was a vicious four footed animal that lived in the wild uplands of the Cladon forest and it was highly sought after for its body parts.

Its skin was sleek and grey coloured with markings of blue and black, though it looked furry it was not. It was leathery, but more flexible and had a silky feel to it.

Senna had filleted the skin off in one piece, the one piece skin was his best trade as the bana and the dark elves made their tunics with them.

The head, complete with teeth, he had bartered to the tribe of Selma; the claws to the Rall people who valued them as talismans, they made necklaces to wear at their throats.

Bheir turned Senna over and pulled his tunic open at the neck. 'He has it.' She said addressing Eils. Eils kneeled down beside Bheir and they removed something from his neck. Eils had it in her hand but straight away gave it to Bheir.

'Put it around your neck Bheir, and keep hold of it until we get back to Arcil.'

I didn't get a look at what it was that Senna was killed for and at the time I didn't really care. Once they had what they were after, we were off at the gallop again. I asked Eils where we were headed and the answer I got unnerved me a bit.

'Lael, once we leave the woodlands of Creroc we will

head deep into the land by the way of Ica and we will be looking for fire.'

She gave me an amused look on seeing my reaction to her words; they had picked up that I had an abhorrent attitude to fire and the mention of it.

I decided to ignore it and gave a positive reply by saying 'Oh that sounds interesting'. I caught Nal giving Eils a knowing look.

At high speed we left the woodlands of Creroc behind and started to gain the high ground - up - up - and ever up, the steeper it got the faster the bana five moved. It felt to me that the warriors were sourcing their energy from the living rock.

Every high peak we reached always led to another higher one; then finally we stopped at a flat topped mountain and abruptly the terrain changed yet again. A huge plain opened up in the direction we viewed and at the base of the hill we stood on I could make out what looked like a giant bowl that seemed to have been had been carved out of the plain.

Suila was crouched down at my side and she informed me that we were looking at the plain of Rinnis. I asked Suila why it was called that.

She pointed out a gap in the mountain range far behind the plain and told me that the red moon Rinnis rises in the gap at certain times and when she does it rains flaming stones from the sky.

I was by this time much accustomed to some of the erratic ways of the tribes and the unnatural phenomena which contributes to the madness of Darwan. But I had to ask Suila to elaborate on her statement.

Suila hailed Bheir to come over to tell me more about the flaming stones; she said Bheir did not believe the burning stones are spat out by Rinnis.

Bheir began to say that Rinnis herself is the herald of the flaming stones, then she took me aback by saying to be patient because Rinnis will be rising between the hills shortly and the stones will come hurtling down - watch and see. I followed the warriors to descend on to a ledge slightly below the peak.

We stood on that ledge high above the plain, looking across at the bowl formation. I was flanked on both sides by Eils, Suila and Nal. Traig and Bheir were forward of us and in the kneeling position. Traig shouted back to me to watch the gap in the hills.

I felt something fantastic was going to happen and sure enough it started after Traig spoke. Rinnis appeared like a fireball between the mountains and her surreal red light reflected along the hills like flaming wings.

What happened next was even more spectacular, splinters of fiery stones in colours of red and blue came raining down from the sky into the bowl of Rinnis. They came crackling down at great speed and peppered the floor of the bowl, we could hear the hissing and spluttering of the stones as they extinguished themselves on the plain.

Bheir shouted, telling me to look up and see where the flaming missiles were coming from. I followed the direction that her hand was pointing and was momentarily distracted by noticing a blemish on Bheir's hand. My attention went back to the sky and where the rocks were coming from.

Traig said. 'Look Lael, the flaming rocks are coming from behind where we are standing, not from Rinnis. Bheir believes that the red moon shining through the gap has nothing to do with the flaming rocks - it is only a spectacular marker.'

Bheir again - 'The rocks are up there all the time but for some reason they only come down at certain times. Something happens up there that allows the trapped rocks to rain down on the plain of Rinnis, as far as we know it does not happen anywhere else.'

Silence came upon all of us as we watched the flaming rocks getting less and less until finally the last of them disappeared in a sparkle of blue flame on the plain of Rinnis. We stood for a while, bathed in the queer ochre light of the moon, and in that space I stood back and observed my companions, especially Bheir and Traig.

The two warriors were together, forward and slightly more elevated than the rest of us. Traig was crouched down on one knee, one hand on the handle of her sword, in her other hand she clutched her long spear which was grounded in the upright position. Bheir was standing by her side, her hand on Traig's shoulder.

Their darkened shapes were framed within the fiery red of the rising Rinnis, it looked so dramatic a picture. In the eye of my mind it looked as if Traig was ready to spring into the heart of Rinnis and Bheir was gently holding her back, her body language saying - not yet!

'Hey air-boy, get yourself back to the stone ground

of Darwan.' The voice which was a perfect mimic of Suilval came from Suila. They took great delight doing a voice over of Suilval when they saw me lost in thought.

I asked her what was happening and she told me that we would be sleeping the night away in the place we were at now, and when Apuss was up we were to go into the plain and pick up 'corac.'

I asked her what corac was and she told me it was the stones that fell from the sky, they bury themselves in the soft dust at the bottom of the plain and by the morning they have cooled enough to scoop up.

I asked Suila to tell me more; she was the one warrior I knew the least about, and also the one that I had never been in a position to engage in conversation, so I kept asking her more questions. I was also keen to learn more about this phenomenon. Suila countered by saying that I was as bad as Traig with the questions - and right on cue the said person asked. 'What are you saying about me, I hope it is good?'

I was left to answer Traig, as the elusive Suila moved away to busy herself elsewhere. I then got my question in before Traig asked what I was made of. I started off by asking what the Bana did with the corac stone.

Traig enlightened me by first drawing my attention to her spearheads, this is what corac looks like after our men have cleaned and polished it. Then she pointed to her long spear saying. 'See here Lael, this head is the usual colour of the corac but look where the side broadens and notice it has a black mark like a teardrop.'

I had noticed the spear and arrowheads before and admired the strange colour which was similar to purple, but I had never noticed the black teardrop on any of them. I asked Traig if there was any significance to it.

She told me that the first one was discovered many events ago, before any of the Bana in this space were born. Indeed, before our mothers mothers were born. One of the men was hard at work polishing a lump of corac when he found it.

At first he thought it was a blemish on the surface and tried to clean it away but after a while he realised it was part of the stone.

It was kept in the queen's lodgings, and after the bana moved from the island of Moula to the lands of Daralonadh it was kept at Arcil. The Arcil bana have it as a token and many of them have the arrowhead with a teardrop painted on their bodies.

I then asked Traig if that was what Senna the hunter stole. In a very matter of fact way she said. 'It was ironical that Senna stole the corac token and I killed him with a spearhead of the same.'

The bana then made arrangements for the night sleep. Bheir was the first sentry so I took the opportunity to speak with her. I asked her if she meditated at all or took time for deep thinking and I was pleasantly surprised by her answer.

She told me that all the Bana, when they are in safe circumstances, go silent. They usually do it at night during the presence of either moon. They sit with their back to whatever maiden is in the sky.

Taking in her own perception of events she went on to say.

'We sit cross legged and because we have the light of the moon behind us we look to the starry darkness ahead of us.

The Darwan night is always busy with bright stars and other bodies; there is a restless intensity about it. We shut our eyes and empty our minds. We feel the earth beneath us, the air around us, and the energy of the night sky above us. It is not only the bodies of motion we feel but also the darkness that holds them altogether.

We accept that we are part of a force that we do not understand, but we use that force to heighten our senses and the belief in ourselves.'

I said to Bheir that I understood what she told me and that I shared her belief because, for all the knowledge I had accumulated from my three world journeys, the moving darkness still mystified me.

I then picked a spot and spent the night in meditation under the red moon called Rinnis.

The morning cry was bright and early, Suila was last watcher and she did the wakening. I have been amazed at the rising of the bana. When they get their shout they are instantly awake and stand up straight away, it's as if they were never asleep.

They eat something called 'Esta' it's a dried fruit of some kind, they carry it on their person and it's mainly consumed first thing in the morning along with water. However on my first journey with Suilval and Ruis they had food wrapped in a leaf and it did not look like dried fruit.

They took their time over breakfast Suila informed me that the longer the Corac lies in the bowl of Rinnis the cooler it will be. There will be other life entities there as Corac is much valued for its use as tools and weapons and also for its beauty.

She carried on speaking, giving me very descriptive pictures of some of the creatures that scavenge for the sky stones. Suila said there are strange beings that are only seen during the falling of the Rinnis firestones.

I was amazed at the length of conversation I had with Suila, in all the time I have been with the bana I have hardly had any words with her. She is a very witty person and I have heard her come out with some really cheeky humour.

She went on to say that the gruflics will be at the gathering but it's not the corac they go for - it's the powdered sand they gather up. She said it with a touch of humour in her speech, making me think that the gruflics always get it wrong.

Then she enlightened me as to why the gruflics gather the sand. They line the bottom of their huts with it because it looks good and you will see today there are minute slivers of corac in the sand.

The slivers of corac glint and flash in the light and the gruflics are drawn to stuff like that. Suila then said that they do a lot of nonsensical things, but very occasionally they do get it right - like once in a lifetime!

Oh another thing, they usually bound in immediately after the stones have fallen and start to scoop up the sand. The stones are still burning hot so the Grufs stand on them quite often and it is hilarious to see them jumping about holding on to their feet.

We wound our way down from the hill we had camped on and crossed the plain that led to the bowl of Rinnis. It was slightly further than I anticipated but when we arrived I was staggered by the size of it.

It was absolutely huge, we stood on the rim of the bowl and I could see a pathway that wound its way inside the bowl of stone, it seemed to go on forever. The bana took off at a great speed with Traig shouting at me. 'Come on Lael, get a move on - this is a great path to run down, it goes on forever.'

So I had to take off after them and joined in on that lung bursting run all the way to the sandy bottom. It was, as Suila said, a vast plain of grey sand, but it glittered with dots of corac picked out by the light of Apuss.

The Bana spread out in a line and began to stab at the sand with their sword points, so totally focused on their search they forgot about me. I had no sword or staff of any kind but I had something else, and that was energy sensing.

I, being so light of foot, hardly reached the solid bottom of the bowl, so I wandered away from the bana and began to focus on what might lie beneath my feet. I had not long to wait before my senses found something that sent a message of tremendous energy through me.

I felt beneath my feet and my fingers touched something that sent a shiver of excitement through me. I picked it up and found it was a stone - but such a stone as I had never seen before.

It was small, just fitting in the hollow of my palm, spherical, more oblate than flat but the colouration was something else. Dark ochre was the main colour but running in parallel all the way around it were two thin lines of violet.

As I turned it about in my hand I could see pinpricks of gold light coming and going all around it. The energy emanating from it was powerful for such a small item. I felt it was a gift from the cosmos and although I was the finder I knew it was not for me.

Traigs voice floated into my space.

'What have you got Lael?'

'Something wonderful Traig, come and look.'

On hearing our voices the rest of the bana showed interest and they flocked around me to see what I had found.

They were well impressed with what I had found and were very vocal in their praise. Eils said she had never seen the like of it in all the fires of Rinnis that she had been at. I gave it to her saying. 'Here pass it round and tell me what feeling you get from it.'

She felt it and juggled it between both her hands finally flicking it in the direction of Suila who deftly caught it with her finger and thumb. She then rubbed it inside of both palms then threw it in the direction of Nal.

Likewise Nal caught it and like Eils juggled it to and fro from hand to hand.

I said. 'Well, did any of you feel anything?'

They all agreed it was very smooth and pleasing to

hold and beautiful to look at but none of them got any sensation of energy from it.

Nal passed it on to Traig who immediately stiffened at its touch. I thought to myself - at last a reaction. Before I could say anything else she turned to Bheir and said. 'I feel a power in this stone that I cannot understand.' And with that said she put it into the hand of Bheir.

Bheir held it in her clenched hand and with closed eyes turned her head upwards to the sky saying. 'This is indeed a gift from the universe and is a treasure to be respected you are very fortunate Lael, for finding such an item.'

'I was the finder Bheir but at the very first touch of it I knew who it was for, it is yours for as long as you need it, it will help you in your meditations. The power is in you and as you develop the stone will act as a channel to energise and enlighten you. Take it with my blessing.'

The corac stone had a long journey through the matter of the universe to drop into the crater of Rinnis.

Its arrival coincided with Lael and the bana scouring for the flaming rocks. The bana had no way of knowing at that time that the giving of the stone to Bheir was the catalyst to a turning point in their society.

In typical bana fashion the others cheered and clapped Bheir on the back, all of them thrilled at Bheir getting such a gift - no envy, only enjoyment, just because one of their numbers gets or does something to bring honour to the race.

The bana returned to their search for corac and I remained in conversation with Bheir for a while. I happened to glance over Bheir's shoulder and saw Eils talking to a very strange creature.

I drew Bheir's attention to the creature and she told me the creature was a 'hoflic' and his name was Dur. She went on to say that they were like land versions of the river gaists. They hunted the plains and forests around the bowl of Rinnis and like the gaists they liked strong drink, unfortunately like the gaists - rot-gut does not agree with them either.

I said to Bheir. 'Where in all of the wilderness does he get puflic?'

She gave an amused half smile as she answered my question. 'Lael there are many rest houses scattered about the lands. Some of them are very good and others are not so good. They all make their own brew and it carries the same name no matter where it is produced - puflic and rot-gut, but none of it tastes as good as the stuff that Elid's pixies produce.

There is a place called the 'Fallen Stone' which is not far from here and when we have collected enough of the corac we will be headed there. We keep most of the corac we find and our men fashion them into arrow heads and spear tips, however we have plenty to barter with and what better place than the Fallen Stone.'

We did a few more sweeps of that dusky plain of Rinnis, until Eils called a halt and said it was time to make a move and enjoy the pleasures of the other fallen stone.

That was met by hearty cheers from the rest of the

band and me included. I was looking forward to seeing the fallen stone, even the name conjured up images of some erratic place in the middle of nowhere.

We retraced our steps at the run and never stopped until we were well away from the plain of fire. We halted at the top of a small hill and the bana began to part the stones they had gathered in equal parts so that each warrior carried roughly the same weight.

They kept some of the stones of lesser quality apart, these were the stones to be bartered in the rest house for food and strong drink. I took time to look around me and I could make out the hoflic in the direction we had just come, he seemed to be in company of another creature.

Then I beheld a wonderful sight at the bottom of the hill to our front. A lochan of clear crystal water, so clear I could see the bottom and the fascinating thing about it was that the loch bed was floored with a myriad of stones.

The colouration of the stones was breath taking, there were red ones with black stripes, white ones with red stripes, grey ones that glittered with silver freckles and pure white ones.

From my vantage point I could see there was a pattern to the random colours, the stones that ringed the shore had a background colour of red and they merged into a circle of orange, the orange faded into a ring of yellow.

There followed circles of green, blue, indigo and finally, in the middle of the lochan, was a mass of violet stones. Within the stone circles the pure white ones shaped like arrowheads all pointed to the centre of the stone circles.

The background colours all glistened with dots of silver and gold bars, streaks of black and white added to the collage. I asked Suila what the lochan was called and if there was any life in it.

Suila said it was called the Beata water and nothing lived in its waters as far as she knew. Elid had told them it was a circle of liquid energy linked to the force of the living world of Darwan. There were many such lochans all over Darwan and they keep the balance of the energies of earth and lower sky.

Nal said that they wash themselves with the water and drink it; it tastes so good and they all feel energised afterwards.

By this time we were joined by the hoflic and his companion who looked like a smaller version of Suilval. He introduced the creature by the name of Doridh-Ler and said she was of the tribe of Ativa.

Doridh-Ler was a slender female and when she spoke her voice sounded like a tender whisper, she seemed a gentle soul and like the others she had been gleaning for corac. The Bana warriors had met her before and started quizzing her about the movements of her tribe.

We then went to the edge of the sparkling water and all of us washed ourselves in the lochan and drank of its refreshing liquid. Immediately after, the bana and I took off for the fallen stone. Dur said he and Ler would catch up later, Ler was to continue on her journey but she would have one drink with Dur before she left.

We ran on the flat for some time, then we ascended onto a ridge and carried on running along the spine until it descended onto another plain - and there it was - I did not need to be told it was the Fallen Stone. It was a round house of stone and it looked as if it had dropped from the sky.

Before I could take in any more, Suila, who had been running at the point, was now kneeling at the edge of the downward slope. She was pointing to what looked like horses tethered behind the building.

Eils uttered with a hint of disdain 'Terk warriors'. Whoever the terk warriors were they did not seem to faze the bana, as we made all speed to the rest house.

The Fallen Stone was a beautiful building; I was stunned by the colouring of it close up I saw that it was made up of many small stones. There were grey, pink, black and white and many of them were stripped and some were spotted with colours that contrasted with the background colour.

It looked as if it had been built by the creator of the lochan we had just visited.

We entered the place and I was pleasantly surprised by the ambience of the interior, it was a mixture of stone and wood and an abundance of plants were strategically placed in little arbours.

There were creatures of differing shapes and sizes sitting at the tables, all engrossed in conversation, some looked up and acknowledged the bana. I knew straightaway who the terk warriors were, they were a group standing apart from the rest of the customers. Tall and dark, long hair pulled back from their brow and tied tightly close to their heads, the remainder hanging like tails down their backs. They wore the same selc armour as the bana, their trews were baggy legged and pulled in at the ankles. A variety of wicked looking weapons hung from belts that looked like they were woven from metal.

They did not pay much attention to the bana by the same token the bana did not pay any attention to them. But I felt a slight tension in the air.

I seemed to be the one who was attracting the attention in the bar, especially from the pretty person serving the puflic, her name was Elva but I was not sure of what race she was. She had a slight resemblance to a shade elf so I asked her to what race of Darwan she belonged.

The bana loaded themselves with foaming goblets and retired to an arbour at the back of the bar, leaving me standing at the bar in conversation with Elva. I had made it clear to the bana I was not going to touch any strong drink.

Elva told me she belonged to a race called the larmid people and that they are a race of nomads who had come from faraway Dargal and settled in the lands around the plain of Rinnis.

Because she resembled a shade elf she was known as Elva as that is what the larmid people call the elves.

Our conversation was broken by an uproar from the terk warriors. I turned to see what had caused the eruption and was surprised to see it was directed at Ler and Dur who had just entered.

I went to meet them and ask them to join me at the bar but they declined, saying that I would get myself into trouble from the terk warriors they said they were used to the abuse.

I stood my ground with Ler and Dur but was aware of the terks surrounding me and one of their numbers began prodding me with stick of some kind.

In a high pitched screeching tone which belied his looks the one with the stick asked me what I was and why was I in company of 'the creatures of the dust'.

I replied in my most adamant manner that I was a spirit of Ulana and the two I was in company with were called Ler and Dur, two life forms that had mutual right in the lands of Darwan.

My statement brought shouts of derision from the terks and a burly looking one with a beard drew his sword and pointed it at my throat, saying.

'I don't know what you are but you might not be so arrogant with your throat cut.'

'And you terk might not look so attractive without a head.' It was the voice of Nal who had come to the bar for another round of drinks.

The beard with the sword answered her back, but his tone had a touch of caution to it. 'This is no concern of the bana ger it is our business warrior, not yours.'

Nal's voice came back slow and easy. 'I am making it my business terk, what are you going to do about it?'

The bearded one was standing between Nal and me and he still had his sword at my throat. I was wondering what was going to happen next and it came in less than a heartbeat, in a blur of motion Traig appeared with her long spear in her hand.

Stabbing her spear into the floor she pole-vaulted between myself and Nal and planted both feet on the bearded one's head, knocking him clean over a table - completely toes up.

Greatly daring, one of the terks made a move for his sword but quick as lightening Nal's sword was at his throat.

Eils, Suila and Bheir had been watching the action and had come forward in time to see the rest of the terks raising their arms to show they had had enough. The one that went for his sword said. 'We do not want any trouble with you, all we wanted was a bit of fun with the dust creatures.'

Eils stepped forward and I could feel the air charged with energy, the terks sensed it as well because as one they all drew back and visibly shrank in stature. Eils stands taller than most of the bana warriors and can be quite intimidating at the best of times.

Her body language as she confronted the terks did not need words to convey the message that was coming. But when the words came they were spoken with such venom that I felt the sting myself.

The way Eils spoke to the terk warriors I was sure the terks felt as if the threats had been carried out already.

She said. 'You might not want trouble with us but you have got it, because from now on the two creatures to whom you have given so much abuse are under the protection of the bana-ger.

If word ever comes to us that these two have been harmed in any way I will take my tribe and decimate much of your warriors, and any that we leave will have their tongues cut out so that they will not abuse any more creatures in this part of Darwan.'

The only life entities in that place who did not feel fear were the Bana five themselves. The terk warriors were first out of the door, carrying their fallen comrade, followed swiftly by some other creatures that had nothing to do with the affair.

Eils, the perpetrator of the exodus, turned to Traig and said. 'Well done Traig; how to clear a bar in one easy movement.'

That lightened the mood a bit and we all retired to the arbour, taking Dur and Ler with us and the five did not waste time in getting stuck in to more drink. Dur was a ready participant so that left myself and Ler to chat away by ourselves.

Ler told me she was from a tribe of solitary wanderers, they had no tribal lands nor did they have any place that they could call a home.

Occasionally, like the fiery rains of Rinnis, the sky would tell them where and when to meet. Then they would congregate away from other creatures and meditate as a group, the time in mind combination invigorated them all and gave them the spiritual mind strength to cope with their solitary existence.

I was so excited by Ler's revelations, especially at the mention of spiritual meditation, that I pumped her for more knowledge and was astounded by her next performance.

Ler told me to watch Dur, so I complied with her wishes and stared at the Hoflic who had started to rise, chair and all, above the table. Poor Dur, he hadn't a clue what was going on; he got a sense of relief when he landed on the table top.

The bana drew back slightly but were not spooked by the event, Suila as usual quipped in with 'High on puflic again Dur.' Dur just sat with a dumbfounded look on his face making no attempt to get himself off the table, and carried on drinking out of his goblet much to the delight of the bana.

Traig said they should buy him more goblets and see if Dur would reach the roof - Nal countered by saying 'Better not feed him much more or he might be having his last drink on one of Rinnis's rings.'

Other than Eils offhand comment to me 'Is this your doing Lael?' They carried on with their drinking after they got Dur back on stone floor.

Ler then told me their power is great but like me they cannot use it to kill, only in defence of themselves or others is it allowable to temporary disable a foe.

I reasoned that Ler could have saved Dur without the help of the bana in the confrontation with the terks. Ler said it was more entertaining watching the warriors in action and apart from Traig nearly knocking the bearded one's head off there was no serious injury.

Ler and her tribe were spiritual wanderers, they wandered far in the direction between Ica and Ulas, they never crossed into Daralonadh but she had heard of Elid Silverhair. I asked Ler what purpose they were pursuing.

Her answer was disconcerting to say the least as she said that she and her band of companions were setting bounds of spiritual defences. They were doing this as their meditary perception had warned them that a dark power was at work.

Ler was very forthright as she traced out the stages of the dark power's effect on the lands. She said tribes and creatures were guided to do things out of their control and Elid Silverhair had put bounds both physical and magical around her lands.

All very noble Ler said, but in doing so it allowed the power of darkness to affect the areas round about Daralonadh. Then you, Lael, appeared as a physical presence, never before has a spirit of passage to the higher reaches been so visible.

We detected your spiritual presence when you first set foot on the earth of Darwan and began carrying out your healing work on the land. We felt the healing energy from far away. We were not the only ones who felt it and that is why the slarcs were drawn to you.

They were guided by a force that felt your energy; that same force wants you, whatever the entity is it knows you are here. The bana are powerful warriors and they would die in your defence but they cannot fight black power. It was born in the magi-weave of darkness, and within the shadow of matter it wandered before the universes were formed.

When Ica and Ulas took shape and began to form dimensional space they worked well together. Ica bent light to her bidding and sent it speeding through the ripples of time on its endless journey to brighten the corridors of space.

Ulas chose the dark of the weave to work with and for a while all was well, then he awoke the slumbering power that had been dormant within the weave for so long.

Ulas was completely unaware that he had absorbed the dark energy that was part of the beginning of all things. The energy had no distinction between good or bad - light or dark, it was created in a vortex of fire and force; it can never be destroyed.

He carried on moulding the elements that would eventually melt in with the light of Ica's work.

Then, when all was at a state of readiness, the dark overpowered Ulas and Ulas became the power. He created out of the elasticity of the weave ethereal beings of various shapes and levels of power.

He relished what he thought was his own power and kept his creations hidden from Ica, not realising that the dark energy had its own purpose.

The weave is the source of power, the shape shifter of all the universes, it is indifferent to good or bad and it gives itself to whom or whatever wants it - for a while.

I was fascinated by what Ler had to say, although I had doubts about me being used as bait, however I had no time for reflection as my conversation with Ler was brought to an end by Eils.

Once again in a good take-off of Suilval she said. 'Come on air-boy leave Ler alone, we have journeys to be going on.'

And that was it once more, I said goodbye to Ler and Dur and followed in the footsteps of Suila and Nal, with the other three of the bana close behind. I thought to myself 'where in this crazy world of Darwan are we going now.'

After a good spell of running through variable terrains we came across a shade elf. He was perched on an exposed root of a tree with his back to the trunk. The bana knew him and engaged him in conversation.

They introduced me to the elf, called Lonesli. Traig said he was the blood brother of Enderli - she added on that he did not share any of Enderli's trickster traits.

The elf conveyed a piece of information which unsettled me a bit - he told the bana that he had come across a force of slarcs lying up in a place he named as 'Estil hill.'

Eils asked if he got close enough to see what their numbers were.

Lonesli answered, saying that he felt the numbers were superior to the bana five and he went on to say that whenever he spotted their movements he melted away into the land.

Nal said. 'Eils, surely we have to go and disperse the slarcs or they will think they can come and go as they please.'

Eils said. 'We will Nal, although they are on the outer fringe of Daralonadh it is too close to our land. We need to give them a hard lesson that they won't forget in a hurry.'

'They must be long gone by now.' I ventured, as truth to tell I did not relish the idea of meeting up with a band of slarcs.

Traig answered my question, worse luck, she told me that Lonesli thought it was a camp for a scouting party she also added that somebody or something must be controlling them as they would not have the savvy to do it themselves.

So off we went on a slarc hunt, Suila out front; the formation was arrowhead, Traig and Eils on one flank and Bheir and Nal on the other flank and me in the middle.

We covered some rough country at a steady pace then we came to a stretch of marshland which wasn't too difficult to negotiate. To the front the land rose to form a long rounded hill, Suila turned and motioned Traig up to her, she gave the rest of us a palm down motion with her hand so we all got down to a crouched position.

I learned later that Traig had got a description from Lonesli of the terrain and although she had passed it on, Suila just wanted the confirmation.

They fanned out a bit and crept forward to the brow of the hill and had a look to see if there was anything there. They came back at the run, Traig to Eils and Suila to Nal and Bheir, they closed in on me and told me what I didn't want to know!

A large party of slarcs was camped below the rise - Traig gleefully said that they are so stupid they have no sentinels out.

I was told to stay behind the line of warriors as they crested the rise, the battle plan was surprise. The bana were going over the top at speed and straight into the slarcs to kill as many as possible before they rallied, and even if they do it won't make any difference.

I never got a chance to voice an opinion they were over the top and in amongst the slarcs before the creatures knew what was happening. I could only watch as if time had rolled back and I was watching Ruis and Suilval dealing with the black plague.

Only this time there were five dealing out death and destruction, and what a spectacle it was. As much as I do not like killing I was held in awe at the speed and effectiveness of the bana killing machine. I understood now how they came by their reputation - they enjoy fighting and I regret to say they enjoy killing.

Then something unexpected happened - two giant gurks appeared on the scene, in the turmoil of battle their presence went unnoticed.

Suila had been fighting on the flank where the slope of the hill was slightly higher than the ground the rest of the warriors were fighting on, with the result she was a bit behind the fighting line.

The gurks had come from the rear, the leading one swooping low on the upsweep of the hill grabbed Suila from behind. Eils, ever watchful of her section even in the thickest of fighting shouted. 'Bana - a gurk has Suila!'

The gurk wheeled slightly to gain height, that's as far as it got. An arrow from the bow of Nal speared the bird through the neck. Before it crashed to the ground it let go of Suila. By this time Eils had run under its belly, she caught Suila - Suila found her feet - they touched hands briefly.

When her arms had been pinned by the gurks claw she had held fast to her battle axe, it was put to good use by hacking the claw that held her from the carcass of the beast. With a mighty throw she sent it flying high in the air and down it went right in the middle of the slarcs in the rear. It must have killed or maimed at least three of them.

I was told later that killing a couple of slarcs with the claw was a bonus, but there was another reason for Suila's action. Slarcs are fierce fighters when they have strength in numbers but they are not organised and they are easily panicked, once they start panicking the air rings with alarm calls.

The same thing happened when I was attacked at Slar-fel, when Ruis and Suilval appeared on the scene and started cutting them to pieces, at the first screech of panic they vanished from me like magic.

When the gurks claw landed among the horde at the rear it caused hysterical wailing which had an immediate effect on their fighting front.

The foremost slarcs turned away from the bana, the bana were then chasing the slarcs. The five were spread evenly behind the fleeing horde, cutting, slashing, maiming and killing - no mercy, just pure blood lust. I was fully expecting them to chase the slarcs until they killed them all. Suilval told me the bana ger are the fastest and most dreadful killers in the Darwan world, nothing escapes them.

As my thoughts were on Suilval's words, I saw that the bana had stopped the chase. By some unseen or unheard command they had all stopped in line and turned back and were now finishing off the dying or wounded slarcs.

For others of this world it ends at the sight of the dead bodies but for me it doesn't end there.

With the demise of the physical body comes the

release of the spirit, even these dark creatures have their nether world. In their dark worldly life they didn't have much in the way of light, but in death their spirits left them in a glorious array of colours.

For as much as I don't like death and destruction by violent means, when I see the departing spirit it makes me glad that in death a release of spiritual energy is freed into the wonder of the universe---
'Have a feather Lael!' Traig's voice takes me back from my thoughts, she hands me a gurks feather and I notice that they all have them adorning their sword belts.

Their mercurial skin and selc clothes are smeared with the dark ooze which is the life stream of the slarcs. We leave the battle field to the dead eaters of the air and land they also have their part to play.

I asked Traig what creatures ate dead Slarcs - she told me Oshic Worms and Bladit Birds; I did not like the sound of them so I did not pursue the question.

In single file we pass through a fertile glen to follow a clear sparkling stream downwards to a loch. In all my lives I have liked the sound of flowing water ruffling over stones on its meandering way to a loch or a river.

At last we came to a stretch of still water and the bana stripped off and entered the water. Bheir ducked under the water and swam off out of sight. Traig was cavorting with Nal, Eils was washing herself down.

Suila was behind me perched on a rock, eyes scanning round about, her turn will come when one of the others relieves her. I was getting anxious about Bheir and I voiced my thoughts to Suila. 'Do not worry about Bheir, she has gone for fish,' replied Suila. 'Why don't you get in the water Lael and enjoy the feel of it.'

'Oh I am going in Suila, I like the feel of water.' So saying I stripped off my tunic and stepped into the water, my translucent blue skin got a few comments from the warriors. Traig fired a broadside of questions at me - luckily the conversation was stopped by the appearance of Bheir surfacing with two large fish, one in each hand, they were twisting about in her grip as she waded ashore - *won't be twisting about for long water creatures.*

Traig was back to the questions she asked about my blue skin and pointed ears, if that's what I looked like on Earth home. I told her I became like that because the spirit I was mentored by was a blue elf and in the spirit world you adopt the features of the spirit form you are most comfortable with.

Her next question was why I didn't eat or drink.

I told her I do drink the water. I also take the dew off the grass, sometimes I will ask the bushes if I can have some of their berries, mainly I take my energy from Apuss, the earth beneath my feet and the great stars of the night. I was in the water by then and Traig had got more interested in the fish.

They were always interested in me and my spiritual ways and they quizzed me endlessly about what I thought was my former life. They do not believe in an afterlife, their only purpose is the continuance of their race, this they achieve by maintaining their dominance as warriors. There is no reward after death, when they die they see what they leave behind as a reward.

The bana made a good job finishing off the meal of fish. Heads, skins and guts all consumed - nothing left.

I noticed when Bheir appeared with the fish that after she shared it out they each took a portion of fish in their fingers and held it up to Apuss before they ate it. I asked Traig why they did it as I knew the bana did not believe in spirituality.

Traigs answer was straight forward she said. 'Just because we don't believe in an afterlife doesn't mean we don't believe in the land we walk on or Apuss who gives light in the day and Ara and Rinnis by night, it is to them we give thanks for who we are.'

After the meal they settled into a conversation time during which they cleaned and sharpened their weapons. Each of them carried a sharpening stone in a small sheath attached to their sword sheaths.

Once again I was questioned by Traig on the subject of my life on Earth, asking me if I was ever a warrior on Earth.

My answer took them by surprise when I answered yes; I had all their attention. The idea of me being a warrior was beyond belief.

The next question raised by Nal was what kind of warrior I was.

I said. 'The warriors on Earth are called soldiers and I became a soldier to fight for the land I lived on, but when the war was over I stopped being a soldier. I did not believe in an afterlife then, although many

Earth people did and they lived by their ideals. Unfortunately many wars were fought on Earth between people of differing beliefs, each one thinking they were in the right.'

Bheir said. 'All the entities that I know of in Darwan believe in Apus and the night maidens. All of the males in Darwan see Apus as a god whilst other males see Apus, Ara and Rinnis as Gods.

We see the goddess in everything because we are female but the males know that. We in turn know what the males believe. None of us would ever fight over it because it is as it is. There is no argument as all the bodies are in the night sky for all to see, it is in the eyes of she or he whether they are female or male.'

Bheir and Traigs dialogue did open my mind to their way of thinking because they had a sound belief in the natural beauty which surrounded them - in sea, land and sky. What better deity to give thanks to but the fiery ball of light that gives the brightness of day. The night sky gives them two spectacular moons and other astral bodies; some that are static and others that move in an erratic manner.

I had noticed when the females referred to Apus and the two moons it was in the feminine. Ruis and any other males, although they acknowledged the moons as feminine, always called to Apus in male terms.

Indirectly they all believe in 'Creation' so whoever the creator of all that we see is - then he or she must be well pleased with the reactions of its life entities.

The bana warrior contribution that they give to their race in Darwan is enough, after death they are fed to the sea - and there it ends.

Right on cue once again Traig, in her usual staccato manner, flew off a salvo of questions. 'So where does it end for you Lael? Where are you going next? What will you do when you get there - wherever it is? Will you take Nal with you?' With that comment she broke off and laughed, the rest joined in the humour, including Nal who added.

'Yes I am going with Lael to the sky and from the starry clusters of Delga I will look down on the bana and with my new found power I will take Traigs voice from her and give it to Gular of the gaists.' That caused more amusement and plenty of comments, it tailed off with Traig herself saying, 'Huh, if Gular gets my voice he will be a great chief amongst the gaists.'

They reckon Nal has taken me for a soul mate from the night in the Cat Bough when we danced all night. Since that night we have had many meaningful conversations.

Nal is next to go to the sacred island beyond the Salacian Sea. This happens once in every warriors lifetime, any other race would call it spiritual time - not the bana - they call it physical loneliness.

The island is uninhabited and it is the ancestral home of the bana ger. In the night sky there appears a heavenly body called Seba - *it sounded to me like a wandering star*. According to Nal, when Seba appears, a warrior crosses the Salacian Sea in a very large boat sailed by the larger than life mariner called big Jon Beet.

As one warrior is landed, the warrior who was on

the island returns with Big Jon to the clan lands of the bana. Part of this regime is probably right of occupancy, as Nal has told me they have on occasions driven off strangers.

I never got the chance to ask Elid or Elios about the spirit form of the bana. They must go somewhere after death, only certain shades and eathie demons dissipate after death, never again to assume any form, spiritual or physical. The bana are sheer physical energy so therefore there has to be strong motivating spirit within.

Eils voice broke into my thoughts and took me back to Darwan again. 'Come Lael we have to journey far before the light of Apuss fades. Elid needs to be informed about the slarc camp we will bypass the gruflic village this time.'

I was going to ask why we needed to bypass the gruflics as I would have been fair pleased to visit them again, they were so much fun to be with. But I was cut short by Traig who told me to get into the middle of the arrowhead.

The bana had taken up formation, this time Eils was at the head, Suila and Nal on the left flank and Traig and Bheir on the right. In dense scrub they formed in line.

The whole culture of the bana is martial, even the way the three tribes live. The queen's tribe live in the Halls of Arcil. Nal described it as a white mountain hollowed out into living quarters and halls. There are six tiers of rooms and halls. Tiathmor has her rooms on the third level as this makes her accessible to the inhabitants of all levels.

Apart from artefacts from their tribal past, her furnishings are no better or no worse than the living quarters of the warriors. I noticed whenever the queen's name was mentioned voices and body language became energised.

Nal told me there is a great space within the grounds of Arcil where the warriors spar with each other. It is also used for celebrations and as a meeting place for the three tribes. There are always watchers in and around Arcil - it never sleeps.

The same goes for the Bana vour and the warriors of the forests and plains. Their bounds are patrolled by day and night.

DRAIGHEAN

We had just arrived back from our adventures and discovered there was a welcoming party at the flat land between the pink plain and the river Losa.

Elid was there and alongside her Ruis and Suilval, as well as numerous gruflics and gaists. The pixies were bustling about dishing up drink and food, Bila was in the act of delivering a full tray of puflic to the river gaists when he was ambushed by the bana.

They ringed him in so that he had no choice but to leave the drink on the ground, whereupon he was picked up by Suila and passed round each of the bana at high speed.

I counted that he was on his fourth circuit before Elid shouted to the warriors to put Bila down, telling them he had work to do and he couldn't do it with Darwan spinning round him.

Nal complied by tossing Bila in the direction of Suilval - a pixie's worst nightmare, the cat caught him by the scruff of his neck and held his face close to hers and snarled a terrible snarl that vibrated throughout the whole ensemble. She then dropped him and muttered something about Bila being a waste product of Ulas.

Bila scampered off in the direction of the Cat Bough, albeit in a rather erratic gait but he still had breath to quip back at Suilval. 'At least I'm a product!'

I overheard Gular telling Ruis that the bana had stolen the tray of puflic that was supposed to be theirs.

Ruis's reply was short and sweet. 'I wouldn't bother them Gular, even if they are in party mood you just might end up in the Losa.'

I saw Eils and Elid conversing together obviously Eils was telling Elid about the fight with the slarcs.

I enjoyed watching the goings on, all the different shapes united under the influence of puflic and rotgut. Then my mind did a fast forward and my imagination took over, what if higher ascendency took the form of every creature of every planet that ever was?

What if they occupied a space in infinity and did nothing but swill strong drink down their throats all day and it was their euphoria that ignited the light of everything?

I was just getting over the thought that out of darkness came puflic and rotgut when Suilval's voice shattered the illusion.

'Come over here air-boy and get some puflic down you.'

I had to decline the invitation and was treated to a

scathing response from the cat.

'What's up Lael got a roasting from the forest faerie after your last drinking spree?'

'Yes something like that Suilval, it was my first and last drinking session.' Then harkening back to my previous thoughts-------*maybe!*

Suilval lost interest in me and proceeded to converse with Enderli and Coonie who had just shown up. Eils told me that the shade elf and the faolwarrior have the unerring gift of sniffing out strong drink no matter where they are.

I turned my attention to Elid, who was standing on her own well apart from the crowd of revellers. She didn't seem to be meditating or in thought communication, just standing as if waiting for an event of some kind.

No sooner had the thought vanished from my mind when an event happened that shattered the ambience of the gathering.

A mighty shape that I recognised as Croin the storm hawk dropped out of the sky, but this time he bore a rider and the rider was as dark as the bird itself.

In an instant all was movement - warriors of the bana and Suilval as one - lunged forward at Elid's side, river gaists and gruflics cowered behind - within that frozen picture of action my eye picked up a subtle movement to the side of me.

It was of Enderli and Coonie vanishing with a flagon of rotgut each.

In one quick agile movement the rider dismounted and faced Elid and bowed his head in respect.

When Elid spoke it was with authority – no hint of

suspicion in her tone as she addressed the Black Elf. 'What is your name elf and what message do you bring me from Cimer?'

'My name is Derca---------'. The sound of his name brought a buzz of interest from Suilval and some of the bana.

The elf called Derca carried on talking. 'I am of the tribe of Lael and I was trusted by the great Cimer to deliver a token into your hand as proof of who I am and it is him I represent.'

Elid replied by calling on Suilval to go forward and take the token from the elf.

Suilval approached Derca and held her hand out to accept the token from Derca's outstretched hand. With the token in her hand she returned and passed it over to Elid then resumed her stance alongside her.

All eyes were on Elid as she took something from inside the shell like container that Derca had referred to as a token. She then locked eyes with the dark elf of Lael and asked of him what Cimer's message was about.

Derca started by saying that Cimer had knowledge of a powerful dark energy that was centred around the Black Island. The energy had been very resourceful in having enchanted certain entities to do its bidding and had built up a good sized army of barbaric tribes.

He went on to say that Croin and he had observed movements of large numbers of creatures from the badlands. When they reported back to Cimer with what they had seen they were told to make haste and head for the Laic lands.

Elid thanked Derca and Croin for their information and asked that they stay to hear what she had to say. By this time many more of the denizens of Daralonadh had appeared so there was a fair gathering at that place.

Elid's words were assertive and very much to the point. 'People of the Laic I have known of dark goings on for some time, I have had much communication with the few that I could trust. I fear we are on the threshold of battle.

Whatever dark power is behind the insurgency must be very powerful indeed in order to mask the movements of so many numbers and hide itself from view. Dark magic is the weapon that will be used and we have few left to wield the power of white magic against it. I have two faeries, Ilo and Tress, who will stand with me.' The mention of the faeries names brought gasps of wonder and comments from the audience.

'I know that Cimer had communication with the faerie folk when I knew him, I am going to ask Croin if he still has knowledge of them, even one would make a difference.

I also know of a powerful entity that resides in a far

off island, this entity has been redundant for a very long age and so it is time it made its presence felt again.

She then looked in my direction and said. 'Spirit Lael I need you to search out this nameless entity. I have already asked Tiathmor for a bana warrior to accompany you and she has agreed. I had planned to have Suilval go with you as well but I need her to take charge of a battle formation.'

Then she gave Derca a penetrating look and asked him if he would guard Lael on his quest along with a bana warrior.

Before Derca could answer Ruis launched a tirade at Elid, screaming out the words at her --- Suilval moved to intercept him but Elid stopped her and said. 'Let him have his say.'

And Ruis certainly did that; he hurled abuse at Elid saying, he was the one that should be accompanying Lael to find the magical entity and Derca was not to be trusted as his dark race was part of the evil that pervaded the land.

Ruis had a wildness about him as he stepped forward to confront Derca, his hand on the handle of his sword. The black elf never flinched he stood his ground and kept his eyes on Elid.

I could feel the tension in the air, I wondered when Derca was going to make his move, by his demeanour he looked detached but all who looked on knew he was ready to strike.

The confrontation was brought to halt by a swift move of Elid's hand which stopped Ruis in his tracks.

When Elid spoke it was with calm authority she said. 'Ruis, you are a loyal warrior and have carried out many tasks for me, however at this time you have misread the signs. Derca has come with a warning from Cimer, this I know to be true as only he and I knew what took place in the bower of Aior anor.

Before we parted after giving love to each other, Cimer cut a lock of my hair and that is what Derca has brought to me. Cimer would have chosen death rather than admit to whom it belonged.

Croin has imparted his thoughts to me that Derca is held in high regard by Cimer. There are many here who were present at the last battle, Ruis you more than any should know that the tribe of Lael fought against the dark host and eventually had to leave their ancestral lands.

The Lael elves have settled in well with your kinfolk the blue elfin - do you doubt them? If you find my words are hollow then I will lend you the wings of Croin and he can take you to the warrior elf himself and there you may debate about Derca's presence here.'

At that Ruis stepped back and bowed his head at Elid, and that ended the heated debate.

Elid got the attention of us all once more by calling us to silence and to meditate as one so that the energy of the strong among us would be shared with the weaker ones.

I got a knowing look from Elid and I knew what she wanted of me. I encompassed all the life forces that were gathered there with the light of spirit, I enlightened the earth we stood on and the trees and the bushes. The spiritual glow invigorated every living entity in that space.

In the calm of the aftermath everybody began to partake of the food and drink again and an air of congeniality reigned for the rest of the day.

I took the opportunity to speak to Croin and to introduce myself to Derca, as I approached them I noticed Elid making her way in the same direction as myself.

She pre-empted me by conducting the introduction herself, I was introduced as Lael, spirit of Ulana, and the black elf as - Derca, high chief of the tribe of Lael and aide to Cimer.

Looking back I think Elid Silverhair was letting me know in a subtle way that Derca was no ordinary elf.

For all his titles Derca was an easy person to speak to, he was interested in my story of the transition from Ulana to Darwan and asked some very pertinent questions about the world of spirit.

Meanwhile Elid had been in deep thought talk with Croin, they broke off and she got my attention saying. 'Lael I hope I didn't take you by surprise when I said you were to be going on a journey to find a magical entity, and that I had volunteered a bana warrior and Derca here.'

Derca said to me 'If it's any consolation Lael, I had no idea I was going on a journey either.'

Elid smiled that smile that was guaranteed to melt the heart of a slarc and said she was certain that both of us would jump at the chance.

I asked which of the bana she had picked to go with us and was surprised when she said that it was my choice - providing I chose Nal.

Derca asked her if Nal knew she was chosen and both us had to laugh when Elid answered - not yet.

A thought crossed my mind and I voiced it to Elid. 'Surely it would be quicker and easier for one of us to fly with Croin to find the mysterious entity?'

'Ah Lael, were it that simple, first of all I need Croin - he will be my eyes and ears and my communication with Cimer. The entity you will be looking for will not listen to anyone but me and I can't be spared at this time. However I have something that I can give you that will let the entity know you have been sent by me.

Trust is the thing that is most dear at this event we are facing, so the smaller the circle that knows what is going on the better. Derca knows the far off lands that will point you the way to the entity. Nal has knowledge of the lands by the way of Ica and is a capable warrior; she is also like Derca - incorruptible.

Lael, I will speak with you later, but for now we must be at the Cat Bough with Tiathmor and her warriors, I have much to prepare before you set off.'

The Sword of Elid

Elid and Tiathmor had retired to the upper floor of the Cat Bough and were having some kind of debate, when they had finished with their conversation we were all summoned by Elid to her bower. All the bana five, Suilval, Ruis and I were present and I knew by the energy that was in the air that something was about to happen.

Elid spoke first. 'Eils I have a special purpose in mind for you and, if you accept, it will probably be the most important duty you will ever be called to do.

It will have far reaching effects not only for your own race but also for all the life entities in Darwan. I will let Tiathmor enlighten you.'

Tiathmor took up the story. 'Warriors of the bana, Elid has done us a great honour by singling out two warriors to undertake tasks. The first is given to Nal, who, along with Derca the Lael elf, will accompany the spirit Lael to where Elid has directed him.'

At this point I noticed Ruis about to argue again, Elid shot a look at him, and whatever was in the look it literally paralysed him. Then I looked at Nal and if she felt any emotion she certainly didn't show it.

My attention went back to Tiathmor, who continued by saying.

'The other one of the five is Eils, who is to be given the sword of Elid.'

Right on cue Traig stormed in with a race of questions that staggered the company with the sheer speed of the vocal tirade.

Tiathmor was used to Traigs impatience and so she waited until her outburst had ended and answered.

'First of all Bheir, give some calm to Traig and I will try to answer some of the questions I think she asked.' This brought a ripple of laughter from the group.

When the laughter died down, Elid stepped forward and took her sword in its sheath and passed it over to Eils saying. 'Take this sword and use it well, it will fend off any dark magic you may encounter.'

Eils accepted the sword graciously and dipped her head in respect to Elid she then said 'How will you defend yourself against a foe that has magic without your sword?'

Elid allayed Eils fears by saying. 'Do not worry about me Eils, the magic is in me and I can channel it through my body or my mace. You are going to be needed when the enemy strikes, as it surely will.

There has been much going on, incidents here and there; small insignificant happenings. Then the tribe of Selma attacked and scattered. Although it was a long time ago, the Crill attack on the Bana might have been the dark energy feeling its way. I believe that the coming anger will be a force to be reckoned with and that is why I am rallying what forces I can.

Whatever power that is behind the attacks will certainly come for me. It needs to defeat me if it wants control of the land.

There are two possible ways into the lands of the Laic, one is through the Daralonadh hills and the other is through the gap of Fochd.

Most of the magic will be concentrated on me and so as I said earlier, I have asked Ilo, the faerie of the night, and her daytime companion Tress to stand with me.'

Even though Elid had mentioned the faeries already at the party of the pink plain, it still caused an intake of breath at the mention of them, and I had to admit I was a bit taken aback at the realisation that faeries were in the vicinity.

I remembered a conversation with Gular when he had described a night faerie but because Elid had never mentioned it I did not take much notice. Although looking back on that event I realise that Gular's imagination would never had painted the picture of the words he spoke to me.

Elid had more to say on the subject and carried on with her battle plan. 'I know there are many who think that all of the faerie folk had left the land after the last battle but believe you me, there are still some that inhabit the lands and they will stand with me to the end.'

It was that last word that hit me the most, up to then it was good learning that the faerie folk were still about. Even as far away as a child on Earth the stories of the faerie folk were told in hushed tones, as if they were real and always close by - I now know that they were. They were the angels of the pagan people and although some of them were known for their mischief making it was a comfort to know there were magical deities about.

I more than most know that one ending means a rebirth, but there is another part of me that still feels for others who have not got the belief in the spirit, and for them an ending of a loved one or end of an era really means - the end.

Elid had a lot more to say about the way she wanted her forces distributed so I focused on what she had to say.

'I, along with Ilo and Tress, will face the main force of darkness at the plains of the Laic. I will have the bana of Arcil behind me, some shade elves and a few faolwarriors. I feel that the dark energy is ready to move so we have to make ready with all speed, that is why I am keeping my own council as much as possible as the less that is made known the better.'

Suilval asked Elid if the sea elves of Meren were to be present at the battle. Elid answered her with an emphatic no, which was met with a dead silence. She then carried on explaining why the elves of Meren were not included.

The words she spoke were sensible and very much to the point. Elid began by telling us that she'd had conversations with Isilis, queen of sea elves, and had a hard job of talking her out of taking her elves into the battle ground.

'After a much heated debate Isilis saw the reasoning of my plans. When I explained that the enemy would be transporting warriors by ships, and as they would bypass the Meren Sea, it would enable the sea elves to block their retreat if we were to win the day.

Murmurs of approval came from those who were assembled. Then Bheir asked a question. 'What if we lose the battle, surely the sea elves will be alone and vulnerable?'

Elid's answer was poignant to say the least. 'I told Isilis that as the sea elves were first in the lands of Meren, it is fitting that they should be last to leave. If anything happens to me I have made arrangements, should the battle go against us then word will be sent to Isilis by a creature of the wilds that is incorruptible.

The sign that she will receive will tell her to sail as far away from the Meren Sea as possible. Isilis has to trust that the spirits of the sea will be good to them and guide their ships to Cimer's shores.

In spite of my words Isilis requested that a small force of volunteers represent the sea elves in the coming battle. There were so many clamouring for a place that she had to hand pick them herself.

The force of sea elves will fight with Suilval and Ruis on the left flank.'

Silence greeted Elids words and although they hung heavy in that space I detected not a hint of fear. All the energies around me were steadfast in the belief that they would prevail and all would be as it is.

Elid Silverhair filled the silent interlude with words of positive actions and an aura of confidence, which bolstered the belief of the group as she continued with the battle plan.

'The force that will hold the Fochd pass will be composed of some of the plains bana, the bana vour, Red Shelcs, Faolwarriors and Shade elfs.'

Then, turning to Eils, she said 'You will be taking the brunt of the magic once they realise that someone is wielding magic on our side.

On the left flank will be Suilval, Ruis, a mixture of the plains and vour bana and, as I have said already, a force of sea elves of Meren.

As I mentioned, I am sending Lael to search for an entity that has very powerful magic, this life entity disappeared many ages ago, it is time for it to move now and breathe life into others.

The search that Lael is trusted with will be so important to the greater good of the land and, indeed, maybe even the survival of the land. As I have already said, Nal of the bana and Derca of the tribe of Lael will be his companions.

I know there are still whispers of distrust regarding Derca the black elf, so what I say next will dissipate all the ill feelings towards him.

Cimer has entrusted Derca with information regarding the force of evil that is spreading throughout the land. Croin the storm hawk has verified Derca's standing with Cimer and that is good enough for me. Tress the faerie could not pick up any evil intent in the mind of the elf. Lael of Ulana felt good feelings emanating from him.'

Elid then turned to Nal and said. 'Tiathmor has given her leave for you to accompany Lael but has left the final decision to you. What is your choice?'

Nal stated 'I go with Lael and Derca to wherever that may be.' Then she turned to Tiathmor and asked who was to take her place, if anyone?

Tiathmor's answer brought a few 'Yip! Yips!' from the warriors. She announced that Rhu was to stand in for Nal. This was a bit unusual, for a substitute to join a five in the absence of one of their number.

As Tiathmor went on to explain that she wanted four warriors, two on either side of Eils, as support while she focused on the magic. Rhu and Eils had fought side by side on many an occasion so she was the logical choice.

Eils, Suila, Traig and Bheir gathered round Nal and congratulated her on the task she had been given. Bheir said that she felt they would all come through and meet again to have many more adventures and drink enough puflic to float a galley.

Ruis then spoke. 'Who or what is this entity that Lael is requested to find?'

Elid's answer was ambiguous to say the least. 'I will give instructions to Nal and Derca where to guide Lael. When they get to that place they will be told where the entity can be found and how to get there.

Elios of Ulana will be in thought with Lael in the event that I am unable to reach him, as all of you have to understand, secrecy and speed are all-important so the words that have been spoken in this bower do not get repeated outside this group. Now let us go outside and put Eils through some practice with the sword.'

With that we knew that Elid was not prepared to say any more on the subject of the journey, but I could not help wondering what kind of entity we were going to be searching for and where was it.

'Come on air-boy we are all waiting for you.'

Suilvals call brought me back to Darwan, I hadn't realised that although my thoughts had been moving my body hadn't, I was lagging behind again and I hurried to join them.

Elid told Eils to take the sword she had given her earlier and feel and wield it like any other sword. Eils did as she was bid and we were treated to display of whirling sword play. She stabbed; slashed; cut and thrust with great speed and dexterity.

Elid held up her hand to stop Eils and Eils complied. She then positioned Eils well back from the company and stood away from Eils but in line with her.

'Now Eils I am going to fire some magic at you, but

don't worry it is soft magic and is only for your practice. As I fire the white bolts at you, the sword will sense the magic and as you move it to deflect the bolts the sword will dissipate the magic, now try it.'

Elid raised one hand and with stiffened fingers sent white bolts of magic towards Eils. The warrior followed Elid's instructions and began parrying the bolts; the faster Elid fired them the faster Eils blew them apart. Elid fired them faster and faster - at Eil's legs, at her head, at her body, at her arms but not one bolt hit her.

Elid stopped and said to Eils. 'Well done, the magic that will be attacking you is black; the sword will sense the dark magic and dissipate it before it harms you. But I must warn you Eils, if there is enough of the dark energy it will overcome you.

I certainly hope that the living entity that I sent Lael and his companions for will rise to the occasion and arrive in time. Now for the short time we are together, let us to the 'Bough' and make merry while we may.'

We all trooped off to the back door of the Cat Bough and the door was opened by Enderli. I had begun to say that Elid hadn't joined us, 'just as well' said Suilval as she would have taken my slippery friend by his long ears and hung him up on one of the branches, he has no business here.

Suilval then hauled Enderli out of the doorway and shoved him behind her before she stomped into the bar. Poor Enderli, every warrior did the same to him until he was left staring at me. I said for him to go in before me, he flashed me a smile and was ready to enter the bough but unfortunately Ruis was behind me, and once more Enderli was hauled away from the door, and he was last in because Ruis took me by the shoulders and marched me in - followed by a most annoyed shade elf.

EADHA

Our journey to find the secret entity began at the rear of the Cat Bough, Derca and I being briefed by Elid and Suilval.

Nal was with her companions, who were imparting as much information as they could about the terrain out-with Nal's knowledge. Traig and Bheir had been the most recent of the bana warriors to have journeyed further than the plains of Cin-edher.

Elid had made it quite clear that the Black Hills of Cin-edher were very pertinent to the journey.

She spoke well to us and began by saying that I had to be very careful with my energy as most of the journey would be in the dark. The light of the stars and moons is meant for meditation and self-healing. It is the radiance of Apuss by day that gives power and mobility to a spirit that has been exposed to the heaviness of Darwan.

Suilval was telling Derca about any likely encounters

that we might have, she had travelled through many dangerous lands in the search for survivors of her clan.

We were joined by Nal who seemed eager for us to be on our way, however before we took off Elid cloaked us all in an aura which felt as if all four elements were present.

In the aftermath we all agreed that we felt as if we were rooted to the earth and the light that surrounded us was like air in motion and it had the heat of fire in it.

Most wonderful of all was when the light dissipated, a very fine drizzle of water coursed over our bodies. The light film of fluid energy washed from the crown of our heads down our bodies to our feet and in that instant the earth released us.

No sooner had our little debate ended - Nal took off, not a word or a backward glance; just assumed the lead, head down and away. I looked at Derca, who gave me an amused look and shrugged his shoulders then directed me with his hand to follow Nal's lead.

I remembered from my earlier jaunt with the bana how fast they could move, and Nal was testimony to my thoughts. She was speeding ahead as if the journey had to be ended before Apuss rose in the morning.

That first night's march from the Sloch made me think I was marching to where I had come in. Before the attack of the slarcs I was wandering with a mind that matched the dismal environment I was passing through.

The effervescence of the elemental aura had stayed with me for a while, but my mind had locked itself to the atmosphere we were passing through and mind and body felt very heavy.

A dreary Rinnis strained through a curtain of Darwan mist, Elid had informed me that Ara would soon be in the sky and her white light would aid my heavy feelings during the night marches.

Derca's voice cut through my muddle of thoughts and stopped me in my tracks.

'Are you all right Lael, your step is not so light?'

He then hailed Nal, telling her to stop and come back to join us. I had not been aware of how far ahead she had got.

Nal doubled back and asked Derca why we had stopped, she paid no heed to me, just carried on to tell Derca that we had a great distance to go and stopping was not going to get us there.

Derca drew her attention to me and said he was concerned that I was not functioning well owing to the speed we were going. He told Nal to cut the pace a bit and see if that would help me.

Nal reluctantly agreed and with a curt nod of her head resumed the lead at a more leisurely pace. Derca took up a position alongside me and engaged in conversation which did me a great deal of good. Instead of focusing on the direness of the night and reinventing my first journey in the land in my head I concentrated on answering Derca's questions.

He asked me all about Ulana, as he had when we first met at the pink plain, he was a great listener. I knew he had reservations about the afterlife, I could feel it off him, but my answers to his questions revived my muddled mind and renewed my vigour.

Nal called a halt by a rocky outcrop and led us to a shallow cave where we were to spend the daylight hours. She told me that it was well sheltered from prying eyes as the overhang of rock shielded the cave from flying eyes.

Then she added. 'You can speak to Apuss all day and nobody will see you, Derca and I won't hear you because we will be sleeping like the stones of the earth.'

We settled ourselves within the cave. I stood close to the cave opening the warriors sat at the back and began feeding themselves. They carry small parcels of food on their person - I had seen the bana feeding on the same food when I went out on the field with them.

Suila told me the most common and efficient food was a mixture of fish and a vegetable made into a paste, she called it 'Atii.' They wrap it up in the leaf of a plant. It must be common to all the tribes as Derca had exactly the same food as Nal. When they finish off the contents they then eat the leaf.

After passing a few words with each other they proceeded to scrape away stones and earth to make a sleep shape. I was amused to see the way they laid the shapes out in relation to each. Their feet almost touched but the body shapes fanned out to either side - very curious!

Nal knew from the time I spent with them that when I meditated my aura guarded my sleep state, so that is why they both got their heads down. I was instructed by Nal to wake them up when Apuss was directly overhead.

Rinnis disappeared with her dreary night and I fixed my mind and eyes to the direction from which Apuss was to make his appearance, asking the spirits of the universe for a brighter dawn.

My prayers were answered as the first streaks of light filtered through the stuffy air, pushing the remnants of the night after the retreating red maiden. In an instant the sky was filled with orange light. Apuss was still below my visual horizon but I bathed my face in his orange light and holding my arms up, palms outward, I gave silent thanks to the abundant life above.

Nal and Derca did not need to be wakened; they both got up well before Apuss was overhead. We spent the rest of the daylight discussing the recent happenings and getting to know each other.

Derca had never trod the direction we were taking so it was Nal's knowledge we were going on. She told us that the place called Cin-edher was within easy reach after Apuss went down, and then Ara would appear low and bright behind us. Then she changed tack and began to tell us about horses that galloped across Cin-edher's plain.

I could not see what that had to do with our journey but Derca seemed very interested, so I entered the universe of my mind and left them to their talk. By this time Apuss had disappeared well behind our refuge and was ready to give the day up.

At last we reached the plain of Cin-edher, it was night when we got to the outer limits and just as Elid had said Darwan's moon was full and bright, low in the sky and lay behind us.

The creatures of Darwan call Ara their happy moon, not only because it determines one of their directions but also it is bright and regular. Whereas Rinnis the red ringed moon is moody and can, at times, have a very erratic pathway - she is also the harbinger of storms.

We had not been long in the plain when Nal pointed out a large dark mass ahead of us. 'There, she said, is Cin-edher, let us move quickly as the wild horses of Edher will be on the gallop soon.'

She had told us of this spectacle days ago and seemed to be quite excited about the event. The horses gather at the dark side of Cin-edher, then as one they all gallop down the plain in the direction of Ara.

On the moonlit flatness of Edher they meet up with the mares and their union continues until Apuss rises in the morning. Nal quickened her pace and I said to Derca. 'Have you seen the horses?'

'Not I, but if Nal's excitement is anything to go by it must be worth watching.' I knew by the way of his speech he was caught up in the bana warrior's enthusiasm. He forged ahead, catching up with Nal.

I could hear them chattering away like two breathless children, I smiled to myself and thought. Here I am in this strange land with two of its most fearsome warriors and all that they are thinking about is seeing a herd of horses at the gallop!

I stopped at that spot for a brief moment and looked at the sky ahead of me; I made out clouds of stars and I knew what was going on within those far off mists of starlight, new stars were being born and soon that would be emulated on this plain in the form of sexual energy.

'Come on Lael we are nearly there.' Nal's cry shook me out of my muse and I caught up with them, they had stopped at the base of a huge cliff, it was the dark shadow we had seen from afar. Nal enlightened us as to where we were.

'This Is Cin-edher.' she said, at the same time patting it with outstretched arms. 'It's a great head of rock that juts into the plain and right across from us is a ridge of high rock called 'The Hasach'. The Hasach runs by the way of Ulas for a long distance and walls the plain in on that side.' As she continued I could feel the energy in her voice rising.

'The horses come from behind the headland and run through the moonlit gap between the Hasach and Cin-edher, when you see them bursting into the light you will be amazed.'

To myself I was thinking that I have seen horses on Earth and in Ulana and I dearly love the sight and touch of them all, but I cannot imagine why Nal is getting so high about horses at the gallop doing what their natural instincts tell them.

Then once again Nal broke into my thoughts with a shout. 'Listen, I can hear them - they're on the move!'

Then I heard them the drumming of many hoofs on the dry plain of Edher and they must have been running fast as the noise got louder in a short space of time. A shout came, this time from Derca.

'I can see them - look they are in the light of Ara.' As I looked down the plain I could see the horses flooding into the expanse of lunar light; I saw at once that these were no ordinary horses.

It was the colours that drew my attention; their bodies touched by Ara they reflected out hues of green, indigo, red, purple and silver, and then I heard Nal shouting again. 'Come on Derca let us ride the Edher horses!'

She was on the run as she shouted and Derca was not slow - he was at her heels. I felt very elated at the sight of the two warriors running abreast of the herd, I knew they were capable of high speed running but I did not think they could keep pace with horses.

I watched as Nal singled out an indigo and green mount; she matched its speed for a while then reached up and grabbed its mane, deftly swinging herself up on its back. I looked away in time to see Derca alighting on a black and red horse.

No sooner was he seated than in a blink of an eye he was standing on the animal's back, I saw him calling to Nal. I didn't hear what he said but she stood up on the back of her horse and called something back at him.

Then I realised what they were going to do. Sure enough, just as the thought crossed my mind they started to jump from mount to mount. I enjoyed the sheer stupidity of the scene, here we were with a mission that if it failed would have dire consequences for Darwan, and Nal and Derca play with horses.

So saying, looking at the scene as I did then, I could not help being awed at the display of agility and strength of the warriors and also the energy I could sense off the horses. Nal, standing tall on a violet steed looking like a silver statue and Derca, seated now on a black stallion like ebony in motion.

On closer inspection of the horses I could see that it was individual hairs that were coloured and also the hair on the body was long and more like thin strands of grass that lay flat against the body. The lead horses were out of sight and my two companions with them, I just hoped that Nal and Derca did not get distracted too much and forget the gravity of our mission.

Then as I watched I saw the pair of them running back along the plain, their shadows dancing in front of them and I could hear their voices carrying through the night air arguing about something.

'Come on you two let us make use of the night while we can.' I tried to inject them with a sense of urgency because as I remembered that we had to be well past Cin-edher before daylight. It seemed to have an effect because they took up position on either side of me and concentrated on the path ahead.

We had made good time but the horseplay had set us back a bit. I had a fair knowledge of the path our journey was to take, as Elid had taken great pains to ensure I knew what route to take in the event I was separated from Nal and Derca.

In my mind's eye I estimated that the journey was going to take longer than anticipated so I put the question to Nal. 'Is there a quicker route than the one we are to take?'

She replied immediately. 'Yes, but it would take us through the 'Shimmering Emptiness."

'What in all the worlds is that?' I asked.

'It is a gap between the burning rocks that nothing can pass through.' As she continued I felt the aggressive voice tones in her speech. In the short time I have known Nal I know when her voice gets angry it usually means she does not understand a situation.

Her next statement caused Derca and me to exchange glances with each other. She said, 'Traig and Bheir journeying through Cin-edher once decided to short cut through the Shimmering Emptiness.

Traig entered first with Bheir close behind, at first the air felt warm and soothing but as they waded in - and that was the word for it because both of them felt as if the air they were wading through was water, it was definitely a force of some kind. They could not see anything even though Apuss was high in the sky and the air was light and normal looking, but still the unseen force pushed against them and it was all around.

Traig said it was like walking through a transparent jelly, then she felt a sucking effect on her body and she began to be pulled ahead, she tried to turn back but the force was too powerful.

Bheir saw what was happening and grabbed the end of Traigs spear and pulled Traig out of the emptiness, but she said it took a lot of strength even with Traig pulling backwards against the force. They cleared out double quick and spread the word amongst the Bana and that is why I chose not to lead you that way.'

They both went silent for a while until I announced that I would be going through the Shimmering Emptiness. I felt it was not my own intuition that led me to make the decision but a voice which I did not recognise at the time.

Derca said he had been influenced by Nal's account of the two bana warriors and I did not blame him one bit. He knew how powerful Traig and Bheir were and if they had difficulties even with their combined strength - well?

Nal had a bit more to say. 'Lael you cannot afford to be trapped in the gap, the land depends on you too much and Elid needs you to help us heal this wounded world. I was instructed to accompany you wherever you went by Elid Silverhair, this was acknowledged by Tiathmor so if you go through the gap I go with you, Derca is free to make his own choice.'

Then the dark elf spoke. 'I cannot let the Bana Ger take all the glory that awaits us when we rid the land of this evil, therefore I will join you in the passage through this strange place.'

I was certain I saw a flicker of relief in Nal's eyes as it was obvious to me that she felt everything would be on her shoulders if it was only the two of us going through the Emptiness. Nal respected me and she knew that I was capable of exuding power when I had to, but she could never get her head round the fact that I would not kill any creature.

Now that Derca had said he was joining us in taking the shortcut she knew that she had backup if things started going wrong.

I then took charge. 'Nal, lead us to this empty passage as we need to make haste to be there when Apuss rises.' At that Nal took off with Derca by her side, I followed behind and fixed my mind on the strange occurrence we were about to encounter.

I figured it had to be some kind of trapped energy, but the question was - was it a dark or light power? I detected a change in the light as we left Cin-edher behind that told me Ara was giving way to Apuss. A short time later Nal stopped and pointed ahead. 'Look, there are the burning mountains.'

We all stopped and looked in the direction she was pointing, and sure enough there in the distance could be seen a range of hills with a gap in the middle and the hills seemed to be glowing, though I could not see any naked flames.

Without further ado we carried on in the direction of the gap. As we got closer Apuss began to rise behind the hills and his brightness overwhelmed the burning mountains.

We stopped to acknowledge his appearance; I to thank the spirits for the morning light, Nal and Derca holding their faces up to him to bathe in his light. Then we were off at a brisk pace heading straight for the gap.

I noticed my two companions had assumed their aggressive attitude, they had that fixed look about them and they were regaling each other with tales of past events.

I was totally focused on absorbing the energy from Apuss as I needed the light of day to boost my spiritual body for the coming affray. I could see the gap in the near distance and also the high cliffs on either side, the cliffs were black and shining and had a smooth look about them.

Within, I saw the flames of fire coming from the very roots of the cliffs, burning up from the depths of Darwan until finally their fiery tongues were halted by the shining black mass.

I called to the warriors to stop and position themselves behind me. I wanted to feel the energy around the gap to see if I could determine if there were any malignant forces at work. We had arrived at the gap itself by this time and we could see the air shimmering slightly within, however Apuss's light was there and all looked normal inside.

Derca commented on the smoothness of the cliffs. 'They would be impossible to climb.' He said as he approached to touch the stone.

'Do not touch it Derca.' Nal's commanding tone stopped Derca in his tracks.

She said. 'When Bheir and Traig arrived at this spot they were amazed that despite the burning within they could not feel any heat from the stone, so Bheir touched the smooth rock with the end of her spear, it was only a light tap and yet the rock seared it and sent the heat right up to Bheir's hand, she carries the mark of it to this day.'

Derca stepped back with the words. 'Then that

would certainly make it impossible to climb!' Nal turned to me and asked why the barrier of flame was there. I could only manage a very wistful. 'I do not know.'

I remember standing there looking through the gap at the clear day air and seeing only the slightest distortion of the view that betrayed the presence of whatever was there. I could not detect any bad energy or malign entities, at the same time I could not sense any kind of energy.

I shouted to Nal and Derca to stand at my side and they dutifully obeyed, Nal on my left, Derca on my right. I explained to them what I intended to do. I held each one by the waist and projected my aura all around the three of us.

I then instructed them to stay at my side, no matter what happened they were not to try to move away from me. 'The golden aura that surrounds us is very powerful and it will shield us from any malignant forces, also any light spirit that is about will recognise the aura for what it is and let us pass.

Derca asked. 'What if the ground beneath us opens up?'

'That is why I have asked you to stay by my side.' I tried to imbue my words with the confidence I felt. 'The spirit aura will support us all.' I meant it - I had all faith in the power of spirit.

As one entity we moved forward, I could feel the latent power of Nal and Derca on either side of me and I wondered what they were thinking about. For myself, I did not think too much because for some reason, as we entered the gap, I felt a sense of calm descend on me and so far I could not feel any resistance.

Then I felt a ripple of thought in my mind, it was pleasant and soothing and I knew I was sensing spirit. I dropped my shield and stopped, at the same time putting the warriors at ease by telling them we were in light energy.

I realised that the shimmer was a mirror of flexible energy. It was powerful enough to stop any dark energy or physical foe, what was seen in front was a reflection of what was behind. Only a very powerful spiritual energy could have created a mirror image that deleted the movements of living creatures.

I was still linked to the warriors, they had held on to me at the waist and calmly walked by my side through the mirage, I told them to stay at my side until I had aligned myself to the energy I felt emanating around us.

Nal was first to speak and I was a bit sharp with my answer. 'Hang on Nal I need to feel the light matter in the air.' Nal took no offence as I was aware of her saying to Derca. 'He's lucky it's not Traig that's asking the questions.'

I came to the conclusion that the light energy was good. I felt there was laughter in the air around us, as if whatever the power was, it was taking delight at our antics. I used my most authoritative voice to ask who or whatever the power was to show itself. Silence, then the air around us bubbled with humour and as it tailed off a voice spoke through the energy.

A very male voice it was too, but it sounded kind in a teasing way. 'I may reveal myself but then again I may not, I will think about it. But I might not come to a conclusion so until I do, carry on into my land, you are perfectly safe.'

We did as the voice said and walked forward into the land encompassed by the flaming hills. In between normal walking we were nudged gently by the air around us, at other times we had to swim our way ahead through the energy and always the gleeful chuckle accompanied these playful tricks.

Then I stole a thought from a conversation with Elios in the MoAraian forest, I stopped and shouted. 'I know who you are – you are Nindril, spirit of the air.'

Once again the air was filled with laughter and like a pixie that had played a trick and been found out; Nindril emerged to us out of the air - and what a sight it was. Still laughing, Nindril took shape as if he had come through a door in the atmosphere.

He was a masculine spirit and bigger by far than any elf, his skin a light blue, a bit darker than the air around him. What made his outline bold was the radiance of Apuss, emphasizing his features and body lines. Nindril was indeed a body shape moulded out of the air.

Nal of course had to break the moment by asking yet another question, and as usual it was straightforward with a hint of aggression.

'Why do you stop the tribes from using the pass?'

Nindril answered in an offhanded way. 'Because I am Nindril, spirit of the air, and these are my bounds. Here I watch and command the air, the wind whistles its information to me. Not often do I leave this place unless something warrants my attention.'

Then turning to Derca he said. 'Dark one, you called on me once when Shuira and I were at odds with one another. We made peace and you were allowed to go on your way - that was after you left the shores of the Black Island.'

Derca nodded in agreement but did not say anything.

Then Nindril focused on Nal. 'Does your fellow warrior still carry the mark of the black fire on her hand? They certainly tried very hard to enter my space and I was very impressed by the strength of the pair of them as they tried to extricate themselves from my energy.'

Nal replied with the usual aggression. 'They would have pulled you out as well and that was only two of us.'

Nindril's answer was a ripple of laughter. Then he spoke to Nal in a more serious manner. 'Your warrior carries the mark of fire and air, ever since she has been susceptible to the air of Cin-edher and the fiery orbs of the night sky, she will be a great asset to the race of the bana ger.'

Nal answered Nindril's statement by addressing us all. 'The air spirit is right in what he says because Traig and I had noticed the subtle change in Bheir after she was marked at the burning mountains. She knows things that sometimes amaze all of us, and at rest times at the darkening she sits and stares at the night sky as if she is seeing messages up there.

At evening Traig and Bheir sit for ages in deep

conversation. Traig can talk the horns off a bos because she has an urge to know everything, so she has taken to pumping Bheir for more information, which she does during their long debates under the moons of Darwan.'

Nindril had a satisfied smile on his face as he listened to Nal's account of the change in Bheir then abruptly he changed tack and asked me what I thought of the Darwan world.

I looked up at Nindril and saw in him the personification of one of the old Greek gods of Earth. I held his steady gaze, taking in the classical face with its accompanying amused smile and started telling him that so far I liked the world, at least as much of it as I had seen.

I went on to tell him that I felt that some parts of the land had more to offer, it had growth but it was poor, not as fertile as it should be.

It interested me that the nights of Darwan were magical and it was then that I fully appreciated the strange world. The night had a mystique of its own, as if it was feeding off the darkness of the cosmos and the luminescence of the two opposing moons. The night sky was in waiting – watching for the opportunity to expend its moving magic into the living world of Darwan.

The ever moving motion of starlight had always been my reality on Earth and Ulana. So it was now in Darwan, when watching the spectacular mosaic of stars, its erratic planets, some with rings of fire and others reflecting the red light of Rinnis. It is a beguiling scenario of universal magic not adhering to any laws or disciplines; it seems to go its own way shaping worlds and mocking time and space as we know it.

At my words Nindril threw back his head and laughed loudly, the peals of his laughter echoed all around and Nal and Derca held their hands over their ears in mock reaction to the noise he made.

'Forgive me for my laughter spirit Lael, it is not intended to demean your words, they are very eloquent. I am the spirit of the air and like the air my thoughts and movements are light. When I hear words and questions with deep, meaningful attachments it makes me feel that life in the air is uncomplicated.

The only time I get a surge of fury is when I have a disagreement with Shuira of the sea and I am sure your companion from the race of Lael would agree with that.' On making that statement Nindril looked at Derca for confirmation of his words.

Derca, as usual not one to waste words, just nodded to Nindril in acknowledgement.

I tried as far as possible to get Nindril to appreciate the seriousness of the quest we pursued. He was a restless, mischievous spirit and he kept playing with the air, sometimes pushing us with it and other times pulling us in all directions.

Nal got hot with him and slashed the air around her with her sword, whereupon Nindril created a vortex of air and spiralled Nal upwards inside it, but not before Derca leaped up and caught Nal by the ankles.

'Nindril! I shouted, with as much authority in my

voice that I could muster. 'Put my warriors down - I need them to guide me to the lair of the Draig'.

At the mention of the Draig, Nindril promptly dissipated the vortex and Nal and Derca came tumbling down. I asked if the two were okay and Nal answered for both of them.

'It will take more than a puff of air to break our bones - right Derca?'

'You are exactly right Nal' Was Derca's retort.

Nindril ignored the remarks because, by mentioning the Draig, I had got his attention at last.

'So darkness must be coming into the land when Silverhair is searching for a Draig. Well you had better sit down and tell me all about it, Lael of Ulana, and while you do that your warrior companions can find themselves food and water.'

He turned to Nal and Derca and in front of them he conjured up a sprite of the air saying. 'This is Scir, a sprite of the warm air, and he will lead you to a lochan where you can hunt fish for yourselves and drink the pure, flowing water that runs into it. Nearby are trees laden with fruit, eat your fill and keep some for your journey.'

Then he spoke directly to Scir. 'Give the warriors the shapes of protection to play with I am sure they will put them to good use when the time comes.'

With a cursory look at me the two departed after Scir - the taste of fish and fruit already in their mouths. I thought to myself that they must be hungry and thirsty as it had been many changes of Apuss and Ara since they had tasted food and water. When I turned round to face Nindril I was surprised to see he had reduced his size in keeping with my stature. He wasted no time in quizzing me about the happenings in the land, quite a lot he already knew but, as he reminded me many times, the spirits do not meddle in the affairs of the creatures of the land unless the air, water and earth of the world is in dire jeopardy.

He then proceeded to tell me about the Draig. I was already excited with the idea of a Draig in Darwan and I listened attentively to what Nindril told me.

'The Draig is Cerenor-Tala, and she lives in repose at her crystal cave on the heights of Elin Broom. Cerenor fought at the battle of the Fochd Pass and has served many masters and mistresses. She is the last of her kind in Darwan and unfortunately her mind has become a mire of despondency.

I have passed over her at times and used my winds to whisper calmness upon her. She has not flown for many an eon but that is what Draigs do - they can lie in suspension while the rivers of age take the races of the land time after time.

There is a rhyme that only three of Darwan know.

One is The Green woman, the second is Ilo the faery of the night, and the third is Elid Silverhair. The words that are known to them are trusted by the Draig, and it is said that whoever recites them will gain the attention of the Draig, but it is no guarantee that she will do their will.

I told Nindril that Elid had told the words to me after the meeting in the Cat Bough and she also said that the only time I was to say them aloud was when I was face to face with Cerenor.

Nindril agreed and added more reasoning why Elid meant what she said. 'The air and the waters are pure, but some of the life forms that inhabit both elements are not to be trusted.

Take care, because the smallest of creatures might be listening, creatures so small and insignificant that you might not notice them, but they will notice you and be sure that any whisper will be passed on to a higher source.

When you pass out of my bounds do not mention any of the information to Nal or Derca. It is not because you cannot trust them it is because you cannot take the chance that your words might be intercepted. Do you understand what I am saying Lael?'

I acknowledged that I understood exactly what Nindril was saying. In Ulana, Roscranna said that if she wanted to know where any creature was she would send messages to the wind, who would whisper it to the birds who in turn would tell the trees and so on --

However in Ulana there were no bad vibrations, all was for the greater good. Here in Darwan I had to change my mind set. I only look for the good in all things and it grieves my very being when I hear the words of Nindril, telling me that I cannot trust the beings of the air.

Gurks I can understand because they are easily seen and I have seen them in action, indeed if it had not been for the swiftness of the bana, Suila would have been carried off by one.

And I had my own experience during the slarc

attack, they were creatures from a worst nightmare, but I recognised them as such and accepted it. Now I cannot enjoy a talk with a skarling bird for fear it may be corrupted by the bad energy.

Nindril took the conversation back to more basic tactics, he said that Derca would know the paths to Elin Broom even though he had never been there, all he needed to know was the direction, when the warriors came back we would speak more about the journey.

We then went into spirit mode and it was good, Nindril stopped his nonsense and concentrated on importing knowledge into me, it was a magical merging of spirituality and after it was over I felt good and ready for the tasks ahead.

We sat for a while in the aftermath; in silence we breathed in the air and silently thanked the universe for all we had. At that point the warriors arrived back on the scene. Straight away I knew Nindril was up to his old tricks because when the warriors approached us they banged themselves against something solid - I guessed it was a wall of air.

The warriors must have come to the same conclusion as me because after the initial contact they sat down where they were and began to eat the fish they had caught. They also started to talk and laugh between themselves and showed no reaction to the invisible wall.

Then they began playing with elliptical shapes which they had tied to their wrists. With the result that Nindril lifted the invisible veil and with a chuckle put his hands up and declared a no-nonsense pact.

I told the warriors about the conversation between myself and Nindril, I also put them straight about the place they were sitting in now. 'This is a spiritual refuge, it is one of a few contained areas in Darwan where no evil energy can penetrate and you are in perfect safety here within the burning mountains. I am taking this opportunity to speak freely - we are on a search of a Draig!'

I paused to see what effect my words had on Nal and Derca - as usual it was not a spontaneous response. But Nal rose to the occasion by saying that one of her kin had ridden on a Draig but it was long before the lives of any bana living on Darwan.

Derca also put in a word, hinting at some knowledge of a Draig. I got the idea that the stories of Draigs were considered to be make believe. 'Tall elf tales' as Suilval would say.

I carried on where I had left off. 'The Draig can be found at a place called Elinbroom, it is a far distant land, have either of you heard of it?'

I got a definite no from both, so I then mentioned another place called Scaravban. On hearing that name Derca said he knew of the place, he had been there during his mercenary days.

I noticed Nal giving Derca a curious look, I must say I was surprised myself at the word, mercenary! I then told him that Scaravban was the way of Elinbroom and also a range of hills known as Greystones that leads to a stretch of waters called Tanaron.

As we stand on the shores of the Greystone peninsula the light of the rising Ara on the sea of

Tanaron will point us to the way of Elinbroom, which is an island of yellow rock.

Derca told us he been to the foothills of Greystones but he had not been any further than that, he had never heard of or seen the Tanaron Sea, so consequently he knew nothing about the island of Elinbroom. I was dimly aware that he mentioned something about a boat but at the time I did not take any notice.

Then I reiterated what Nindril had said about discussing place names. 'There must be no mention of where we are heading or the names of places we are going to. Even huddled together we cannot trust what we cannot see.'

I asked the two if they had any questions and received bland expressions from both and a slight shake of heads. They do not waste words!

Then my attention was directed to the elliptical shapes that the warriors had on their wrists. Nal stuck her one in front of my face. I saw the shape was metallic looking, the colouring seemed to alternate between dark and light. On the metal I could make out a combination of inscribed shapes.

The background was a spiral overlaid by a zig-zag lightning streak and at the end of each point was an arrowhead. I asked Nindril for what they were intended.

He replied in very dramatic tones. 'It is a defence against dark energy and it will give your warriors a chance to escape. I know they are quick in movements, so as it takes great dexterity to use the energy deflectors I thought that a dark elf and a bana warrior would be an ideal pair to try them out.'

I was a bit taken aback by Nindril's last remark. 'You mean nobody else has used them, so how do you know they will work?'

The answer came back sharp and abrupt. 'Because I am Nindril of the air and I say it will work.'

And then as an afterthought he added. 'You can only deflect the bad energy it cannot be directly reflected back from the elliptical shape to the bearer. Your warriors will adapt because they are fighters from birth and I suspect they have already worked out a strategy, judging from my observations.'

'So where is the source of the deflector's power?' I asked.

'The power is in the air; the motion of the spiral; the energy of the lightening and the accuracy of the arrow - you will see.'

Nindril's flippancy in regards to important matters unnerved me a bit and his lax attitude did not go unnoticed by the warriors.

Derca put my mind at rest when he told me Scir had given them all the information beforehand.

We spent the day in the refuge, Nindril and I in deep conversation with each other. The warriors, after they had eaten, fell asleep. We had already decided that it would cause less attention if we travelled by the light of Ara and slept where possible by day.

When Ara rose in the evening we were transfixed by her light as it reflected off the black crystalline rocks surrounding the refuge, another visual wonder in the frustrating world of Darwan.

As we prepared to leave, Nindril informed us that in

times of confusion he would allow an air spirit to help. He said that he had made contact with Shuira and she agreed that at any time if we were lost by the waters a water sprite would direct us.

Outside the mountains of fire we waved goodbye to Nindril of the air, he disappeared up into the night sky and we heard his laughter from a long way off.

Scaravban

We did not leave by the way we came, Nindril had taken us out by another route although we all agreed it looked exactly the same in every detail, the only giveaway was Ara, she was shining brightly in front of us which was the direction we had to take.

Derca led the way as he knew the route to Scaravban, Nindril had instructed him to keep the light of Ara in our faces until she was high overhead. When that came about he would recognise the features of the land and would know where he was.

True to form, when Ara was overhead we had arrived at the shores of a great loch and Derca instantly recognised it. 'This is the Loch of Brona; we hold its shore until we come to a small group of hills. We can spend the light of Apuss by sheltering in one of the many caves that riddle the cliffs there.'

It was a punishing journey from the burning hills to the caves by the shores of loch Brona. No worn path to follow, just broken rock and bog, but we made good time and found a decent cave to hole up in.

Although Ara was still the sentinel of the night she was low in the sky, and because the warriors still had the taste of fish in their mouths they wanted more. Derca volunteered Nal to hunt the fish, without hesitation she dived straight into the waters of Brona and appeared in no time at all with a sizeable fish.

As Nal got to work with her knife dividing the fish between herself and Derca, I asked Derca if he left Nal to do the fishing on purpose.

Derca's amused reply made me smile as well.

'I fish and journey on the water not in it, anyway the bana are good at it, they can stay under the water for ages and can swim very fast.'

We spent the light of Apuss in a cave further up the rocky steep, the warriors slept as I sat in meditation. A curious excitement had taken me over it was the knowledge that a Draig was alive in Darwan. The world of Earth had many tales to tell of dragons, such were they named on earth.

I had never seen or heard of any Draigs in Ulana and now the prospect of meeting one in this strangest of worlds exhilarated me. Cerenor-Tala of Elinbroom, even the name and the place enhanced my imagination.

The light of Ara was well up as we started off again in the direction that Derca led us and as usual we went at a cracking pace, which was ever upwards. We came to a field of broken boulders, a mess of irregular, shattered stones that looked as if some giant with a mighty hammer had been at work on it.

It did not impede the two warriors any, they skipped and hopped over the crazy rocks as we traversed up the hill and I followed in their wake. High up, just at the ending of the sloping boulder field, we could just make out a slender path that spiralled its way round a lonely hill.

We stopped before reaching the pathway, all three of us enjoying the surreal brightness of Ara. Looking upwards I caught sight of a bird and I remembered it was the same as that Suilval had commented on during the walk through the lavender snow.

I asked Derca what kind of bird it was and he told me it was a 'sluin' he also added that it was strange to see it so far from the sea as they spent most of their lives on the sea. They only come ashore to breed on the coastal cliffs.

We had our eyes on the bird when I told them Suilval had made the same comment ---------------- next thing the bird that we had been watching seemed to have hit a brick wall and then it dropped like a stone, it hit the rocks in a burst of feathers and blood with an arrow in it.

I looked at Nal who was in the act of slinging her bow - I was shocked - I turned to Derca - 'why - why - did she do that?'

It was Nal who answered my question. 'Derca is right and so was Suilval, the bird should not have been so far from the sea.'

'So you shot it!' I said in disbelief, at the same time giving Derca an appealing look, I was wasting my time there as he had an amused look on his face.

Then Derca spelled it out--------'Lael, what Nal did is not as callous as you think, remember the words of Nindril - do not trust some of the creatures that inhabit the air - lookout for unusual events'-------

His words were left hanging as I thought over what

had just occurred, as far back as my being escorted to the Sloch we had been spied on. There must be someone in our midst that has been corrupted.

I knew they were right but I did not have to like it and I said so, they were not bothered in the slightest, they were even debating taking the dead bird with them to eat later.

I told them if they ate it they might digest the corruption and become the dark energy's latest recruits. That ended the discussion, Nal retrieved her arrow and we continued on our way.

It was a hard slog to what I thought was the top of the hill, but it was a false summit, another peak loomed up, silhouetted by the light of Ara. As well as the physical march, my mind was in a mire of confusion regarding the idea of a traitor in the group.

Derca's voice took me out of my muddled thoughts by saying we had to speed our pace as Apuss would be in the sky shortly and we would be caught out in the open.

He was right, it would not do to be stuck in the daylight on a slope as exposed as the one we were on. The two warriors then set off at high speed. Elios' words came back to me on that hillside; Remember Lael that in some parts of Darwan the air will feel heavy on you and you will be at your most vulnerable during those times.

Her words rang true on that hillside as I felt as if I was swimming against the air, heaviness came over me, the like of which I had not felt since that first footfall in Darwan.

Nal looked round and realised I was struggling, she called Derca to stop and they both rallied round me.

I explained what was happening to me and told them I needed to stop and refresh myself with a meditary slumber to absorb the light of Ara. They did not argue and just asked what they could do to help.

I told them I needed all round exposure to the light of the prime maiden Ara, a cave or a hollow in the side of the mountain was no use, I needed to be out in the light! I found a place almost at the edge of a sheer drop and proceeded to meditate.

Nal told me much later that she and Derca positioned themselves behind me and stayed on the alert all the time I was recovering.

I was fully recharged with energy by the time Apuss rose and along with the warriors I thankfully bathed in the light of his radiance.

We sat in a crevice in the rock and had a debate about the sluin bird and what power had enslaved it. Elid and Elios had mentioned dark energy but neither of them had put a name to it.

Nindril had not put a name to it either, which sent my thoughts in two directions. I voiced them to the warriors.

'Companions, we now know that there is malignant force at work in the land and I think Elid has had knowledge of it for some time, I also think she knows where it is coming from.

From my conversation with Ler at the Fallen Stone I gleaned some very interesting information about the goings on in the land. This has led me to believe that whatever entity is behind the evil doings is not of Darwan.

The knowledge I have accumulated from the enlightened entities, coupled with the vision I got during my journey with Suilval and Ruis, has enhanced my belief that the evil has come from the dark energy that binds the stars.'

I waited to see what effect my words had on the two warriors. I wasted my time, I could have waited until the end of Darwan. The faces never changed, they just stared back at me; no questions, no facial expression.

I broke the silence. 'Have the two of you anything to say?'

Derca answered. 'What difference does it make as we still have a journey to go on?'

I said 'The difference is that if I am right and the power does come from the sky dark-side then it will be very powerful. If it gets to us before we get where we are going then that is the end for all of us.

What I am saying, is that the two of you can head back to your tribes and I will go alone and hope I reach my destination before the evil gets me.'

That brought a very aggressive reaction from both of them - they both yelled at me saying. 'We could never turn back'----------- Derca said. 'We started with you and we finish with you!'

Nal joined in. 'Derca is right, neither of us could face our tribal companions - ever - if we left you on your own. We will stay with you to the end, Derca and I belong to the greatest fighting tribes in the world of Darwan, do not underestimate us Lael.'

I countered by saying. 'It is powerful black magic I am talking about, you cannot fight it, and you will be dissipated before you are able to fire an arrow.'

Nal replied immediately, brandishing Nindril's devices in my face she said. 'We have the air spirits protective discs - they will give us a chance.'

Derca said. 'We have to try Lael, even if only one of us gets through to where we are going then there is a chance, if we give up now there is no chance.'

They had both adopted a determined stance and having said their piece they stood staring at me, defying me to say any more about going alone.

I put my hands up in mock surrender and said. 'So be it to journey's end.'

We stayed in that crevice until Apuss left the sky - Ara rose and was so bright she gave a day time look to the landscape. She brought with her renewed energy for me and my two companions.

We took off with a spring in our steps - just as well as the terrain we were going through was the worst we had covered so far.

The first hill we climbed was fairly easily but its companion on the other side was higher and its slope was covered in scree.

The hill itself was layered with small round stones, floating on the top of the stones were bigger flat ones. We had to double our efforts, springing from one to the other as every time our feet hit the flat stones they slid backwards.

By the time we reached the top it felt as if we had climbed the mountain twice, although it was fun watching Nal and Derca zig - zagging across each other, sometimes sharing the same boulder then splitting in opposite directions.

All traces of the serious conversation of the daytime was long gone as they cavorted up the hillside, each one trying to outdo the other - they well and truly live in the space they occupy now.

It was easier going down the other side, however the descent did not last long as once more the way was upward.

Making our way up a steep rocky path we were shouldered on one side by a craggy wall of grey stone, marbled by streaks of black and silver. The path broadened and the gradient dropped slightly; then I sensed that there were life forms about and I quickly relayed this to my companions.

Immediately Derca shouted "rock phantoms" and drew his sword, Nal followed suit without pause. What happened next would have been wonderful to behold in different circumstances, but then it could have had dire consequences had it not been for the reflexes of the warriors.

Out of the solid rock appeared a gang of two legged creatures wielding huge stone clubs, they melted out of the rock wall as if they were part of it, streaked and coloured they completely matched the cliff face they had been hugging.

However, I saw straight away they were not made of stone as Derca's first slash cut one of them in half.

Nal was straight in with a stroke that cut another one down the middle but then I watched in horror as another being rose from the side of the path and knocked Nal over the sheer edge of the cliff.

The speed of Derca's movements were something to behold, he slashed a phantom out of the way with his sword, at the same time slithering sideways over the edge, grabbing Nal by her hair tail.

Keeping hold on his sword he gripped the edge of the rock by using the heel of his weapon as a brake - swung Nal up by her hair back onto the path and as she rolled over the edge she cut the legs off an advancing rock phantom.

By this time Derca, sword in hand once more, cut another phantom down. Then a strange thing happened, the rest of the rock beings threw down their weapons and got down on their knees and started wailing.

Derca said 'It's all right Nal, they are cowards and they rely on surprise to overpower their prey, although I am amazed that they took us on knowing full well who we are!'

'What are you saying Derca?' I asked.

Derca replied. 'Even had I been alone they would never have dared attack me, and considering I am in the company of a Bana warrior it reads to me of sheer folly on their part.'

I answered Derca's statement straight away, 'It is the dark energy driving them, they have no choice but to go with it as their will has been taken over by a strong, evil power which overrides all fear and caution.'

I approached the few that were spared, Nal and Derca wanted to kill them all but I wouldn't have it, instead I decided to try and heal them.

They were cowering against the face of the cliff, as I

came to them I used the spirit aura to descend on them and it calmed them down and allowed me to touch them. Their outer skin was hard, almost like the stone they were copying.

I stepped back and spread the light from my fingers up the centre of their bodies to their throats and heads. I felt a resistance, but not too much, whatever possessed them hadn't used much power to enslave them and probably never visualised anybody trying to free such a spineless lot.

The dark energy fled from them without a fight, but I knew I had marked myself and the main power would know that a healing spirit was about.

I was not the only one who thought that, both the warriors had worked it out for themselves. Nal just looked at me and said. 'We have to run now and not stop until we reach the place we cannot name.'

Derca backed her up by saying. 'Nal is right, we journey by the light of Apuss as it makes no difference now. We do not rest until we sight the place we seek.' By the time we had spoken the few words of a plan the rock phantoms had disappeared into the refuge of the rocks from whence they had come.

Derca said that he had never ventured as far as the summit of Greystones, he had marched his party of elves back the way they had come.

No more to be said so we took off, single file up the rocky steep, Nal leading, Derca and me behind. It did not take us long to reach the summit of the ridge and from the top we viewed a huge slope of grey smooth stone, not flat but it was as if the rolling waves of a sea had been turned to stone.

Dour and dull grey there was not a green patch anywhere, it was well named Greystones, dull and featureless, like the phantoms who inhabited it. No crags or rugged rocks just smooth grey stone, sweeping down to a distant curved flat plain.

We crossed an expanse of flatness between the wavelets of stone; it just went on and on in featureless monotony. Even the air was grey, Apuss's light was oozing through a curtain of fine mist that had just appeared.

The only sign of life we saw were strange flat creatures that blended in with the stone around. When we disturbed them they took off at great speed on their short legs, their tails wagging from side to side.

We came out of the mist and made out the distant plain we had first seen, now its curve more pronounced than ever.

We could just make out that in the centre of the curve was a peninsula of dark grey rock, like an arrowhead it cut into the sea, pointing straight ahead into the fringe of a moody blue ocean.

There was no land horizon, just an endless sea all around, only the arrowhead of stone -a lonely silent marker waiting for any life form to heed its direction.

Holding the same formation we started to run down the mountainside, and then we had company of the worst kind. It was Derca who saw them first and shouted the warning -gurks!

I looked back in time to see four gurks that had just

crested the rise. Derca was very vigilant to have seen them as the colouration of the giant birds matched the stone of the hill.

I had hardly taken in the scene when I saw the leading gurk crash into the hill in an explosion of blood and feathers. Nal -- quick as a flash -- had taken the gurk out and was now sending another arrow in the direction of a second gurk, but it was not the bird she targeted - they carried riders.

I caught Derca in my peripheral vision heading towards the gurk carcass and wondered what he was doing.

Everything happened so fast, the air filled with the shrieking of the gurks, Nal bringing one down, Derca killing a rider and Nal furiously firing arrows at the remaining gurks. With astonishing speed she took all four of the giant birds down, Derca's reflexes were as lightening as Nal downed the birds, so Derca darted from one to the other killing the riders.

The side of the hill was spewed with feathers, bones and blood and the shrill screeching of one of the dying gurks was like a dirge to the departing spirits of the dead creatures. In spite of the bloody affray played out in front of me I still took time to wish the passing spirits well.

Unlike my companions, who were in the act of decapitating the giant birds, blood up to their elbows and whooping to each other in the throes of their violent acts. They revel in their sheer physical energy and the two complemented each other during the gurk ambush. Nal as usual was recovering her bloodied arrows.

However it was a short respite because, from the shelter of one of the huge wavelets of stone, appeared a sizeable host of black elves. But it was not the black elves that held our attention.

Occupying the centre of the host of elves was a weird looking grey shape which seemed to be floating along. The shape forged ahead of the black elves, heading straight for me it paid no attention to Derca and Nal, who had closed up to me on seeing the enemy.

Derca shouted to me to stay behind himself and Nal, I screamed back at him saying. 'Run! Save yourselves - it's a demon of magic you are facing and you cannot fight it.'

Nal answered me with a touch of venom in her voice. 'We will see about that.'

What happened next took me by surprise; the sheer speed and dexterity of the two warriors and their fearless attack on the demon was beyond belief.

Nal and Derca moved forward towards the demon and as they approached it they moved away from each other, widening the angle between them and the demon. The demon kept coming, confident in his magical dominance. Raising his arm he fired a black bolt at Derca.

Quick as lightening Derca deflected the bolt in the direction of Nal, who deflected it straight back at the demon. The demon visibly shuddered at the shock of his own magic hitting him but managed to let fly another one at Nal.

Nal, matching the speed of Derca, deflected it to the elf who hammered it at the demon stopping it in its tracks. The demon fired another couple of bolts but they were very weak compared to its first salvo, but the deflective power of the warriors seemed to get stronger and they were closing in on the demon.

With a shrill cry of anguish the demon turned and fled. The dark elves, having witnessed the power of Nal and Derca, must have thought they were sorcerers so they turned tail and ran after the demon. I knew Nal and Derca were hyped up and were about to chase the enemy, so I shouted to them to turn about and follow me 'Run Derca, run.' I shouted the same to Nal who began to run after Derca.

My work done I turned tail and fled after my two companions, who had stopped a fair distance down the hill, crouched down with their backs to the direction we had just come.

I ran between the two of them shouting at the top of my vocals. 'Run as fast as your able - we have to get off the hill and make for the sea.' They reacted instantly and were alongside me charging down the hill to the plain below.

At the bottom we were still running side by side, and never stopped until we reached the arrowhead. It was a great sensation running down the mountain, the shared energy added impetus to the mad rush to get to the sea.

We stood together on the peninsula like three sentinels, gazing across the blue of that great expanse of water which had now become silent. Nal broke the silence by saying, 'What is to happen now Lael, how can we cross the Tanaron Sea and how long until the enemy find another demon and chase after us?'

I told her that the enemy would be confused for quite some time, and as for the crossing I had nothing to say. My mind went back to when Derca mentioned the boat, but it had seemed so unimportant at the time. I suppose I had thought *sea - boat - must be boats by the sea?*

I kept looking back up the grey hill but could see no movement, I knew the sight of the grey demon being wasted by Derca and Nal would have shocked the elves and put them out of the fight for a while. But it would not last long and I did not want to take any chances. I certainly wanted to get onto the sea and away before the enemy recovered.

I turned to my companions and just shrugged what else could I do as I hadn't thought as far as to plan for the crossing. I imagined that we could see land on the far side and maybe swim the short distance. But Tanaron is not a sea, it is a mighty ocean and we needed transport.

I looked at Nal and Derca, I never get tired of looking at them; they never complain they never lose their tempers, *thank the stars.*

Nal was a tall, slim warrior she had unslung her bow and had it longwise in front of her, leaning slightly on it. The mercurial blue skin the occasional tattoos of her tribe on legs and arms reflecting the light of Apuss. Her selc armour covering her breasts and pelvis, the woven metallic throat and neck guard, sword and daggers at her belt she had that familiar stoic bland look on her face.

And alongside, only slightly taller, the figure of Derca; his arms folded in front of him, so different from Nal in looks and stature. The hair pulled back from the forehead, the dark yellow skin, tight fitting selc armour on his upper body, and the baggy black mariner's trews pulled tight at the waist and ankles. The deadly duan at his waist; the bandolier of elfshot across his chest and as always his head slightly to the side.

I so loved those two warriors, I would be broken hearted if anything happened to them and I told them so. Nal said. 'What is the love that you speak of Lael? I do not know it.'

Derca's answer was. 'We have a bonding that we feel and know, we accept the feeling but we have no word for it.'

I replied using my earthly experience to explain a word that I did not use too often while I lived there.

'Love is a word that surpasses all, it is far more meaningful than words like - devotion - loyalty - faithfulness and hope.'

I couldn't help but smile at the two looking back at me with the "Well, what next?" look on their faces. So I cut short trying to explain away the love word.

Nal turned to Derca and said. 'What about the sea spirit Derca, can she be reached?'

I looked at Derca and said. 'That's the answer Derca! Remember what Nindril said about him and Shuira making peace? I can speak to the air and the air will carry it to Nindril who in turn will reach Shuira. I have the name of the trustworthy air spirit and he will deliver the message to Nindril.'

I stood on the extreme point of the rock and entered my meditary state, focusing my mind to run with the wind, I felt the energy of the air entering my thoughts and I answered the whispers I felt in my head. I told the warriors that the air spirit, Scir, had heard me and the sea would be touched by the wind of thought.

Apuss had left the sky and we all had sat on the point of rock and, as the light of Ara watched over us, we looked on that flat peaceful water. It was being polished by the yellow moonbeams of Ara. Nal said. 'We could dance on that water it is so flat and solid looking.' Then at her last words the waters rippled with movement and fish broke the surface.

At once Derca's exited voice shouted. 'It's the mer's of Shuira - Shuira is here!'

Hardly were the words out of his mouth when two figures hurtled out of the waters and landed on the shingle below us.

Derca's voice lost its enthusiasm when he saw who was with Shuira. 'Oh no, Azirema is here, she will take one of us to the sea.'

I never got a chance to reply as one of the sea entities called out to us. 'Come down to the water's edge, warriors of the land.'

We bounded down from the promontory and faced Shuira and the one called Azirema. I felt instantly energised by their company, they were without any doubt powerful spirits and we had nothing to fear from them despite Derca's response.

Shuira spoke first. 'Well Derca we meet again and once more you seek my help.'

Derca bowed his head slightly and thanked Shuira for answering the call. He also bowed to her companion and voiced her name. As he said her name I felt vibrations of foreboding in his tone.

He stood back slightly and introduced us as Lael, spirit of Ulana, and Nal of the bana-ger. He named them as Shuira, goddess of the waters, and Azirema, spirit of the dead.

Shuira spoke first. 'Derca you have nothing to worry about with the presence of Azirema, she is not here to take any of you we have both come not only to help you but also to speak with the spirit form of Ulana.'

I noticed that Nal had remained silent and her behaviour seemed remarkably subdued, as if she was transfixed by the sea spirits. I was taken aside by them and communication was by thought only.

Shuira started the conversation. *Lael, it pleases us that a spirit of Ulana is helping the world of Darwan and that is why we have both come, we need to give you as much information as we know - Azirema will explain.*

Azirema came into my thoughts. *Lael, as you know there is a dark power controlling some of the tribes of Darwan we do not know what it is although we have a good idea where it has come from. The dark entity has not shown itself on the waters, if it had I would have taken it but because it is keeping itself clear of the seas and rivers we can only conclude that it knows of our existence and that tells Shuira and me that it is not ready to deal with us yet.*

Shuira again. *We both know that whatever it is, it has come from the darkness of Ulas and it will be accompanied by many forms of evil energy. These other energies will take many forms, Azirema took an eathie demon that dared too close to the shore, unfortunately it was one of the few entities that have no after spirit so it just dissipated in her power.*

Azirema. *I wondered if the entity was sacrificed to see if we were on the alert, knowing if we captured it we would learn nothing from it.*

Lael. *So where can this being hide itself, surely the air and the waters must have an idea?*

Shuira. *Lael, Darwan is a very large world, the spirits of the air and waters have knowledge of it. In the faraway parts there are creatures the like of which you have never seen, but nothing seems to be amiss with their goings on.*

The only habitations that are being affected by the evil energy are those who live in or by the lands of the Laic. The Black Island has been veiled by an energy that has confused the air around it - nothing has touched the waters, however our bounds are the waters and that must always be so. We cannot interfere with the beings of air and earth.

Azirema stepped onto the shoreline of the Black Island at a place called Cail-dur, but it was blinded to her by an invisible power so she got no information from her visit. Azirema and I think that the evil entity sees Elid Silverhair and her adherents as an enemy that has to be vanquished before it can continue with the oppression of the rest of Darwan.

Azirema. *Furthermore we think that the entity possibly knows about you and if that is true then it will certainly try to trap you. It cannot kill you, but if it is powerful enough it could contain you and that would be like imprisonment for all time.*

Shuira and I think that you are maybe meant as bait, Elid is using you as a diversion, because whatever the power is its attention will be on trying to find out whereabouts in the land you are, if it has not found you already. While its attention is on you Elid can muster her forces.

Lael. *Elid would never knowingly expose me to danger, she is in constant communication with Elios and Elios would never allow me to be used without my knowledge and anyway what about Derca and Nal, they would die in my defence?*

Although Ler of the wandering people said to me that the dark power had knowledge of me when I first entered Darwan.

Shuira. *Elid is not only fighting for her own lands but for all of Darwan, so she is using all the forces that she has, so do not judge her harshly. Let us deal with the event of now. I will leave a pack of mers with you, Ara has now given way to Rinnis and her red light will shine on the stone point and on the water of Tanaron that is the way of Elinbroom, once the mers know the direction they will take you to Elinbroom. Now we will talk to Derca and the bana warrior.*

We came out of thought and joined Nal and Derca. Straight away Azirema went up to Nal and fixed her with her violet eyes. 'Nal of the bana, whatever the outcome of your journey you will meet with me in the sea, I feel you will come out of the battles and live long, so until then farewell.' Then she was gone and not a ripple on the quiet water to show she had entered it.

I looked at Nal and had a quiet laugh to myself as I had never seen a confused bana warrior, but I was looking at one now.

Shuira then spoke to the two warriors. 'Derca and Nal, you are both able warriors but it is only the beginning for the two of you because within your tribes you will rise to become great leaders and will be renowned in the land for your wisdom and knowledge. Now ride the mers, they will love it and so will you. Enjoy the freedom of the sea you are safe in my domain.' Then, like Azirema, she was gone.

The Crossing of the Tanaron Sea

I think we were all a bit delirious from meeting two of the most powerful spirits in Darwan. However, I got a clue as to where the bana's spirits go after death with the words of Azirema to Nal.

Derca looked at the sky and said. 'The moons have changed over, let us now follow the pathway of Rinnis, we should get in the water now and get acquainted with our mer friends.' So saying he jumped into the sea closely followed by Nal. I watched them for a while I had a feeling that this crossing might be the last journey the three of us would have together for some time.

Then the sea glowed with the sheen of Rinnis's light and Nal shouted to me to hurry up. With a lingering look at the sky I joined my companions, who by this time had chosen their mounts and were astride them. Shuira had given us more merfish than we needed, they like each-others company and the more of them there are together the more they like it.

Derca shouted to me, telling me that a mer will pick me, not the other way about, so I entered the water and floated on the surface and sure enough one of the mers nuzzled up to me and then swam underneath so I could mount him easily.

When he rose to the surface with me on his back I sat astride of him and held on to his dorsal fin, which was quite close to his head. I felt as if had instantly refreshed - emptied of all thoughts about what was going on or what lay ahead, I let my immediate thoughts go the mer I was astride.

Oh mer, if only you knew what my feelings are now, I am so at one with the placid sea reflecting the red light of Rinnis and the energy I am getting from your body, I wonder if you are female or male.

Imagine my surprise when the mer answered me in thought?

'My name is Lefin and I am female, and I am glad you are at one with my energy.'

The sound in my head was softly hissing out the words, they were soothing and unhurried and I felt great joy at the contact I had made with Lefin. She was still in my head.

Your companions are mounted on two males, the one the female warrior rides is called Vir, Derca rides Cin. The one who leads us down the pathway of light is called Orisa and is female, the one behind is male and he is called Uil.

So Lefin you know Derca, have you met him before?

During their great exodus from the black island I was one of the mers who led him to the Tears of Apuss. Shuira has been impressed greatly by Derca's conduct during his journeys through life and has aided him more than she has any other entity.

I had to ask Lefin why Shuira was so impressed by Derca and what was so special about him.

Lefin's answer was thought for thought for what I

was thinking, she said.

Derca is a fierce warrior and is quite merciless with his foes at times. However he is all for his people and will go the ends of Darwan for them, the tribe of Lael is his life's blood. He is a very popular warrior and leader and the children like him because he takes time to speak to them. He only takes from the land and sea what he needs, no more no less.

As I deliberated on the thoughts of Lefin I became aware of Nal and Derca yelling at each other, what I saw reminded me of the ride of the horses of Cinedher. The bold heroes were standing on the backs of the mers and were play-acting again.

Lefin, will they upset the mers by what they are doing?

Lael, the mers will join in the play, the males are prone to boisterous fun and energy, look behind - I can feel Uil coming up fast as he doesn't want to be left out.

As I watched, the mer called Uil sped past us and shot in between Vir and Cin, recognising that sport was in the offing. Nal and Derca used Uil as a stepping stone and swapped mers.

The mers knew they had like spirits on their backs so the three split and started cavorting about.

I heard Nal shouting to Derca. 'Watch this Derca!' She had her bow in front of her at arm's length then she did something incredible - judging the speed of Cin she leapt upwards and somersaulted twice before landing back on both feet on the back of Cin. Derca yelled back in appreciation. 'Good one Nal, now get your eyes on this.' He straddled Vir and held on to his fin, as if he had picked up a thought signal the mer charged ahead at great speed and Uil came thundering up alongside. Then both mers dived below the water, I looked across at Nal still balanced on the back of Cin and she just shrugged her shoulders at me.

I thought. *What in the name of Iaphalon are they doing now?*

As if in answer to my thoughts both mers shot out of the water high into the air - Derca still clinging to Vir. As they reached their high point, both mers lowered their heads ready for the downward plunge and in that brief space of time Derca jumped from Vir to Uil and down they went for another go.

I looked across at Nal and saw her shouldering her bow and knew she wanted in on the action.

I switched thought to Lefin again. *How long are they going to keep up the antics Lefin?*

All the way to the shores of Elinbroom Lael, they feel the returning energy of the two warriors and that will exhilarate them even more. Uil is the usual instigator of the high spirits and that is why I had him at the rear. I will rein him in before we reach the Draig's island.

Shuira has already banished Uil to the sea of Arie for shooting out of the water and leaping over the fishermen's boats scaring them to death. She told him that the merfish are her chosen companions and as they are close to her they have a duty to show respect to those who inhabit the waters, and also those who work on the waters in order to feed themselves.

What happens in the sea of Arie, Lefin?

Very little Lael, that is why he was put there to allow him time on his own, enable him to be comfortable with himself and lose the desire to annoy other entities with his antics.

But surely Lefin there must be other creatures in the Arie Sea that he could play with?

It is a sea of new birth, far away on the other side of Darwan the sea bed is made up mainly of rocks. Forests of tree weed reach upward almost to the surface of the water.

The life forces are very small and hide in the nooks and holes of the rocks. There are large patches of sand where flatfish live, spending most of the time beneath the sand. He did try to snuffle them out of the sand but the flat fish just dug themselves deeper and he soon got bored with their unresponsive attitude.

I love the place, the tranquil waters exude peace and harmony, the fronds of tree weed shimmer with the slow movement of the waters and the colours of the rocks reflect the light of Apuss as he reaches down to the sea bottom. We feel the new life forces coming into being all around, it is a magical time for us to be there.

I was with her in thought as she described the Arie Sea and my mind broadened with hers with the realisation that Darwan is a giant planet. Dargal and Daralonadh are mere specks in the great scheme of things.

She told me that they are the shepherds of the newly evolving sea life; they take it in turns to watch over the creatures that inhabit the waters. *The males of our species very seldom go there, Shuira put Uil to the sea thinking it would calm him a bit - but it didn't, I think he's worse than ever. Look at him now - he is in his element all right, especially as he has like-minded entities that can return his energy.*

Oh! I can identify with that Lefin, my companions will rise to the occasion but they can switch on a deadlier energy when required. To look at them now you would not think they are two of the most capable warriors on the planet.

Yes Lael, I can see that is so, but it is not so with Uil, he needs to switch off what he is in order to be what he should be, and that is of use to others. I feel Shuira will put him somewhere to serve a master or mistress that will put him under pressure and make him realise that his power and energy is to be put to use in helping others.

So what about you Lael, have you visited below the waters since you came to Darwan?

Lefin's question took me by surprise and I think my answer had the same effect on her, especially when I added on that I had never been below the waters in Darwan or Ulana.

Would you like to journey beneath the waters Lael? I can take you there as we have time before we reach Elinbroom. All I need to do is alert Orisa to what we are doing and anyway we will be swimming in the same direction.

After a pause in thought to Orisa, Lefin told me to hold on and hold the breathing. She did not nose dive, a very delicate submerge took us into a serene world beneath the Tanaron Sea.

The red of Rinnis shimmered through the surface giving a surreal look in an already surreal environment. As we swam, many marine creatures came up to see what was sitting on the back of a mer. The warm waters brought back a memory from a long time ago - of comfort and warmth and life beginning.

A company of jellyfish appeared and started to dance around us, it was truly amazing to see their fluid movements against the background of red.

Then all too soon we surfaced, and yet again I had felt I had passed from one world to another.

I had a peaceful journey on Lefin's back, switching on and off in thought conversation with the passive merfish. She told me they were not fish, only the entities that fish on the waters call them that, they are the Merevra or Mers for short.

She understood when I went quiet that I was in meditary sleep and so did not communicate until I sent a thought out first.

Virtually all the length of the journey Nal, Derca and the mers kept up the fooling around, the sheer physical energy of the group was wonderful to feel and see. As Rinnis gave up the sky for the emergence of Apuss they quietened down and we all got back in formation.

Uil, with a bit of gentle nudging from Lefin, returned to the rear of the group. I was convinced he winked to me on the way past, what he did do was flick some seawater in my direction with his tail.

Orisa slowed the pace down, ahead we could see the high tops of Elinbroom as the false dawn gave way to the true light of the rising Apuss, and in respect to the god of the sky we all held our faces to the light and thanked him for the day.

It was a colourful place - Elinbroom - it was mostly yellow higher up, in the lower region colours of red ochre predominated. A range of jagged white-topped mountains made a curve in the horizon.

Behind it stood a most impressive peak, the yellow of its lower bulk just appearing above the points of the lesser peaks. The yellow stone glowed briefly below the peak then it was lost in the sparkling whiteness of the high top.

Derca said it was crystal white on all the mountain tops, not snow, he had seen the wonder of sparkling whiteness before.

Before we parted on the shores of Elinbroom Lefin

said that Cerenor-Tala resided on the highest mountain in Elinbroom, which was the crystal topped peak we could see. As the mers swam away, one turned back and balanced on its tail it then did a back flip. Nal said. 'I wonder who that was.'

We turned away from the sea and made our way through red ochre stone to a pass between a curvature of hills which led to the main peak of Elinbroom. We trekked through the winding pass for a very long time; we could not yet catch a glimpse of the crystal peak though at every twist and turn we expected to see it.

I heard Derca say to Nal that the moons changed over when they started their journey so Rinnis will be in the sky for many nights. He also commented on the peaceful change over as when Rinnis rules the night, the first two nights are usually very turbulent. I do not know how they keep track of the change overs they are so erratic.

Apuss began to dip and the evening dark started to close in. I decided to stop and rest up and told my companions to take it easy for a while as I wanted some spiritual meditation. I had hardly started when I was hailed by Nal.

'Lael, come quick and see this.'

I turned about and saw Nal and Derca staring ahead of them, but I needed no answer to what it was they were looking at. The crystal tower of Cerenor-Tala had been set on fire by the red light of rising Rinnis, like a flaming torch it flickered and shone, kindled by a myriad of tiny crystals.

As one we bounded forward and started to ascend

the slopes which would ultimately take us to the lair of the Draig.

We stared at the peak of Elinbroom its white crystalline pillar had become an energetic show of fiery light. Just as Derca had said - peace reigned when Rinnis the vibrant red daughter of Ara had taken possession of the night sky and was setting the high tops of Elinbroom on fire. Like a mighty flaming beacon in the sky, the lair of Cerenor-Tala drew us ever upwards.

FEARN

It took us all of the night of Rinnis and half the day of Apuss's light to ascend the yellow mountain of Elinbroom, it was so steep in places that we had to climb. The rock itself was gritty, not smooth, I described it as yellow sandstone. My companions had never seen the like of it anywhere else nor had they heard of the name I gave it.

We had stopped on a plateau of the yellow sandstone, a broad path led up from it and there, sprawled in front of a very large cave, was the creature we sought - Cerenor-Tala. She was asleep, the massive head slightly to the side showing a row of awesome sharp pointed teeth, we paused for a spell to look around before we disturbed her.

The abrupt change from yellow sandstone to the sparkling beauty of the white crystalline pinnacle that housed the cave of the Draig was like entering another world. Yet again another magical happening on my spiritual journey, will the enchantment never cease?

Long had the Draig slumbered, until the day I and my two warrior companions awoke her. Like her kin in other worlds who had to leave because the life entities feared them, she was left to bear the pain and remorse of being the last of a line of creatures who had served other beings to help them rule worlds.

From the heights of Elinbroom I, Nal and Derca looked down on a river winding its way through a plain of bleached yellow stone. A fiery sun beat down on an indigo sea and beyond, pointed hills rose like the teeth of the dragon herself. Both Nal and Derca were moved by the striking beauty of the place but both agreed there was a coldness about it, Derca said the clear crystals looked like dripping ice.

There was an air of despondency all around; then I felt the powerful intake of air from the mouth of the Draig and I shouted to the warriors. 'Move! She is going to fire-out.'

Instantaneously Nal and Derca moved – one to each side of the pathway. I levitated upwards just as the Draig fired her first salvo of a blue white fire it wasted the stone pathway and peppered the air with pellets of molten rock.

In the voice of the mind I addressed the last Draig of Elinbroom by her ancient name. 'Hold, Cerenor-Tala, Draig of earth, air and fire! I am Lael, spirit of Ulana I come to you in the name of Elid Silverhair, ruler of the lands of Laic.'

After a long pause - as dragons tend to do - a light, silken voice floated into my thought waves. *If you are what you say you are, you will be able to tell to me the rhyme that I gave to Silverhair.*

In thought I delivered the ancient rhyme which described the melancholy mood of the Draig and would hopefully gain her trust.

Here must I lie in cold Elinbroom from whence in ages past I saw the sea - silent -eternal. A ribbon of blood the river - conical hills by the way of Ica and Ulas. At last may I leave this body of fire and fury to live in the stars forever more.

Cerenor reverted to voice. 'Are you coming to hasten me to my end, spirit of earth? What task does Silverhair require me to do now, I hope it is the last one I carry out as I am tired - so very - tired!

Speak to me spirit and tell the two with you to snap out of their fighting stance.'

I turned to my friends and told them to stand down. Derca complied immediately - not so Nal.

With the absolute belief in her race and herself, she faced the Draig with the words. 'It will take more than a spout of flame to make me stand down Draig.'

The Draig once again paused and looked as if she was delving into past events before she answered Nal. 'I know by your name and your markings who you are little warrior, I carried your mother's mother on my back at the first great battle of the Fochd plain.

She was a great warrior who fought well on that day, her name was Nal-ester and like you she was a bow master. I see her yet, a tall, powerful warrior who approached me and asked if I would honour her by carrying her into battle.

Deadly was her aim that day as she stood on my back, bending and swaying in unison with my flight, with practiced ease she loosed her arrows into the evil throng.

And now one of her offspring approaches me with impunity.'

I was ready to interject on Nal's behalf but she beat me to it. Addressing the Draig by name she began.

'Cerenor-Tala, if I may be as bold as use your name, I did not intend to offend you. I know at times I am too quick with my tongue but it is the habit of ages that makes us stand up for our race.

The name and reputation of the Bana ger is all important to us and we would gladly give up our lives for it. I bow my head to you Cerenor-Tala, and as my ancestor was honoured by you in ages past so also would I be honoured to serve you in any way.'

So saying Nal dipped her head and held the position until the Draig replied, after another lengthy pause.

'I accept your words, and depending on the demand of Silverhair I may have need of you. But I warn you if you consort with Draigs you may have to give up your life earlier than you wish for.' Then Cerenor turned her attention to Derca.

'I noticed elf that you were not prepared to be burned back to the dust that made you.'

I had noticed myself that Derca had edged to the side when Nal made her declaration. Although in my head I knew Derca had probably seen and done too much, so being roasted for a reputation didn't come into it.

Not waiting for an answer Cerenor continued,

quizzing Derca. 'Why is an elf from the race of Lael in the company of a spirit of Ulana called Lael?'

'I do not know the answer to that one Draig, all that I know is that great Cimer asked if I would do a duty for him and that is why I am here.'

'Ah! Said Cerenor - first Elid Silverhair and now Cimer gets a mention, something is about to happen and I hope it is not what I think it is. I will give you the same question spirit of earth.

'Why are the names linked? One from a world between the first and second veil the other from a world which lies between the third and fourth boundary? There has to be a meaning or a reason behind it.'

I could not answer Cerenors question because I had not the slightest idea about why our names should be of interest to her. Mine was given to me by Roscranna when I first arrived in Ulana.

Derca just shrugged his shoulders, as far as he was concerned his race has always been known as the tribe of Lael and even some of his clansmen carry the name Lael.

'Somewhere there must be a mutual belonging - all will be revealed no doubt' said the Draig of Elinbroom. Cerenors tone intimated to me that the reason would become apparent at a later date.

Then she asked what the reason for my visit on behalf of Elid was about and I began in voice as Nal and Derca do not talk in thought.

I said that Elid has felt for some time that things were not right as she has never had trouble in the Laic land, but rumours from without has prompted her to take action ---before I could say more on the subject I was cut off by the Draig.

Cerenor answered, albeit rather dryly. 'It might have been more like it to take action when the tribe of Selma were wiped out.'

This time it was Derca who answered. 'You are well informed Cerenor, for one who has slumbered for so long.'

Turning her massive head in Derca's direction she said. 'Ah so you have a tongue in your head dark one?'

'Yes Cerenor, I have.' Said Derca. 'And I also have thoughts and they tell me that what we will face will be like no other foe we have fought before.'

Cerenors reply was ominous to say the least. 'Your thoughts are true to the mark dark one, I fear the black child of Ulas is amongst us.'

'Who in all the worlds is the black child of Ulas?' I asked.

Back came Cerenors answer 'She is Ulas-darg in the old tongue, also known as the mindbender and sometimes Dulsie Ular - an enchantress and a very powerful witch.

She was spawned in the great cosmos when Ulas was at his most powerful, but she was secreted away before great Ica scattered the dark forces.

It was she who was behind the forces of evil which culminated at the Fochd pass. Elid and the Green woman vanquished her dark energy. However they had not possessed the power to destroy her completely and now she has returned more powerful than ever, this could be a job for a Draig before she bids farewell to Darwan.'

At that statement Cerenor seemed to pick up, her eyes flashed with excitement and her whole demeanour changed before our eyes, her head reared up and her great bulk started to emerge from the Crystal cave.

The voice tone was soft as before but it carried conviction. 'Come little warrior, let us see if you have the spirit of your ancestor - climb aboard my back and we will fly through the air above Elinbroom and scatter the skarling birds, and if we are lucky we might waste a passing gurk or two.'

With that she squatted down with her upper body and shoulders to enable Nal to jump onto her back. Nal did so with ease and took up position slightly in front of Cerenors shoulders and the base of her neck.

I said to Cerenor. 'Is it safe for Nal to ride without a harness of some kind?'

'Lael, how long have you been in the company of the bana? Surely you have realised that they are easily on a level with the elves as far as dexterity goes. They are so coordinated that they can match my every movement and fight at the same time.

However we have a device called a wipping cord which Nal will wrap around her waist, the other end will cling to one of my scales. The cord does not need to be tied as it will hold fast by its fibres to Nal and my body, it will never let go unless one of us expires.

Our energies are linked through the cord and it will allow Nal to feel my every movement as if we are one. No need for her to anticipate my every twist and turn because she is linked to me in mind and body.'

So saying, Cerenor turned to Derca and said. 'Dark one, I am going to ask you to enter my crystal cave and fetch the wipping cord for me, very few creatures have entered the cave of a Draig and lived to tell the tale.

You will be renowned among elves as being one of the few who walked back out again.' Then as an afterthought she whispered out 'Unless I change my mind.'

Derca did as he was bid without hesitation and much later he told me that the cave of Cerenor the Draig was the most beautiful place he had ever been in. It was bejewelled with sparkling crystals.

It was a gigantic cavern inside and all around it there were shining colours - roof, floor and walls - crystals of all sizes and shapes, some of which had designs the like of which he had never seen before. He also mentioned that the air inside the cave felt fresh and fragrant and likened it to the air on the peaks of the DaRinnis Mountains.

He also saw some strange things on crystal shelves, and again they were items and symbols that were unknown to him, as well as peculiar markings emblazoned on the walls. On the far wall there was an effigy of a Draig, though it did not look like Cerenor, and in tandem with the surrounding crystalline twinkling, the eyes of the Draig shone back at him as if they were alive.

On one of the Draig's painted claws hung the

wipping cord that Cerenor spoke about, he removed it, and as he did so he felt as if the Draigs eyes were watching his every move. He commented on the lightness of the wipping cord to us on his emergence from the cave. Again Cerenor explained the significance of the cord.

'This is the cord that binds us.' She said. 'It will link Nal with me to make us as one. Energy will flow between us and we will be in magical unity; you will find there is more to Draigs than blowing hot air.'

Then the whispering stopped and we all went silent, in that sensitive pause we were unified and I sent the aura of light out to touch each of my companions and was reassured by the returned energy that said we would all come through the trials that lay ahead.

Cerenors voice broke the silence. 'Enough talk, come Nal let us stir the upper air of Magical Elinbroom.' Hardly was the comment passed than the two were spearing their way through the atmosphere. I was amazed that such a heavy shape could propel itself and a passenger at such a speed.

Still climbing and now silhouetted against the blue light of the upper reaches, Cerenors shape could be seen as clearly as if she had been painted on a canvas. Having reached the zenith of her climb it looked as if she was frozen in motion, wings outspread, head, body and tail in a straight line. I shouted to Derca. 'How does Nal stay on her back at that impossible angle?'

Derca answered and by his voice tone I knew he was impressed. 'I have ridden with Croin the storm hawk, but never once did he achieve the angle of ascent such as Cerenor holds now.'

As we watched we could see Nal bending and swaying as if she was part of Cerenor. I suppose she was indeed part of the Draig, being joined by the chord as they were. Nal was shooting off imaginary arrows, in position with the bow unslung, sighting the weapon, pulling on the string and envisioning falling targets.

Then the trance was broken and the aerial display came to an abrupt end as Cerenor, like an arrow herself, shot out of the sky and was at our feet in a trice. Hardly had she landed than she hit me with a question.

'What now Lael of Ulana, where do we go from here?' She had adopted her lazy position once more and it was hard to imagine that the sleek shape that had entertained us with her flying expertise was the same one that was slumped in front of me now.

All I could manage was a feeble. 'I don't know Cerenor, I thought I had it all planned but now I feel confused and unable to make any kind of decision. I don't even know where the witch that you speak of resides.'

Then Derca spoke. 'But I know where the witch's lair is. The sea spirit told us that Azirema took an eathie demon on the shore at the fortress of Cail-dur and she said that the dark energy emanated from it. Also, Croin told me he had seen a shape which was female with one other - a male on the ramparts of Cail-dur.

We have no power to wield against a witch but a Draig could cause death and destruction to the fortress and all those in it. Surely that would be the way to go?'

Cerenors reply was to the point. 'Yes Derca, that would be the way to go but I have been summoned by Ener Elid of the line of Aronis, and to her I must go for whatever reason or plan she has for me.'

Derca said. 'Then we must all go to the Laic and leave the decision making to Elid, after all it was she who sent us to seek out Cerenor.'

I knew that he was right and that part I was easy with, however I knew that we could not all go back. We would have to split in two and that was not going to be easy because it would have to be Nal who would have to accompany Cerenor, and she would have a lot to say on that score.

I also had a feeling of foreboding about what was going on in the land; it was no longer a trail of adventure I was on. The consequences of my actions from now on could determine how the coming warfare played out.

Cerenor must have sensed the serious turn of my thinking as her silken voice tone broke into my thoughts. 'What now Lael of Ulana, are you ready to command a Draig?'

I replied to Cerenors question with a renewed confidence. 'Yes Cerenor I am, you along with Nal should make haste and go to the aid of Elid and let her direct you.

I feel the dark energy that is on the move is not confined to one force; there is movement I sense from the direction of Ulas and also from the way of Ica, although I am sure Elid knows of this.'

Cerenor looked directly at me and fixed me with a deep penetrating stare - I was transfixed by her eyes. As she spoke her words to me the eyes that I looked into had seen so much from the very beginnings of life.

As I listened to her, my eyes were seeing what her eyes had seen - many, many events ago.

'Lael, see with my eyes from a time long gone - once again see the fiery curtain that you saw on the peak of enlightenment. This was the dawn of all our journeys, that mighty fire signalled all our beginnings. I do not know what caused the barrier of fire, I can only guess that two powerful energies collided and created the fusion of fire and light. Who knows Lael, there might be another Draig and a spirit having the same conversation as us on the reverse side of the flaming light. See with my eyes as my kin and I fly through the black mass of moving, living energy, in and out of the burning orbs of fire which you see as the flickering lights of stars. We were headed for the worlds that great Ica had created to breathe the life of fire into them. Each one placed close to a burning orb so the light and heat would maintain a balance. On your Earth it was called 'Sun' in Darwan it is known as 'Apuss' the moons of the night stole the light of day to show the coming life entities that they were not alone in the darkness.

As you get closer to the dark power you have to trust that you will not be alone, I will make sure of that. Now attend to your little warriors, they look for your instructions.'

Once again the visions of the past merged into my space in time and I thanked Cerenor for the insight and the comfort of knowing that I would be watched over.

Hardly had the words left my mouth when they were

challenged immediately by Nal.

'I was asked by Elid to lead and defend you if need be, to her request I am held by my word and my honour.'

'Nal, in the daylight of Apuss you pledged your servitude to Cerenor-Tala, by serving her you serve Elid and myself but more importantly the land of Darwan, Derca will accompany me to the Black island.

It will be your duty to fight with Cerenor for the greater benefit of the land and its inhabitants. Just think Nal, you will be renowned among the bana as the warrior who fought on the back of the last Draig in Darwan.'

I knew by Nal's tone when she answered me that I had convinced her.

'Then I will go with Cerenor.' she said. Then turning to Derca she held out her bow to him. In acknowledgement of such a singular honour he unsheathed his sword and handed it to Nal. They then took possession of their own weapons.

Only warriors of different cultures who have high regard for the fighting prowess of another do this. It does not happen often - especially from the Bana!

Formalities exchanged, Nal and Derca parted company, Nal leaped up onto the back of Cerenor and attached herself to the Draig with the cord of energy. The great Draig took off without a backward look from either of them.

I watched until Cerenors shape disappeared and then turned to speak with Derca, only to find he had already gone in the direction we had decided to take.

I looked again in the direction Cerenor and Nal had gone, then back to Derca's departing shape. I knew by the way he was holding himself that he would have rather been with Nal and Cerenor heading for action.

Instead he was stuck with a goody-goody spirit who was going head on with the most evil and powerful witch Darwan had ever seen, and he doesn't know how he is going to beat her. It was probably the words going through Derca's head and at that place in the land they were certainly my thoughts.

I was not even sure that the evil entity would be in Cail-dur it could be that she was leading her demonic legions in the direction of the Laic as I thought about it.

We walked in silence for a long time after we left the peak of Elinbroom. I left Derca to his own thoughts as he was missing the company of Nal. Apuss had dipped close to a distant mountainous horizon by the time the two of us spoke.

Derca said he recognised the terrain in the distance and although he was not familiar with the land we were tramping through he had walked the distant hills in events long gone, but he said no more on the subject.

Cerenor had told us that although Elinbroom was an island it had a fording point which separated the Tanaron Sea from the Lost Sea. We would be able to wade across to the land on the other side when the waters were still. She said Derca would know when the tide was still.

We carried on through the daylight of Apuss till we

came to a long slim curve of land, the land kept curving round till we were parallel with Elinbroom itself. We assumed that the lost sea was now between us and the isle of the Draig and the open sea on the other side of us was the Tanaron Sea.

We continued on our way to a point where the spit of land had straightened out and we could go no further as both seas had met. Looking sideways from the point we observed a very flat landscape.

The shoreline dead across the water from us was a grey shattering of rock and boulders with no pathway or peninsula to mark where the ford could end or start.

Derca said that the sea marks on the sides of the spit we were on told him the tide was running away and he would have to watch it carefully for a while.

Then once again we both became silent; each one of us alone in our individual world of thought, never a word passed between us; I looking across to the other side and Derca crouched watching the waters.

We had not long to wait, Derca stood up and said. 'The sea has quietened we now have still water till the tide moves.'

Having made his statement he looked straight across from where we stood and entered the water and I followed in his wake.

We were up to our knees in water but the sea bed we walked on was flat and free of any impediments. Derca kept his eyes fixed on a point on the other side, using it to keep his direction and to keep us on the submerged bridge.

We were not far from the grey rocky shore the water

was getting deeper and had gotten very cold. Derca said the tide was making inwards and possibly taking a cold current with it. We started to move more quickly and by the time we reached the boulders we were already waist high in the water.

We had to crawl up the rocky foreshore as it turned out to be steeper than it looked from the water level. Derca never halted as we got on level ground and almost sprinted through an empty plain of sparse vegetation, dappled now and then with dark green spongy moss and clumps of sorry looking reeds.

Apuss was poised on the horizon almost ready to pull down the dark curtain of night, Derca was still speeding ahead like a dark silent effigy of his self - silhouetted against the glare of the setting Apuss.

Then Apuss dropped behind the land leaving the terrain black. Derca, well ahead of me by this time, disappeared into the darkness.

The dying embers of Apuss's light streaked the sky with shards and slivers of red light, drifting clouds on the fringe of orange glow fed the darkness over the land.

I was so busy admiring the evening glow I had forgotten how far I had fallen behind Derca. His shout jolted me momentarily - I called back telling him to stay where he was as I wanted to watch the dark sky before the red maiden rose.

I heard the resignation in his voice when he answered and I could imagine him sitting cross-legged and shaking his head.

There is always a gap of pure darkness between the setting of Apuss and the rising of Ara. Rinnis is a hasty and erratic moon, at times she is above the land before Apuss has left the sky. On that night only the eccentricity of Ara's daughter would know, for some unknown reason Rinnis did not appear and all I could see was a clear starlit sky.

But standing in that place looking up to the starry sky - some fixed in strange looking patterns others moving in pulsating light, I could float upwards and spend eternity within the celestial mist of colours - all that is the universes; so much movement and so much mystery.

Invigorated by the cosmic night I took off to find Derca and exactly as I imagined he was sitting cross-legged on a rock. He does not say a lot but I know Derca loves the night sky; he has never shared that information but I have observed him being absorbed by it.

Rinnis had risen by the time we arrived at the side of a river flowing through a deep gully and as I looked down into its brooding black waters, which were reflecting the light of the red moon - I felt a stab of anguish.

Something terrible happened in that place - I sensed its ominous presence. As I looked closer, the reflected light of Rinnis appeared as though it was coming out of the water and not reflecting off it.

Derca said the way we were walking was bringing back memory, he said the guita elves drove a party of shade elves and their children into the waters and fired arrows into them - none survived. When he walked away I stayed and gazed into the dark river for a while imagining the horrific scene and blessing the place.

> *Dark – brooding – flowing river*
> *Cold – remorseless - fluid motion*
> *Sustaining life – taking life*
> *Nourishing – flourishing – relentless*
> *--------Uncaring*

A long time later we came to a rushing stream of white water, Derca said. 'We will stop here for a drink and rest for a while. We must have a plan in order to fulfil our mission no matter how foolhardy it may be.'

Derca then squatted down and cupped his hands in the water, splashing it over his face before he took a drink. I followed his example - then something strange took place, for a brief space in time the stream stopped flowing, the water in the pool stilled and became like a mirror. I sensed Derca at my side - silent and watching, ever on the alert.

The waters shimmered and the figure of a water sprite took shape. With a motion of her hand the sprite tickled the water with her outspread fingers then raised them in a sweeping motion which followed the curve of the stream.

As she fell back into the waters the echo of her laughter could be heard mingled with the now rushing, bubbling water. We looked at each other and as I met his eyes I knew we shared the same silent wonder, we laughed spontaneously and that broke the mood.

We walked side by side following that meandering stream; the appearance of the sprite had renewed our sense of purpose. We had never really lost it but the parting with Nal, and even Cerenor - although we only just met her, had unsettled us.

They were flying directly to battle with the dark forces, while we were on a journey that had no plan, no backup and no idea what we faced. I knew Derca did not fear death his only fear was that he might not be able to protect me from whatever we had to face.

I looked at him and thought I really don't know much about his history. From the very moment his feet touched the earth after he dismounted from Croin he had received a blasting from Elid, and I myself was aware of the fear and distaste that had emanated from the crowd around me.

When Elid was convinced he was indeed a messenger from Cimer she had accepted him for who he was. Not so Ruis, who shocked all around by his attack not only on Derca but on Elid herself. Then the Bana started taunting him, along with a few of the shade elves who hurled abuse at him.

Not once did he retaliate with words or actions, through it all he bore it with great fortitude. Much later Nal had said she had observed Traig and Bheir watching Derca closely and they said to the rest of the bana that their opinion of Derca was that he was a force of energy for the greater good of all.

I never felt any evil intent from Derca in fact it was quite the opposite. I felt a real strength about him, not only physical but strength of character - he had presence, integrity and loyalty.

He was an elf who served a powerful leader, Cimer

of the blue elves. He also rode a storm hawk and they were friends. Elid told me that the storm hawks chose their riders and were very astute in reading the character of other creatures.

I needed to know Derca's story and now was the time, so I asked him outright to tell me about his journey of life up to that time and place in the Laic where we first met. It was a fascinating tale and he told it in the voices of the many colourful characters he spoke about.

GORT

Derca's Story

The last war ended at the battle of the Fochd pass, Derca said he and his clan were fighting as mercenary soldiers alongside Cimer and his elves. During the breakup of forces in the aftermath, all the tribes returned to their lands - all with the exception of Cimer and his elves.

They carried on marching through their ancestral lands, stopping only to pick up their families on the way. They were joined by fragments of other tribes such as gruflics, river gaists, white goblins, shade elves and faolwarriors.

Another strange lot hung on to them and Derca described them as being very like shade elves but bigger and more powerful, they had handled themselves very well on the battlefield. They were called Garglas warriors, tall and strongly built their weapons were long two handed swords which they wielded with devastating results.

Cimer was very impressed by the fighting prowess of the black elves of Lael. He told Derca of his plans to lead his people out of the known lands and find new places to live. Croin knew of a place that would be ideal for the elves to settle in and so had agreed to lead them there.

Cimer invited the tribe of Lael to accompany him on the exodus. However, if they were not ready to depart now, then whatever event under Apuss occurred that made them feel it was right to move, they should look for his elves and himself. The tribe of Lael would be welcomed wherever the Blue Elfin had made their home.

Derca returned to the black island with his warriors, of the forces that fought on the side of evil from the black island, the dara-guel elves were spared and allowed back to their lands on the black island.

They were content for many spans of time but gradually got bolder, and so they started raiding the Lael lands again. Although the dara-guita elves did not take part in the war they were close kin to the dara-guel, and willingly joined the guel elves in the raids on Lael territory.

The tribe of Lael fought back and pushed the invaders back to their own lands but it came with a heavy price to both sides. It became clear to the clans of Lael that continued fighting to protect their lands would result in many deaths on both sides.

The Lael elves had no king or leader and they were essentially tribal, each tribe occupied various parts of the land. The ver-lael, which was Derca's tribe, lived along the coast. The macel-elves lived in the fertile plains between the sea coast and the mountains. The einn-elves were the mountain people and they were the clan that bore the brunt of the attacks from the guel and guita.

Each tribe was watched over by a chief, under him were a number of sub chiefs and they in turn watched over a community of families. Rank was not important, chiefs were responsible for the families under them; the tribal family was all important. The chiefs spoke for the people and whatever decisions had to be made would only be made with a majority vote.

It was a majority vote that favoured Derca's idea to sail away in search of Cimer, high king of the Blue Elfin, he was sure that Cimer would welcome an alliance with the tribe of Lael, all he had to do was find him.

The only clue to his whereabouts came from the great mariner, 'Big Jon Beet.' According to Jon his boat had been driven by the wind further than he had ever been before. All night the wind had howled like a thousand faolwarriors. Come the morning the wind had abated and he and his crew witnessed a magnificent sight.

Dead ahead of the boat Apuss was making his appearance. Flaming red was he, licking the now mirror-like waters with tongues of fire. Between the mariner and Apuss was a barrier of sea cliffs but the redness penetrated through the cliffs, the tongues of flame had turned to droplets of amber on what was surely a pass through the cliffs and he could just make out the masts of ships disappearing into the amber waters.

Then it was all gone, ships, entrance and the pathway of light. Big Jon referred to it as the 'Pass of the Tears of Apuss' and was convinced it was the ships of the blue elves.

He added that the pass was more like the entrance to a giant cave, as the two headlands were joined by a rocky bridge, Apuss and any ship had to be dead in line to see the passageway.

Part One of the Search for The Tears of Apuss

It was agreed by the high council and the women and men of Lael that Derca, with a handpicked crew, would sail away in search of Cimer.

If they were successful in finding where the Blue elves had settled and contact was made with Cimer, then any decisions that had to be made out of negotiations with the blue elves were to be made by Derca and his crew on behalf of the tribe of Lael. They were trusted to do all in their power to secure land and friendship with the blue elves.

Derca and his crew sailed away from the haven of Ver-lael. There was no farewell parade or crowd present as it was thought to keep to normality as much as possible so secrecy was the order of the day. Not a word was said to any traders or travellers that sailed into the havens of Lael.

Anybody asking after Derca would be told he was on a voyage to find new places and cultures to trade with, this was not an unusual journey for Derca and his crew as their ship 'The Ector' was well known in the faraway seas of Darwan.

It was Derca's intention to follow courses that Big Jon had told him about, he was heavily reliant on Jon's information about the sightings of the ships that bore the blue elves but he knew Jon's knowledge of seas and ships was second to none.

Jon had assured Derca that although he had only seen the topmasts of the galleys he had recognised the pennants of the blue elves. Derca held onto a hope that he might meet the mariner somewhere between where he was now and wherever the mystical pass of Apuss tears was.

As they lost the land and entered the belly of the Tuathen Sea the air changed drastically and hardly had they got the galley's head into the wind when they were blasted by a storm. They hardly saw Ara or Apuss for many an Araen.

The cyclical handover corresponds roughly to Earth's moon. Whereas the moon of Earth has a twenty eight day period, the moons of Darwan have fourteen days each. An Araen is the cycle of the rising moon Ara and the rising of the ringed moon Rinnis. Ara hides while Rinnis rules the night sky.

Occasionally during the transfer they both occupy the sky and pass each other in contra motion. Occasionally, after many cycles, neither of the two moons is in the sky for two nights, thereafter both moons appear for two nights - although at times Rinnis the fiery daughter of Ara disrupts the celestial sequence.

Food was in short supply as they could not cast their lines due to the ferocity of the storm. Water was saved from the squalls of rain which hammered the boat during the day and impaired visibility. The sail was holding grimly to its cross members and the rigging was bearing up well, they had no choice but to go with the wind and trust in providence.

At night the switching between Ara and Rinnis was at times hard to discern because of the heavy rain which wet the night as well as the day. Ara is a very luminous white moon and Rinnis the ringed moon is reddish. Easy to see in a clear starlit sky but not so easy when the visibility does not go much further than the top of the mainmast.

Derca had to keep track of time by the occasional glimpse of each of the moons. He only had the faded light of Apuss trying vainly to penetrate the drab air during the day. The same with the moons by night and with them the fleeting glance of different colour gave him a reckoning of sorts.

Derca said he was mesmerised by the sea, not only the mountainous waves but the water coloration, greens, blues, grey and white breakers driven by the force of the wind, an ever changing mosaic of water on either side of the boat, kept alive by the incessantly powerful storm-tossed ocean.

The noise of the wind and sea was coincident with the visual picture. He saw the wind as a wild creature whipping the sea into a frenzy as it tore at the surface of the water so that the sea reached up into the air as if to drag the wind down into its depths; a terrible raging fight between air and water, each of the elements trying to assert their power over the other

Awesome as the storm was, there was more to come as a most dramatic event took place which gave added impetus to the wildness of the night.

Rinnis was red and furious, the darkness behind accented her brilliance as she glared down on the frenzy below; her aura of fiery energy seemingly unleashing the elements of sound and light.

Smashes of thunder gave way to jagged spears of lightening that streaked the night sky all around, but none dared pass in front of the red maiden.

The wind never ceased its shrieking torment but the night display was obscured at intervals by ghosts of mist which teased the eyes of the mariners. Then, in an instant, slicing wind shredded cloud and ripped the sea to forge ahead in a tempestuous rage.

Derca and his crew were getting weaker, the more the storm raged so only staunch resolve kept their morale up. There was absolutely no peace on the ship as it bucked and rolled in the boiling motion. The relentless battering by a wind that knew no direction made keeping the boat afloat an exhausting duty.

Often they cried to the spirit of the air to make peace with the spirit of the remorseless sea. Until finally their cries were answered when one night Rinnis appeared very red and very clear, before she dipped below the horizon. Apuss followed suit when he rose, bright and fiery for the new day. The wind had stilled ---- the motion was ever present but the broken water had gone.

No land could be seen in any direction, not a bird in the sky, not a boat on the sea---nothing to give a clue to where land may be. They set about to put the boat in order as best they could; the sail was mended and damaged rigging replaced. They put lines over the side to catch fish as all had been at starvation level.

Then all at once the rolling motion of sea began to flatten. The air got very still --- the water took on the appearance of a polished mirror. Apuss's light reflecting off the now calm ocean hurt the eyes.

The boat ceased to move, not one of the crew moved or spoke as they waited in expectation of something, their breathing as still as the water beneath the boat. The silence was broken by a shout from the elvess Trera.

'Mers! mers!' All eyes looked in the direction she pointed. Scything through the water with her entourage was the mer elfess spirit of the sea called Shuira. Derca said the speed they came through the water was incredible. Coming alongside Shuira vaulted aboard the Ector and stood on the deck. One other mer elf came aboard and stood beside her leader.

Derca had met Shuira long ago and she had appeared as suddenly then as she did on that day. Her previous visit was to give him clear cut instructions where not to fish or intrude into a certain area while Rinnis was in the night sky.

She did not tell him why and Derca never asked. He carried out Shuira's instructions to the letter and made it known to his clan that the region of sea called the 'Weelic' was not to be entered at any time when Rinnis was present, it was a command that every galley master of the tribe of Lael obeyed.

If ever the elves needed help it was now and it seemed as though their cries had been answered by a visit from the Great Spirit and another who looked if she was on even status with Shuira.

Derca said Shuira stood taller than him, long limbed and sleek of body the fingers of her hands were splayed and webbed as were her feet. Her frontal body colour was a melting of blue and silver, her back was a darker blue, barred with black and green. Her facial looks were sharp with good bone structure. Her ears were pointed in the elfin way but more swept back and the black shine on her scalp looked like hair but it was in fact her skin.

When she spoke it sounded as if she was hissing out the words. To Derca she said. 'Long time since we last spoke. I think you are very lost, would you accept my help?'

Derca replied in a manner that befitted a powerful spirit entity such as Shuira. 'I am honoured to have you and your companion aboard the Ector, if we can serve in any way you only need ask and you are right, we are very lost and we readily accept your offer of help.' And with that said he bowed his head as did all of the crew.

Shuira paused before she replied turning slightly to face all of the crew she introduced her silent companion. 'This is the Azirema' --- at the sound of that name there was sharp intakes of breath and a few utterances - *The soul taker - mer angel - sea devil.*

Azirema stepped forward and held her hand up for silence. She was tall like Shuira and almost identical in looks, the difference was in the eyes. Her eyes were like deep pools of violet water and they held Derca and his crew in a trance-like state as she spoke.

'I am known by many names, to you this day I am Azirema and you have no need to fear me. I guide the souls of drowned mariners to their spiritual homes. Sometimes I take living creatures to join with us in the waters of this world we call Darwan. At any time during your ordeal in the storm I could have taken all of you but Shuira said otherwise.

Her far reaching perception told her that the safety of the Ector was paramount to the greater good of the land, so you were spared. However a price has to be paid and that is that I take one of your numbers to the sea.'

The crew of the Ector stood in silence, watching Azirema as she approached them she walked down the line of warriors, stopped at one and asked. 'What is your name elvess?'

The warrior answered and her voice was strong and clear. 'I am called Norrin and I am a warrior of Lael.'

Azirema held out both her hands and said. 'Then come with me Norrin of Lael, and I will make you a spiritual warrior of the sea.' So saying Azirema took Norrin the elvess into her arms and in front of all, Norrin changed and became like the mer.

With Azirema leading they both entered the water and as they did so a light breeze ruffled the sail. *Ever after when mariners wanted wind for their sails they would call to Norrin or Whispering Norrin as the Lael elves called her.*

Shuira addressed the crew of the Ector saying. 'Elves of Lael you have been well favoured by us spirits of the waters. Do not worry about your warrior, she now goes on to greater levels and will forever swim the great oceans of Darwan.

For you Derca and your crew, you may carry my effigy on your sail until the day you are called to the eternal life of the spirit. Now tell me where you want to be?'

Derca was staggered by events that had taken place on the deck of the Ector but he had the presence of mind to thank Shuira for the honour bestowed on his ship. He then described the place that they sought and asked if Shuira knew of it.

She told him it was known to them as the pass of the yellow shore.

Shuira said she would tell her mer-fins to take the Ector to the pass of Apuss's tears and they would guide the ship through. Thereafter he should keep the landward side of yellow stone and to keep that shore for a full night of Ara, in the following light of day you will know where to berth.

Shuira then dived over the side, Derca watched the waters where she disappeared and a strange feeling came over him. The feeling that he would call on Shuira one more time before his life race ran out.

The crew had been watching the Mer-fins they were large playful fish that were just as happy on the surface as below it. Grey with dark colouration on their backs, easily identified by the prominent snout and the large dorsal fin.

The rest of the daylight of Apuss and all of the night of Ara was spent following the mers. It was a very serene voyage the light wind that was blowing was enough for a leisurely cruise and to provide for himself and his crew a peaceful interlude after all the dramatic events that had taken place.

As Ara left the night sky the mers altered course, they made a sharp turn and slowed their pace. We followed suit and as the Ector's head lined up with the direction our guides had taken the mers stopped and took up position on either side of the boat.

At that part in his story we stopped and had a drink by the side of a fast running stream, a noisy - bubbling melody of water. We sat there by the swift flowing torrent - it seemed to be at one with Derca's story.

He started his tale again but this time he moved ahead to speak of the exodus.

The Exodus

Derca's elves had left the Black Island on a night that the Darwan sky was lit by Ara and Rinnis for five days, this happens once in twenty and ten cycles. It was known as the time of 'Edila' and during Edila all the tribes of the known Darwan lands feasted, danced and generally had a good time.

Because they were an island race part of the celebrations entailed ships laden with males, females, children and sometimes animals sailing out from their havens. The boats were decorated with coloured banners and followed a chief's galley which at a predetermined distance from the shore lay at anchor.

All the other ships then sailed in-line astern until they formed a great circle round the chief's flagship. After the review, as it was called, the boats all returned to their havens and the celebrations continued on the land.

This was very much the case on the Black Island, Derca knew the guita and guel tribes would be wasted on strong liquor for many days and nights. So even if they came out of their stupor earlier than usual it would be too late to do anything about it.

As they sailed away from their ancestral homeland the elves beheld a spectacular sight in the night sky. Many blue twinkling stars had formed the outline of a ship, a random ship in a sea of stars, the elves of Lael could not have asked for a better omen.

Ahead of them they had the bright star Linar to guide them, ships from all around the coastline of Lael filled with males, females and young ones of the clans of Lael sailed away from the shores of their Black Island of Lael forever.

All the ships captains had their sailing orders, which were simple enough - that they were to follow Linar until the rising of Apuss. Keeping Apuss behind them throughout the day would keep them on course for Liner's night time guidance.

This was to go on for four nights of Liner and four days of Apuss. On the fourth day of Apuss as she descended, her blood red reflections on the water would point them in direction of land.

The red waters show a stretch of narrow water between two hills, it looks more like a hole in the cliffs as the two hills are joined at the top by a natural bridge - this was known as the Pass of Apuss's Tears.

Once through the gap the pilot ship would lead the fleet to a sheltered bay easy to recognise because of its yellow stone coastline.

The ships were to anchor within the Tears and wait until all ships were present. Water and herds of bos were plentiful on the land so the wait for slower ships would be comfortable.

The leading ship was piloted by Reiren, high chief of the clans of Lael - behind him in lines of three abreast were the galleys filled with the families and stores. On the flanks of the serried ranks of the ships were the war galleys, two for every four rows of three, these were the fighting ships and it was their job to herd the large fleet to their ultimate destination.

Just out of sight behind the armada was Derca's ship with his warriors this was the tail ship whose job was to shadow the fleet and to ensure they were not being followed.

On the afternoon of the fourth day one of Derca's elves spotted a ship in the direction in the way of Ica. Derca decided to alter course and close up to the vessel which was barely visible on the far horizon. By the time they had got close enough to the other ship to identify it Apuss was starting to dip, Ceara who was the elf that first spotted the ship shouted ---------

'It's the Oliv-Losai Derca.'

Derca agreed. 'It's big Jon all right, he will have seen the banner of Lael and knows we are no danger to him. Close up to the Losai and we will have words.'

Hardly had Derca spoken when they saw the stem of the Oliv-Losai turning in their direction, it did not take long for the two vessels to meet up. The boats remained apart but close enough to jump aboard. The gun'le of the Losai was slightly lower than the galley, Derca shouted to big Jon. 'Can Ceara and I come aboard Jon?'

Big Jon gave a wave of his hand and howled back. 'Aye come aboard the two of you.'

Derca and Ceara as one sprang from the deck of the galley and landed on the rail of the Losai, running down the rail they jumped onto the deck where big Jon stood.

'Showing off again Derca?' He bellowed as he advanced to welcome the two elves. 'What brings you to these waters or should I say what mission are you on now?' At the same time he shouted to his two sons Gat and Mora to sort out food and drink for the guests. 'Come down below friends and we will have the comfort of a snort of rotgut and fish from the waters of mer'. So saying he led the elves down below deck.

When they were seated and had a dram of rotgut Derca and Ceara took it in turns to tell the story of the exodus and why it came about, the sons had joined them at the table by this time and had laid the fish meal on the centre of the table.

Big Jon and his sons didn't touch their food as they sat in silence, listening intently to the elves describing the events that had pushed the tribe of Lael to leave their homelands to cross the sea of Crom to lands unknown.

Big Jon motioned them to help themselves to the food; after the guests had taken food Big Jon then took his share, before the crew, as was the right of master of the vessel. For a short time they chewed the fish and tasted the rotgut - nobody spoke, such was the emotion.

It was big Jon who finally broke the silence. 'So Derca where are you headed, I know you of old so there must be somewhere you have in mind and that's a mighty big fleet of Lael galleys we spotted a while back.'

Derca's answer was immediate. 'You were dead right Jon when you said you saw the ships of the blue elves slipping through the pass of Apuss's tears. Ceara and I sailed through the gap of red water but we did not anchor in the bay but kept on going.

We followed Shuira's instructions by keeping a shore of yellow rock on our shadow side. We had land to both sides of us for two risings of Apuss then gradually the land on our steering side began to fall away and finally we were left with open sea. We held the shelter of the shore for another four days until the land became mountains and the shore line consisted of high cliffs.'

'Just like your homeland.' Jon put in.

'Exactly, and it was not long before we came to a break in the cliffs, an opening that led to a sheltered bay. It was an incredible piece of luck that we spotted it and had we not been sailing so close to the land we would have passed it by.

We anchored in the bay and left a crew aboard with instructions if we were not back in a certain passage of time they were to take the Ector back to the gate of Tears and wait a spell.

Ceara and I with six of our clan waded ashore onto a sandy beach, when we were all out of the water we gathered in a circle and thanked the spirits of the air, sea and the land for our good fortune then we turned our faces to Apuss and absorbed the energy from her light and the goddess of the sky returned our thanks by flaring briefly.'

At Derca's statement Big Jon and his sons gasped and they all voiced praises to Apuss.

The elf continued with his story but could not disguise the excitement in his words. 'As we stood there on that golden beach Ceara named it 'Edila."

Jon looked at Ceara and said. 'You named it after the 'Time of Edila' and that is when you departed your island, because of the celebrations it was easier to slip away unnoticed.'

Derca laughed and said. 'Yes Jon and to make it better Ceara conjured up a ship in the sky to send us on our way. Not only is he a much feared warrior he is one who can read messages from the wind, his words and thoughts are well respected amongst our people.'

Gat and Mora were so taken by the elves that they had been hanging on to every word Derca and Ceara had said and this latest statement just blew them away.

Mora, his face a picture, said to Ceara. 'Are you a sorcerer?'

Ceara laughed and replied in a light hearted tone. 'No Mora I am not a sorcerer, I am an elf who has been gifted by the spirits and I use my gifts to help my fellow clanelfs as much as possible.'

Big Jon spoke again. 'Come, come elf men, I am anxious to hear about your exploration of this new land.'

Ceara took up the story. 'We split into two groups of four after we thanked great Apuss. Derca took Aril, Torma and Dara; I took Serl, Gera and Sera-ni.'

'An elder elfess in a black elf fighting section of males - I thought the elder females were always in charge of an all-female section?' Jon's question was answered by Ceara.

'It is not that unusual Jon, some of the elder elvess take charge of male sections - they are easily the match of the male section leaders. They are strong and very fast they also have an intuition which is quite uncanny and Sera-ni, whom I mentioned, is certainly on equal status with the Bana.' Ceara's statement had impressed Big Jon who held his fists up in support of what he had heard.

'We had decided to split into two groups because it would allow us to explore the surrounding land in as short a time as possible. Derca's group was to head in the way of Ulas for as long as Apuss was in the sky then as she dipped the group would rest and eat while they waited for Ara to show them the way.

They then followed Ara until he gave way to Apuss, then they switched to the way of Ica.' Once again Big Jon cut Ceara short.

'So your group went the opposite way to Derca's - followed Ara - then to Ulas and met somewhere in the middle, you explored the land in box shapes - very clever and the speed you elves go meant you covered a lot of ground.'

'Right again Jon, we found the land very rich in bird and animal life; thick forests and high hills and a coastline of unforgiving cliffs. We also encountered a surprise but I will let Derca tell you about that.' Ceara held his palm towards Derca.

Part Two of The Search for The Tears of Apuss

'We came out of a forest onto the shores of a lochan and there perched on a rock was a blue elfess, our presence didn't seem to bother her in the least.' At that Derca held up his hand and said. 'I know what you're going to say Jon - and I agree, you were right about the blue elf ships passing through the gap of tears because we have met the blue elf clan.

And another surprise for you Jon, the elfess we met answered to Mirna who is ----' he paused for effect holding Jon's baffled expression.

Jon couldn't contain himself anymore. 'Well?' He bellowed.

Derca put him out of his misery. 'Well here's a surprise, she is none other than the daughter of Cimer.'

Gat and Mora both shouted in unison at their father. 'Jon who is Cimer?'

Jon replied, but his voice tone intimated that he was taken aback at the mention of Cimer's name.

'Cimer is a great chief of the blue mountain elves, he led his race long ago, after the dark wars, to a land far away and was never heard of again, until now that is.

So Derca, you and your clan are at the point of no return through the gate of tears to another beginning, a new land, new friends and powerful friends at that. So where are your galleys?'

'As we speak our ships with all our people aboard should be entering the gap of Apuss Tears where they will rest up for a while in the crescent bay within. They wait for our galley to lead them to Edila. We have left the Black Island and we have all sworn that no matter what happens we will never set foot on the stones of Lael ever again.'

But big Jon wanted to know more. 'I'm still waiting for more news of Cimer, did you meet him Derca? Where does he live and who is the mother of his daughter? And another thi----'

Jon was halted in mid-sentence by Ceara. 'Before we go any further Jon we want another shot of your rotgut, it may be a long time ere we share a drink together and our throats are getting dry with all this talk, am I right Derca?'

'You are very right Ceara, come on Jon you are not usually slow with the refreshments and we need to move soon before Ara moves the tide.'

No sooner had Derca spoken than a flagon of brew

was placed on the table along with bread and more fish. Jon apologised for not attending to them sooner, but he said his head was still reeling at the news of the tribe of Lael leaving their island and then the reappearance of great Cimer - it was all too much to take in.

They ate and drank and for a while the conversation was light hearted, with Jon's sons quizzing the backside off Ceara, who seemed happy to feed their curiosity. He was enjoying their youthful exuberance; however Jon had to get back to the saga of Cimer.

'Right you pair, I want to know more of Mirma and Cimer before you take off.' So saying he filled all the goblets up again and raised his one in a toast to Elid Silverhair and her pixies who do a good job making rotgut. They all joined in on the toast -shouting out. 'To Elid and her pixies!'

After another two snorts of rotgut Derca got round to finishing his tale of the meeting with Mirma. He could see that big Jon and his sons were desperate to hear the tale to its end so he didn't drag it out any longer; and Ara waits for no elf.

'Yes Jon, where was I?'

'The meeting of Mirma - Cimer's daughter.' Jon was hungry for the story and Derca knew it.

Ceara also knew Derca was winding Jon up so he stepped in. 'We arrived just as Mirma was telling Derca who her father was, she was not at all intimidated by the presence of so many of us. We introduced ourselves individually and she took to Sera-ni at once. Then Mirma asked if they would be happy for her to escort them to Cimer.'

Ceara turned to Gat and Mora and said. 'Brace yourselves boys for what I say next. Mirma appeared to be on her own but she was not, she gave out a loud piercing whistle.

The next thing we felt was a great disturbance of the air then a huge black shape landed almost in the midst of us, needless to say we formed a defensive line and drew our weapons.'

Taking the lads by surprise with this twist to the tale, Ceara jumped onto the table at the same time drawing the duan and adopted the defensive position. It was too much for the boys they yelled out. 'What was the black shape Ceara?'

Ceara shrugged off his aggressive stance, sheathed his blade and sat down again. 'It was a giant bird as big as a gurk but fiercer looking - feathers as black as night and a beak that looked as if it would pierce stone. It was a black storm hawk.'

Silence reigned - then Big Jon spoke. 'Aye Derca there are queer things going on these days, your tribe leaving the Black Island; the appearance of Cimer and Storm Hawks. I haven't heard mention of them in many an age. Anyway, get back to your tale as I am anxious to know about Cimer himself.'

Derca took up the story. 'Mirma laughed at our reaction and asked us to sheath our weapons. She then introduced us to the storm hawk that was known as Croin. Mirma then proposed that we should set off to meet her father in the land of the blue elves. I said the warriors of our ship will be getting anxious as to our whereabouts, so how far was it to the place where Cimer lives? My question was answered by another whistle from Mirma, as she did this she tilted her face to the sky and blew out the whistle long and slow, it seemed to resonate in the air for a time after she stopped.

Then far up in the sky another black shape appeared, just a black dot to start with then as it plummeted from the sky we saw that it was another storm hawk, and easily bigger than Croin.' There was a sharp intake of breath from Gat and Mora and big Jon leaned further over the table.

At this point Ceara took up the tale. 'Mirma introduced the new arrival as Oren and continued by saying. Oren is female and my usual companion but Croin here was closer so he answered the first whistle. Might I suggest that you choose two of your elves to accompany you to meet Cimer, I will ride Oren with one other and you and one of your companions can ride with Croin?

At this big Jon boomed out. 'By the spirit of the seas Derca - you didn't trust yourself to Nindril of the air?'

'Now Jon, Nindril is kind to our sails as we go about our business in the waters so why would he not be with me in the air?'

'Well that's true, but he can be mischievous at times, and speaking for myself I would rather have a heaving deck below my feet than have my ass tickled by the feathers of a storm hawk.'

Ceara remarked. 'You have a way with words Jon.'

The conversations with Big Jon and his sons were most enjoyable, the elves could have stayed all night but the tide was almost on the turn so they had to bid farewell to the big mariner and his sons. As a parting gift Jon gave the elves a basket of fish, which they received gratefully then they boarded their own vessel and took the tide.

As they bore away from the Oliv-Losai, Derca watched Jon's boat from the stern of the Ector. Ceara joined him and asked him what he was thinking about.

'Oh I am thinking about many things Ceara, mostly about our move but also our island home that we have left behind.'

'You are not having doubts Derca?' Ceara slapped his friend on the shoulder as he asked the question. 'Remember the Bana ger left their island long before we thought of moving.'

Derca sat on the rail of the boat and looked at Ceara he paused for a while before he spoke. 'No doubts Ceara, but I worry about the island itself. I hope it does not become a bastion for evil.

The guita elves were burrowing deeper into the earth and I wonder for what purpose and who is behind it. You know as I do that the guita tribe are strong and powerful but they are not renowned for their thinking ability. Whatever is going on it is someone or something else behind it.'

'You worry too much about the land Derca, it was there before we were and it will still be there after all the dark elves are gone. We are headed for a new beginning, a new way of life, and for once neighbours we can get on with.

This is our time Derca, look back no more. Forward is the prow of our boat, we have the sign of Shuira on our sail, so my friend look ahead and enjoy the life that awaits us.'

Ceara spoke words of wisdom and Derca recognised them, he turned and faced forward. His crew were all facing the direction the ship was taking and they were laughing and talking about the new land they were headed to. He turned to Ceara and said. 'You are right Ceara as usual.'

Derca told me during the drinking spree with big Jon and his sons that he never actually got round to telling him about his one to one meeting with Cimer

I had to laugh at that as I could imagine the frustration of Big Jon when the effects of the rot gut wore off. So I asked Derca about the outcome of the meeting between him and Cimer.

Derca was deposited by the storm hawk right outside Cimer's lodge, Cimer was standing there and it felt as if nothing had happened in between.

They stood in silence for a long time regarding each other, both looking for traces of what they were, within the eyes of both men was the telling of the mind-sets.

Elves and storm hawks also stood in silence, waiting in expectation for the silent interrogation to end. When it did it was with both men laughing and clapping each other on the shoulders.

Cimer addressed the motley crowd by proclaiming that the Lael elves were friends and would be treated as guests as long as they stayed. He then called for the great lodge to be made ready.

He then asked the storm hawks if they would take the news to the outlying tribes and invite representatives of each clan to make haste and come to a grand meeting at the great lodge of Pitalonagh.

By this time there was fair sized population of various life entities gathered about, some had never seen black elves before and were keen to see and speak to the warriors of Lael. There was much commotion and more beings of the land filtered into the crowds already there.

Derca and his elves were swept along with the crowd in the direction of the grand lodge where great stone tables were being laden with food and drink. Above the melee Derca could hear the sound of the blue elves' war pipes thankfully they were playing tunes of joy and revelry.

After the third day of Apuss events had slowed down, the main thrust of the meetings in the grand lodge having been settled in quick time almost if it had been pre-ordained.

All tribes had called for the elves of Lael to come and settle within the Tears of Apuss. They had even agreed where the black elves could live, taking into account that the three tribes all had different environments. Derca and his tribe were to have the coastline where they landed; the Macel-Lael were to have the huge plain and forests adjoining Derca's tribe. The Einn-Lael, or mountain people were to be settled away from the other two tribes far by the way of Ulas. Further still were the mountains of the storm hawks so they would not be isolated.

Derca said the Einn-Lael were used to being isolated, they were the tribe that bore the brunt of the attacks from the geala and guita elves. They were undoubtedly the fiercest clan of all the elfin races they proved that long ago at the Fochd pass.

The Landing

The black elf population of Lael were met on the shores of a place called Arta du by Cimer and many of his people.

The welcome was warm indeed, for each ship a party of blue elves had been delegated to help and settle the passengers. They would be responsible for the settling of the dark elves from the party on the beach to the permanent living areas.

Cimer himself addressed the tribe of Lael from an elevated position on the top of a sandy mound his booming voice was heard by all.

All was quiet as Cimer voiced a declaration of unity. 'We of the tribe of Liath welcome the tribe of Lael to their new lands. We are of different tribes but we share common ancestry and though the names of the fathers and mothers of our past have been lost in the mists of time we are still linked in mind and body.

Elf for elf, strength in unity and an inherent belief in the day spirit of Apuss and the night spirits of Ara and Rinnis.'

After Cimer had spoken a great tumult arose from the assembled elves, shouts and cheers accompanied the drums of the black elves and the shrill screams of the war pipes of the blue elfin.

All along the shoreline of Arta du temporary shelters had been erected, fires lit and food prepared. Havens had been marked out for the individual shipping communities and the same for the forest and hill families.

Although the actual time of Edila had passed a new one came to being and it was named in memory of the coming of the Lael elves. It was called 'Arta edila' and the first celebration at the first landing was the party of all parties. Derca said the bay where they first landed and named Edila was at the extreme end of their newly acquired territory and was held sacred by the Lael elves.

As well as the blue and black elves, many other life entities appeared. Some had made long journeys to join in the celebrations. There were gruflics, river gaists, white goblins, gargs, faolwarriors, shade elves and other unrecognisable creatures.

He also said that he saw a band of the same creatures that he had seen at the great battle of the Fochd Pass. They had the build of faolwarriors but bigger but they also had an elfin look about them.

Mirma told him they were cave elfs and lived in the Anich Mountains, which were also home to the storm hawks.

Croin and Oren had appeared with some more of their kin and they caused a stir with the younger black elves. As the partying got under way the storm hawks were in great demand, flying young elves along the sands of Arta du.

Another surprise was the appearance of two faeries amongst the throng; by their very presence a sense of security and hope prevailed.

Powerful entities as they were, they walked through the revelry laughing and talking to all, even the gargs couldn't help their faces breaking into a smile at such wondrous beings.

By the time Arta edila was over many friendships had been formed between the newcomers and the many races that had appeared to welcome the Black elves of Lael to their new land.

Derca had become very friendly with one of Cimer's household elves by the name of Cendor and it was a friendship which carried on through many events of good times and tragedies.

He then went on to tell me about Mirma and her part in the lead up to a fierce battle.

Mirma's Story

Mirma was very young when she accompanied her father to the lands of Dargal, which they knew as Tirangorm, it was a fantastic world to grow up in. She would forage far and wide within the bounds that the blue elves had made, and sometimes outwith which did not please her father.

Her father, who was Cimer king of blue elves, could not stop her from exploring the lands as he recognised she was a free spirit. So they compromised, she would have a tracker on her tail.

This would be one of Cimer's elves and he would give her plenty of her own time because the elf in question would follow a good distance behind. By his skill he would track her so that they would know exactly where she was at any time.

Mirma agreed reluctantly, but in her mind she knew it would put her father's mind at rest and the land out with the settlements was a still a stranger to them, there might be dangers out in the wilds.

The elf that Cimer entrusted his daughter to was called Renil he was a superb tracker and a fierce warrior. He had fought in the front line with Cimer at the last battle and was one of the kings closes friends.

With the appearance of the Lael elves, Mirma made new friends and her wanderings ceased for a time. Cimer was easier in mind when she had the odd urge to wander off because she would head by the way of one of the Lael settlements.

However a time came when Mirma took off on one of her longest walks of exploration. She left the elf settlement and crossed over a mountain range that her father had called after her - the Mountains of Mir.

She then followed the river Avin all the way down through the Raglan plains to the sea of Sol. She bypassed the coast of the sea elves of Lael and lingered for a while with a community of macel elves.

There were blue elf settlements in the Mountains of Mir along the banks of the Avin, the Raglin plains and all along the coastal cliffs of the Sol Sea. So she was not alone and she was well known among all the elfs of the land.

At the mouth of the river Avin there lived a colony of river gaists who had arrived with the blue elves during the exodus. Mirma stopped with the gaists because she found them good fun especially the gaist children, they were so cute. Mirma used to think what a shame they had to turn into adult gaists.

After she left the gaists she made her way up the rugged cliff coastline of the sea of Sol. She came across a settlement of white goblins and was welcomed in by the inhabitants.

Mirma did not stay long with the goblins, much to the dismay of the young goblins as they all adored her and were amazed by her pointed ears. They kept pulling her ears, so much so that she thought they must have stretched beyond their usual size.

Before she left, the chief goblin of the tribe told her that when she came to a rocky promontory which resembled a gurks head she was not to go any further. He said the 'Gurks Head Rock' marked the border of the lands that Cimer claimed.

Beyond the rock the coastline and the land got very rugged and almost impossible to pass through, known as the cutting rocks because the boulders and cliff faces have sharp edges to them.

The goblin warned Mirma of another danger, beyond the cutting rocks the land sloped down to fertile plains and soft undulating hills. The country was home to sker goblins and further on to the way of Ulas was the homelands of the gel demons. They were not demons in the true sense of the word but they fought and behaved like demons.

Ever warlike, the two tribes had been engaged in raids and skirmishes with each other for as long as they had been neighbours, although never actually in open warfare. However a strange peace seemed to have descended on the two tribes of late.

After thanking the goblins for their kindness Mirma set off for the Gurks Head Rock in anticipation of seeing it because of the description. Mirma had never seen a gurk, she could only visualise one from elf talk.

It did not take her long to find the rock formation, even though she had never seen a gurk she recognised it because it resembled the head of a storm crow. Not that she would be imparting that piece of information to Croin and friends.

She stood on the head of the rock for quite some time gazing seaward; where she focused her attention to the lands and coastline where the sker goblins and the demons lived.

It looked inviting, especially the coastline which stretched a long way from sight; it was lined by ochre coloured cliffs, white sands lay between the cliffs and the blue sea; so much colour, so calm and so devoid of any kind of living entity. Surely such beautiful scenery could not disguise evil.

Mirma's mind was made up, she hit the beach at a trot, determined to see what lay at the end of the cliff lined shore. As she got closer her vision made out a sheer cliff feature which protruded into the sea.

The cliff that jutted into the sea had different coloration from the ochre cliffs and was also higher. The height carried on into the land then disappeared in a curve out of sight.

There was no turning back, Mirma's curiosity was in control - she had to see what was beyond the wall. The ochre cliffs were easy to climb as she shinned up a rocky spout with no difficulty.

Once on top she did not take long to reach the

rocky parapet, because that is what it was, a huge stone rampart curving out of sight on the landward side. As she approached a sudden feeling of unease took her which made her cautious.

Curiosity was still in her head but caution was in command as she closed up to the rock wall in a stealthy crouch. Carefully she slithered up the sloping wall and looked over, what she saw made her gasp and duck her head.

Taking a breath she ventured another look. On the other side, within the ring of rock, was a huge bay and on it were ships of a type she had never seen before. The shoreline below the cliff was alive with fierce looking creatures moving about as if practicing some kind of movements.

She had hardly taken in the events below when strong arms grabbed her; clamped her mouth and pulled her from her perch.

Still holding her a voice whispered. 'It is I, Renil, keep quiet - sker goblins have very acute hearing.'

Mirma nodded her head and Renil released her. Before she could say anything Renil got her to her feet and keeping his words to a whisper he told her to crawl with him to the edge of the rampart.

She nodded in acknowledgement and followed Renil's lead, hugging the smooth rock as if it was her best friend. Slowly they got their eyes in a position where they could see what was taking place all the while careful not to skyline themselves.

Their black hair blended well with the strange rock formation that was darkened all along its rim. There was so much activity going on below, with some warriors practicing battle drills and others loading stores on board the galleys which were moored just off the shore.

The boats were not familiar to Renil, even the skiffs which were being used to transfer goods from shore to ship were odd looking. One thing was clear, the forces below were preparing to strike, but where?

In the eye of his mind Renil went through a process of division and placement - the number of warriors below far exceeded the amount of space in the fleet of galleys.

Therefore he surmised that there was an embarked force and a land force was being assembled, and by the warriors he recognised there was only one way they were headed ----- in the direction of Ica to the lands of Cimer.

Slowly the two elves slid down from the parapet. Renil motioned Mirma to run ahead and to make all speed as he matched her speed from behind and ran her back in the direction she had come. They did not halt or speak until they reached the other side of the Gurk's Head.

When they stopped, he turned and faced Mirma and spoke, not in anger or haste, but very slowly and deliberately.

'We have just witnessed an army making preparations for an assault on our lands, we two have to alert our people. We will carry on to the settlements of the white goblins and from there you must whistle to the wind and call for a storm hawk.'

They sped on and in no time were at the first of the goblin houses. On seeing two elves appearing at high speed it did not take much working out on the goblin's part that something was up.

A goblin called Fer spoke first to enquire what the haste was about and he listened attentively to what Renil told him.

'Fer, you must gather all your people together and head for the lands of the Lael elves, you will be safe with them. I fear there is a large army of goblins and demons ready to make war on us.'

Renils calm assurance rubbed off on Fer and his companions as they took in his words and without more ado he moved off to spread the word --- Fer muttered something about 'So that's why they stopped fighting each other.'

Renil turned to Mirma who was completely at a loss for words and probably a bit of fear had crept in. He took her gently by the shoulders and spoke softly to her, calming her as much as he could as he needed Mirma to communicate with the storm hawks.

Her words came out in a bubble of dialogue, what Renil could make out was that Mirma was afraid of what Cimer would say to her, he would be so angry - it was her fault - she should have listened to him - what am I supposed to do now?

Renil shook his head at the frantic rave and said to her. 'I think Cimer might be more interested in the army that might be approaching and he would be well pleased that you warned him. Now will you take some calm off me and whistle up a storm hawk?'

Mirma calmed and turned and faced Apuss and after a few deep breaths she whistled into the air long and slow.

They waited by the house of Fer on their own, the goblins had all gone out of sight - they did not waste time clearing out. Renil told Mirma that when her hawk arrived she was to fly directly to her father and tell him exactly what they had seen at the end of the ochre coast.

Renil then said he was going to alert the Lael elves, he would soon overtake the goblins and he had already told them to warn the outliers on the way.

They had not long to wait when Oren the female storm hawk alighted beside them, she knew by the look of Mirma that something terrible had occurred, or was ready to.

Renil said. 'Don't delay, tell Oren once you are in the air.' He watched as the great bird took off and found her direction then she headed at speed for the habitation of Cimer.

Storm Hawks can communicate in voice and thought and when Oren was informed of the events Mirma had witnessed she put out her thoughts to others of her kind.

By the time they had reached the land of the blue elves there were many hawks in the air escorting Oren and Mirma.

Cimer was standing by the great lodge when his attention was caught by the sight of a flock of storm hawks heading directly for him. The leading Hawk had a rider and it looked very like Mirma. Something was very wrong because hawks do not flock unless they are on the move somewhere; they usually fly solitary or in pairs.

Picking their spots clear of the huts all the storm

hawks landed, Oren landed as near as possible to Cimer and Mirma dismounted. She ran to her father and started to tell him what she had seen.

Cimer listened in silence and when Mirma finished her tale he gazed at her and nodded then he looked around. Many of the blue elves had gathered because of the presence of the storm hawks in the air and they had heard what Mirma had said.

Cimer's elves looked to their king to hear his words there was no fear or doubt in their eyes as they waited for his response.

In silent contemplation Cimer regarded the storm hawks who were staring back at him - impassive - silent - waiting.

When he spoke his words were fearless and carried conviction, he was a warrior of many battles and a king of a powerful race; he also had strong allies.

'My people, once again an enemy has gathered and is heading for us or our neighbours, we are fortunate that we are forewarned of this event and therefore have time to prepare.

However speed is essential. Mirma tells me that Renil is on the way to make the elves of Lael aware of the enemy as they might be the first to be assaulted since the tribe of Lael guard the coastline and the plains and hills beyond it.'

He stopped as another storm hawk landed close by, it was Croin who was king of all storm hawks and close friend of Cimer and Derca of Lael.

Cimer addressed him directly. 'Croin you have no doubt heard of the events that are taking place by the way of Ulas, I need the wings of you and your kin.'

Croin said. 'I respect you for asking Cimer but there is no need, we are here and many more can be here if needed. Tell us what we are to do and we will gladly comply.'

Cimer thanked Croin for his support and went on to tell him what he wanted the hawks to do.

'Make haste to all the inhabitants of our lands and tell the warrior clans what is going on, if Renil hasn't already done so. If you can fly some of the leaders back to me, especially Derca, I would be most grateful.'

And yourself Croin, can you fly as near to the Black Rim as possible and keep a good height so that the warrior force below will not be aware of you. If possible you may see how the forces are to be distributed and what direction they take.'

Croin dipped his beak and without further ado took off immediately and headed for the sky above the Black Rim.

Cimer then turned to his elves that had gathered in great numbers about him, alerted by the flock of storm hawks.

He addressed them and his words carried the power of a warrior king, his resolute tones carried through the air and were heard by elves making their way into the settlement.

'Elves and elvesses, words have reached me of coming events that give me great concern. A vast number of galleys have been seen beyond the rock of the Gurk's Head, also many armed warriors were observed making their way out of the Black Rim.

We have been fortunate in our time here and we have lived in continuity with the land, sea and air, only taking such as we need. We have moved from lands once before - we will not be moving again!

This time we are not alone and we have a great advantage - the storm hawks - they will be our watchers in the sky. Even as you listen to my words the hawks are alerting our forces by the coasts and forests, they are also watching the movements of the force that I will call an enemy.

We are fishers of the sea and harvesters of the land, many of our kin are shepherds of the trees in the great forests of Arta du. Others are solitary wanderers of the hills and mountains.

Whatever calling they answer to there is one that calls louder than any other - the call of the clan and the warrior spirit that makes us who we are. I ask that every elvess and elf that can carry a sword arm themselves and prepare for battle.

All the young of the tribe are to be sheltered in the caverns behind the waterfall of the Fion waters. Runners carrying the blue banner with the white lightening symbol are being dispatched to the length and breadth of the lands to alert all of our people to the imminent confrontation.'

Cimer got no further with his speech as the huge winged shape of a stormhawk descended - hovering briefly to allow the elves below to move out of his way. On landing his mighty wings were hardly folded when off jumped two riders who were instantly recognised and acknowledged by the surrounding crowd.

The unique style of dress and the yellow skin colour identified the riders as black elves, both were well known to all in the lands of Arta du. They approached Cimer who welcomed the twosome and shouted out their introductions to the assembled crowd.

An elf called Cendor shouted back. 'We would never have known!' That brought a ripple of laughter from the assembly.

Derca and Seri-ni were in fighting order - the males wear bones in their hairtail (rumoured to be parts of their ancestors) the female warriors shorten their hair for impending battles.

Both black elf warriors were resplendent in selc armour and were fully armed and ready for anything.

Derca stopped recounting his story for a while; the rushing stream we had been sitting beside had ceased its headlong flow and was stilled as if waiting for Derca's story to end. He cupped his hands and took a few swallows of the sparkling water then carried on talking.

'You know Lael, I have been fighting all my life and most of the time it has been for the freedom of my race to go about their lives in peace. When we joined up with Cimer's elves and settled in our own territories it was the longest time that the race of Lael had never been embroiled in conflict.

It was an idyllic time in Arta du, we had settlements

of creatures all around us and the Einn clan even had white goblins and gargs integrated within their bounds. We all were as one with each other.

When Ecril the storm hawk arrived with words of warfare I should have felt disappointment that peace was about to be shattered. But that was not so - I felt an energy filling my mind and body, Sera-ni was near-hand and I shouted to her to get her fighting gear on.

She never asked why, just went to her habitation and donned her selc armour and in that space got a fellow elf to cut her hairtail off. By the way she accepted my words it was as if long awaited expectation had come to pass.

While Ecril waited, I told Ceara what was going on, the appearance of the storm hawk did not cause a stir as they were frequent visitors to our lands.

As I put my fighting gear on I asked Ceara to have certain members of our tribe sent out with our gathering symbol - a black banner with the yellow star of Shuira. Also he was to organise the gathering of the young ones and shepherd them to Cimer's stronghold.

Ceara said he would get the ships crewed and get them out to sea so that they would not be locked in, he would get Dender the elf healer to take care of the young.

I could feel that the vibrations from Sera-ni and Ceara were the same as what I had felt myself, it was what I would call - a battle lust. My mind and body made a transfer from the unreality of peace to the reality of war when it should have been the other way round.

Lael! Is war a never ending reality? Is the space between wars only a respite for the next one? Are ideals and visions of peace only excuses to vent energy and death on others?

I have no answer to what I am saying to you, but I do know that when we were not at war we enjoyed the serenity of living in peace. Yet when Seri-ni and I took off on the back of Ecril all my thoughts that I had of peace and serenity were blown away as if they were nothing but false illusions.'

I had listened intently to what Derca had to say and I could only tell him that he was most probably right in some of his words, he had been fighting all his life and so it had been a way of life for him and his tribe. However, the longevity of the peace that he had experienced in Arta du proved that it was worth fighting for.

Derca made no comment and continued with his tale.

'Along with Cimer and some of his chiefs we all congregated in the longhouse. I had been there many times before and I was always amazed at the collection of artefacts that were hanging on the walls and displayed in arbours here and there.

All were objects taken with them when they left their homelands and I could not understand why Cimer and his elves took things like stones and bits of trees. I asked him why he took the rocks, as surely there were plenty to spare all over the lands of Darwan.

He told me that they were the foundation of the land of his and his tribe's birthplace he showed me stones taken from the sea and the land and from the highest hills. They did not shine like crystal but they were all different colours and were pleasing to the eye.

He gave me a small round stone the colour of ochre, it had two bands of blue round it and when he gave it to me he said that there will never be another stone like it. For all the stones that are in the Darwan world never will two be the same, each and every one is unique to itself and to whoever picks it up and keeps it.'

Once again Derca paused with his story as he produced a small pouch made of selc skin. He handed me a stone which he had taken from the pouch and asked what vibrations I got from it.

As soon as it touched my hand I felt the same vibration that I had got from the stone of Corac that I found in the plain of Rinnis. Like its counterpart, now a possession of Bheir, it had come from a far off time, having had travelled eons to get to this place. By Derca's previous description I surmised it was the stone Cimer gave him.

It was elliptical, not round and it was so very smooth, the coloration was distinct - deep ochre and the slim lines that swept round the curve were violet. It was slightly bigger than Bheir's stone but contained the same energy.

Derca accepted my words and confirmed that Cimer had given him the stone and he had carried it on his person ever since. Then he carried on with the tale of the gathering of the tribes.

'The longhouse filled up quickly, mainly with blue elves but a sprinkling of white goblins and faolwarriors were mixed in with the crowd. Segments round about the walls of the longhouse were removed so that others outside could hear and see what was going on.

I stood beside Cimer and watched the crowd, there was a muted murmur but no shouted questions aimed at Cimer. They knew the instant Cimer got information he would relay it to them, and they had not long to wait.

The beating of powerful wings was heard and I turned outwards in time to see Croin alighting on a bank overlooking where most of the crowd had gathered.

Croin addressed Cimer, asking if all were ready for his information. Cimer told him that all the assembly were waiting for him.

Croin did not waste his words, he told of two columns of many warriors heading out from the black rim. One armed force took the direction to the mountain lands of the einn lael.

'The other force is headed for the ver lael and there are ships making way down in the direction of the ver lael. It is my thoughts that they intend to ambush the ver lael from land and sea.

By defeating the ver lael it would leave the macel lael exposed on that flank and if the force that looks set to engage the einn lael defeats them - then the macel lael will be exposed on both flanks.'

Croin went on to say that he flew into the settlements of the einn lael to warn them as it looked likely they were to be the first target. He gave the same account to them and warned them to retire to the lands of the macel lael.

He then gave one of his cruel laughs and said he had wasted his words on them because the einn had no intention of retiring in fact they are going to take the fight to the enemy.

'One of their chiefs called Berda said they made preparations when they first settled in the mountain lands. The weak link in defence is always the pass between hills but sometimes it can be a strong point for defenders. He went on to say that as there was only one pass from the direction of any enemy so it was easy over a period of time to make defensive preparations.

Those defences consisted of walls built on either side of the pass; many visiting beings had assumed they were boundary lines as it was common practice in their homelands of the black island.'

Once again Croin gave out his cruel laugh and said the einn clan had placed stones in certain places in the walls which they called pull-stones. Once pulled in unison all the dyke stones would roll and tumble down into the pass squashing any beings caught below.

'Some of the einn clan are going out-with the pass to face the goblanic horde, engage them for a while then make a pretence of running away. They are swifter by far than any of the enemy so they will clear the pass before the boulders start rolling.'

Derca laughed to himself after he had related that episode and said, all about shook their heads and had a good laugh at the sheer simplicity of the tactics. He also said they knew all about the boundary walls but never knew or heard of 'pull stones.'

When Croin had finished his tale, Cimer commented on the einn elves by saying that it looked as if they were taking care of the flanking move themselves.

He then went on to say that he would despatch some of the blue elves to back up the einn lael. The same for the macel; and for the maritime enemy the ships of the blue elves would support the fleet of the ver lael.

Cimer and his retainers would be joining Derca's land forces. He asked Croin if the hawks could fly above the battle arena and watch the goings on, just in case there were any variables.

He was also going to ask Esar amit the faerie if she would make an appearance in the event that the enemy had magical aid.

As Derca spoke about the ensuing events I could feel hyper emotion in his voice and body mannerisms. One of Croin's hawks had appeared and reported that the goblin -demon force were approaching fast towards the einn lael. They seemed to have rushed ahead of the other enemy forces.

I could hear glee in Derca's tone as he said that it knocked the enemies flanking movement out of line. Then events happened quickly, every elf took to their battle stations on their chosen ground and prepared to meet the enemy. The enemy by this time had realised that elves had been warned, but according to the hawks the horde had not slowed down.

Ceara had moved fast, the war galleys of the ver lael were already at sea fully crewed and ready for action. The ships of Lael could sail very close to the wind and were very manoeuvrable.

When they and the enemy closed up Ceara saw that the ships of the opposition were packed with warriors, leaving not much deck space. The ships were broad beamed and clumsy looking, definitely not fighting ships.

It was an embarked force that expected to be landed somewhere; the demon army had not envisioned a sea battle. The masters of the Lael ships must have been smiling to themselves as they looked at the sluggish armada.

Another factor in favour of the Lael elves was the wind. Nindril had been kind to them, giving them superiority. Ceara held his ships back from the approaching enemy, ever alert and watching. His eyes were not only scanning the demon armada but also the coastal cliffs of his tribe.

The enemy were not ready for what happened next. The sky above them nearly went dark as showers of arrows poured down on them mercilessly. Blue and black bow-elves rained volley after volley on the defenceless demons and goblins.

Ceara's fleet made their move, to the sound of the persistent beat of the drums the rowers turned the ships into the tidal race; wind and sea combined to drive the war galleys of the black elvin amongst the distraught enemy

What the arrows hadn't achieved, the elf shot of the black elvin accomplished, as the slick moving war galleys turned and twisted among the goblin fleet. The black elves of Lael jumped aboard the boats of the goblin warriors, dealing death to the remaining few.

Absolute slaughter, not one was left alive to tell the tale. The blue and lael elves were glorious in their victory. They had vanquished a very ruthless enemy.

Virtually the same thing happened on the landward flank as the einn elves succeeded in trapping the demon horde within the pass and, together with a deputation from the macel, chased what remained of the enemy force all the way to the Black rim.

At the Black rim they encountered a backup force of sker goblins, demons and grendelon warriors. But the hackles of the einn and macel were up and no force of any kind could halt that murderous assault.

After burning the dead of the enemy the einn and the macel claimed the black rim and the lands round about for the tribe of Lael. They chased the families of the goblins and demons to the furthest extremities of their former lands and there they were allowed to stay, as long as they behaved.

The einn clan wanted to wipe the lot out, but listened to the reasoning of their macel kinfolk. The macel reckoned that the gual and guita tribes of the home island would have done exactly that. The tribes of Lael are every bit as fierce, but they draw the line at the slaughter of the young and helpless.

The main thrust of the enemy marched down through the middle of the land killing and plundering as they went. The force numbered more than twice that of both flanks put together.

Cimer and Derca met them at the plain of Evity, where a strange encounter took place as the time of Rinnis was nearly on them - the enemy halted. Goblins and the like are fearful of the red maiden's light.

The elves held their position out of arrow shot, the goblin horde had already lit fires as had the elves. Cimer had some of his elves out-with on both flanks just in case!

During the night of Rinnis the elves and elvesses danced in wild abandon to the sounds of the drums and pipes. The flames of the campfires seemed to be in tandem to the dancers - enhanced by the red maidens flickering light they flared and stretched as if in obedience to the sky goddess.

Much shrieking and wailing could be heard from the goblin side, they were also dancing and playing strange sounding instruments. Derca said that most of the antics were intended to invoke the support of Rinnis for the coming battle.

Then as suddenly as the night began so also did it end, and right where Cimer and Derca chose to stand their ground, Apuss rose; his light bright in its intensity behind the elves.

The almost blinded goblin horde marched towards them. To the sound of the drums and pipes the elves spread out in extended line then the extreme end of each side curled inward in a pincer movement.

A bloody affray ensued, the warriors of the middle ground were fighters and fought well but they were no match for the joint force of blue and black. The fiercer the fight became, so also did the shrill mystical cry of the pipes rise to the energy of the battle and the steady beat of the drums were like a barrier of sound at the rear - no retreat.

Derca went silent and stared ahead as if he was reliving part of his tale, I looked into his face and for the first time I saw a great hurt cross his features briefly, then it was gone. He said that in the aftermath they were told that Ceara had been lost.

No elf had seen him killed, the last that was seen of him was at the steering arm so it was presumed he had fallen into the sea, maybe hit by a stray arrow.

Derca went on to say that he found out the last sighting of Ceara and where the ship was at that event. Using his knowledge of tide and currents he came to a reckoning where Ceara's body would most likely be washed up.

He searched and searched for many an Araen but to no avail, the sea did not give up the elf that was Ceara. Derca settled for the idea that Azirema had taken him.

He went quiet for a while then carried on with his tale. He said the einn elves had made the decision to extend their bounds on behalf of the clan. They maintained that the black rim was a strategic point of the landmass as it had all round views because of its height advantage.

It was also a natural harbour, completely obscured from the landward side and almost completely hidden from eyes on the waters. The great curve of the rim turned itself by the way of Ica so that the entrance to the harbour lay between the coastal cliff and the end of the rim.

The einn elves did not care much for a harbour, they only claimed it for the tribe. As far as they were concerned the ver and the macel could do what they wanted with it as long as a watch was maintained on it.

They retired back to their mountains and glens and set about clearing the pass. They had plenty of help from their co-settlers - the garg people and the white goblins. The macel Lael melted back to their forests and plains as they had as much interest in the black rim as the einn had.

Derca said part of his own tribe and some of the sea people of the blue elfin shared a part of the coastline that was starting to get crowded as a result of many children being born in both tribes.

It was an ideal place for the maritime people of the two tribes to settle down in and it was met with great enthusiasm. So preparations were made to transport them to their new habitation.

It was a time of celebration, the coming together after the hard fought battle was good for all. Once again a move signalled a new beginning and a new territory was established.

Representatives from all the living creatures in Arta-du and beyond flocked to the land around the black rim to welcome the new arrivals. Much dancing and drinking took place but the focal point came when the faerie Esir-amit blessed the new occupants and their land.

At the mouth of the harbour on the seaward side there was a very large black boulder. I remember it well after the battle - the einn elves had their eye on it but no matter how hard they tried they could not shift it.

They even had a few of the gargs with them but they met their match with the black boulder, they all said the stone would not speak to them so they could not manipulate it.

During the festivities Esir-amit was seen staring intently at it, she always drew attention whenever she made an appearance and this was no exception.

Those that were closest heard her say something but could not make out the words; however a loud sharp noise diverted their attention to the black boulder.

To the amazement of all about, the black stone had split wide open and revealed a sparkling array of white and indigo crystals which glittered fiercely in the light of Apuss.

All around who saw the happening were staggered by the beauty that was the inner life of the black boulder.

Esir-amit spoke loudly so all could hear.

'I have released energy from a stone that was buried in the earth beneath the sea before any living creature walked the lands of Darwan. I give my message to all the tribes this day to remember that out of darkness there will always be light and what is lost will always be found in some form or another.'

She finished by saying. 'Come people, and take in the beauty of the stone and be comforted that the light of faerie will always be with you.'

And there Derca's tale ended. I was fascinated by the story but something or someone was missing. There was never a mention of a female partner or children so I asked him if he had a female companion and young ones.

Derca gave me one of his rare smiles and said that the sea was his constant companion he was passionate about his boat, his crew and sailing the great seas of Darwan.

Most of the crew had been with him since he first got the Ector, a mingling of elves and elvesses. I asked him if all the ships carried elvesses and he replied by saying that it was common to have mixed crews. Some boats carried all male crews but by the same token others carried all female crews----------

He stopped and stared ahead and told me that he recognised a prominent hill in the distance. I followed the line of his arm and saw the hill, it was red and very pointed -almost a spearhead. I asked him if it had a name.

Derca brightened up when he gave me my answer. 'Oh yes Lael I know that hill very well, although I am not used to seeing it from this direction.

It is called the Red Stora and is a very distinctive landmark when we used to sail from our island. Now I have a land marker and because I know the setting and rising of Apus and the maidens we now have a positive direction to follow.

Come Lael, we must make haste; although we have direction assured we have a long way to go.'

And that was it no more said, Derca took off at speed and I followed at the tail. We ranged through flat land, forests and hills and never halted once

UATH

The Battle at The Fochd Pass

Cimer asked Croin if he was willing to recommend four storm hawks, each one carrying two elves or elvesses. Although not a mighty force at least the hawks could create panic among the gurks and the elves on the ground would appreciate their presence. Croin immediately volunteered himself but Cimer held his hand up and said he had another task for him if he was willing to do it.

Before the conversation was carried further they were interrupted by Esir-amit who told Cimer and Croin that she would be flying to the Laic with Riora the red hawk.

Esir had the immediate attention of both elfin king and storm hawk and they listened intently to what else she had to say.

'I have had Tress and Ilo in my thoughts and I know

their intentions; they will be standing with Elid Silverhair to the very last. We three along with Enir-isl are the only faeries left in Darwan who can trace their direct line to Illis-ri the starlight wanderer.

We are the daughters of Ica, the angels call us by that name and because we are Ica's daughters and we know she will guide and protect us through the storms of battle.

Enir-isl and I agreed that one of us had to be along with them as their presence in Darwan might well come to an end. So it is that I asked Riora if she would carry me into battle telling her that it could be her last journey as well.

She readily agreed to accompany me to the Laic lands and accepted that it may be her last flight. Riora rejoiced with the idea that she would be involved in such an epic episode in the planet's history and, like her first ancestor of the red feathers, have the power to help another.'

Croin nodded in approval, Riora was always Esir's choice if she needed to be flown out-with the lands.

Cimer said 'Well Esir, it is your journey and I will be sorry to see you go but I wish you and Riora well - whatever happens.'

The elves of Cimer and Lael, along with their adherent clans, had been strengthening the defences round their lands and were readying themselves for war. Cimer knew if Elid's forces were defeated then sooner or later the darkness would descend on them. They had been keeping a close eye on the lands of Urtha that was home to their former enemies. They seemed to be getting on with each other in a more civilised way and neither Esir-amit nor Enir-isl could detect any bad vibrations that dark forces would emanate.

She said to Cimer 'If Ilo is standing against the dark entities then I must be there with her and if we fall, then we will fall together, our visible form will leave Darwan but in higher spirit we will merge and be united in the starry clusters of Illis-ri, back to the faerie dust that bore us.'

Cimer had to agree, faeries go their own way as they are not subject to any entity or place. Esir-amit would be sadly missed if anything were to happen to her.

Cimer then turned his attention to Croin and said. 'Croin, I must ask you yet again to carry out a task for me and that is to go on the hunt for Derca and his two companions.'

Croin answered in good humour. 'What! Do you mean I have to go and dig him out of another hole?'

Cimer answered in the same tone as Croin. 'He may well be in a hole along with his companions, so you may have to dig them out as well.'

Croin said. 'I have organised Reglan to carry the black elf of Lael called Era and a blue elvess called Lirl.

Nerli will fly with Torma a blue elf and Lith an elvess of Lael; Brana a blue elf called Cirin and Virda a black elvess. It seems fitting that although we cannot risk embarking a force then we have to represent ourselves albeit in small numbers.'

Cimer threw up his arms in mock surrender and said. 'Well, looks like you have organised the hawks and the elves - what can I say, you have even given thought that in the absence of Derca a black elfess and an elf of Lael should be included in the coming battle.

They both watched the storm hawks taking off with their individual riders; Cimer's gaze lingered on Riora and Esir-amit and wondered ......

Esir-amit and Riora

The storm hawks flew at a great height and took up a flying formation with Riora leading, out on the flanks were the storm birds Nerli and Brana. Bringing up the rear was Reglan.

Esir-amit was in thought communication with Riora giving her directions and having general conversation with her.

Esir-amit and Riora were known to each other, the faeries were to be seen often in the elfin lands of Arta du visiting Cimer. Riora had carried Esir many times and that is why she had asked to go on the journey.

Esir told Riora about her ancestors and how the red markings came about, of course Riona knew about the story but to hear it from a faerie who was there at the happening made the hearing of it more exciting.

As you know the order of creation began with the Draigs. After that great Ica formed the angels and it is said she modelled them on her own shape.

Then she made us - the faery folk to populate the many worlds then after us your kin - the Storm Hawks. Many other species came after, as the mighty universes slowed their movement and light energy started to eclipse the darkness.

It was a fascinating time to live through, with the vastness of space to wander in with few restrictions. Only certain areas guarded by the angels in the far outer reaches were barred to us.

My kin and I were formed within the space mists of a cluster called Illis–ri when Ica formed our first ancestor, faerie and star cluster bore the same name. My ancestor was also known as star wanderer.

Ica's plan to fill the darkness with light was working well and she had great joy watching her creations enjoying the living light energy that merged well with the moving darkness.

She gave us an energy pattern which followed the contours of our shape, it extended outward from our visible bodies. Every movement we made was simulated by the power source, it was like a path being cleared ahead of us - energy allowed us and the Draigs to fly through the emptiness of space.

Ulas had been at work also but he preferred the inner darkness that penetrated the far flung wilderness of grey dust and black movement. He did much in the way of experimentation - his most deadly creation was the wells of darkness.

They were portals of great power that sucked anything into their inner blackness and once in - never seen again.

That is where your forbearer made an appearance - Der was a female storm hawk gliding through the space dust of Ior-n when she noticed a funnel of dust being pulled out of the cluster by some unseen force.

Der followed it and saw the dust disappearing into nothing but something else a lot worse was being sucked in - a Draig was struggling against the force.

We all know a Draig can only be destroyed by fire but equally the portal could transport it to places unknown and - the well could contain wild fire. Der acted quickly and flew straight for the Draig and hooked her mighty claws into the scales of the Draig, the power of both sets of wings was enough to lift them away from the well of darkness.

Der said she looked back and saw space dust at the entry of the well of darkness and it looked as if it was suspended before it vanished in less than a wingbeat.

The Draig was known as Erar the fire, and it was she who gave the redness in your feathers for all to see and know.

Then Esir-amit asked Riora if she was ready for the coming battle. Riora knew what the intimation of the question was about. She answered Esir defiantly.

I have been fortunate in life, I love the land I live on and the air I fly in. I am honoured to carry the markings of my ancestors. If I am called to the eternal light during the battle, then I know my spirit will live on at a higher level.'

Spearhead

Eils was weaving and turning among the shades, stabbing and slashing with the sword of Elid. The blue light that emanated from the blade bit into the foul beings dissipating them to where ever they go. Traig, Bheir, Rhu and Suila were on either side guarding against slarcs, sker goblins and dara guita elves. They would not leave her side even though the odds were overwhelming.

On the left flank Suilval and her mixed force were holding well against a strong force of slarcs and gurks and grendelon warriors. The faolwarriors arrow men were hampering the gurks but the bows of the faols lacked the power and accuracy of the bana weapons.

There were also a company of red ghals who were visiting the Laic at the time Elid was drawing up her battle plan. They asked to be included in the force that was to head for the Pass of Fochd. They had a good history with the shade elves and that was the reason they were in the Laic at the time.

They were a mixture of male and female warriors and very fearsome looking, not as tall as the bana but more muscular, they all had red hair. The females wore theirs closely cropped and had some kind of thin needle like plant woven through the hair. The men wore their hair in the same fashion as the black elves except there were no bones in the pigtail.

Their armament was the usual assortment of spears, swords and bows. However some of them had whips rolled up on their belts but they were no ordinary whips. Closer inspection showed a deadly addition - small barbs protruded from the body of each whip.

The leader of the ghals was a female called Sersa and she was a leader in every sense of the word. Her position was alongside Traig right where the action was. Wielding two curved swords she cut down many a slarc and sker goblin.

After the battle she said how much she enjoyed fighting alongside the bana, especially Traig who kept up a nonstop tirade all the time she was dealing out death and destruction to the enemy.

Three of the male warriors were watching a

swooping gurk, quick as anything one of the warriors snared it by the neck with his whip the other two held on with him and brought the gurk to the ground where the three of them then hacked it to death.

Suilval had crossed over from the left flank where she had left a very competent bana warrior called Rana in charge. Elid had asked her to keep an eye out for Ruis but so far he had not been seen by any of the warriors on the left or centre forces.

After scouting around the right flank quizzing some of the warriors she established that no entity had seen Ruis during the fighting or in the lulls in between. Knowing that the left flank was in capable hands she joined up with a mixed force of bana and elves from the sea of Meren.

The sea elves were a small representation of their tribe and were integrated within the ranks of the bana. In their homelands by the sea they lived side by side with the tribe of bana they were now fighting with. These were the Bana-ger-vour and their leader was Sarl. She was also a blood sister of Rhu.

Apart from the black energy that Eils had to deal with in the centre, the right flank had by far the worst job as they had to fight two tribes of Black Elves as well as goblins and other wild entities.

The bana numbered half the force of the black elves and they now had Suilval, a few red ghals; a sprinkling of shade elves and a contingent of sea elves - against such a deadly foe it was going to be hard work.

The fighting started not long after Apuss rose and

continued all day. By the time Apuss gave way to Ara heavy losses were suffered on both sides, the dark forces retired to lick their wounds.

Eils shouted to Traig. 'Traig go and tell our sea people to hold their ground - they are not to chase after the enemy.'

Without a word Traig was off in the direction of the bana vour, Eils then asked Suila to go and check out how the shade elves had fared then she turned to Bheir. 'Come Bheir, we need to talk.' Bheir followed Eils to a small hollow behind their lines.

Holding Bheir by the shoulders Eils said. 'Of the bana five we two have been together the longest therefore I need you to feel the might of the sword so that if I am called to the sea you can use the magic.'

Bheir replied. 'Surely we will see Apuss rising many times before that happens.'

Eils said. 'I fear the enemy only tested us today and they were surprised to find we had magic on our side. The next onslaught will be aimed at me - all the dark energy will be concentrated on taking me out of the fight.

So Bheir I ask you, before I am overcome I will try to throw the sword of Elid in your direction, you must run with it to the water of Fochd and dive deep where their magic can't reach you, only river gaists and sea elves can match us in the water. Find Tiathmor or Elid and give it to which ever one you find.'

'I would wish to finish my life alongside you Eils, rather than run from the battle, but if that is what you want then that is what I will do.' replied Bheir.

There was no hint of sentiment or fear in Eils voice when she answered back. 'Nal has gone on her journey and you will have your one. It would be better if we five fought and died together but I will have Traig and Suila by my side so I will not be alone.'

The two walked to the front line and were met by Traig, who straightaway asked 'What do you two know that I don't?' Bheir put her in the picture as Eils went to find Suila.

'You will never have another war partner like me.' Was Traigs answer as she walked away, Bheir shook her head and said 'What no questions?'

Dark clouds appeared from the direction the enemy had retreated to, sounds of wailing and howling could be heard then the air was ripped apart by a high pitched scream that lingered on and on until it finally dissipated over the forces of light.

Silence for a moment then one of the red ghal warriors shouted. 'I thought Suilval was on our side.' That brought some laughter to those of the gathering who heard it.

Then the enormity of the dark energy became apparent, in the middle of the approaching horde was a weaving mass of shades and ghouls, above them hovered the black gurks of Cildur. The sound of the black elves drums were omnipresent in their steady beat as they marched forward feet thumping on the plain.

The Firedraig

The firedraig soared over the mountains and plains of Darwan powered by her great wings, the air itself lent its winds to aid her flight and as she approached the Laic Elids thoughts reached her.

'Cerenor-Tala firedraig of Elinbroom, it pleases me to feel your presence for you give us hope for what we are about to face. You must pass over us and go with all speed to the pass of Fochd as our force there needs you the most. Tress and Ilo will stand with me to form the Triad, it is the only way for us now.'

The mighty shape of the firedraig appeared over the Laic and flew low over Elids warriors. Nal lifted her bow over her head with both hands and got a mighty cheer from the Bana. Gruflics danced with delight and shouted for feathers, river gaists stared in awe, Elid caught Cerenors thought.

'Our day has almost come Silverhair, I feel that both of us have reached the end of this stage of our journey, whatever the outcome may be I hope the tree of destiny is kind to both of us - farewell daughters of Ica.'

Then the firedraig and her rider were lost to sight and thought.

The Trio of Light

The energy of the dark magic was too much to contend with, wave upon wave of shades, plasins, witches and a myriad of lesser demonic entities were taking their toll. They came fast and furious, the black masses hurtled their malignant powers against the faeries.

The main thrust was on Ilo the dark forces hit her in a maelstrom of hate and anger. They realised her power was great and they had to smash her. The blue power of Ilo was indeed great and the dark forces were hit by it head on, many were dissipated forever, others were drained of their powers and ran from the field.

Elid knew they would be overcome - it had been a foregone conclusion, the storm of dark forces was too much and the three were too little. She stood in the centre, Tress and Ilo at either side of her; they had fought well.

The enemy fell back but not because they had given up. Elid knew they were reorganising their masses for a final, all empowering charge. The serried ranks of dark elves and slarcs were being brought forward, the dark servants of Urais ular would forge ahead of the elf-slarc army to sweep away Elid and her two faeries. Then the dark elves would fall upon the creatures of the Laic.

Elid wondered if they realised the arcil bana were lying low behind her in the forest. Quick as she was to appraise the situation, her thoughts were quicker, they were directed to her two faeries and they responded immediately and came to her side.

When they were gathered she sent Bila to fetch Tiathmor. Bila and his pixie band had been sheltering behind a rock during the fighting they would not go away to safety. Before he went she gave him a gentle reminder who he was to speaking to.

Elid spoke to the two faeries - 'Ilo, Tress - this next onslaught will be our final event in Darwan, our stay here is nearly over. I ask you to join me in a trio of light, with our combined power we can create a wave of energy that can devour everything in its path, and of course us as well.

I know there are no more nights for me in Darwan and I know that what I ask of you is perhaps not what you intended, if you are not in favour I will understand.'

Both faeries spoke in unison. 'We are with you Elid anor, if by our last deed we free the land from this dark grip then so be it.'

Then Ilo spoke again 'I feel a thought from not very far away, give me space so I may hear the voice in my head, it is familiar.' Elid and Tress remained silent.

After a pause of silent contemplation Ilo spoke to her companions. 'We are to be joined by Esir-amit she is riding a storm hawk. I have told her about the triad of light - she said they will fly from behind and hopefully fly straight into the power of light energy.

We are powerful as we stand now but with Esir-amit and a red hawk there will be no escape for any of the dark powers. They will be decimated forever within the clouds of dark matter.

Elid held the two close to her and whispered to both. 'Together we will stand in light then after, when we go our separate ways, may our journeys continue ever upward until we all merge again in light.'

Tiathmor's voice came to them. 'What's this I see, getting amorous with each other? There is a time and a place you know. I am not surprised at Ilo - but you two!'

Tiathmor had come with her companion in arms - Ari. Elid explained her intentions to the two bana warriors. She told them that the light power would burn away the dark spirits but would also finish the life essence of the trio in Darwan.

She also enlightened Tiathmor to expect a storm hawk and rider flying over her force of warriors heading for the light.

Then you Tiathmor must take the bana forward and finish off the slarcs and elves. The slarcs will be in dire panic with the light energy, the dark elves will stand and fight to the end, you must finish them all off.

Tiathmor and Ari listened to Elids words, faces impassive. Finally Tiathmor spoke. 'So you three flowers will be blooming in the MoAraian forest shortly?'

'No Tiathmor I don't think we will be headed back that way, we three will be destined for other worlds. The power of the triad of light will project our spirits to wherever we go we will not retain the shapes we have now.' Elids statement provoked a short silence, until Ilo changed the mood.

'Aw,' said Ilo moving suggestively around Tiathmor. 'Will you miss us? Who knows, we may meet again.'

'No I don't think so, one world is enough for the

bana, we lived by the sea and we will return to it in death.'

Suddenly the sky darkened and a loud clamour was raised from the direction of the enemy.

Elid said. 'Come faeries, we came in light and now we go in light.' Ilo blew a kiss to the bana warriors then joined her two companions forming the union of three.

The black horde came on, led by a Dara-sith, a powerful she-devil. Shrieking and screaming like so many demented winds the tide of black energy swept down on the trio.

The Words of Tiathmor, Queen of The Bana

What can they do against so much evil, where did it all come from, were we blinded with our own sense of security that we did not see events taking place that were not in the flow of the land?

Had I not heeded the powerful words that Elid spoke before the conflict began, I would have led the bana against that heaving mass of evil.

As I watched the enemy closing in, the Triad of Light came together in an embrace of bodies, their arms and hands pointing straight up to the sky. A blue light started to emanate from them. Remembering what Elid had instructed I turned my back to the field of battle as did the warriors under my care.

Then we saw the red hawk and rider that Elid spoke of, it flew low over us. A mighty black bird with red wing feathers and the luminosity of the rider that she carried was startling to behold.

The sky held its blue-black broodiness - as if watching for an event. Then streaks of silver blue light pierced it like so many daggers. The blue light was swiftly followed by shards of green and ochre, colours which took over the sky completely.

I could hear the malignant screams had been silenced and new sounds were coming to our ears. They were sounds of agony and terror, hardly had we heard the death cries when the air and light around us changed dramatically.

The colours intensified until all about was red, such red as I had never seen before. Apuss setting on the Salacian Sea was pale in comparison to the red I saw that day. The air felt as if it was being torn apart as it rippled over us and at times thunder-like noises added to the confusion of the elements.

Then abruptly all went silent and the land and sky around us was bathed in a white light so bright and so peaceful --- then it was gone.

I turned about and saw a land that had been scorched to the bedrock, nothing moved in that black scarred tunnel of earth and stone. No evil entities, no slarcs, no moabs or gurks flying about.

Of the Triad of Light? Only the place where they had stood was left, no trace of the Triad and no trace either of the hawk and its rider. I named the rock that the three took their last stand on - "Halion" meaning spirits.

Then I spied movement to the far right of the plain. It was the rear-guard of black elves. Instantly I called the bana to action. We crossed that blackened plain and chased them to a place called Dur-nos.

They turned to face us there, like us they had been staggered by the events of the battle. But like us they were warriors and they stood their ground and fought well. Their speed, strength and agility were exceptional.

We were pleased to win against such a formidable foe. None of them surrendered, all chose to die where they stood. It was not their fault that they were corrupted by the darkness, their natural aggression and hatred of the tribe of Lael had laid them open to enchantment.

It is the custom of the black elves to burn their dead. In honour to a warrior race we gathered them together and made burnings. We have certain of the bana who are fire makers so they were given the task.

We had our own warriors who had fallen during the battle, so we had them to prepare for their last journey to the sea. Among them was Corel, the longest serving bana warrior of all the three tribes. Many tales had been told about her prowess as a warrior and also the sweetness of her singing voice.

Seeing Corel being prepared made me think on Bheir and the rest of my warriors. Had they fared well at the Fochd Pass?

The Battle is Over

Cerenor came in behind the forces of good, she had already enlightened Nal to what she had intended to do. The idea was to fly low over the forces for light and hit the wielders of magic head on.

She had warned Nal to keep as low as she could behind the Draig's head as a stray bolt of magic could knock her off. True to the stubborn streak in the bana warrior, Nal said she would stand up tall so that all would see it was a warrior of the bana that was facing the enemy.

Cerenor had to put her straight by saying. 'Little warrior I will tip you off my back into the ranks of your kin and attack the evil host myself if you do not follow my instructions.'

Rather than be unceremoniously dumped into the lines of the bana, Nal promised to obey the words of Cerenor. She was to keep her head down until Cerenor wasted the main thrust of the black magic then she was free to shoot as many of the enemy as she could.

The Song of Draigs in the Voice of Nal

I was honoured to be the last of the bana warriors to ride on the back of the last Draig in Darwan. On the way to the battle field she told me of Draigs and their place in Darwan and other worlds and so I tell the story of Cerenor-Tala in her words as she spoke them to me.

She was created by great Ica in the second universe within the heat of a pulsing star named Cerister.

Stories and legends have not been kind to Draigs, they tell of how firedraigs were hunted down and killed. At the words she spoke I could feel the rumblings of power in her body followed by a short burst of flame as she spat the words out.

'In the physical world of Earth where the human form of Lael lived they told tales of men in metal suits wielding swords like needles who killed off many of the race of Draig. I tell you Nal, my kin on Earth would have melted them to the very rock they stood on before they could have flickered an eye.

Others tell stories of magicians who chained us to rocks and bled us for our knowledge and wisdom. Huh! We would have worn them around our necks like a pendant by the very chains they tried to ensnare us with and carried their withered bones for all eternity.

No one entity can kill a Draig, we were born of fire and we are the living embodiment of fire, the light of Apuss is fire. In the black magic matrix of space, fire burst through and brought light to the darkness.

In the ensuing fight between light and dark, so powerful was the energy that was produced it caused a mighty explosion - the explosion rippled on through many eons until finally two forms took shape. One was Ulas of the dark and was the male side of the black matter the other was Ica the feminine side of light.

Between them they fashioned the worlds that would bear life - one could not do without the other. Ica realised that to bear life, worlds would need light and heat. The dark magic matrix was needed to keep the balance and Ulas was content to live and work in the shadows of space.

However Ica wanted life forms to inhabit the

forming worlds and she was tired of being shrouded in the everlasting darkness. More of the light in the explosion had inhibited her. Ulas had absorbed more of the darkness and was unconcerned about light.

Ica gathered light energy about her and formed the Draigs and into us she breathed the everlasting fire. Our mission was to go far into the darkness and set the dark orbs on fire, this we did - we were the creators of the stars.

Round about certain stars were little worlds that were set aside to bear life entities, we had to fly around them at great speed to set them spinning so that every part of the world would at some time feel the heat. When we had done that some of us landed on each world and there we bored into the core of it and turned the hardness into molten rock, then we retreated upwards and lived in the caves and high mountains until the worlds heated up.

Great Ica came to each of the many worlds and put an invisible shield around them, we were guardians of the worlds and watchers of the forming life entities. We were accepted among the early life forms, they were in awe of us, they knew we looked after them and we lived in harmony for many, many eons. But eventually in some worlds as life forms evolved they gathered more knowledge and expertise and with the coming of the new intelligence came arrogance.

Draigs became feared and viewed as a threat to the now, so called, superior species. We left most of the worlds of our own accord much to the joy of the inhabitants who regaled their children with stories of

Draigs being slain and chased into the heavens. One world even called a twisting constellation of stars in the night sky after a so called banished Draig. One day they might know the irony of it!

Ica bade certain Draigs like me to stay hidden in some of the worlds, yet again to help in time of danger from out-with.

Draigs do not die Nal - we were born of fire and we are consumed by fire when we are called as I have been called now. This is my last battle little warrior, then I go to the everlasting light unless a higher power has other ideas. But not yet, get yourself ready -we are almost at the point of battle.'

As the Draig approached the battle front from behind Elids forces she could see the dark energy was concentrated on one point and that focus seemed to be a bana warrior with a sword who was bearing the brunt of the attack.

'Now spawn of Ulas let us see what you do against Cerenor-Tala, the last Draig of Elinbroom.' The first blast of fire took away the shades nearest the sword maiden and sent all who saw the fiery beast into a paroxysm of fear and panic.

Cerenors hackles were up as she swept over the evil throng firing gouts of fire and molten stone; as she did so she could feel her rider's energy on her back and she knew Nal was dealing out punishment with her bow.

Ahead she saw a huddle of sinister shapes and instantly recognised the forms from an age gone by. The Ula sith, powerful demons of the past, were the driving force behind the shades. It was they who transmitted power through the shades, staying well away from any force who might be their equal. If the tide of battle turned they would be free to retreat in safety and fight another day.

'Not this day you won't, this will be your last battle ever because I am going to send you into black infinity with my magic fire. Nal! Get your head down now and watch because you will never see the like of this again.'

The Ula sith sent slivers of magic at Cerenor but they were no match for the Draig of Elinbroom. Cerenors blue flame licked across the battlefield like burning quicksilver. Like a flaming tide it engulfed the sith and burned them to oblivion, never to reform again.

The Draig, sensing more dark forces on the other flank, made an about turn and came in behind a huddle of black moabs and eter-phantoms who instantly unleashed a battery of magic at the Draig.

The Draig, in a fury of fire and energy, deflected the black power like water off a gaist's back and sent a lethal ball of blue energy which totally vanquished the demonic foe.

Then Nal, like an avenging angel, began firing arrow after arrow into the enemy on the ground. Elids forces had surged forward after Cerenors work was done and were engaging the enemy on both flanks.

Nal was fired up and shouted to Cerenor to drop her into the fighting so she could battle alongside her race.

Cerenor flew low over the enemy, friend and foe alike scattered in all directions to avoid the mighty beast as she touched down to allow Nal to jump off. Then with a mighty roar she was off, leaving Nal running in the direction of Suilval who was dispatching goblins to wherever they go after death.

Before she reached Suilval two black elf warriors engaged her, but Nal was glorious and the euphoria of fighting on the back of a Draig had energised her beyond normality. With swords in both hands she somersaulted over the black elves and hammered both blades through their skulls.

Meanwhile Suilval and some bana warriors had vanquished the goblin horde and were dealing with a force of black elves. As Nal closed up to them a familiar staccato voice hailed her from behind. 'Did you fall off the Draig Nal or did she ditch you?'

She had hardly turned her head when Traig and Suila appeared on either side of her Suila followed up and said. 'We did not want you to be lonely so we left Eils with Bheir, let's do some business.'

As one the three got among the throng alongside Suilval and the other bana warriors - all magic dissipated - they began to drive the black elves back. It was all physical energy from both sides, bodies moving and motivated by the sheer will to destroy the opposition.

All around the battlefield warriors were fighting like beings possessed, totally absorbed in their own prowess of body and mind. The dead and dying were all around, the smell of death melted in with the clinging reek which was still rising from the ground after the Draig's burning.

Apuss had tired of the hideous goings on and had

long since vanished, leaving the night to Ara. The Maiden's light gave a surreal slant to the fighting - the ground was still trying to shed the blackened wisps of smoke from the scorched earth.

The fighters looked as they were battling in a dark haze interspaced with flashes of moonbeam. The mercurial skin of the bana warriors reflected the light making their movements stilted and more rapid looking than usual. The black elves seemed to vaporise into the blackness with only glances of the yellow skin on their face and hands to show they were there.

Suilval alone held on to the light, her furred body shone with the energising power of Ara, a devastating physical entity wasting all that got in her way. She was on a predetermined path and it was Suila who sussed out what her intentions were, in between the fighting she shouted out to Traig. 'Suilval is headed for Rinnis Dur.'

No sooner had Suila communicated her words to Traig when the air cleared and dead ahead, caught by the light of Ara, was the legendary warrior - Rinnis Dur.

Standing tall on a flat rock, in one hand he carried a wicked looking axe and in the other he grasped the deadly duan sword of the black elves. Rinnis Dur was waiting for someone and that someone was closing in fast.

In hand to hand combat warriors are not only energised by their own euphoria but also by the opposing side's vibrations. When two sides clash, the energy is shared and it carries on into the heat of the battle. The heat is the product of all the individual warriors expending all their power to win or survive. Sometimes it comes quickly and at other times it can go on for days, but always there comes a pivot point when one side as a whole senses the drop in energy of the opposition. This is where a transfer of energy takes place, one side takes the others energy and their vibrations increase and victory for them is usually assured.

Rinnis Dur was a veteran of many battles and sensed that his forces were losing ground, however he was not going to leave the field. Sometimes the outcomes of battles can be dictated by single combat.

He had positioned himself at the rock surrounded by his elves and had singled out his opponent - Suilval!

He had watched her cutting a swathe through his forces, fur and selc armour absorbing the energy of Ara. Suilval, friend of the sorceress of the Laic and much admired warrior by the elves and the bana ger.

He would kill her as he had killed others like her in battles long past. When they saw their great warrior fall, his elves would seize the chance and turn the energy about.

In that part of the battlefield warriors on both sides felt something was about to happen. Black elves and goblins looked in the direction of Rinnis Dur - elves and bana warriors looked at Suilval. The fighting began to fizzle out and cease all together as warriors of both sides looked on in anticipation of a dual that would end in the death of one of the two greatest warriors in Darwan.

The arena was set; Suilval was at the ring of warriors, the black elves facing the cat warrior parted in front of their chief leaving the two staring at each other.

Suilval padded back and forth in front of Rinnis Dur, snarling and brandishing both her swords at him inviting him to leave his perch.

Rinnis Dur stood motionless staring at Suilval, his eyes boring into hers, not a word did he speak nor did he make any movement with either weapon. Only the most observant might have noticed a slight tightening of his hands on the hilts of both weapons. The bana had formed themselves in squares and were watching the event, eager for the contest to begin. Suila whispered to Traig. 'He's bracing himself for a charge.'

Suila's whispered words came to pass in the blink of an eye. Rinnis launched himself at Suilval in a dazzling display of speed and coordination - both weapons came hammering down on the big cat.

Suilval answered his charge by crouching down and taking the brunt of the charge with her own weapons. They broke and began circling each other feeling the others energy and looking for any sign of weakness. Once again Rinnis attacked with both weapons raining blow after blow which Suilval parried with equal force.

Nal said to Suila and Traig. 'Suilval is choosing her moment.'

Traig answered in a slow deliberate tone. 'Rinnis is not going to get a quick death.'

In the eerie light of Ara the last battle was being played out between two powerful entities, each one confident in their own superiority. All eyes were on them as they continued to hack at each other.

During the fast and furious stab and parry both warriors seemed to be on equal footing; if anything Suilval looked as if she was on the defensive. Then in a move that caught the elf chief by surprise she deftly closed her two weapons together then pushing outwards caught Rinnis's blades - using the space between she kicked violently up with her foot and caught Rinnis under his chin knocking his head back.

Sweeping her sword outwards she cut Rinnis's axe arm off at the elbow and retreated back to see the effect.

The effect was almost instantaneous as Rinnis lunged forward, his sword twirling in front of him scything the air as if he wanted to cut the light of Ara into ribbons. Then he switched to a downstroke with the Duan; fast as he was Suilval was faster.

She crossed her weapons and caught the black sword between the two blades - using her upper blade to sweep the duan to the side she crouched low and swept her other blade down and out severing Rinnis's leg below the knee.

There were moans of despondency from the black elves roundabout but none dared to break the code of single combat.

Nal murmured to Traig with a touch of glee in her voice. 'You were right Traig she is making the most of it.'

Rinnis Dur faced Suilval displaying no fear or even pain as with a roar he attempted to move forward.

The cat threw her short sword at him with such power it pierced his selc armour and took him to his knees.

Still alert for any sudden movement she approached her enemy and cut off the hand that held the sword. Grabbing Rinnis by his hairtail she turned him round to face his elves and slowly severed his head from his body.

Such a clamour arose from the black elves when they saw their leader fall, but Suilval wasn't finished.

Holding the head high above her head she snarled loud and long then she shouted. 'Here is what's left of your leader - take it with you and leave the field or die where you stand.' After removing the three black feathers from the hair tail of Rinnis she hurled it amidst the black elves and waited for the response. The sea elves and the bana had grouped behind her and they also were waiting for a response.

The response came from an elf called Desta - he asked if they could take the remains of Rinnis Dur from the field.

Suilval answered him in no uncertain terms. 'You can take Rinnis and your dead and when you finish the burning you will leave the land of Daralonadh and return to your Black Island and never leave its shores again.'

IOGH

After the observation of the Red Stora we had run and run - it seemed forever, I had to stop on one of the nights when Ara was at midpoint in the sky. Derca understood I had to meditate so he as usual stood guard, while I absorbed the cosmic energy from the endless universes.

We ran for another day and night then on the next day when Apus was high in the sky we halted and Derca said we were at the land close to a crossing to the Black island.

He said. 'We need to cross the waters to Cail-dur, so what now Lael?'

I said I would ask the air for help so I moved off to take a stance on a rock.

Derca had seen and done many things in his life. Through it all he always had the love of his land and the welfare of his people close to his heart.

He had fought battles against the other tribes that inhabited the Black Island. He had fought as a mercenary with Cimer and his elves in the great battle of Fochd Pass.

In their new land of Edila they had to stand by the blue elves and fight to keep their lands from fierce tribes that came through the mountains of Lergar.

He was hailed as a hero and a great warrior by his people. More than that he was held in awe by his race due to the fact that Shuira the goddess of the waters had boarded his ship and spoken to him. Derca took it in his stride - saying he always had good and capable elves at his side.

Now he was perched on a boulder on a hillside along with a spirit being from the divine world of Ulana. His mind reflected on past journeys - all the trials and tribulations that had taken him to the rock strewn hill he sat on now.

He cast a glance at Lael, the spirit who was lost in meditation as he called it. Even after all the time they had spent together Derca wondered at who Lael was and what he was trying to do.

As the thoughts ran through his head Lael shouted to him saying it was better if we moved before Apuss went down.

Lael told Derca that Nindril had been contacted and word would be put about that they need help to cross over to the black island.

We were both astounded by the speed the message had been conveyed but were not expecting the transport that appeared literally out of the sky. Huge black wings drummed the air and for a breath Derca and I were in shadow as mighty Croin landed beside us, and he was not alone.

A blue elfin bowman leapt nimbly off Croin's back,

Derca ran forward and took the elf by the shoulders saying. 'Cender how is this possible?'

Before Cender could answer Derca had turned to Croin and more or less asked the same. 'Where have you come from in so short a time?'

Croin's answer was to the point 'From the air, where else Derca - have you lost your reasoning since we last met?'

Derca laughed at Croin's sarcastic answer and replied in kind. 'Well now that you are both grounded you can tell me the truth before I do lose my reasoning.'

Before any of the two could answer Derca motioned me forward and introduced me to the blue elf. 'Lael this is Cender my good friend and comrade in arms, we have had many fights side by side and drunk many goblets of puflic together.'

Cender gave me the customary slow nod of the head and asked why my appearance resembled his race but before I could answer he fired another question at me. This time it was to ask why my name was the same as the tribal land of Derca's people. Then he followed up by saying. 'Are you a mixture of all the elfin races?'

Croin gave me a knowing look and said. 'Cender is the blue elves answer to Traig of the bana.' He then switched his attention to Derca and directed his speech to him.

'Great Cimer instructed me to hunt you down as he feared you were standing into danger, Cender offered to go with me as an extra pair of eyes, there is great activity going on in the lands of Daralonadh and none of it good.

Cimer has put all his tribes on the defensive and he cannot spare any great numbers to help Elid's forces---------------'

Croin's words were cut short as he looked to a point behind us and announced. 'Ah! The traitor joins us.'

We all looked to our rear and I gasped out. 'That's no traitor that is Ruis' - and yet as I said it I realised it was not Ruis as I knew him. The strapping warrior with the fine features had gone and in their place had appeared a wild eyed elf that looked as if all the guilt in Darwan was etched on his face.

He had a purposeful look though and the words he spat out made it clear what his intentions were.

'Get out of my way Lael - I am going to kill this traitor elf of the black.' To enforce his threat he stepped forward and drew his sword.

In response Derca and Cender, standing on either side of Croin drew their swords.

Still confused by the events taking place I could only say. 'What are you saying Ruis, Derca has been my guardian, he is helping me to find a way of ridding Darwan of the witch of darkness.'

At my words Ruis turned on me - his eyes filled with hate and spoke words that didn't make sense.

'You are not going to kill my mistress, she has chosen me as her companion to rule alongside her and you have no power to stop her.' He finished off by pointing his sword at Derca and screamed out. 'He is the enemy, he and Cimer, it is they who have broken the land and he has killed Nal.'

I turned to Derca and said. 'What is he talking about

Nal is very much alive, has he lost his senses?'

By this time Derca had adopted an aggressive stance and the words that he spoke carried intent.

'No Ruis, it is not I who is the traitor but you, Croin saw you in an embrace with the she-devil on the pathway to Cail-dur. He carried the news to Cimer and that is why I was dispatched to the lands of the Laic to warn Elid about you.'

At that point Ruis launched another tirade at Derca and Croin. 'Ulas take you and your pet crow, it is already too late - the forces of Dulsie will destroy Silverhair and her allies.'

Then turning in my direction he said. 'And as for this spirit of Ulana who thinks he can do something about it!'

Croin's raucous reply spoke volumes. 'Derca' let me pick him up and I will drop him from a great height onto the stone nest of his black mistress of Ulas.'

Derca replied in a slow tone to Croin's threat. 'No friend, this is to be settled between him and me.'

You and Cender must fly with Lael to Cail-dur, what Lael can do once he is there is beyond me, he has not got the power to match the witch but he seems to think he can do something.'

Ruis seemed to be more crazed than ever and his voice was not his own as he responded to the words of Derca. 'Yes Lael fly to your destiny and meet Ulas-darg in her casil and there you will be drained of all your spiritual essence and contained in darkness for ever.'

'Go now! Quickly mount Croin both of you and do what you must, I will attend to this creature who once was an elf.' The urgent tone of Derca's words spurred us to do his bidding and in less than a heartbeat we were taking to the air.

My last sight of Derca and Ruis was of the two closing to contact. 'I made my thoughts clear to Croin in thought. *Croin I fear for Derca's life, Ruis is crazed and he may have some power from the witch at his disposal.*

Croin's thoughts came to me and they carried connotations of reason and a staunch belief in Derca. *Ruis has served his purpose, the enchantress has left him to his fate and that is to die by the sword of Derca.*

You must prepare yourself Lael for what lies ahead, I will fly us as low to the water as I can, that way we will have some protection from the waters. Ulas-darg cannot project her power too close to the waters because she knows the spirits of the sea can intercept it.

Nindril of the air is a good spirit but he is too fey in his manner and is easily tempted to foolish antics with the result he can be confused if a power is strong enough - not so with the powers that rule the waters, they are ever vigilant.

Croin by this time was flying very low over the sea of Crom. Cender behind me remained silent as he had been since we left Derca and Ruis. His energy was strong so he obviously shared Croin's faith in Derca.

Then Croin came to me again in thought. *Lael, the black island is heavily protected by guard ships and foot patrols so it is practically impossible to get to the shore undetected. The only place that is not guarded is a neck of waters called the 'Roarans' beneath which is a twisted reef. This reef, in conjunction with the tidal surge between the black island and the lesser island of Girta, causes great turbulence in the waters making it impossible to navigate.*

By the time we get there the light of Apuss will be fading and by the aid of the wild waters we will touch the land right under the witch's nose.

True to form we landed on the neck of land that Cail-dur stood on and there to front of us silhouetted by the last of Apuss's light was the ominous shape that housed the witch of Cail-dur.

I was a bit elated by the fact we had reached the casil undetected and I thanked Croin for his help.

His answer unnerved me a bit when he replied to my words.

'Lael you can be sure she knows you are here, no matter how secretive we were Dulsie has allowed us to come this far. Cender and I are of no interest to her, it is you she wants.

I am going back for Derca, Cender is going to stay with you, he will enter Cail-dur with you if you so wish?'

I answered as best I could. 'Go your way both of you this is something I have to do myself - whatever way it ends.'

Croin nodded and looked at Cender for his answer.

The reply was short and to the point. 'Here will I stand and wait for whatever happens -go Croin and get Derca, who knows we may stand together yet.'

Croin gave me a last look and dipped his beak then he was gone, lost in the intermediate darkness between the going down of Apuss and the rising of Ara.

I looked at Cender the blue elf and my mind went

back to Ulana and my mentor of my early days as a spirit. He was a blue elf of the mountains, not unlike Cender but that was another age in another world which seemed so far away now.

'Look out for yourself Cender, may you come out of this event and live in peace all your life.' It was all I could think to say before I turned and faced Cail-dur. Cender said nothing but he lifted his hand in a farewell gesture.

Ara had risen by the time I was ready to head for the Cail. I paused to look down on the witch's lair, beyond which I could see the Crom Sea. The light of Ara had made a pathway of mystical brilliance on the waters. I felt I could have made an escape along that mysterious way.

The dark castle was perched high up on a cliff by the sea, even the rock promontory that held it looked as if it had been wedged into the land by something other than the force of nature.

Across the bay was a range of hills, one rose higher than all the rest, it had a watch tower on it. All round vision to the sea and land was had for the watcher for Cail-dur, from a distance the tower looked like a giant skull wearing a crown.

The top of the tower was crenelated then it narrowed down to the level that enclosed the watchers. Two rounded holes, like sightless eyes that faced the sea, gave a wide arc of sight. On the next level was a stone veranda and behind it a gaping hole to allow entry.

I followed a narrow winding stone path which twisted so far round on itself that I almost went back in the direction I came. Not a tree or bush or any other kind of plant lined that wasted walkway to Cail-dur.

I fully expected to be met by some foul fiend or demon as I cautiously picked my way down the steep snaking path. That was another quirk of the route to the lair of Dulsie. It dropped all the winding way to well below the entry point to the Cail-dur then it reared upwards in an astonishingly steep gradient and widened out at the fearsome looking door which marked the entrance to Cail-dur.

Grotesque stone faces glowered at me from the lintel at the top of the door and the effigy of what I imagined to be of the dark god Ulas himself was ingrained into the timber of the door.

The shape in the door looked as if it was coming out of the wood but was being held in by an unseen power that did not want it to manifest. Hooded and cloaked darker than the wood that bore it, a face that was barely visible in sideways profile and yet it conveyed such an air of hideous and menacing intent.

I did not want touch that door, even looking at it I began to have doubts about going through with entering Cail-dur. So much went through my mind in that lonely place but uppermost in my thoughts were the companions I knew were relying on me to do something.

Elid and Nal, Cerenor and Derca; they might be all gone by now and there was I dithering at the threshold of the dark power. I pulled my spiritual intent together and was just about to push the door with my aura in front of my palms --- when the door swung open of its own accord.

Intense evil and darkness was the expectation I had in my mind as I made my way through the stone arch which led straight into Cail-dur. I glanced at the door and was shocked to find the gruesome profile had turned the other way and I felt the baleful stare from the one exposed eye in the shadow of the hood.

I found myself in a corridor, it was well lit and warm, and unexpectedly a smell of pine was in the air.

Then I was at the entrance to a hall, I could see it was dimly lit and I was aware of shadowy drapes hung about, no tables or chairs were visible and I had a feeling the hall rose to a great height.

As I entered the hall I could see where the source of the light came from, six burning torches. Two hung on the back wall and two on each of the walls to the side.

The light reflected off the floor making a dais of colour giving the impression of a stage being set. I was not intimidated at all by the surroundings, in fact it was not the witch cavern I was expecting, even the air felt warm and sweet smelling - then in the blink of an eye she was there.

Tall and noble looking - wearing a cloak and hood both of which were immediately cast aside to reveal a body that looked as if the whole of the fires of creation in miniature was revolving over her.

The background colour of her skin was dark purple and all around it was a fantastic movement of tongues of fire licking round her body. Between the serpentine blades of fire were the dark red stars, planets and moons of Ulas the dark.

Only the face had no movement, it was the same colour as her body skin, and was beautiful to behold. On one side it had a red lightening streak running from her temple across her cheek to disappear at her throat into stardust.

Her hair was braided platinum and on it she wore a helmet of black, on one side was emblazoned a flame of red that looked as if it was real fire. In one hand she held a sceptre of silver, at the top end shone the same flame that adorned her helmet.

As I looked closer at the sceptre my eyes caught a flicker of movement, a thin coil of dark matter twisted its way endlessly around the shaft of the wand.

I was hypnotised by the sight of the witch of Caildur she was the most beautiful and powerful woman I had ever seen, more beautiful than Elios, more powerful and seductive than Ilo.

Her lips were mouthing messages to me but no words were spoken, the ambience of it all flowed through my very being, I was entranced by that spectacular female; I could not move and I could not speak.

The needs of desire were in me, I could feel an agonising want as I watched that hypnotic, fiery mosaic of the dark cosmos flowing itself around the body of Dulsie Mindbender. Not once did she speak through the seductive movements of her mouth, she didn't need to I was enthralled by the exotic, wondrous display on her body.

Her lips were still mouthing messages to me but I could not make them out. I was so entranced I did not realise I was moving steadily closer to her, because I so wanted to hear what her enticing lips were saying. She was firmly fixed in my mind in that space of time as a spectacular child of the universe and not capable of any evil.

I had to get closer, see the eyes, read her lips as they mouthed my name. I am pure spirit - she is a fallen elf. A union of the two of us could heal her - bring her back to her true self! I need to taste her lips, look into her eyes and be as one with her. The moving cosmos of her body had me spellbound.

A voice inside my head urgently whispering to my inner self - I don't want to listen, my focus is on Dulsie. The voice persists - I recognise Elios and I falter at her words.

Lael! She has entranced you with her body pictures- you feel as if you are one with her in the universe but you are not - you are of Ica and she is the child of Ulas. Do not look at her face and body, look through to the sewers of her mind, see how they run with malice and hatred - lower your eyes to the body and gaze within - do it Lael - you have the power of the spirit!

Look within and see for yourself the vile black essence of evil which courses through her body - see the rancid, putrid fluid gurgling down through her stomach. Can you see it Lael? The filth doesn't stop there it gutters its way down through her vile parts.

Would you want to unionise with that? She is no forest faerie she is a witch of the highest order; a destroyer of tribes; a corrupter of life entities; a hater of all things spiritual - Lael!

Do you hear me - resist! Help is nearby.

Elios words hit home, I saw Ulas-darg for what she was, in that instant all was still. Hardly a flicker as my aura started to became defensive, in the same breath the witch realised she had lost me.

No intimacy now, she stood stark naked facing me. The face contorted as if her fury couldn't decide which element to unleash first, thunder or lightening - thunder won.

'That whore from the forest has got to you.' The voice pealed through the chamber, shaking Cail-dur to its foundations. Then she raised her arms and shadows came alive behind her.

She aimed her sceptre at the wall beside me and a burst of flame came from it spreading itself across part of the wall at my side. The voice of Ulas-darg spoke in tones that threatened to shatter any kind of thought that I had left in my head. Then it lowered slightly so that I could listen to the horror that was to come.

'See the fire in the wall spirit of Ulana, remember the Earth that bore you, now watch and see it die. My dark servant is there already and has begun to destroy'-----------------

I was not prepared for what I saw, I could only see in the visual plane pictures that transferred to my random, fearful utterances of voice and thought------
----

A bloody red and treacherous plain - came to life in the flaming wall
As I gazed in the flames of fire - I saw the moon on its darker side

The lunar mass alive with explosive red - wretched and writhed in warlike dread
And in the living flames I saw tortured faces - pain and sorrow plain to see
A demon in black a mirror held - its fiery breath the smoke dispelled
At the glass I looked in fear - at images both far and near
Streets of blood and heat of death – crackling, hissing, dying earth
The mirror shone in flames of fire - my mind was kindled by illusions glare
In reflected horror I saw the end of all mankind - lifeless Earth and barren moon
Consumed by fire and now dust--------------swept away in cosmic wind
From terrors edge I stepped back from that wall of licking, crackling, fiery light.

A voice from a long way off - distant - persistent - pulsing - in my head. Elios commanding, demanding, telling me to look away from the flame, it is an illusion the Earth is not touched, put your aura up - now - now - now!

I was too slow - my last thought was *'How long will my defences last here in this cradle of evil.'* I never felt the stream of black energy that hit me.

Semora's Kiss

Before she was struck down Ulas-darg felled me with a bolt of black power. I was hurtled backwards and ended up on my back, I felt I was suspended in an energy of cold black remorseless time.

It's the only description I can equate it to, my body was cold, colder than it had ever been before and all around was swirling darkness. Out of the black mist horrific looking shapes began to manifest and as they did their empty mouths opened wide.

I was enmeshed in silence - no sound at all pervaded my space of dread, even from the mouthing of the demonic entities no sound came. Then words from the past came to enhance my cold shock -------- Evil cannot kill you, but if the power is strong enough it can contain you for all of eternity.

Never to see the light of suns by day or the stars and moons by night, no more cool air, no more to taste the water of a flowing stream. As if that wasn't punishment enough I was to spend eternity in silence with a pack of demons.

Then the demons stopped their weird antics and began to get agitated, in my torpid state I was aware of other entities. Grey shapes appeared and lined up beside my body and through the greyness I could discern fine features and one of them had a crown on his head.

The grey shapes surrounded me and linked arms, facing outwards to the demons. They were chanting something, I still couldn't hear but I could see their mouths moving. The demons were writhing and twisting and I could tell by their wide open red mouths they were howling and very angry.

Then everything happened at once, clarity of vision - an elfin king with a gold crown -elfin and faerie faces and beyond, demonic, twisted, torn, ugly black shapes mouthing their agony.

Sound returned in elfin chants ------ **ICA IS THE LIGHT - ICA IS THE LIGHT** - and in the background the last demented shrieks of tortured darkness ------------ then the warm touch of the angel.

I gazed into the face of the angel and Roscranna's words came back to me in her description of the angel she met at Satus. 'The most beautiful face I had ever seen.'

Lying where I was on the stone floor of Cail-dur staring at that face I passionately agreed with Roscranna and could only ask of her, her name. Then she was gone!

Then I was aware of Cender bending over me. 'Come Lael let us get out of this place and breath the air of Apuss, he has been waiting for us since Ara left the sky.'

We left by the way I came in and it felt a long time ago since I entered through that hideous door. I did notice then that it was gone, only the door posts and lintel left. As we passed through the gap, Derca appeared at the run sword drawn and ready for action. He stopped short when he saw the two of us and the look on his face was something else.

Cender got his words in first. 'Taken care of Ruis as I knew you would Derca - we have just taken care of the witch of Cail-dur in your absence.'

Derca sheathed his sword and for the first time since I had known him he laughed long and loud, it was a laugh of relief and of course at the stupidity of Cender's statement.

'Come let us be off this place, Croin awaits at the

top of the pathway and we can tell our tales of the happenings in his company, there is much to tell.' With that said he turned and led the way out of Caildur.

The light of day in the three worlds had never felt as good as it did on that morning of Apuss. I lifted my face upwards and was kissed again by the mighty god of the sky and I felt so blessed among mortals and spirits.

The huge shape of Croin was waiting at the place where Derca said he would be, I thought I caught the glimmer of a smile, if that was possible on his great beaked face, in respect he dipped his beak at me.

Cender told the tale as he saw it. 'I crept along the passageway not long after you entered, I thought if I was to expire then it was not to be skulking in the dark like an eathie demon. I got to the hall as the witch struck you down.

Then everything happened at once, the roof of the hall blew apart and an entity with wings descended - the winged creature caught the witch in an aura of light and the last I saw was Dulsie trapped in a spiral of bright pulsing energy vanishing through the hole in the roof.

The entity looked straight at me and I was staggered by the appearance of it, although her wings were folded she was hovering slightly above the floor. I say her! Because the shape was female in every respect.

I was held by her intense beauty and by the skin on her body, the background colours were dark purple and indigo and across that fascinating body and face a moving picture of the cosmos flowed all around.

On hearing Cender's description I thought to myself - *once again the duality of the opposites appears in the greatest goodness and the worst evil.* I listened intently to what he said next.

The flying creature came from the sky of that I am sure - and yet her wings were more like slivers of black and silver and they did not move like a bird's motion. They were more like an energy that accompanied her.

I looked at you Lael and saw your body lying on the cold hard floor of Cail-dur your lightness had gone. Darkness and shadow enveloped all of you and your face was contorted in great horror.

I moved towards you but the creature held up its hand and I was rendered motionless, it then stood over you and swept its hands over you then it kissed you. When your lightness returned the entity looked at me and smiled a smile that nearly melted me to the place where I stood, then it vanished the way it came.'

Derca and Croin were staggered by the words of Cender and I could see they were bewildered by the description of the winged creature so I took it upon myself to enlighten them as to what it was.

'The creature, or entity as Cender called her, was an angel, one of the messengers of mighty Ica herself. Her name was Semora and were it not for her I would be condemned to eternal darkness.'

Then reality hit me - what has happened to all my friends, I was so wrapped up in my own survival that

I had not spared a thought for my companions who were probably fighting for their lives and the world we stood on. I voiced my thoughts to Derca.

'Derca for a brief moment I felt the energy of many spirits leaving their physical bodies but what or who they were I cannot tell. I can only imagine a battle has been fought.'

My thoughts were immediately answered by the soft whispering tones of Elios and I remained in the listening mode. My companions sensed what was happening and remained in silent union with myself.

Lael, all the dark forces have been vanquished - the magical union of the triad with added support from Esir-amit and the red storm hawk that carried her were successful in defeating the enemy.

Cerenor-Tala, the Draig of Elinbroom, completely wiped out the evil entities at the Fochd pass.

You have done well for your part in ridding the world of Darwan of the black witch.

All your friends have come through the battle unscathed and I have instructed Croin to pick you up after you have time with the two elves.

He will take you to a place where you will await Nal of the bana, who will be accompanying you on your final journey in Darwan. I will speak to you again before your journey ends.

And that was that after all the events that had transpired – well at least all the strange characters that I knew came through it all. I passed on the words of Elios to my companions. Derca and Cendor immediately turned their faces to Apuss and thanked him for ridding the land of the evil and for sparing their friends in arms.

Even Croin gave a reaction of sorts he lifted his beak to Apuss and gave out a raucous cry - minus the cruelty.

Croin preferred the solitude of the air and took off, leaving myself and the two elves. I immediately quizzed Derca about the fight between him and Ruis.

'What took place Derca? Where is Ruis?' I was relieved to see Derca in one piece but I wanted to know where Ruis had gone.

Derca answered me by first jumping on to the top of a prominent rock where he stood for a while before answering.

Derca leaped down from the rock and stood in front of me saying. 'Ruis is dead, I killed him but it was not easy. I fought the greatest one to one battle of my life at that place on a rock such as this one.'

'What happened to his body - is it still lying where you killed him?'

Derca answered me, but before he spoke he went back atop the boulder he had just come off. He had a faraway look in his eyes as he recounted the events leading to the death of Ruis.

'Ruis fought like an elf possessed, his speed was amazing, his arms that wielded the blades so powerful and his movements so co-ordinated. I knew I had to use tactics that would throw him off balance. I moved from offensive to defensive time and again. I leaped from rock to rock and somersaulted over the top of him, he was quick and good but I was more experienced.

It was a long time ago since he had fought against a

foe that was his equal. Whereas I had been fighting all my life against powerful enemies and had sparred with Nal of the bana during our journey, so I had the advantage there.

The blow I dealt him came from a rock like this one here where I stand. Ruis came at me leaping from boulder to boulder, I watched as he launched himself off the last boulder in order to spring up to face me. I timed it to perfection, as his feet left the boulder I moved, jumping sideways I passed him in mid-air and sliced my blade through his upraised arm, cutting into his neck bone.

His body collapsed and I was on him, severing his head from his body. As I watched, a misty shape rose from the body of Ruis and spiralled upwards; I watched it until it disappeared into the sky. Then I heard a voice I did not recognise in my head. The voice said to me. You have done well Derca of Lael now stand back from the body of the fallen elf.

I stood back and in front of my eyes the body of Ruis was consumed by a fire that came from nowhere, all that was left but a mark of scorched earth to show where he had lain.'

I spoke to Derca again. 'The spirit of Ruis was taken back to Ulana and will be placed in the isle of tortured souls. His body was taken by fire by the guardians of the universe and its dust scattered in the dark clouds where life and death are as one. The physical body of Ruis is no more.'

Derca stood silent for a while then he turned to me and said.

'Lael, I swore once that I would never again set foot

on the land of the Black Isle and now I recognise the folly of making emphatic statements. We know not what lies ahead of us and it is just as well - the space we occupy now is enough to live in.

Like a galley sailing on the water it is good to look back on its wake to assure us our course is true. But after a while the ruffle of the wake is absorbed by the sea around, so like our past that merges with the past of others we are guided to where we are now.

The entanglement of so many lives over so many eons of time, and in your case Lael three worlds, make me so aware of the mystery of life - of all entities be they good or bad. We are survivors of all the pasts of so many lives and as such should be grateful for the light of Apuss by day and the appearance of Ara and Rinnis by night.'

Then, taking Cender and me by the shoulders, he pushed us in a forward direction and declared. 'No more deep thinking, come friends let us walk and rejoice as we have come through it all. We have much to talk about before we part company, Croin will find us when he has had enough of his own company.'

Casualties of War

In the aftermath the warriors began the trek from the battlefield to their homelands. The Bana were carrying their dead back to the sea. All the other clans burn their dead on the field of battle.

The badly injured were carried in litters by their comrades to wherever their homes were. All the Bana five had survived the battle, they had gathered round Eils who had recovered, due to the help of Cerenor.

The Draig had stayed with Eils and Bheir until the battle was over, she had put Eils into a trance and completely removed the small amount of black energy that had seeped into her system during the battle. Eils and Bheir thanked Cerenor for saving the land and all the inhabitants in it; if she had not appeared things would not have gone well.

Cerenor replied by saying. 'I can heal as well as waste the malignant carrion that miss-use magic for the ways of Ulas.'

At that point Suila drew the group's attention to a band of shade elfs and faolwarriors who were carrying two litters between them. They all looked at the occupants of the litters and Traig said. 'That is Enderli and Coonie.'

Suila asked one of the faolwarriors how badly injured they were.

A faolwarrior called Erman answered her in a very scoffing tone. 'This pair of hind-enders are not injured, they are comatose with rotgut - they missed the battle, we found them lying behind a boulder with many empty flagons beside them.'

At Erman's statement the Bana nearly collapsed with laughter, Traig said. 'Enderli will never be allowed to forget this occasion, it's easily his best trick so far. Imagine if the war had been lost and they woke in a land of shades and demons.'

Nal said. 'If the shades ran out of rotgut they could have hung Coonie and Enderli upside down and drained them.'

Suila added on after glancing at the departing pair. 'By the looks of those two, the shades would have enough from Coonie and Enderli to last them for a few Araens.'

Even Cerenor had something to say. 'Well, after all the devastation that has occurred their non-participation has brought forth the joy of laughter.'

Then she addressed the bana five. 'You are fine warriors you all have integrity and a sound belief in yourselves. Today you fought and won a battle, Eils did well to wield the magic sword of Elid as long as she did with no protection.

Understand my words warriors, even with good magic, self-protection is important. The power that you have can come back into you and weaken you considerably. That is why Eils collapsed as she did, if she had not been as strong and resilient she would have fallen long before she did.

Remember warriors you are all of a race and whatever or wherever you go, the bond will always be strong no matter how far apart you may be.

I felt the essence of Ilo, Tress and Elid leaving the world of Darwan, maybe some of you saw the light in the sky over the Laic lands. That signalled the end of the battle and also the end of an era of magic.

On the field of battle today I felt the ascendancy of Esir-amit and the red draig hawk of the Liagh Mountains.

Esir's mind was with the faeries of the Laic as she and the red hawk merged into the light energy, creating an invincible power that vanquished everything pertaining to dark energy.

Energy cannot be destroyed but it can be converted and carried away within the purity of light and taken back to where it was created. There it will be integrated with the force that it was separated from and the balance will once again be maintained.

Hardly were the words out of the Draig's mouth when Traig rattled out a question. 'Why did she take the storm hawk with her and why had the black hawk red markings and wh'------------' Cerenor stopped Traig in mid flow. 'Hold there little warrior, if I could spit flame at the rate questions fly out of you I would be a mean fighting creature.

Nal has told me all about her companions in arms and I would hazard a guess and say you are Traig, am I right?'

'Yes Cerenor Tala, I am Traig of the bana.' Traig looked up at the Draig from her kneeling position and put on her listening ears.

'Well Traig I am happy to meet you, you ask many questions because inside you have a fervent desire for knowledge. In a time far ahead the only weapons you will carry will be the knowledge and experience you will have in your head.

You and the warrior standing behind you with her hand on your shoulder, by the name of Bheir, will become great warriors of wisdom. You two alone will be responsible for taking the race of the bana ger into a new age and this will be a foundation for the rest of the world of Darwan.

You are fortunate to be part of a race and culture that take pride in each-others doings, no envy or greed taints you or your comrades, you would die for each other if you had to.

Before I depart on my journey I will tell you this, not all the magic has left the lands of Laic; you may find the next bearer of white energy very different from the last one.'

With that Cerenor raised the hackles at the sides of her neck and stretched her mighty wings, blew a plume of flame into the air then she was off.

As they watched Cerenor flying off, Nal muttered. 'I hope that last blast of flame burnt Nindrils ass.'

They all chuckled at Nal's quip then all five walked off to join their clan and head back to the coast and their window on the world ------ the sea of Meren.

LUIS

Croin eventually came back for us and took us off the Black Island, I was squashed between Cender and Derca - Croin said one of his neck feathers was heavier than me.

He dropped Cender and Derca off at a shade elf settlement and it was there that I said my farewells to them. It was a happy parting and no great words of wisdom were passed.

Croin took me to a place he called Methia and to my great delight all of the bana five were there - it was so good to see them all. Croin said he had to go as Derca and Cender would want to get back to their lands.

But before he left he spoke to the bana awhile, mainly to ask about the battle they fought. He also filled them in about my part in the witch's downfall and that brought a few - yip - yips from the bana.

As he flew away I waved and the bana cheered and whistled after him.

Croin was hardly out of sight when I was

bombarded by questions from Traig, one in particular interested me. She asked if the angel that Croin mentioned controlled the movements of afterlife spirits.

That caused a pronounced silence from the rest until Bheir agreed with the question that Traig had asked. She went on to enhance the question by saying - why are some entities capable of thought transference and others have magical powers?

I had to admit I had not much knowledge of angels, only what Roscranna told me and of course my own recent experience with one. So I explained what I did know and that was that the angels were guardians of not only the worlds but also the layers of stars and the corridors of time.

'The stars of the night sky are endless and within them are boundaries, I do not know how many there are but each boundary has a guardian angel. Roscranna told me that Seronis had said that the angels did not communicate directly with the spirits; that was left to the guardians of each and every spirit world.

There are many types of energies in the earth, waters and the air; within some of these energies are channels that link certain life entities to one another through the mind.

The five of you share a physical energy and you all have absolute faith in one another, although you do not talk in your heads - yet! You all know each other for what you are, it is all about knowing and knowing is a step to enlightenment of the mind.

Who knows, maybe some of you might be able to

contact each other through the mind and at a great distance.'

My little speech was received in silence, a sure sign that I had given them something to think about - and not one question from Traig.

Nal started to walk away from me so I said goodbye to the four warriors and wished them well on their journeys. I hurried after Nal and asked her why she did not stay until her companions left.

Her answer was simply put. 'They know where I am going and I know where they will be, now let us head for the Salacian water.' So side by side we set off on yet another journey.

Most of the travel was spent passing through bare undulating hills and open woodlands. I had such a buoyant feeling, all the trials and hardships I had encountered on my journey of further enlightenment were getting closer to fruition.

I relayed my enthusiasm to Nal and was most surprised by the reaction I got; she was highly motivated by her coming journey and told me tales about journeys the other bana warriors had gone on.

I let her carry on with her stories and listened with shared joy at all of the many and various events she spoke of.

Finally we both retreated into ourselves and just walked and enjoyed the quiet of the surrounding landscape.

We heard the rumbling of the mighty ocean before we saw it. We breasted a round bare hill and there it was - a huge expanse of royal blue water as far as the eye could see, flat as the Beatha loch but even in stillness there was sound. It was the sound of eternal motion, no matter how calm or how silent the land round about; the sea always spoke to those of us who had an ear to listen.

I turned Nal. 'It's beautiful and not in the slightest bit wild.'

She answered me in no uncertain terms. 'Lael when that sea gets angry you will know all about it, remember Derca's tale about the voyage of the Ector.' Then in a lighter tone. 'Look down there Lael, it's the Oliv-losai.'

My vision of the Oliv-losai up to that point had been of a drab craft the like of which the gaists use on the rivers. I stood in wonder for a breath of time to take in what I saw.

The Oliv-losai was lying alongside a pier which had been whitened due to eons of salt spray and hot sun. The hull of the boat was ochre red which accented the fine lines of the ship. Topside the well-scrubbed woodwork was mostly white. A wheelhouse with a cabin attached to it was at the aft'er end. A mizzen mast was behind the cabin, it had a boom with a topping-lift and I could make out a terracotta coloured sail wrapped between the two.

At the forward end was a main mast and boom complete with sail, also terracotta coloured. A jib was prominent at the fore peak. No figures could be seen on deck.

The boat lay still at its moorings and the whole of the vessel was reflected in the water.

'Look.' I said to Nal. 'You would think there was another boat stuck to the Oliv-losai upside down, so clear is the water.'

Nal crouched down and regarded the scene below then said. 'You would think some power had polished the world as we see it. So shiny is the sea and the colour of the boat and the pier and rocks, Apuss is kind to us.'

It was on that bare promontory in the midst of nature's shinning beauty that Elios came to me for the last time.

'Lael you are on the edge of the great water. Here begins your journey to the upper reaches of spiritual enlightenment. Jon knows where to take you, he will sail you to your destination. He will drop Nal off at the sacred isle of the Bana; she will accomplish much before she is swallowed up by the great waters.

The voyage will give you time to meditate on your time in Darwan. You may not be aware of it but you have had an effect on all the life entities that you came in contact with.

You have healed a great part of the land itself by your depth of feeling and love for the natural world. Already a great forest has flourished and stretched far beyond its former boundaries and it will carry your name until the rivers of time merge at their final destination.

These are events that have yet to come, for you Lael the real journey begins now. May peace and love go with you until you come to journeys end.'

These were the last words I heard from Elios the faerie.

Nal was regarding me with her bland stare. 'Were you talking in your head Lael?'

'Yes Nal I was in conversation with Elios, she has told me Jon knows the way to the green island and she wished me well on my journey.'

How can she know these things when she is in different world from us?

'Such is the way of the spirit Nal, there is virtually no barrier to thought transference but having said that, on the path that I tread after the Salacian Sea I will be alone with my thoughts, and the only way after that will be ahead and upward.'

Whatever Nal thought she didn't voice it, she got up from her crouched position and headed down a path which led directly to the haven below us. *So many events had come and gone -*

We reached the boat and there was still no one about so Nal jumped onto the deck and drew her short sword and rattled it against the deck house.

Noises from below told us that someone was aboard and that was confirmed by the sound of footsteps coming up from the depths of the ship.

Before any figure emerged a deep booming voice sounded forth. 'Aye aye, is that my new shipmates I hear?'

Then a body emerged and it certainly matched the voice. I don't know what Nal was thinking but I wondered how the shape managed to get up through such a small hatchway.

I had never met the man but this could only be big Jon Beet - and what a size he was, easily the biggest man I had seen since my time in Darwan.

He came forward to us with arms outstretched and hands open. 'Welcome to my boat spirit Lael and warrior Nal, we shall have good stories to tell each other. Come - come down below and have some fish and drink and tell me of the events that have passed'.

We followed Jon down below and I marvelled at the agility of the man as he lightly shinned down the steps to the cabin below. His feet had no sooner touched the lower deck than he yelled loudly. 'Gat, Mora, get up - we have guests c'mon - c'mon lets have you.'

Two shapes appeared from spaces that looked as if they had been carved out of the sides of the boat. They were beds of some sort and by the look of the two who answered Jon's call they had been fast asleep.

They gazed at me in astonishment but their expressions changed when they saw Nal.

'Gat, Mora - this is Nal of the bana and we will be taking her to the sacred isle of her tribe. The other guest is Lael, a spirit of Ulana we will be dropping him off at the Green isle of Erisdel.'

Mora asked Nal if she had been fighting. Before she could answer him I broke in.

'She was fighting all right, firing arrows from the back of a Draig and after the Draig landed she joined up with Traig and Suila and fought with them against the remainder of the enemy.'

The faces of Gat and Mora were a picture as I elaborated on the tale of the battle. However they would have to wait for more details as big Jon gave them their marching orders.

'Come on lads, get topsides and cast the ropes off, we need to catch the tide.'

The lads didn't need a second telling, they went

scuttling up the trap and we could hear their footsteps on the deck as they hastened to their tasks.

I stood with Nal by my side, both of us looking at big Jon and in the ambience of that cabin which had witnessed so much, images floated across my mind.

'My feeling is that the tribe of Cimer and the black elves will have much to do with the unknown lands. The bana warriors will move again and Suilval will probably drift with them. A new entity will appear in the Laic lands and Daralonadh will become a place of spirituality and learning.

Such is the physical existence of life - ever wandering - ever wondering and so slowly heading towards spirituality. It comes to all sooner or later, most meet it at the point of death but some get it early in their physical life. They are very gifted and are influential in spreading goodness by their presence alone.'

MUIN

Nal was standing on the bow rail when she drew my attention to a speck on the horizon. 'Lael, Jon has told me that my island of Moola is what we see ahead of us, it won't be long before we reach it.'

I had been in silent meditation in the after part of the ship when I was alerted by Nal and as I looked at the faraway isle I felt a pang of emotion. The time had to come when we would have to say goodbye.

I had already said my goodbyes to Derca, Suilval and Cerenor but it was a shared farewell and I still had Nal to accompany me. Now it was drawing closer to the final parting, as I came to Darwan on my own so I would leave it, and as far as I knew it would be on my own.

However her enthusiasm at seeing her island took me out of my moment and I joined her at the bow where we stood together and watched it draw closer.

It was higher than I imagined and as we got closer I saw that the mountainous region was in the centre of the island, high pointed hills with the treeline stopping short of the summits. The whole range of hills was covered in forests of green, copper and orange, the colouration was spectacular.

Below the mountains the lesser hills were dappled with purple and green, and as my eyes were drawn down to the plains of Moola I made out some of the stone obelisks that the bana men had erected. They were standing on an elevated rise and I could see they were tall and equally spaced from each other.

Although they were all the same height, each one had a different shape and some had openings in them, I could see right through some of the holes. I asked Nal what they were for.

I was a amazed at her reply, she told me that the 'Brudair' ask the bana warriors to take notice of the risings of Ara, Rinnis and certain stars in relation to the markings that are incised into the plain in front of the stones.

She went on to tell me that the bana men made replicas of the stones and their positions relative to a stone floor in front of the halls of Arcil. Each warrior has to check the lines of Moola and in company of the Brudair when they return to Arcil they look for any shift that may have occurred.

Nal ended the conversation abruptly - as usual - and gave the island her full attention.

Yellow cliffs curved down to the white sands of a beach that stretched for miles on either side of my vision. The blue of the inshore water made sharp contrast as it licked the white sands.

High in the sky I could see birds soaring on air currents, short bodies but very long slender wings, I asked Nal what kind of birds they were.

'They are the sacred birds of the Sonder Mountains. They are protected no one is allowed to hunt them.'

I asked Nal why they were protected, knowing full well the bana eat any animal that walks, any fish that swims and anything they can shoot out of the air.

Nal couldn't tell me, she said that they have always been sacred to the bana and that's all there is to it.

Big Jon shouted to us. 'Nal, this is your journeys end, you have to get off now.'

Bheir had told me when the bana reach the island the boat stays offshore in shallow water, no one except the bana warrior who is to be the keeper of the island may go ashore.

And that was it, Nal leaped into the water, nothing else but her weapons and the scant clothes she wore. Not a backward look, just a raising of the bow in her hands as she waded through the gentle surf, she left me without a word of goodbye.

The Bana warrior who had done her time in Moola came tripping along the beach and into the water to greet Nal. They stopped and held each other by the shoulders and words were spoken that we could not hear, then they parted.

Jon grinned when he saw my bewildered look then in his loud haly-racket voice he roared. 'Well it saves a sentimental farewell, although there would not have been any tears from her.' He nodded in the direction of the departing Nal. 'They are a queer lot right enough, give me Derca and his elves any day.'

Jon turned his attention to the incoming warrior 'Well how have you been faring San?'

San, who reminded me of Suila, jumped aboard the boat and answered Jon's question in the style of Suila. 'Okay Jon! I notice you haven't lost your voice since I have been away.'

Jon answered back and I am sure he lowered his voice an octave. 'Aye and you haven't lost your wit San.'

San came right up to me and introduced herself, we had hardly spoken when Jon - his voice back to thunder again, told San to go below and join the lads who were at their supper with plenty fish to spare.

Off she went and I was left at the bow on my own staring at the island, Nal had vanished from sight. I must have kept that stance for longer than I thought because I became aware of the boat's movement.

Gat was at the rudder and Mora was setting the half-sail, the Oliv-Losai slipped silently out of the bay and soon had its head into the open sea. I sat for a long time at the bow in the stillness of my mind and the accompanying soft sound of the water as the stem of the boat pushed it apart.

My thoughts floated in memory of three worlds. My first journey on one of the great seas of earth ----------- my first voyage on the magnificent ocean of Ulana ---- and now most probably my last sea crossing in Darwan ---- or ever.

I crossed the waters of all my lives

To look back on reflected joys

That mirrored youth and carefree days

On a shore now that was a vision of my past

My mind and eyes left the waters and became filled with the light as I gazed upward at a white incandescent sun high above. It was by far the brightest I had seen Apuss in all the time I had been in Darwan.

I live in the light and the light lives in me, but no matter how often I think on light ascendancy I still wonder if I become part of the fusion of light will I miss the ability to sail on a sea or climb a mountain or fly through the air on the back of a storm hawk.

I do believe in the effervescence of light and the merging of spirits to keep it bright and pure, but self-doubt gnaws away at me. Am I ready to give up my ability to move and because of my self-guilt am I good enough to go any further in spirit.

Why is it that self-doubt follows me through all the worlds I have travelled? Though a voice from afar comes misting into my mind, they are words that Elios had repeated to me many times.------------- *Lael do not resist your thoughts of doubts, remember they are not there to drag you down they are there for you to focus on. Whatever level you are at whether it is in an earthen body or an Ulana spirit or going through the passage of Darwan.*

You were connected to the great universe when you were on Earth you were connected even more in Ulana. When you are in the last stage of your journey through Darwan you must trust wholly in the spirit and remain connected. Connection to the universe is the meaning of life no matter what form anything is ------- a spirit, a physical body, a stone, a tree they all share one thing and that is connection to the universe. When you are merged with the light then that is the ultimate connection.

The memory of her words refreshed my mind and I instantly connected to where I was and thanked the universe for the natural beauty that that was all around me.

I was hailed by the voice of big Jon. 'Aye Lael, what world are you in - mine or somebody else's, come aft-by and give me some company, the lads are sleeping.'

So I trotted aft and sat by big Jon Beet and when I got there the 'Beet' gave me the rudder and vanished down below with the parting words. 'Keep the head of the boat on Apuss.'

Three risings of Apuss and three of Ara and I was nearing the land that I was to be put ashore on.

It was Mora who alerted me that the land was dead ahead. In his excitement to tell me he shouted three times -------- Lael the land ---- Lael the land ---- Lael the land! I stood on the bowsprit and held on to one of the stays and watched the faint green shape on the horizon get bigger and bigger.

I had been refreshed in mind and spirit and I had the dark nights of the Salacian Sea to gaze upward and connect with the mighty universe. Just looking at the clear night sky is all you need do to connect your 'self' to the life giving universe.

Now ahead of me is another place I have to connect with, I have received no information pertaining to the land or any living entity on it. I quizzed Jon about it and he was no more informed about it than I. In fact he said it was the furthest by the way of Ica he had ever been on the Salacian Sea.

He had received a message from Elid Silverhair long

back telling him if all went well he would receive instructions from a sea elf of Meren called Iorla.

He had been hailed by a war galley whilst cruising off the Meren Sea in an area that was called 'The waters of Adine'. The elf called Iorla asked if she could come aboard. Big Jon added on that he was not going to say no to that lot.

Jon also remarked that she was armed for battle and the galley looked as if it was ready for a long voyage. She did not waste time telling him that he was to take a spirit form with him when Nal of the bana was making her journey to Moola. She gave him the course details from Moola to the land he was to drop me off at --- no more no less.

He said that the sea elves are a fine tribe to deal with; he had been to their shores many times. He also said they are masters of the waves and can handle anything from an elf skiff to a war galley.

Big Jon told me that an elf skiff is hardly a boat at all, it's a board with slightly upturned sides and a keel of sorts. It carries a light sail which the elves handle by movements of a swivel boom.

'They are one elf craft, mostly used for skittering around the coast; no good for me as I would hardly get the sole of one of my feet on it.'

With that said he planted one huge foot on Gat's hind end and bellowed. 'Isn't that right boy?'

Gat agreed from where he had landed - half way up the deck.

After my dialogue with Jon I stood at the bow of the boat to enjoy the solitude, it was not long before the slim image of green in the far distance took on shape. Even then as I looked ahead my mind could not help but to take backward thoughts.

It was not doubt, fear or regret that made my thoughts go back to all my journeys to this almost final part. In all of the three worlds there had been identities that I could relate to - even my body shape held its upright position although the rest of my senses were heightened to their zenith, but that I could accept.

The thought of ascendancy excited me no end, but what form would I take - what memories would I retain - what reality would I be in - so many what ifs ----

I dismissed the thoughts of events to come and concentrated on the ambience of my present reality. Gat and Mora were down below sleeping. Big Jon was manning the rudder, silent for a change.

The sea was flat and calm with Apuss's light a pathway to the green land.

Then without warning shapes shot out of the water. I instantly recognised them as my friends from the Tanaron Sea. Leaping and cavorting in the path of the boat their energy swept all over me.

Big Jon's booming voice came from the stern. 'Aye Lael, you must be well in with Shuira for her to send the mers to escort you.'

Then Lefin was in my thoughts, but before I could respond one of the mers flew out of the water right over the boat deck showering Jon with seawater.

Once again big Jon's voice boomed out as he shook his fist at the Mer. 'I will catch you by the tail one day.'

Yes Lael, I suppose you have guessed who that was - some things never change. I doubt if he ever will. We all wanted to accompany you on your last sea crossing - from all of us - go in love and light.

I sent my thoughts to all of the mers and called them all by name, each and every one acknowledged me. They stayed with the boat for a long time then in a final display of water antics they were gone.

The vision of land took form and before long the Oliv-Losai was grounded at the bow end. But this parting was more civilised than the last one on Moola, Jon and his two sons waded the short distance ashore with me and wished me well on my journey wherever I was going.

I looked back at the departing ship and waved again at the crew, big Jon was at the rudder looking back at me, Gat and Mora sitting on the rail of the stern. Sar was sitting cross legged between the two. They all waved back and Gat spun himself round the stay of the mizzen mast as a farewell to me.

I stood in the stillness of myself, glorying in the feel of the earth beneath my feet and the white light of Apuss. My eyes took in the fast disappearing boat it looked as if it was skimming on top of the water not floating in it.

Water shining on endless ocean

Polished mirror silver sea

Lonely ship pursues its course

Heading home to friendly coast

After I had sent my thoughts of farewell to the sea I turned and felt the green embrace of the tree lined shore, it beckoned me with a welcoming ambience. A shimmer of movement from the trees directly in front invited me to pass through.

The inside of the forest was a sight to behold, from the tops of the high trees Apuss speared through leaves, branches and plants making a pathway of light in a direction I was obliged to take.

A melody of birdsong was all around and shapes of creatures flitted in and out of my vision, one in particular. Out of memory and like a snapshot through many veils of time ------ my dog of Earth, Brin the German shepherd who saw me fall in the earthen forest of Lael.

She came right up to me, tail wagging and making howling noises. The feel of touching her head and big ears gave me a peculiar feeling that only seconds had elapsed since I saw her last.

And as on Earth all the way back through the long corridors of time, with its many twists and turns, Brin ran ahead of me once again and I had no option but to follow.

I followed Brin for a long time and it was so enjoyable watching her sniffing and snuffling about the forest floor. Then she stopped and gave me the same quizzical look that she gave me on Earth - and just disappeared.

I called and called but got no response, I thought to myself - am I moving forward in time --- I cannot be moving back --- or can I - surely worlds and galaxies cannot move in opposition to each other - but in the mystery of space anything is possible.

I tried to project my thoughts to any friendlies that may be about. I knew they must be around somewhere because there was heavy spiritual presence in the forest.

All the time I was trying to connect I had the curious feeling that my mind path was being blocked by something or someone.

Your thoughts won't go anywhere out or in this wood, spirit of Ulana, unless I clear the way.

The voice was in my head but I could not see the body shape. I voiced my request. 'Show yourself entity.'

The voice laughed in my head.

I do not show myself to any being unless I so wish. This is my forest, I hear and see everything just like your guardian in the MoAraian forest.

I was encouraged by the mention of the forest of Ulana so I asked the bearer of thoughts and voice if she knew Elios.

Again I heard the intense voice in my head, with its vibrations of amusement and mystery.

Elios and I walked the forests of Ulana and Darwan when the stream of time was in its youth. She was Erim Elios, faerie healer of life entities and I was Aior anor--------------At the sound of the name of Aior anor I broke into her thoughts and said ----- 'The Green woman companion of Elios.'

Aior anor appeared behind me and I was a bit amazed at first impression, not what I expected. She was tall like Elios but there the resemblance ended, I noticed something straightaway that I had never seen before on any elfin or faerie spirit.

Aior looked older, not old - old, but most definitely her features were more mature looking than others of the spirit.

Although older looking she radiated a rare beauty that I had never seen before, her skin was as russet brown as the trunks of the trees about her. She had a noble face and eyes that shone with delight.

But by far the most striking feature was the green hair! The shade of it changed with the movement of her head from emerald to dark then to moss green. Enhanced by the light of Apuss the hues of green were ever so lightly touched by threads of auburn.

Her legs were bare as were her arms, all she wore was a plain skirted tunic, around her neck she wore a cord of brown material and from it hung a drop of green crystal.

And that was Aior anor, as true a vision of natural beauty as I had ever seen, no staff of power had she in either hand. The power was within and it exuded all around, every living entity was alive with her energy.

All the time I was looking at her, she was regarding me with an amused expression on her face, it matched exactly the vibrations of the thoughts that I received from her during mind contact.

When she spoke her voice tones matched the song of the wood which had been pleasantly humming all around since I entered it.

'Lael have you no questions to ask me, have the wonders of the mystical wood of Erisel robbed you of voice?'

I did find my voice and the first question I asked was about the appearance of Brin and the feelings I experienced during the encounter.

Aior answered my question by asking me one. 'Lael when you looked to the night sky in the worlds you have been on did you ever see anything that formed a perfect circle?'

She answered for me saying. 'No, the universes are full of ellipses, spirals and oblate shapes, even light and time do not move in straight lines. Only humanity and certain other world creatures have the circle and straight lines.

They formed the circle to aid them to understand how to arrive at solutions or to find their way on their seas and the heavens. The circle is equated to life, fate and even time itself, it is easy to understand because it states the obvious.

There is no obvious understanding of time, the mighty universes are alive with corridors and doors of time and they do not run in straight lines; nor does the life journey of a world form a circle. Time is the illusionary guide for the machinations of humanity,

The spirit of Brin reached Ulana not long after you did. All I did was open a door in space time. Brin appeared to welcome you for a brief moment then I put her back through the door she came.

There is such a spiritual ambience in the forest of Lael, many happenings have taken place there; in its growth history it is very connected to the galaxy it lives in.'

My next question had been turning over and over

again in my mind so I asked why spirits like Aior and Elios had not been called to the light before now.

She smiled an even broader smile and said. We were not first to take shape in the great scheme of Ica and Ulas. The Draigs were first born and then another race of spiritual entities that populated another dimension, one of whom took you back from the darkness.

'Oh! The angels! So they came after the Draigs - I remember well the kiss of Semora on that day.

After my exclamation Aior continued to enlighten me about the hierarchy of ascension.

'Lael you have heard the expression ------- the first shall be last and the last shall be first. Well that holds true as far as the entities are concerned in this continuum. The Draigs will be last to join the blinding light of Ica. We have all remained to guide the young spirits in their journey to light.'

Then I asked. 'Where did Cerenor go when she left the field of battle?'

'Ah!' Said Aior. 'Cerenor-Tala is another story - who knows what Draigs get up to.'

And that was all she said on the subject of Cerenor-Tala, the last Draig of Darwan.

'Come Lael, let us wander through the wonderful woodland of Erisel as there is much to see and think about.

The energetic, elliptical and sometimes erratic movements of the universes can be likened to cities, towns and villages on your world of Earth that grow outwards and upwards connected by roads and railways and airways.

So it is with Universes, galaxies, worlds, planets and wells of darkness, they are all connected by corridors of time within the great movement of the magimatrix of dark energy.'

'Come with me and I will show you where the energy is that keeps Erisel in its place of serenity.'

I followed Aior through the greenery of Erisel. Truly I felt I was back in Ulana, such was the euphoria of my spiritual wellbeing and the company of the Green Woman made it complete.

We came to a vast clearing in the forest and right in the middle of it stood a tree that was so magnificent it must have been the greatest tree I had ever seen in all my lives.

It was gigantic and spectacular in its beauty, it would need three trees of Ulana to make that giant of Erisel. Aior said because of its coppery colouring, Apuss in the morning makes it a golden splendour. In the evening he turns it red, to the beholder it looks as if the tree is on fire.

The tree is called Erisendal and it has its roots in the very heart of Darwan. The land lives and breathes through Erisendal; he is the great protector of this - the forest of ascendancy. The Green Woman did a pirouette with arms at full stretch as she made the statement.

I had to ask Aior a question before she carried on with her story of Erisendal.

'Tell me Aior what is the connection that Darwan has with Ulana and the higher ascendancy, and where does Earth fit in with it. Darwan is such a planet of contradictions and yet I feel at times there is much identifiable with Earth.'

Aior fixed me with green eyes that had probably witnessed the dawn of man's time on Earth and completely ignored my question. 'Lael your time is here, this is the start of another journey, one that takes you on to higher ascension of spirituality.'

I had to come clean to Aior about my thoughts on the higher reaches. 'Aior I understand why the upper reaches need the spirits to feed the light but I do not think I'm ready to give up my spiritual body or deny myself the sight of the stars by night and the sun by day.'

Aior's reply shook me a bit as I was not prepared for what she told me next.

'Oh Lael who said ascension meant ever upwards, sometimes you have to go sideways to learn a bit more before you venture any further to blend with the light. Believe you me, where you go next will be every bit as colourful as the worlds you have been in already.

The spirit world of Ulana is the home for earthen spirits and that is what it is. The doors are open for spirits to enter after death. Some gifted earthen humans can pick up vibrations of thought and sight and take occasional messages from spirit.

Those messages do not pass through the doors of spirit, everything that is - vibrates to a tune.'

Aior motioned me in the direction of Erisendel's massive trunk, the closer we got to it the more vibrant I felt. What an immense feeling of energy coursed through my already enhanced spiritual body. Anor led me under the tree of the universe and under its gigantic branches she bade me sit down.

I did what she told me and then sitting alongside she went on to say that my meditation in that place would be very different from all of the meditations I had ever had up to that point.

Anor said. 'Lael up to now you have heard of various versions of how the universes were formed. Each and every one has accepted that in the mystery of the darkness the life forms of Ica and Ulas took shape. Some life entities have differing ideas of how the darkness itself came from.

Now Lael you have a chance under the tree of Erisel to meditate on that beginning and see what pictures come to you. I will be by your side throughout your meditation so be assured you are not alone when your subconscious mind is detached from your spiritual body.

Through the magnificent canopy of the mighty tree of Erisel I could make out one or two stars and planets in the night sky. I felt the whole of the universe was stilled as I sat in that space in time.

I felt my mind ever so slowly being pulled from my body - a gentle soothing withdrawal from the worlds that I had known. I was in the beginning of creation and through the eyes of my sub-conscious I beheld a blackness that was so deep it felt heavy.

I felt through the eyes of my mind that the blackness was moving around me and was substance not darkness. Then the heaviness left me and I saw a magnificent sight at a great distance from me.

Two huge convex bands of blue pulsating energy facing each other - the black void between kept them apart. I could see a slight difference in one of the bands; its blue energy was tinged with white.

Then a happening that was so fast and violent - both bands crashed together and in a blaze of confusion so many colours filled my visual plane. Then the colours turned to shapes and sped off away from me.

The movements in my visual plane were happening so fast it was hard to grasp what was going on. It looked like many universes were being formed but the curious thing was they were not as one. The whole starlit entity split in two and formed up on either side of the original explosion which was still burning.

Then clouds of vapour obscured my vision, at intervals the haze cleared and the blackness was revealed again - shapes appeared through the veil of blackness as if the dark matter had been torn to allow them through.

The shapes appeared and disappeared in fast and furious motion - I had hardly time to focus on any of them. Vague memories of a dark haired female with a mace - a red blunt looking shape with a gaping mouth - a luminous green blob came close and as its luminosity faded I caught sight of a slim figure with pointed ears.

I did not feel any fear at the events unfolding in front of me I just felt a great connection to a never ending sequence of energy and ever evolving life; space so full of wonder and mystery - ever moving.

As my mind floated back to conscious reality I was aware of Aior watching my reaction, she put her arm around my shoulder and slowly walked us out from under Erisendal.

Standing well clear of the tree she said. 'I am now going to explain to you what ascendancy means. I know Elid in her last message to you spoke about connection now I am going to tell you what connects us all.'

All the time Aior was speaking she was pacing around, sometimes touching the bark of Erisendal other times pushing at the air with the palms of her hands then rubbing my cheek with the back of her hand - always moving.

'We are all part of the living, moving, mighty and wonderful universes and what connects us to the rest of everything else is something called " The spinning energy", I call it the " Tingling energy".

'Imagine Lael, when you were a child on Earth and you were on a beach of pure silvery sand, you were cupping the sand and letting it run through your fingers and it was so smooth it ran like liquid.

The reason it ran so easily was because each grain was so tiny and the space between each grain was equally tiny, so there was hardly any resistance to the flow.

Now, so that I can form a picture in your head we will remain on the beach on Earth but this time I want you to visualise yourself pinching some grains of sand with your fingertips. Go a stage further and place the grains in the palm of your other hand and try to separate one grain and push it away from the rest.

Now look at the grain, it is so tiny you can hardly see

it, then picture in your mind a boulder as big as yourself. That boulder is now the grain of sand in relation to the tiny speck of spinning energy I am going to talk about.'

Aior anor was moving around touching, feeling, breathing and radiating energy all the time as she spoke to me about the spinning energy.

The proportion of a grain of sand being like a boulder, the size of me alongside a grain of spinning energy was mind blowing and that was nothing to what Aior anor came away with next.

'You, me, trees, seas, lands, planets, stars and galaxies are formed by these spinning grains of energy. When Ulas and Ica worked together they created the grains of energy out of the dark magic matrix of space and put together the stars and planets first.

Life came along later in many forms and inhabited worlds that had environments to suit their physical needs or spiritual requirements. Although conditions in one world suited the beings that lived there, the same conditions might not suit a life entity from another world. However they do share one thing and that is the grain of creation.

Right Lael, back to Earth again but this time you are in the forest of Lael ready to enter Ulana. But before you expire stop a moment and magnify your sight a thousand times, look at your body and see it alive with spinning grains of energy.

Now you have entered Ulana and if you had been able to see your spinning energy you would have seen that the grains were spinning faster than they did in your earthen body. When your spirit was released, the grains of creation spun at a higher rate and it was able to pass into Ulana.

In Ulana everything spins at the same rate so the whole of the world is in tune, all are connected. On Earth the spin of the grains of creation are lower so an earthen shape in physical form cannot pass through to another world.

She laughed and said. 'That is why certain sprites on earth called humanity "the heavy people."

So Lael you can only be led to the door of any ascendancy, but if your rate of spinning energy is not on a level with the next level of spirituality then you are not ready, it is as simple as that.'

Not once did she ask what I saw or felt during my meditation but because my conscious mind was alive with the pictures of what I had seen it was easy to take in the fascinating facts I was learning from Aior. She carried on as to why things can develop and I just listened in wonder at her words.

'Did you ever wonder why others saw you in Darwan when other spirits that passed through were invisible?' I nodded in agreement.

'The reason you were seen was because as you entered the tunnel of light you were diverted through the spiral of colours, the speed of your spin was altered so the lower level enabled you to exist in visible form in Darwan. Whilst other spirits followed their level of spin or tune and passed through to the next veil.

You asked Elid once about certain life entities in Darwan that you had never seen in Ulana. You also had feelings that in some there was identification with Earth.

During the upheaval in the outer reaches between Ica and Ulas the universes were in imbalance. Remember the gruflics owed their existence to appearing out of a hole; well they were not far wrong.

Tunnels and spirals were inadvertently opened and creatures of different spin were sucked into worlds they should not have been in. The black elves and the bana were Earthen beings and should have entered Ulana at their allotted times, that is why you remembered remnants of their past lives on Earth.

The earthen forest of Lael and its surrounding hills and lochs were one area where a portal existed. More than likely the Black elves and the Bana were transported from there.

Eventually Ica drove Ulas into a well of darkness and she set about to put things right in the galaxies. The life forces in Darwan seemed to be adapting well with the change so Ica put certain faeries and elves amongst them to help with the continuity of the eccentric world that was Darwan.

She put in place the corridor of energy which allowed higher spinning spirits to pass through Darwan so they could see the development of the world. However a door which Semora found and closed after she destroyed Dulsie had allowed the malign spirits to gain entry for too long.

Now Lael is your time for deciding, it is not uncommon for spirits to remain in Erisendal with me. Some lived and breathed the forest for a while and when they were ready they moved onward and upward to a new level.

Others realised they were not ready for ascension and decided they wanted to return from whence they came and so I arranged for them to make the backward journey.

There is no success or failure in the spiritual progression, it is always a state of readiness and that is what it must be, what it always must be.

So Lael, what is it to be? Come with me and I will introduce you to someone who might influence you just a wee bit.'

Once again I followed in the footsteps of the Green Woman and wondered what or who am I going to meet now. I had not long to wait we emerged from the forest to what I can describe as a bowl of greenery.

And right in the middle stood the mighty form of Cerenor-Tala the Draig of Elinbroom, the massive head turned to face us and her thoughts came to me in that instant.

'Lael - spirit of Ulana we are well met in this place, come close to me and share your thoughts.'

What a surprise to see Cerenor again and I rushed up to her with the intention of giving her a very big hug. However Cerenor is a very big Draig so I settled for a stance in front of her very large head.

I said. *'Cerenor it is so good to see you again and I have a question to ask.'*

'Ask away Lael and if I can I will certainly answer you.'

'In the last conversation we had on the jewelled peak of Elinbroom you told me I would not be alone - was it you who alerted the angel?'

Cerenor threw back her head and laughed or - maybe a sound akin to laughter as she reverted to voice.

'Lael I might have left a thought with Semora the angel, however she told me that she had been watching the machinations of the witch. The laws of the universes are watched over by the angels and when powerful transfers of energies are felt the watchers are instantly alert.

The black witch of Cail-dur was clever with her enchantments - it began with the subjection of the black elves, namely the tribes of guita and gual. She turned them against the Lael elves over a period of time.

Although the gual and guita elves were always at odds with the Lael elves it was more in the form of raids into the territory, usually for livestock or whatever they could steal.

Over a period of events the raids were tempered by hatred and a lust to kill for no other reason than the complete extermination of the tribe of Lael.

It is fortunate for Derca's tribe that they decided to move away from the Black Island as they would have eventually been overcome by the shadow power. That is exactly what she wielded in the beginning - a shadow power; a slow moving enchantment that infiltrated the mind of some of the tribes and certain individuals.

Now Lael answer a question for me - tell me about

your life on Earth?'

I took my time in answering because I was struggling to remember where I had heard Earth mentioned before.

'Sorry Cerenor, I do not have a memory of such a place, I remember a place called Ulana but have no knowledge in my mind about it.'

Cerenor gave me a knowing look and said.

'It is over now and we begin another journey. We may go to a place together or singly, it could be a parallel move or an upward move, it all depends on our individual readiness.

Whatever speed the spinning orbs of creation attain going through the portal will decide where we go - it is all about speed Lael - speed and energy. Just remember wherever you go there will always be the angels watching over every living entity.

Now we follow the Green Woman for she will guide us through the stone portal.

The Orb of Ascendency

Apuss had left the sky but there was no light in the darkness, Ara and her maiden were elsewhere. The pinpricks of starlight seemed far, far away - the canopy that was the window of the universe was motionless.

The flickering of stars, the erratic movements of comets and other celestial bodies that were so prevalent in the night sky of Darwan were stilled as if in waiting -----

I alone knew what the waiting was for, I led Cerenor and Lael along the pathway of infinity to a high top at the edge of a mighty ocean, even the sea was silent.

As I expected, to our front appeared a large orb which glowed with colours of purple, blue and indigo in constant swirling motion. All the colours melted in a fusion of whirling energy at the centre of the orb.

At the top of the orb glowed the whitest of light which began to reach upwards in a spiral of pulsating energy.

At either side of the orb stood two gigantic rocks, one was dark red and was alive with the glitter of white crystal - it looked as if some of the stars had come down to watch.

The other rock was white on the side nearest the orb, its other side was blue, inscribed on it was a lightening streak of bronze crystalline light reaching from its base to the top.

I motioned the two forward and told Lael to climb onto Cerenors back. When they were set I told them if they were to be separated in ascendency it would happen in the spiral of light.

I watched Cerenor and Lael entering the orb. No sooner had the tail of the Draig vanished when the orb and the spiral of light dissipated in a blinding flash. I was left looking through the gap where the orb had been.

The two rocks were standing as before with the crystals all aglitter, the sky had come alive again and I was aware of the roar of the mighty sea.

The words of Aior Anor (The Green woman) to Erim Elios

NUIN

Epilogue

After the great battle the tribes returned to their respective lands and resumed normality as much as possible. Even in victory there had been tragic losses and none more so than the loss of the three faeries and Elid Silverhair, Lael and Cerenor.

At least the spirit Lael and Cerenor knew exactly where they were going and no doubt got there. But the trio, they spent all their energy in demolishing the dark forces, so was anything left of their spirits, had a greater power taken them at the last instant?

Something was now missing in the land, the presence that was always there unseen at times and at other times very visible. The flirting of Ilo, the calm assurance of Tress and the bold personality of Elid - all gone!

The Cat Bough was still serving puflic and rotgut but it was no longer the rip roaring place that Elid Silverhair owned. Suilval's visits were very occasional, even Enderli and Coonie had taken to drinking with the gaists in the burrows by the Los river. The bana had all but forsaken it.

The gruflics did not fully understand what had happened but they felt the change around them. They had stopped teasing the gaists, much to the delight of the said beings who were the only ones that hadn't changed their habits. They were still the Cat Boughs best customers.

Then from voices unknown, whispers were heard, some said it was the wind that carried them, others thought it was the spirits of the faeries. Whatever the source, whispers turned to rumours then rumour found a time and a place.

"A day after the next rising of the red moon Rinnis a new owner of the Cat Bough would be appearing."

A buzz of excitement thrilled through the land and the tribes waited with impatient anticipation for the rising of Rinnis.

Curiosity and intrigue made the clans head for the Cat Bough after the rising of the moon and they were surprised by the amount of former friends and companions in arms that had turned up.

Nal of the bana had already come back from Moola so the original bana five along with Tiathmor and Rhu were present.

Suilval, Enderli and Coonie, the river gaists and a contingent of red selcs had appeared and many more recognisable faces were gathered.

Stories old and new were swapped, puflic and rotgut consumed by all and soon the place was buzzing like old times. Enderli tried to get information out of the pixies but it was clear they were no wiser than the rest.

Toasts were given to Elid, Tress and Ilo and also to Lael and Cerenor, Nal proposed one to Derca to whom she owed so much.

Then the raucous noise dampened a little as a bright white light slowly filtered into the Cat Bough. It seemed to permeate through the walls and roof. Conversations stopped as all looked around to determine where the light was coming from.

The stone door of the Cat Bough flew open and in the midst of the dazzling light a figure could be made out and as it moved forward it took the shape of a tall female. A comforting silence hung within the white light of the bar. The occupants felt no fear or alarm at the sudden appearance of the strange woman.

The vision became clear as the woman moved inside the Cat Bough, her face looked as though it had been sculpted out of white ice, the piercing eyes were as blue as the Salacian Sea, high black eyebrows that looked as they were painted on with a fine pointed brush. The hair was short and dark it had a feathery look about it and an iridescence of dark blue and green filtered through it.

About her neck hung a necklace of silver adorned with slim bars of black shiny stones the silver centre piece at her throat had a diamond shaped black stone.

The slim body was garbed in a white, figure hugging costume and around the waist a belt of silver hung loose at one side. A scabbard attached to the belt contained an article of some kind but whatever it was it had not the shape of a knife or a sword.

In one hand she held a staff which had a black stone set at the top of it. Although the white was as pure as the snow on the DaRinnis Mountains, on closer inspection very intricate black symbols could be made out randomly etched on her costume and staff. The blue eyes swept over the company giving such an aura of peace and calm, she held the assembled company in awe. Only Tiathmor, queen of bana managed to gasp out ---

'Srola Arl Du - the white witch of Erldie!!!'

LOVE YOUR JOURNEY THROUGH LIFE

SPECIAL PREVIEW OF

Con-j.

THE STORY AFTER LAEL

Eils looked out from her vantage point high up in the halls of Arcil her hand resting on the pommel of the sword of Elid. Many happenings had occurred after the war with Ulas anor, her mind drifted through the passages of Apuss and Var.

Tiathmor and many of her eras had long since gone to the sea and now Eils the heroine of the Fochd pass was queen of Bana. At the start of her reign an atmosphere of tranquillity had prevailed till a time of Edila occurred. The effervescent warrior Rhu had approached Eils and announced that she was going to explore the wilderness in the way of Ulas.

Eils had asked Rhu why she felt the need to go to the wilds and when Rhu gave her the answer, she understood.

'Eils' she said. 'I have tried so hard to settle down but the war has stayed in me, I need the exhilaration of discovery and the possibility of mercenary fighting, some of the others feel the same way as me but we ask that your mind will be with us in what we do.'

Eils remembered the walk with Rhu's band of warriors to the edge of the Meren Sea and as they boarded the ships she said her farewells not only to Rhu but also to Sula, Nal and Traig and many more of her tribe.

And now looking down to the courtyard something else niggled at her, a young male was sparring with a female warrior and handling himself very well.

Eils was aware of Bheir standing at her side and posed her a question. 'Well Bheir what are we to make of this?' Gesturing with her hand palm up in the direction of the sparring couple.

Bheir answered in her soft deliberate manner. 'This youth will be no farmer or stone mason, he will challenge us for the right of men to enter the arena of the warrior. The day will come when men will seek equal status with the female warriors of the bana ger.'

Eils nodded in silent agreement and said to Bheir. 'And who better to lead the charge than—Con j son of Rhu.'

They watched the young male warrior dispatch the female bana warrior, who promptly bowed her head in respect.

The young male acknowledged the respect but added on with a touch of arrogance. 'Who's next?'

Eils turned to Bheir and said. 'Bheir go down below and take the bite out of that pup.'

Watching from her lofty perch she watched Bheir approaching Con-j, the young warrior was taken by surprise by the appearance of such a noble warrior.

Bheir said to Con-j 'May I have the honour to be next or

are there bana warriors lining up to test your expertise?'
Con-j regained his composure and dipped his head as a sign he accepted and with dazzling speed he attacked Bheir. In the blink of an eye Con-j landed on his hind-end with a "What happened" look on his face. Bheir's sword at his throat and her foot on his sword arm.

From her high vantage Eils chuckled at the befuddled look on the face of Con-j, not for the first time Eils had seen that bemused look on the countenance of a sparring opponent of Bheir's.

Bheir comes across as silent and deep but below the surface is coiled energy that can leap to the surface in the blink of an eye. Eil's had often thought that there was a latent power within Bheir that she had kept hidden. It was as if there was a magical element to Bheir's thinking that co-ordinated the speed of her movements.

But magic was not apparent in the Bana lineage, that was strictly for the faerie folk and certain others ------ still Cerenor Tala hinted at special talents which she saw in Traig and Bheir-------------------'Eils!' The cry came from the warrior Hasrir, pointing upwards with her spear. 'A storm hawk and he has a rider.'

Instantly many bows were unslung and arrows pointed at the hawk and rider.

Eils voice rang out loud and clear. 'Stand off bana I recognise the hawk and rider. Then she ran down the stairway and into the courtyard. Before she got to the courtyard her intuition told her that this was no social call. She remembered vividly the last time a storm hawk and a black elf appeared events in the land were never the same again.

The hawk had landed and the rider was in the act of

dismounting Bheir and some of the older bana were welcoming the hawk and rider.

Eils stood back from the crowd and cried out. 'Well Derca and Croin what news have you brought to this peaceful land of Daralonadh?'

The bana warriors parted to let Derca through to face Eils – Derca and Eils held each other by the shoulders and gazed at each other through the years each feeling that past and present had merged. When they broke apart Eils told Derca to announce his news to all around.

Derca turned and faced the bana.

'Warriors, during a very angry storm some of our boats were driven far out into the sea by the way of Ulas. All but one returned and when the sea calmed down we scoured the waters for the missing boat. The winds had retreated to the upper sky so they had left the sea with unbroken water. Croin and his kin helped in the search for the galley but to no avail and to make things worse a storm hawk went missing. She was a young female called Aigr and had not a lot of solitary flying experience.

Croin thought that she had been caught unawares by high winds and had flown too far by the way of Ulas. He was right because it was not long after she arrived back to our shores accompanied by another bird.

Aigr had indeed been driven high and far in the direction of Ulas, she spotted an island of high mountains and made for it. She picked the highest peak to land on and as she did so she found that she had company.

The other bird turned out to be a bloodhawk and was male his name was Rill and he had an interesting tale to tell. Bloodhawks are solitary wanderers they do not flock like stormhawks nor do they fly over areas populated by land creatures. However Rill, like Aigr, had been carried off course and much to his dislike found he was flying over the Badlands of Jalardun.

He could see much going on down below, it looked like the land creatures were fighting each other so he turned away from the melee below. He had not flown far when he spotted a black gurk attacking a warrior.

The warrior looked as if it was wounded and had its back against a rock - it looked like it was just managing to keep the gurk at bay with its spear.

The bloodhawk told Aigr that Gurks are the scum of the air and deserve everything that comes to them. He dropped like a stone on the unsuspecting gurk and killed it instantly - he pulled it away from the warrior and ripped its throat apart.

The warrior was wary of him but he assured it that he meant no harm and so the spear was dropped. The warrior said its name was Seri of the bana ger'-------------------------
Such a cry went up from the assembled bana, all of them knew her name - she was a warrior of the Arcil bana. Eils shouted for quiet so Derca could finish his tale.

ABOUT THE AUTHOR

I was born in a small fishing village in the north of Scotland, where we were a community in our own right. My mother's family were all fisher folk and boat owners and could trace their ancestry well back for hundreds of years.

My father's folk were of the same ilk; so I was treated to some fascinating stories during my growing years. I passed some of these stories on to my own daughters – with embellishments.

I went to the fishing myself when I left school then I did a spell in the Marine Commandos, after which I entered the oil industry. That was my main career till I retired at the end of 2015.

I have written stories for the enjoyment of my family - however, Lael is the first book I have written.

Printed in Great Britain
by Amazon